Mason Sabre

Mason Sabre

Dedications

To those who know me truly and still don't disappear.

Exile
Mason Sabre

This book is a work of fiction. All characters in this novel are fictitious. Any resemblance to actual events or locales or persons, living or dead, is entirely coincidental.

Author: Mason Sabre

Also by Mason Sabre

Watch Over you

The Rise of the Phoenix

Cade

Dark Veil

Hidden

Death Awakening

Broken Snow

Cuts Like an Angel

Seraph

She Promised

Exile

Mason Sabre

Chapter One
Stephen

Stephen Davies.

Stephen …

Davies …

He said his name in his head slowly. Just an echo of who he used to be.

Nicholas Mason.

It didn't quite have the same ring, and its very presence came with a weight too heavy in Stephen's heart. He cast his eyes back to the window, staring at the pitiful image of his reflection.

It was dark outside. The streetlights sped along in a blur of colour—one bright yellow line of nothingness. He tried to focus but was unable to keep up with the images as they sped by.

Reflected in the glass in front of him were his many companions—nine of them—prisoners, just like him. All heading to the same unknown, merciless place. Stephen had as little desire to speak to the other prisoners as they did to appreciate the beauty they were missing beyond the confines of the bus.

Destination Exile—execution and the main parade of yet another *Other* dead for the *Humans* to drink, cheer and relish in their own sickening *Humanity*.

Such a feast for them.

Stephen clenched his jaw and rested his shackled hands on his knees as visions of his blazing body filtered into his mind again. God, how he hoped that when he was executed, the stench of his burning flesh would remain in their nasal cavities for days and that the image of his guts and intestines pouring out would stay in their minds for years to come. The wondrous mental impressions of Stephen Davies.

He tsked in his mind. No, not Stephen Davies … Nick Mason. He hadn't yet had time to become accustomed to his new identity—not that he ever would. His father's vain attempt to save his life. What a fuck-up that had turned out to be.

Stephen tried not to feel pity for himself, or even anger at being boarded onto this bus with *Others* such as these. He was not like them. He didn't belong here.

His name did appear on the execution warrant—that much was true—but the rest … it was just bullshit. He was not a criminal. His only 'sin' was sacrifice. His muscles bunched under his shirt as he balled his hands into fists and pulled the silver chains encircling his wrists taut. The silver seared his skin, leaving marks as if he had just been branded with hot iron.

Sweat beaded along his forehead and ran down the nape of his neck. It left a cold trail under his collar, a sliver of a worm travelling down his back. Fire raged underneath his skin at the injustice of all of this. Angry red welts puckered on the skin of his wrists where the binds held him tight. Pain met fury under his flesh, sending his *tiger* back into his cage. Now was not the time to shift. He tried to keep his legs as still as possible, a vain attempt to ease the pain in his ankles as the negligent driver sped along and managed to hit every fucking bump in the road, each one of them jarring, causing the silver to bite a little deeper. The bus rattled and lurched again. Moans and cries rang out from some of the others. The driver smirked, taking great pleasure in the pain he was causing. *Fuck*, he really hated *Humans*.

Hours rolled by on the tedious and drawn out journey, and the only thing that Stephen had to occupy his mind was the view outside the window. It had grown darker now, even the lights had vanished. Eternal darkness lay out there. How much farther was it to their destination? He wasn't privy to that information anymore.

Oh, how the mighty had fallen.

He almost laughed at his predicament. If Cade could only see him now ...

Fuck no.

Cade would fucking die trying to save him if he knew. Same went for Raven—of course, that was after he had laughed at him and downed a shot. Just the day before, Stephen had been at the top of their society, the leader in his own domain. He controlled and commanded. Now? Nothing. Just like the rest of them. No better than an insect germinating in a rotting world.

These fellow passengers were not his equals. He was not like them. Yes, they had started their journey on this bus with him, but they had been loud, brash, uneducated strays. They yelled their demands at the unsympathetic driver and guards, doing nothing more than inciting gleeful laughter and initiating random beatings. The hours had broken them all, one by one. *Humans*—the weaker of the species—yet here they were, controlling powerful beings such as *Others*, holding all the power. Armed to the teeth, they used chains and rods to enforce submission. Each of Stephen's companions now stared out with the same expressionless face.

Splatters of blood and other bodily fluids marred the floor, adding to the stains that had been painted there during earlier 'first class' transportation services such as this. Stephen pitched forward as the bus came to a stop in the same jerky manner that he was becoming accustomed to. Their 'professional chauffeur', with his overgrown belly, sat close enough to the steering wheel that it pressed into the rolls of fat, just so that his pudgy arms could reach. He hit a button and the hydraulics hissed into life. The door slid open, and the overweight driver slipped off his seat, wheezing, a cigarette nestled between his lips. A joke passed between him and the guards, and he coughed out a raspy laugh. Maybe death would come swiftly for him in the next decade, Stephen thought.

The driver paused at the anchor to which all the chains were attached. With a malevolent grin, he gave it a violent tug before checking it was still secured into place. Winces and groans echoed around the confines of the bus as limbs were pulled to awkward positions and the metal gouged and scorched flesh. Stephen gritted his teeth as it seared his skin, but remained silent. The driver laughed as he disembarked the bus. Images of the driver's petrified face and the sound of his death cries flashed through Stephen's mind as he started to imagine escaping his bonds and getting his hands on the fat piece of shit.

A *Human* boarded the bus, a vicious beast. Tall, bulky and muscled. He held his shoulders back, chest pushed out, gun in his hand at the ready, trying to make himself look as intimidating as possible. Stephen may have laughed if he were not restrained in his seat. He didn't fear being beaten, but the silver he was chained to meant his system was weaker, which portended slower healing from any serious damage that might be caused. Stephen had to keep his target in sight. His aim was to escape—that would not be possible if he let himself get beaten to the point he would miss the opportunity of escape should it present itself.

The *Human's* heavy footsteps echoed through the

silence, every head lowering for fear of some sort of reprisal. Stephen reluctantly bowed his head, playing possum.

A second man boarded the bus and came to stand next to Stephen, his gaze boring into the back of Stephen's head. No fucking *Human* ever dared to stand this close to him. Stephen fought the urge to look up and make eye contact— Stephen Davies bowed down to no one—but knew this was one time he had to stifle his pride if he were to get out of this alive.

The stench of fear dripped off him—even though Stephen was shackled. He wondered what the man would do if he knew who the shifter next to him really was. He was already nearly pissing his pants. If Stephen were to sneeze, it was very likely he might just suffer the indecency of losing control of his bladder. Of course, Stephen would pay dearly for that accident. God forbid the *Human* experienced any humiliation. Fear was a powerful tool that gave strength to the weakest of beings, Stephen had learned.

Against his own egotistical urges, Stephen stared down at his scuffed boots. He didn't react when the *Human* grabbed his arm, even though the feel of his sweaty palm against Stephen's bare skin made the corner of his mouth twitch in disgust.

The man ran a scanner over Stephen's new tattoo—a gift acquired upon his sentencing to Exile. The barcode was his name tag imprinted on his arm. No longer the hunter, but the hunted. Branded cattle with a marker to show who owned him.

The *Human* spat on the floor next to Stephen as he waited for the particulars to appear on the screen, and Stephen's hands balled into fists as he stared down at the disgusting splatters of saliva that now desecrated his jeans. What he could do to him if his hands were his own. It would not be saliva that Stephen would be wiping off his jeans, of that he was sure.

"Nick. Mason. 932416." Stephen wanted to congratulate him on being able to read. His pseudonym—a mere face to his true identity. He was certain the *Human* had no fucking idea as to who he really was. Not that it mattered if Stephen didn't manage to escape execution.

The man began to say something, no doubt an attempt at a joke at Stephen's expense perhaps. Another misdemeanour Stephen could add to the long list of things to get retribution for. But the *Human's* words were cut short by the sound of screeching metal. His head snapped back as he watched the roof of the bus being peeled back as though it were nothing more than the foil on a stick of gum.

Stephen blinked to make sure he wasn't hallucinating when he saw what it was that had so effortlessly just torn off the entire top of the bus. Vaguely, he heard the stunned exclamations from the rest of the prisoners as a young girl landed daintily and soundlessly on the floor in front of the *Human* next to Stephen. She rested a small hand on Stephen's head and pushed his head back down with a strength that belied her delicate build. "Do not look at me." Her voice was childlike, mellifluous. For reasons he couldn't quite explain, he kept his head down. Maybe it was shock, or the palpable power that emanated from her, but he had enough sense not to look again.

The *Human* gulped, lifting a shaking gun towards her. "D-Don't move," he stammered. "Hands …"

The tell-tale snap of a neck being broken resounded in the sudden silence of the bus. It was not the content of the Human's bladder that hit the floor, but the *Human* himself, his dead eyes staring up at Stephen unseeingly.

Stephen stayed absolutely still, his mind working a

million miles a second. What kind of creature had strength such as this? Her small hands reached down and snapped the chains that held him in place as effortlessly as the roof she had just destroyed.

She slid her bony hand into his. "Come with me."

He dared not disobey.

Chapter Two
Eden

Nights were the worst. Like bam, darkness comes, and then suddenly the temperature drops and winter comes in uninvited with all its god damn damp and freezing glory. Eden Matthews wrapped her arms around herself, rubbing her chilled flesh—for all the good it did her—as she leaned back against the equally cold wall.

Cold. It was always so damn cold. The band that held her earmuffs in place slid down for the hundredth time in the last hour. She really needed new ones. Of course, she needed money to get new ones. She yanked them down off her head, again, her numb fingers fumbling as she struggled with the overused and overstretched clasp that was meant to hold them in place. Tape—she could get some tape and fix them. But then … that was the money thing again.

With a huff, she shoved the earmuffs back onto her head and positioned them over her freezing ears. She slid down the wall slowly, preparing herself for the moment her ass touched the cold hard ground. She had to sit somewhere. She sure as hell wasn't going to sleep standing up. As she lowered herself to the ground, she brought her knees up to her chin. Her ankle boots caught her eye. "Seriously?" She lifted her foot up for a closer inspection and thumped the loose sole, the mouth of her boot flapping. "Fucking great." She'd get glue tomorrow and fix that, too. At this rate, she was going to be Frankenstein's monster held together by tape and glue, drastically falling apart at the seams.

She pulled her bag closer, dragging it across the ground towards her. She wanted to love this bag, she really did, but every time she saw it, her fists clenched and her memories burned. She'd wanted this bag for months—ever since she had first seen it at the market. Handwoven and decorated with lilies … now all it did was remind her of him. *Him*—that was his name because he didn't deserve anything else. Him. The fucking shit who had brought her here and then left her ass high and dry when he had taken every last penny she had and disappeared. This was more than a bag. This was a memento of the most stupid decision she had made in her entire life. She'd left her family for him. She'd …

She shook her head abruptly. "Stop it." No. She wasn't going to think about him. He did not deserve it.

She blew on her fingertips and rubbed her hands together for a moment before rummaging through her bag for her bottle and the bread roll she had saved—her last one. It was a fight between her stomach and her mind; if she ate it now, then tomorrow she would have to go and get more, and that meant breaking and entering. Which was fine, of course. She could do that. But *Humans* … god, they were everywhere. Fleas in society. And then there were the sweepers … they'd haul her ass in and chain her up just for being too hungry. She held the roll in her hand and stared at it, fraught with the indecision.

The old bridge she sat under was the one that was once used for trains going to the main facilities in Exile. Now, it was nothing—old and decrepit and ready to collapse at the slightest breeze. But it was where she liked to sleep. It was safe and quiet and protected her from the wind. No one could get to her without her seeing them first, either. Surrounding her was land, but it was gated off with high metal fences that ended in spikes about seven feet up. A set of steps ran up the side to the top of the bridge—that was the only way up or down, and she positioned herself so that she could watch them. She stared into the darkness of the steps and brought the bread to her mouth. A sudden clank at the top had her pausing with the bread roll halfway to her lips. She angled her head and leaned forward slowly, putting the bread down on top of her bag and pulling her fingerless gloves from her hands. Something scraped on concrete, and Eden's heart strummed in her chest. She swallowed hard and placed both of her hands on the ground. It vibrated under her fingertips, small stones bouncing, suddenly animated. Her eyes grew brighter, shimmering with golds and browns. The earth under her hands grew warm and cracks slowly broke the surface.

"Who's there?" No answer, but the scratching got louder. She squinted, but the top steps were dark ... too dark to see anything. "Answer me before I send your ass crashing."

The scratching came again, louder this time, faster. It was moving. Eden followed the sound through the darkness with her eyes and raised her hand, ready to strike. The pungent aroma of damp earth wrapped itself around her. Something jumped out of the darkness, teeth flashing. Eden fell back, hands raised, her cast ready on her lips ...

Then it barked.

Eden blinked, then a short laugh escaped her lips. A fucking dog. That's all it was. Just a fucking dog. "Jesus Christ." She lowered her hand to the ground and released the energy there, letting it shoot into the compacted soil. It sliced through the earth and pushed up a twisted green stem, a stark contrast to its bleak surroundings. She sagged against the wall and closed her eyes for a moment while she regained her composure and let her heartbeat settle once again.

A dog. Unbelievable. There weren't many of them roaming around these parts. But this one ... it was small ... a mongrel by the looks of things. Black and shabby. It padded over to her and plonked itself down on the ground, tilting its head to one side, tongue lolling. She scowled as she looked at it. "Don't even try your begging thing on me. I ain't got anything for you."

Above her, passing over the bridge, was the main road that was now used to get into the Exile building. Locals called it Death Towers, because once an *Other* went in there, they never came out. A chimney billowed smoke out once in a while, thick black plumes that turned the air foul, filling it with death. Every time the alarm sounded, a wailing through the quiet, heads turned and glanced at the chimney. It reached high into the sky, a monstrous mouth spitting out what had once been an *Other*.

Tonight, it was quiet, the sky clear—which was why it was so damn cold. But that was it with Exile ... everything was dull and dark and dingy. Even the names. How inventive the *Humans* were with what they called things, she scoffed. Exile island, Exile Prison ... well, actually, they called that a correctional facility, but all *Others* knew, it was more like torture. It was a couple of miles at the end of the long road, but that was the only thing in that direction—another reason for this bridge.

Eden chewed on a thumbnail as she glanced up high, the dog making himself at home by her feet. There wasn't a cloud in sight, the night sky filled with shimmering, bright stars. Her eyes fell on one of the stars that seemed to be moving, and she squinted to get a better look. A shooting star? She pushed herself up, frowning. No, this was no star. Not a plane, either. Nothing flew over these parts. Not at night, at least. The only way to reach Exile was by boat.

The silence of the night crept away with the rumbling of wheels on the tarmac above ... a wagon?

Exile

Forgetting the dog, Eden crept to the stone steps and crawled up them until she was sitting hidden in the dark shadows. A flash of surprise went through her at the sight of the facility bus. That wasn't due this time of night. She had been sleeping here long enough to know the comings and goings of things. There had to be something damn special on that bus for it to be travelling at this time. It came to a stop, and Eden gripped the railing tighter as she leaned over to look, making sure to keep herself out of view. The doors opened with a hiss of the hydraulics, the sound loud in the quiet night. There were a few prisoners on the bus, all of them men, including two Human guards and the driver. From the other direction, lights bobbed and grew bigger as another vehicle drew closer. It pulled up in front of the bus, and Eden was able to recognise it as one of the sweeper cars. She ducked, heart pounding. Fucking sweepers. She rubbed at the tattoo on her wrist absently, a prize from the last time they had caught her and branded her.

The overweight driver of the bus got out, cupping his hand around his mouth to light a cigarette. He hobbled towards the car, blowing blue smoke out into the air. "Can we help you?" he asked the two men who got out of the car.

They wore dark green uniforms and black jackets, boots tied to their ankles, guns resting in their hands. "You have some property of ours," one man said. "Prisoner 932416."

The headlights of the car shone brightly against the driver's fat stomach. "We don't have any orders to do a drop-off."

The middle-aged man with a receding hairline who had spoken before turned to his companion and nodded. The other man, shorter, but no less built in muscle and power, reached into his top pocket and pulled out a folded piece of

17

paper. He handed it to the driver, his expression stern. "Now you do," he said curtly.

The driver scowled, clearly unhappy about the unplanned drop-off. He puffed on his cigarette and walked away shaking his head. He folded the paper and shoved it into his pocket without reading it. What did it matter? If they wanted one of the filthy *Others*, they could have them.

The shooting star in the sky gradually grew larger, but none of the men on the ground seemed to have noticed it. This was definitely not a falling star, Eden thought. She moved back, and she barely contained her squeal as her leg hit fur. The dog yelped and Eden quickly crouched down. "Shh," she whispered, running a calming hand through its matted fur. One of the guards shot a look in her direction, and stared for a moment before finally turning back to the bus.

The taller guard boarded the bus first, and then the shorter one followed. They walked slowly, cautiously, and Eden smirked. They were scared. They stopped at each prisoner, looking for the one they wanted. All the while, the light above was moving, approaching fast. Eden held her breath and moved down another step, pressing herself into the wall as the light landed silently on the top of the bus. Her eyes widened. A swan—a beautiful swan—tall, larger than any she had ever seen. It stood there with its wings spread out then rose, high, stretching, its feathers shimmering in the light, and then abruptly, it slammed a wing down on top of the bus. Only … it wasn't a wing, she realised. Before her very eyes, it changed, transforming itself into a young, slim girl. Eden gasped as she watched her rip away the top of the bus, peeling it back with no effort at all.

"Shit." She slid back down the steps, tripping over her own feet in her haste. Whatever was about to happen on the bus, she was not going to be part of it. *Hell no.* When she reached the bottom, she turned to her things … her bag. It lay open on the ground, the dog standing next to it, her bread in its mouth between its teeth. "Hey. No way … come on," she whispered vehemently. "That's my bread." She stepped closer, but the dog raised its top lip in warning, a slow grumble coming from deep within its throat. "Yeah? That's how we're going to do this?"

It wagged its tail slowly, with uncertainty, then bit down on her bread.

"Don't …"

Before she could do a thing, the dog had knocked its head back, dropping the roll deeper into its mouth. Eden lunged for it with a curse, but the dog dodged her and nipped around to the other side.

"I hope it gives you bellyache," she ground out furiously. "Stupid dog."

She picked up her bag, shoving the spilled contents back in. "Great." The bottle of water lay on the ground on its side, its contents seeping out, soaking the ground. "Just bloody marvellous." She snatched her stuff up and threw it into the corner. Now she was hungry with no food and no way out.

She plopped herself down and curled up on the dirt. With a heavy exhalation, she closed her eyes.

Whatever was going on above her, she was keeping out of that, too.

Chapter Three
Stephen

A lamb to the slaughter—that was the image that popped to the forefront of Stephen's mind as, for whatever reason it was, beyond his own judgment, he followed the girl, the thing—whatever she was—off the bus, allowing her to lead him from his seat. His stiff legs ached from sitting so long confined to one position on the bus, waiting to reach destination hell. He arched his back and rolled his shoulders to work out some of the kinks as he walked. What he needed was to shift and run. The girl wasn't waiting around, though. He let her drag him behind her, his eyes roaming over the other prisoners on the bus as he passed them. His stare met each and every one of theirs. They were as meaningless to him as he was to them. He fought the urge to wave and wish them a safe and pleasant journey before disembarking.

The gutless *Humans* who remained didn't move—cowards hiding behind their weaponry. They stood frozen, their wide-eyed gazes trained on this young girl as she walked past them. Maybe they were braver than Stephen thought—they weren't that afraid that they wouldn't look at her—or maybe they were just foolish. The top of the bus gaped open, and darkness peered back in, the stars shining brightly high above them in the night sky. She had just peeled that metal away with no effort at all. The dainty hand holding his could most likely crush every bone in his big hand with just one powerful squeeze.

The fat driver stood by the bus, pressing himself back against the cold metal, probably hoping that Stephen and the girl wouldn't notice him there. With such girth, however, that was an impossibility. Stephen wondered whether he now regretted eating all of those pies. He paused and angled his head at him, and the man let out a pathetic little whimper and kept his eyes averted, too afraid to meet his gaze. Stephen regarded the feeble excuse of a *Human* with an edge of contempt. Had his mother been proud of him? Did she look upon the fat filth and feel the joy at what she had bred? Stephen lifted his arm so that his sleeve could slide down and surveyed the damage; puckered red skin that glistened where the chains had pressed in. He lifted his eyes to meet with the fat man's, a humourless smile spreading across his face as he heard the *thump, thump, thump* of his racing heart.

"We don't have time for this," the girl urged, tugging on his hand.

Stephen turned to look at her and tried to pull his hand from her vice-like grip. It proved impossible, which was disconcerting—she was so young, just a child.

"You can spare a second," Stephen said flatly.

Vibrant, glassy eyes stared back at him. "We must go," she said. "We have to go."

Stephen nodded at her but didn't move. Whatever it was inside him, driving him, it demanded he stay. His hand still in the girl's, he turned to face the fat man once again. The guard slid sideways, trying to edge away, fear rolling off him in waves.

"I w-was just doing my job," he wailed." I-It wasn't my fault."

Stephen's free hand shot out and his fingers wrapped around the *Human's* throat, repulsed by the way the folds under the man's chin rested on his hand, his grimy stubble grazing across his skin.

Nine lives flashed through Stephen's mind, each one of them a lightning strike of colour smashing into his temples.

The girl released his hand and took a small step back as he fell to his knees, gasping for breath, his throat burning, chest tight. He couldn't get enough air.

Terrifying death throes and screaming resonated in Stephen's head. Someone was crying, another pleaded for their life. Stephen lifted his head, and his eyes shot open. He found himself in a room, the colours tinted, and he had no doubt that his eyes had shifted; no longer the pale green and gold, but bright like fire. His *tiger* rose to the surface, ready to fight and feast upon the fresh kill.

A child was sitting in the corner—small, puny—a pitiful thing with nothing but rags for clothes, his matted, bloodied hair sticking to his sweaty head. Blood and dirt covered his face save for where his tears had run down his cheeks and streaked his skin clean. He held his knees to his chest as he sobbed, his eyes staring straight ahead at some unseen horror. The smell of blood and sex violated Stephen's senses as he turned to follow the boy's gaze. A girl, his sister no doubt, beaten, defiled and slaughtered. But that wasn't the horror or the thing that repulsed him the most—it was the eyes he saw, black pits in the head of the creature who had done this. Eyes were windows to the soul—and the darkness he witnessed now left him breathless.

Stephen fell forward, catching himself on the ground with his free hand, but his vice-like grip never loosened from around the fat man's throat. Stephen's gaze lifted to the man's and shimmering gold-green locked with dull brown. The fat man shook his head jerkily, his eyes widening and the stench of fear rising higher.

He knew what Stephen had seen.

He knew what Stephen had to do.

Exile

Stephen exhaled slowly and his teeth extended in a partial shift. His eyes changed completely, tilting the world, the presence of the *tiger* within comforting.

The fat man gurgled in Stephen's grasp, his chubby fingers clawing at Stephen's wrists. His scream fell away to silence as he desperately kicked out with one short fat leg. Stephen slowly rose to his feet, and the man bucked and shoved in a vain attempt to get away, wriggling like a fish caught on a hook. Death was near, but still he fought. Stephen tightened his grip, bones fracturing under the pressure of his hand. Claws pierced flesh, and blood trickled down Stephen's arm, staining the orange fur that poked through his skin red.

After a long moment, he let go abruptly and the fat man dropped to the ground.

No one moved.

The *Humans* stood staring at Stephen as he wiped the blood from his hand down the front of his shirt. He would have used the *Human's* shirt rather than his own, but the man's own clothes were now soaked with blood, and Stephen had no desire to infect himself more with the stench of the *Human*. He hadn't meant to kill him, but he felt no pity for having done it. Energy surged through his veins. Not the unspent kind, not the kind that wanted release when he had to shift, but the good kind. That kind that comes after a good run and the body is pumped. That's what he was—pumped. He could take over the world right then if he wanted to.

He hesitated. The voices in his mind— loud, static noise always in the background that he would ignore—they were gone. That only happened around Cade and Gemma. Stephen tilted his head back and closed his eyes, waiting for them to come rushing back.

Nothing.

Relief coursed through him, but the images he had seen when he held the *Human* didn't dissipate. They ran through his mind, wild and vivid, the girl's screams and the boy's tears echoing in his ears.

Stephen turned to the young girl next to him, who stood there staring at him with an unreadable expression on her face. His eyes narrowed as he stared back at her. "Who are you? And what the hell was that back on the bus?"

"We don't have time to waste on this," the girl said.

"Then tell me."

"The sweepers will do their rounds soon, and what do you think they will do when they find this?"

"Piss their pants hopefully and know that I have arrived."

The girl scowled at him. "You are not at home anymore. This," she pointed to the bus, "is just a pointless array of powers of the *Other* kind."

"*Humans* are dead," Stephen stated flatly. "It isn't pointless."

The girl scoffed. "Spoilt little rich boy. Always the same. Think you had it bad before? Think that you arrived here in some unjust way? Well, boohoo." She stepped right up to him—something anybody else would have thought twice about doing after his little display with the *Human* before. "So you got caught up in your sister's shit and now you're here. It doesn't make you the hero, so get down off your pedestal. You don't get to be boss here. Here, you're simply Nick Mason, escaped convict. Deal with it and do as you're told, or stay and face the sweepers and see what they say."

Stephen glared down at her, jaw clenched. She was just a fucking child. How the hell did she know his shit? "How do you know about Gemma?"

Exile

The girl raised an eyebrow at him. "I know a lot of things, Nick, or should I call you *Stephen*?"

He narrowed his gaze at the mention of his real name. Who the fuck was this girl? There was no way she could know the shit she did. It would seem his father's attempts to send him to Exile with a new identity had failed already. He had not long stepped on Exile soil.

Girl … that was a light description of her. She was dainty, and yes, she was young, but she exhibited power and knowledge beyond comprehension. She was a total mystery to him. The cockiness in her stance made Stephen want to tell her where to go, but she had got him off the bus and he did have his freedom at the moment because of her. "Who are you?"

She cocked her head to the side as she looked at him. "A friend. Which is about all you have right now, and right now, I am telling you, we have to go. The sweepers are out and we won't hold them off. That execution order of yours will come fast into fruition before you can even think about getting your claws out and showing off like a spoilt child. We have to go. *Now*."

Go? He had no idea where they were going, much less who this girl was and why he should be going with her. He was going to wake up in a moment. He was sure of it. This girl was no older than Evie, his baby sister—the one who hid in her room and practised make-up and sulked when she got called to do chores. That's what this girl in front of him was. And she expected him to follow? What a joke. If this was Evie, he'd be grabbing her by the arm and telling her to shut up and do as she was told, not the other way around.

The girl started to walk to a car parked at the side of the road. The guards shrank back as she passed them and Stephen followed. He wasn't quite sure who of the two they feared more—him or the small girl who had just ripped off the bus roof and beheaded a man. The fleeting thought that the men on the bus were being surprisingly quiet crossed his mind, but it was quickly dispelled when he spotted his bag in the back of the car. He frowned, having no idea how it had got there. A little presumptuous of her, he thought irritatedly. Every sense in his body told him to get his shit and leave. He didn't know this girl. He was grateful she had got him off the bus, but he'd have eventually found his own escape—without her help. He didn't owe her anything. And where the hell was she about to take him anyway? Did he really want to find out?

The car was an old relic. Patches of pink dotted it where the bodywork had been fixed up. One of the front lights was smashed, and the other held no glass at all. His eyes fell on the door on the passenger side—it didn't match the others.

He watched in bewilderment as the girl got in behind the wheel. "You're driving?" he asked incredulously.

She shot Stephen an all too familiar glare—the one that sent a thousand needles through men's eyes, and made them want to retract whatever stupid thing they had just dared to utter. He was sure girls were taught how to do that stare.

"You're like … eleven," he blurted.

"I'm fourteen," she shot back.

Stephen threw his arms up and rolled his eyes—yeah, because that made it okay then.

"Get in the car."

Death by child.

No, not happening.

"I'll go my own way from here. I thank you for your help, though." He opened the back door to pull out his old, grey satchel. It only held a few necessities—it seemed few belongings were required when heading to Exile to be executed. But it did hold a change of clothes, and Stephen was dying to get out of his *Human*-infested, bloodied shirt.

"You'll not make it out there alone," the girl said shortly.

Stephen closed the back door and flung his bag over his shoulder.

"Maybe not," he said casually, and with a curt nod, he turned and walked away from her. He had no clue where he was going, but he had escaped execution for now, and that's all that mattered for the moment. He breathed in a deep breath of new air ... and freedom. Freedom from not just the bonds on the bus, but the bonds that had been his life before.

No longer heir. No longer obliged to do things that were expected of him. He could go left or right. He could walk in any direction ...

But which one would lead him to the right place?

Chapter Four
Helena

Artificial lights flashed, big and bold—as artificial as the morals of the *Humans* who used them. Beams shone into the night sky, chasing away the darkness, sending out a beacon that something big was happening—something major and important. Helena spotted the lights on her drive there long before she had got to the destination. They stood out in the night, drawing curious citizens from their homes to see what was going on. Everyone knew that that was the road which led to the prison and, whether *Other* or *Human*, anything in that direction was not good. Helena approached with dread, pulling her car up behind one of the police cars that were already there. Men stood around talking, none of them paying her any mind as she sat in her car—well, none until Lee noticed her.

Always Lee.

Nephew and right hand to Gregory Norton himself, Lee Norton was not somebody you messed with. Norton Industries were one of the up-and-coming leading corporations in the world, already making Norton one of the richest men on the planet. And much as she despised Lee, Helena was smart enough to know that having him as an enemy would mean the end of her medical practice in Exile. Norton practically controlled everything here. If she needed to be overly nice and friendly to the asshole, then it was a small price to pay in order to continue to be able to help *Others* and keep her practice running.

A leering smile spread across Lee's face as he caught sight of Helena. She breathed in deeply, squared her shoulders and cut off the engine. Forcing a smile to her lips, she opened the car door.

"Lee," she beamed as she got out of her car, ignoring his outstretched hand.

"Helena," he breathed, his breath thick with the scent of whiskey and cigars. Helena reached up and fastened the top button of her blouse. The breeze always came in from the north, cool and crisp, its delicate icy fingers slithering in under the thin fabric of her blouse and causing goosebumps to break out along her arms. But not all of it was from the cold. Lee's cold blue eyes fell to her breasts and lingered, and Helena fought the urge to cross her arms over her chest.

"So, what's going on?" she inquired, forcing his gaze back to her face.

"Best you see for yourself. Damnedest thing I've ever seen."

She frowned at his statement and started towards the bus, making sure to keep a distance between her and Lee. He kept moving closer, however, until she had nowhere else to go. The bridge rose to the side of her, and the drop down was not where she felt like going. Lee's elbow brushed against hers, and she cringed inwardly.

The area around the bus buzzed with people—noise, lights and endless amounts of chatter blended together into an indistinguishable din. The clamour turned to hushed whispers as she and Lee got closer, faces turning towards them and gazes fixing on Lee.

The man in charge—Thomas, she thought he was called—offered her a hand. "Dr Barnes," he said to Helena.

No, Thomas was his surname. He was the one in charge of the clean-up. "Everything is ready for me?"

He nodded. "None of the men have moved. There's no response from any of them, even though they are most definitely alive."

"Shame," Lee scoffed. "Maybe we could fix that."

Helena ignored Lee's jibe. She didn't share his views on the *Other* kind. They were people, just like she was and he was. Her eyes roamed the vicinity until they fell upon a pair of legs sticking out from under a sheet. His pants were dark in the centre, clearly having lost his bladder at some point when his death had been imminent, but as she got closer and the stench rose up to meet her, she realised that he had lost more than control of his bladder.

Two men were coming out of the bus—the grey metal monster—carrying a gurney with another covered body on it. "Human?" she asked Mr Thomas as they walked past them.

"One of the guards," Lee said grimly.

"And the man on the floor?"

"Driver," Thomas said.

Helena wasn't the one investigating this, but one guard? "That's all that were here to transport these men? One guard and one driver?"

"There's another guard at the other side of the bus."

She nodded slowly. It was not her place to ask questions or to be told details about the crime. She had merely been called here to give medical attention—she knew that—yet she still dared to ask, "Who raised the alarm?"

Lee took hold of Helena's elbow and urged her forward before Thomas could think about replying. "These men need your attention.

Helena was not going to give up that easily, however. "Who raised the alarm if the driver and the guards are dead?"

Exile

Lee scowled as he continued to propel her forward, not happy with her questioning. Despite himself, he answered her. "There was a transfer on the bus. Two officers came to pick him up. Shit went down and they left and raised the alarm."

"They weren't armed?"

Lee shrugged, a sign that he was not willing to say more.

Fine. It didn't matter. What did matter was these men on the bus. Nine prisoners—*Others*. They all sat face forward, none of them moving. Not even the lights or the bustle around them roused them from their trance. "How long have they been like this? They haven't moved at all?"

"Since we got here," Thomas said. "We can't get them to talk."

"We need you to tell us what is wrong with them, being the expert and all." Helena didn't miss the sarcasm dripping from his words. It was no secret that Helena worked mostly with *Others*, even though she was *Human*. *Others* here didn't have doctors of their own, but someone had to give them medical attention when they needed it. They fascinated Helena. The way they healed, the ways in which some of them were indestructible whereas others had weaker powers. Perhaps what helped them could help *Humans,* too. On that, she and Lee agreed; the *Others* held power in their blood.

On the bus, five men sat on one side and four on the other. "One of them is missing?" Chains lay on the empty seat, snapped. On the floor, another set of chains, also snapped.

"That was the transfer," Lee said.

"Who were they transferring?" She stared at the space where the last prisoner should have been, and a sense of foreboding plagued her mind. Those binds were silver. This was a shifter or vampire. But they were snapped, and neither of those species could have done this—they would have been weakened from the silver. "Where is he?"

"We don't know, and these fuckers aren't talking." He leaned into one of them, his face close. Helena tensed. She was all for supporting *Others*, just like she was also for the support of lions, but she wasn't about to stick her face in front of one of them and think she wouldn't get bitten. But the man in front of Lee showed no reaction. Not even a blink. The corner of Lee's lip curled into a smirk. He slapped the man across the face, his eyes fixed on the prisoner's as the head snapped back into position. "No one is home."

Helena's hands balled into fists at her sides as she watched the display before her, helpless to do anything. "And the one missing?" she asked coolly, distracting Lee from his game. She knew first-hand what Lee was like. He loved power. He loved intimidation—except with her. It got him nowhere, and he knew it. But she knew his games. He puffed out his cheeks and gave the prisoner one last look-over before getting back up again.

He grabbed the file and flipped it open. "Nicholas Mason," he read out. "*Tiger*. Up for execution for the murder of several *Humans*." Lee's expression hardened and he shook his head in disapproval. "These are the precious *Others* you want us to understand?"

Helena met his gaze square on. "Just because one *Other* goes on a killing spree, doesn't make the rest of them bad. How many *Others* have you killed?" she replied lightly.

His brow smoothed and a smile curved his lips, his eyes lighting with the game. "Touché, touché." That was the thing with Lee; the only reason he was interested in her was because she was the only one to ever say no to him. Oh, he was handsome enough—he knew it, too. Big, well-built, he always worked out, took pride in himself. His sandy blond hair made him look like there was a beach somewhere missing its lifeguard. His features were well-defined, his jawline perfectly formed, mesmerising, blue eyes—but there was a coldness, a malice in them that could chill you to the bone. Not the kind of man she wanted too close to her. "He is a *tiger*, and he mauled them to death for no reason."

Helena didn't buy that. There was always a reason—usually with *Others,* it was that they had been backed into a corner. Of course, there were bad ones, just like any species, but she liked to believe that everyone had some good in them. "You know it wasn't for no reason."

"You don't know that it was for anything. He is a *tiger*; *tigers* kill things."

"They're the most magnificent creatures of such beauty. They don't kill unless it is a necessity."

Lee smiled, making the hairs at the back of her neck stand on end. "Careful, Helena, or we might start questioning your loyalty. You're talking about real *tigers*, not the kind driven by the mind of man. Man is much crueler."

Oh, that was true.

She pulled a pen torch from her top pocket and went to the first man on the other side of Lee, turning her back on Lee. She was done with this conversation now; it wasn't a line worth walking. She shone the light into the man's brown eyes and checked his pupils. No reaction. She took the man's wrist in her hand, pushing the chain back so that she could get to his pulse. His skin was red and raw from where the silver had bitten into him, holding him in place with its razor-sharp teeth. Prisoners or not, the sight tugged at her heartstrings. Most *Others* were criminals because of the problems that *Humans* gave them. What was this man's crime? Theft? Maybe he was hungry. Murder? Maybe one of the *Humans* had done something to provoke him and he had had no choice but to defend himself. She kept her thoughts to herself, though.

"Can you grab me my bag? It's on the backseat of my car," she asked Lee.

"Your bag? You're not here to treat them."

Helena blinked hard and exhaled slowly before forcing a smile to her lips and turning to Lee. "I know, but this man's wounds are going to fester."

Annoyance flickered across Lee's face, but he smiled back at Helena, as fake and as forced as hers. "Maybe we could go out for breakfast in the morning?"

"Maybe we can," she replied equably, turning to continue her perusal of the prisoner. Oh, she knew his game very well—the subtle hint of bribery underneath his words. "Would you please get my bag?"

"I'll send someone for it."

She nodded, throwing him a cool smile. "Thank you."

That was better than nothing, she supposed. She turned her attention back to the prisoner. Welts had already begun to form on the clear skin where she had pushed down the chain to see his wounds. She ran an apologetic thumb over it, but the man didn't seem to notice. She pressed her fingers over his pulse and timed it with her watch. Slow … like he was sleeping. Helena frowned at the man as she set his arm back down to rest on his leg and went on to the next one. She held his wrist and took his pulse. It was the same. She went to another prisoner, and another, but it was the exact same thing with all of them—unresponsive pupils and a slow pulse. "It's like they're asleep," she said in bewilderment, standing back up and turning to Lee once more.

"Maybe we can put them out of their misery while they sleep," Lee said. "They're already out of it, and nine *Others* out of this world would make it a better place.

"Are they all booked for execution?" Helena cut in, ignoring his ruthless words.

Lee flipped through the book, his smile waning as he did, the prospect of delightful murder being dashed as he examined each sentence given to these *Others*. But then he stopped, the corners of his mouth lifting, his lips peeling back into an evil smile. "Two of them are," he grinned. "Our good friend, Nicholas Mason, and Luke Irving." Lee grabbed the scanner from the dashboard. Every prisoner had a new tattoo—their barcode. No longer people, but numbers. "This one," he said victoriously when the scanner found Luke. The man was bound in iron. This wasn't a shifter, but one of the Fae. "He's out of it, too?"

Helena nodded reluctantly. "They all are."

"Good. This one can go back to your lab."

"I have no use for him."

Lee smirked. "Yes, you do." She was beginning to hate that smirk. It always meant trouble; it always meant that Lee had come up with an idea that would no doubt repulse her. She gritted her teeth. Actually she already hated that smirk, but it was beginning to imprint such visions in her mind that her skin crawled every time she saw it. It always meant trouble—something that would delight the malice inside Lee, and something that would repulse her. "We can use him for testing."

"I will not test on people."

Lee shoved his fingers into the man's hair and pulled his head back so that Helena could see his face better. Luke didn't move, or even respond. Whatever had taken them all down like this was powerful. "This is not people. *Others* are

35

not people," Lee spat, his words dripping with hatred. "They're monsters ... creatures. Accidents of nature that do not belong here."

Helena said nothing. She didn't agree with Lee, or any of them. Others weren't monsters or creatures. In fact, she suspected that they were creations of evolution. Not accidents. In a world that was on its way to destruction, people needed to be tougher, stronger. They needed powers if the race was to survive. Were they *Human*? To Helena they were. Not segregated from humanity like people would claim. It was fear talking, that was all. Fear in every political leader's toolkit because they did not understand, and they could not control this product of Mother Nature. *Others* would survive this new world, the world that was being starved to death. They had purpose. *Fae*, she believed, were the healers of the world. It was no coincidence that they were linked to the different parts of it. They came in four kinds: fire, earth, water and air. All the things that the world needed in order to heal. It was no coincidence. "What is it that you expect me to do?"

"See what you can synthesise from him. He is water."

"Weaponise him?"

"You're a fast learner, Helena. Smart. We make a great team."

"I try my best," she said, ignoring the latter part of his statement, even though her mind screamed for her to tell him to get lost. Snapping at him was a little slice of victory, but it would come with dire consequences. She knew that.

Lee let go of the *Other*, thrusting the man's head down. He moved closer to Helena, and she took a step back, backing up until there was nowhere left for her to go. He wasn't touching her, but his presence was enough. It took everything she had not to leave the bus or push against him. She smiled sweetly at him, trying not to look intimidated.

"We work well together, don't we? I love when it is you who gets to come and work with me."

Helena gave a slight nod. "I enjoy the work, you know that."

He stared at her for a moment. "You'll take this man back to your lab for me, won't you?"

She knew the words under his question. She had no choice. She had her own office with a laboratory in it. It was *her* place—hers long before she had worked for Lee and Norton. Lee thought he was the boss, but really he was the right hand man, the doer of dirty work, and god did he love that part. "Of course," she said, betraying her screaming mind. But the alternative was that Lee would have her shipped to Norton Industries to work with them, and she liked her offices. She liked that she could help *Others* without question. "Put him on a stretcher, and I'll take him back to my laboratory."

A Cheshire cat grin spread across Lee's face.

Chapter Five
Eden

If *Humans* were one thing, it was efficient. The people on the bridge, the bus, the chatter, they'd all gone quiet—deathly quiet—and that wasn't a good thing, by any stretch. Pretty soon, the *Humans* would come. They'd clear out all the bodies, remove the bus, and they'd be down by the bridge like a fucking rash, and her ass would be hauled in the back of one of those vans faster than she could cast shit against them.

Eden pressed herself against the wall, head down, ears trained on the sounds above. *They always come back for one last scare. Always*. How many movies had she seen with her sister, and knew the bad guy wasn't dead? How long was it good to wait, though? That was the real problem. She craned her neck, angling it so that she might hear something better. She pressed her hands into the cold stones of the bridge supports—manmade shit that had come far from being part of nature now. She could barely connect with the fibres inside to get her answers. This was why witches were failing. Bloody *Humans* and all of their creations, taking away the most natural things that fed into them. She pressed herself into the wall as she shimmied sideways, walking an imaginary ledge towards the steps. The dog was no bloody use. He circled her, making her efforts seem pointless. "Shoo, you little thief." She wagged her foot at it, but the dog lowered its front paws, stuck its backside in the air and wagged its tail in response. "I'm serious. Get out of here." She swung her bag out towards him. "There's no food; you ate it all." The dog tilted its head, mouth open, panting.

"Whatever." He wasn't going to help. He'd probably get her caught.

Eden slid herself along to the steps, taking each step sideways. It must have looked odd to anyone who could see her, but she didn't care about that just then. What she cared about was what she would find up top. The last she had heard was the man and the woman talking. He wasn't going with her—that was what he had said. A car had driven off, and then there was silence. That was all there was.

She dropped her bag back over her shoulder, adjusting the strap so it was secured around her. Having obviously realised Eden wasn't going to feed him, the dog scampered up the steps. "Hey, wait," she called after him in hushed tones. But he slipped past her, her fingers grazing his fur. He disappeared from sight, and she waited—for a bark, or howl, or growl, or something that would indicate it wasn't safe to go up yet—but silence prevailed. She closed her eyes in frustration and uttered a quiet oath.

The scents of the earth were thick, deep musky scents holding the promise of a new day. "Please let me make it to another day." She took each step slowly until she reached the top, but even then, she wasn't sure if she wanted to look out. Images of a bunch of grinning faces waiting for her sprang into her mind. She'd probably have them waiting, and they'd kill her on the spot. "Stop it. Just stop it." She peeked out, only enough that she could see, her eyes roaming the area. There was a bus stopped in the middle of the road; the lights in the main cabin were on and inside sat some men, all staring one way. The dog had padded till there and was now sniffing at a man lying on the ground next to the bus. He lay on his back, and Eden's stomach lurched when she realised he had to be dead. She dared to take another step, rising on tiptoe, her eyes on the men sitting inside the bus; but not a single one turned or moved. They didn't even seem to bother about the dog who was sniffing around the steps. This was one of the buses of Exile prison—a transportation bus. She had seen them before. That meant … She raised her eyes again to the men and swallowed, her hands gripping the rail at the tops of the steps. They were prisoners. Her gaze caught sight of yet another body, closer to her—she hadn't seen it before, her mind too busy watching the dog. He wore a green uniform with boots that secured the bottom of his pants, laced up to the shins—a prison guard.

If the guard was dead, why didn't the men move? From what Eden could see, there was no one else around. No one there to stop them from escaping. Thankfully, they hadn't. For sure at least one of them would have come down the steps looking for a place to hide, and she was in no mood to fight off the unwanted attentions of a horny prisoner.

The road they were on was long. It was part of the appeal for her. It meant that she wouldn't be disturbed—not by people, at least. The road led to the prison, that was it. No other destination. The opposite way led into the small town. Small town meant that there were a few old houses and one small shop that was nothing but useless. Eden climbed out of the stairwell, keeping her eyes on the men. Oh, yeah, one would suddenly see her and then she'd be screwed. Well done, Eden. But none of them did. Even the dog paid her little mind. She screwed up her face in revulsion when she saw that he was licking up the blood around the man on the ground. Even she wasn't that hungry, although her stomach gave an angry growl, protesting the lack of food it had been given in the last few hours. That was the dog's fault, of course. If it hadn't been for him, she'd have eaten the bread, drunk her water, and probably be sleeping now.

Exile

There was nothing else for Eden to do but leave. *Humans* would come soon, so she couldn't wait around here. Another spot for another night. Her legs ached—she'd walked far today, and she was bloody tired. She fastened her coat up and shoved her earmuffs back into position on her head.

As she set off in the opposite direction to the prison, she saw someone walking ahead of her—the faint silhouette of a man. Maybe the one she had heard talking. Had he done this? Although Eden was far away from him, she stooped low in the darkness to follow him. He walked along the edge of the road, on the tarmac. There were no pavements to walk on here. No footpaths or even dug-out trenches. It was just mud or road. He held a bag, slung over his back, the kind of satchel someone might take with them when off on a trip.

Along the road, the muddy bank at the side eventually became inclined. Even farther down the road—over three miles long—the incline led to water. As she followed him, Eden kept her eyes on the woods beside them. This far up, the area was thick, trees running all the way to the prison and around the back—a dark cloak, giving promise to something lurking in the darkness.

The man she followed was tall. Big. She could see that even from where she was. The kind of man anyone would want on their side in a fight. He wore only a shirt, his arms bulging against the fabric. His hair was dark, cut short, but then all the men on that bus had short hair. It was cut to stop infestations of lice. Not that *Others* had lice, but the *Humans* feared it, so off went the hair.

The road came to a crossroads suddenly, and the man stopped. He had four choices really—he could go back the way he had just came, though that would lead him to the prison— or take one of the other roads that led to different places and destinations within Exile. Most of them lost to nothing, all of them secluded, and likely not a single one of the towns he would come across would take him in. Maybe prison was the better choice, after all.

The man didn't move, enabling Eden to get closer. She crouched lower with each step he took, muttering a curse when her foot slipped off the edge of the road and a pain-filled splits had her landing on her hands. She froze when she caught herself, staring at the man. He was yards away now, but if he had heard, he showed no indication of it. Eden lowered herself down the side of the grassy bank. Long grass parted, allowing her to hide.

The sound of scratching against stone shot Eden's heart into her throat. Hastily, she put her head down, a cast rolling off her lips, calling to the earth to hide her and protect her. She called for the man not to see her just as he turned, his eyes roaming the area. The scratching grew louder in tandem with Eden's heartbeat. She stayed in her awkward crouched position, absolutely still, waiting …

The scruffy dog padded along the road, tail up, ears flopping. Eden released the breath she had been holding, relief washing through her like a tidal wave.

Bloody dog.

He sniffed at the ground, following a trail of something with his nose as he neared Eden. He wagged his tail, walked in a circle around her, then lifted his leg and aimed. Eden slapped her hand over her mouth and sucked her stomach in, trying to make herself as compact as possible so that the dog would miss her. *The little shit*.

She glared at it, willing it to run.

"Hey, fella," the man's deep voice called out, and Eden's eyes widened in alarm. He'd seen the dog, and if the bloody mongrel didn't get away from her soon, he'd see her, too. The dog looked at her, panting happily.

She scowled at him with pursed lips. *Get lost*.

The dog whimpered forlornly for a minute then bounded off towards the man. Eden peered over the tall grass just enough so that she could see, making sure to stay hidden in the shadows. This was fast becoming a habit. The man crouched down, hand out, but the dog hesitated, sitting himself down a small distance from the man. "Yeah, I wouldn't get too close, either," he said to the dog as he stood back up. "Which way do you recommend?" The man's voice was that kind of deep baritone that was calming, sexy. His accent was northern, that roughness to it that just screamed some kind of mischief. It ran delicious shivers down her spine just to hear him talk. She imagined that his voice alone had got himself into a number of panties.

He started to walk away, then paused, casting a look over his shoulder at the dog. "You staying here, then?" The dog tilted his head in response, tongue lolling. "Well, I'm going this way." The man chose left. Not that it mattered. Any choice was the same—refusal and rejection. He'd learn soon enough. She had. She wasn't a prisoner like him, but she was homeless in a place so controlled and guarded that she was constantly sure it was just minutes before she was caught.

When the man was out of sight, Eden pulled herself back up and dusted herself off, wiping bits of grass from her skirt and tights. She pushed her bag back around so that it rested on her back, and tiptoed towards the crossroads, crossing the road so that she could hide at the corner.

The man was gone. The dog, too, she realised. Eden peered down the lane to the left, but all that was there was endless darkness. "How long did I stay there?" she muttered to herself. It hadn't been that much. The length of road she could see was long. "Good luck, mate," she said into the darkness. He would need it. No matter which way he went, he was *Other*. He'd be shot on sight if the *Humans* spotted him. She straightened and turned to go the other way ... and walked straight into a rock-solid wall of muscle. Iron fingers curled around her wrist, spinning her around while a strong arm slid around her waist and yanked her back so that she was pressed tightly against a firm, brawny chest, his grip vice-like.

She stifled a scream.

"Why are you following me?" The words were whispered in her ear, the gruff voice making her skin break out in goose bumps. She flexed her hand to cast, and the grip on her wrist tightened, pushing the bones together until they felt they were at breaking point. She bit back a whimper. "I wouldn't do that if I were you," the man said. "Now, I will ask you again. Why were you following me?"

"I wanted to know where you were going," she whispered back. The stubble on his chin brushed the side of her face. He was nature himself, deep, musky scents so ingrained in him that he smelt like the earth. He was a shifter. Only shifters held those scents, the aroma of earth and animal and man all rolled into one. Beautiful creatures, but dangerous, too. Only a fool would underestimate a true shifter.

"Why?" he growled.

"I was bored."

He wrenched her tighter to him, pulling her arm up and holding it behind his head, pinning her small hand against the small hairs on the back of his neck. She strained to balance, standing on her toes. "I'll ask you one more time. Why were you following me?"

Exile

Eden tugged at her hand even though she knew it would be useless. "You're hurting me." Her pulse throbbed under his grasp, the blood in her hand strumming to the sound of her heartbeat. He let her go a little, not much, but enough that she could retain some circulation. Her fingers tingled as blood rushed back into them. "I saw the bus," she panted. "The *Humans* ..."

He went dead still. "Yes?"

She tried to shrug, but the man's grip tightened, threatening to cut off her circulation once more. His heart beat steadily, his chest moving with slow and steady breaths against her back, the warmth of his body seeping through her clothes to heat her skin. Her gaze fell on the arm that held her around the waist, and she suddenly realised he was injured. Blood oozed from a gash, not so much that he would die from it, but it had to hurt. "I can fix that," she said breathily. "Your arm."

He splayed his fingers out across her stomach, turning his wrist so she couldn't see it. "It's fine. It'll heal. You saw the bus?"

She shook her head. "I don't know. I just saw the bus; I saw the thing that came down from the sky." Whatever it was, she'd never seen anything like it before. The swan had been bright, like a star, so high up, and then ... it was a girl. Definitely not a shifter, though. Shifters couldn't fly. "I saw what it did."

"That still doesn't tell me why you are following me?"

"I don't know." He pressed her hand, squeezed her wrist, making her call out. "I mean it. I don't know. I just got away from there before the sweepers came."

"Sweepers?"

She tried to pull away from him, but he yanked her back. "You don't know what sweepers are?"

45

"I do."

"Then you know it isn't something you want to get hold of you." When he said nothing, she said, "I really can fix your wrist."

"I don't need any of your witchy crap on me."

"Witchy crap?" She gritted her teeth. In her bag, she had bottles and tubes of things. Potions, lotions, things that she hoped to sell, or at least use to get herself into one of the towns. "Can you let me go now?" For a moment, she wasn't sure he would, but then he let go abruptly and stepped back. Eden stumbled forward, catching herself so as not to fall. She took a deep breath and turned to face her assailant.

Shit.

"She stared at him, gaping. She'd never seen such a gorgeous man before. She'd never seen eyes like that. In a daze, she reached a hand out …

He moved back, frowning. "What are you doing?"

"Sorry …" *Shit*. She shook her head. What was she doing? *Focus, Eden*. His wrist. Right. She reached into her bag, and his whole body tensed as if to attack. She held up one hand in a gesture of peace, and slowly took out a small bottle with the other and offered it to him. When all he did was stare at it, she unscrewed the cap "It's just a balm. It'll help your wrist." Still nothing. "Fine. Be a baby." She tipped the bottle into her palm, depositing a small drop of liquid. "See," she said, holding her hand out to him. "I didn't melt. Give me your arm." Still nothing. He didn't stop her, though, when she reached out and grabbed hold of his wrist. She pushed his sleeve up and smothered the wound in the balm. The wounds looked sore, and there were traces of silver on them. They would fester if he wasn't careful. His skin heated beneath her touch, warming flames of fire.

"What the hell …" He yanked his arm back. "What the fuck did you do to me?" The sores were redder, angrier. The man glared at Eden as the blood welling in the cuts bubbled and turned black. "Witch …."

"Wait." She put her hand up to stop him.

The black turned to grey, bubbling over and spilling itself down in silvery lines from his wrist.

"It's the silver. It draws it out and stops it burning you. That is why you don't heal well from silver. It seeps into your skin." Eden picked up her bag and pulled out a tissue, holding her hand out; again, he didn't move. She reached for his wrist and he didn't resist. She gently wiped at his wounds and watched as the silver slowly came away. Reaching into her bag again, she pulled out a bottle of distilled water and poured it over his skin—water and silver pooled on the ground. She poured it until the water ran clear, then she let go of his arm. His healing was slow, but his skin knitted together as they watched, the wound closing, like a shifter's always did, until the wound appeared to be weeks old.

"You're welcome," she said to him when he turned his arm over to inspect it with knitted brow.

"I didn't say thank you."

"No, but I was giving you the benefit of the doubt that you might actually have some manners."

"I don't."

She glared at him. "Never mind. I'll let you be on your way."

"You live near here?"

"I … umm …"

He raised a brow.

"I don't really live anywhere."

"You're homeless?"

Eden pursed her lips for a moment at the condescending tone. "Well, so are you, Mr …?"

"No one." With that, he turned and walked away, leaving her standing there. This time, in her sights again. She watched his retreating back, glaring at him, unsure whether to carry on in that direction herself or to go another way. But there was no other way to Fortvania, and that was where she needed to be. A town at the other side of the island.

She'd be free then.

Free from all this shit.

Chapter Six
Stephen

This was Exile—endless roads of nothingness. Well, not nothing exactly, Stephen realised; the lane was lined with old twisted trees and grass long past a good cut. It hid and housed weird women and dogs that lurked in the overgrowth and followed you for no other reason other than they were bored. Aside from that … there was nothing. No *Others*, no cars, no wild animals to stalk and kill, but perhaps most importantly, no *Humans*. Thank God for small mercies.

Stephen inhaled a lungful of fresh, clean, *Human*-stench-free air. Crisp and pure and invigoratingly cold against his face. Scents of fresh heather and the damp earth filled his nostrils, comforting the *tiger* deep inside with a feeling of home. Exile was a quiet place—he was thankful for that—but the downside, of course, was that this meant no house, no bed, no sanitation and no bearings.

But then, what did a bed mean? Or a shower? What couldn't nature provide for him?

Stephen often wondered what it would be like to live his life as his *tiger;* now was as good a time as any to find out. He'd asked his father once and had been met with comments about how it could be arranged if he didn't step up and face his responsibilities. Ironic. Stephen let out a low chuckle. Stepping up to the plate and dealing with his responsibilities was exactly the reason he had been exiled. "So much for that one, Dad."

He turned off the lane, only to find himself on yet another one, equally as desolate. Well, this was just peachy. Exile wasn't such a bad place if one liked solitude and the

49

same dismal surroundings. Stephen stopped, letting out a long breath when he came to yet another crossroads. There was a pattern forming here. Maybe it would be wise to start marking the trees to ensure he wasn't simply walking around in circles. They all looked the damn same.

He turned slowly, taking in his surroundings. Each choice was no different to the other. Just more empty lanes. More of nothing. More darkness with no destination. At least the girl wasn't behind him any longer. Stupid witch. Had she really thought that she could sneak up on a shifter? On Stephen? That he wouldn't know she was there? He'd picked up her scent a long way back, but had patiently waited to see what she would do.

Stephen chewed on his lip absently as he surveyed his surroundings. Where was he even walking to? It wasn't like he had a destination in mind. He wasn't going home; that was for sure. He let his bag slide down his arm and land on the ground beside him, then he yawned and stretched, clasping his hands behind his head for a moment before rolling his aching shoulders. The pain in his wrists really had gone.

He pushed up his sleeves and frowned at his almost healed skin. "Witches …" It didn't change anything, though. They were still witches. Still creatures at the bottom of the line.

An earthy smell caught Stephen's attention; there was a stream or some kind of water source close by. The air was redolent of fallen leaves and damp, water soaked ground. The rich scent—nature's perfume—was so inviting. The thought of the cool water against Stephen's naked, heated skin sent shivers across his flesh. It was so close; he could feel it.

Stephen picked his bag up again, but this time, he

didn't haul it over his shoulder; he carried it loosely beside him. With every step he took toward the trees, the scent of water grew stronger—earthly scents that called to him and created a longing inside, not just to swim, but for home, too. Stephen exhaled slowly. It was stupid. It really was. Yet he still felt the pangs of loss in his chest. No matter how much he told himself it was just for now, shit would work itself out, he couldn't shake the pull to go home. Even the voices in in his head had calmed and left him. After all this time wishing they would shut the hell up, they had—and it was eerily strange. Like the gentle hum of a refrigerator that is only noticed when it ceases.

Venturing into the shade of the trees, he used his senses to follow the scents of the water. He walked until the road faded from view, until all around him was nothing but woods and trees and the tranquil darkness that came with it.

Finally, the stream. It ran softly, its gentle current brushing against the sides—undisturbed and especially appealing to Stephen's *tiger*. He climbed up and over the weathered trunk of a fallen tree, the top of which rested across the water and on the other side. He leaned down, letting its coolness rise up and touch his skin like a delicate cold feather. He closed his eyes. Gemma would love this …

He scowled at himself. He had to let all that shit go now. He had to forget his old life. With an abrupt shake of his head, he tried to bury the thoughts of his life before Exile from his mind.

Dumping his bag on the ground beside the torn out roots, Stephen lowered himself to the water's edge. The ground was covered in small stones, bits of rocks that had crumbled over the years. Kneeling by the edge of the water, he cupped his hands together and drank from the stream. He hadn't realised how thirsty he was until the water hit his mouth—he gulped it down greedily. It was cold and refreshing, a contrast to his burning skin. The energy running through him from everything that had happened since that day—the day he had protected his father and screwed himself in the process—was unspent and bordering on becoming unbearable.

He'd not been able to shift since then, and his *tiger* roamed under the surface, demanding release. He splashed more water onto his face, soaking his shirt. He couldn't get enough as he scooped more and more into his waiting mouth. *Fuck*. He was so hot. He desperately needed to cool. He needed to shift. So many days on that bus, days with those people. He yanked his shirt over his head, hard muscle rippling as he moved. Throwing the shirt to one side, he started to splash water over his head, washing away the stench of *Humans* that lingered, and the heat that seared his skin. Water dripped down his shoulders and back and the night air clung to his damp skin, cooling him down. Only then did he sit back on his haunches and let out a breath of relief.

The scars along his arm, under his tattoo, throbbed to the beat of his pulse. They did that sometimes. Little rivers of, not pain exactly, but a gentle pulsing that reminded him they were there. He rubbed down his arm, pushing the skin so the lines of his tattoo became distorted. Sometimes he half expected the tattoo to be moving, the feeling in his scars so great.

The cracking of a twig behind him had Stephen's head snapping around. He lunged to his feet in one fluid movement and scanned the darkness, his senses searching. His eyes locked on the darkness. Trees reached out, reaching over each other, their twig fingers entwining together. The mud had fallen away from the base of the trunks of some of the trees, exposing roots that stretched out towards the water. Soon these trees would fall over, too—maybe with the next storm. Stephen squinted against the darkness. She was hard to see at first, but she was there. A wisp of a woman. Stephen lowered himself to the ground, his eyes trained on the target.

She wore a long, white, flowing dress, something a woman would wear on a hot summer's day, not in the middle of the night, alone in the woods.

"I can see you there," he called, leaning forward. "Come out."

Quietly, hesitantly, she moved closer, laying a delicate hand against the side of one of the trees as she peered at him. His chest tightened at the sight of her, and he stood back up slowly, their gazes locked. Her chestnut hair fell around her face in long, soft waves, creating a beautiful frame that made Stephen's heart stop. He couldn't take his eyes from her. The sheer beauty of her brought a lump to his throat and a quickening of his heart. His mouth parted as he sucked in a raspy breath. The tree still hid part of her and he watched with bated breath to see what she would do.

She lowered herself to the ground, kneeling, making no sound as she moved—not even the sound of fabric could be heard against the ground. Silence echoed around them with oppressing force.

"Are you okay?" He dared to step closer. "Do you need something?"

She gave no indication that she had heard him as he continued to kneel quietly. Her gaze fell to her hand, then he watched as she placed something on the ground and pushed it, letting it roll towards him. He knelt, mirroring her and caught it without thinking. A small, glass ball. When he raised his head again, the woman was gone.

"Hey." He lunged forward to where she had been, but

he had barely taken two steps when the world started to spin, his head growing heavy inside. It was suddenly an impossibly great effort to keep his eyes open, as if he hadn't slept in months. His mind grew foggy, his limbs not wanting to function. "Fuck …" The ground rushed up to meet him as he fell forward, suddenly too weak to hold himself up. He landed on his hands and knees, the glass ball still tightly clenched in his hand. Vaguely, he realised the woman was now standing next to him. She delicately stepped around him, and he strained to lift his head to look at her. "What have you done to me?" he said hoarsely.

He reached for her, but she stepped away, out of reach. Stephen's hand dropped back to the ground. Fighting with the forces of nature, he was incapable of resisting gravity as it pulled him to the ground, his big body falling heavily to the hard earth. He blinked up hazily at the ethereal woman just as she turned her back on him and left.

His thoughts were like fleeting birds in his mind—there one moment and gone the next. He couldn't grasp one, couldn't form a sentence to shout out. Everything around him grew silent. He let himself breathe; it was the most he could manage. The hard pebbles and sharp stones pierced his bare chest and the side of his face as he lay there, unable to move. He blinked long and hard, but his vision blurred, becoming pieces of a jigsaw that meshed together and created a blanket of darkness across his eyes.

***

The soft drip, drip, drip was the only sound he could hear. If he had the strength, he would have got up and cursed whatever it was making such a dreadful noise. It wasn't that it was loud, but the constant repetition grated against his nerves as he lay on the cold ground.

Stephen blinked, forcing his heavy eyelids open,

squinting with the effort. He blinked long and slow as he licked his dry lips, the chapped skin stinging at the contact with his tongue. He forced his eyes open, breathing through gritted teeth. How long had it been since he'd had something to drink?

His stomach rumbled with recoiling horror at the thought of a drink. It wasn't just that it was empty, it was a pit of vacant hollowness that screamed to be filled. He had no way of doing anything as his hunger lashed through him; a hot poker stabbing and twisting inside him until he could do nothing but roll onto his side and pant.

Food—it was all he wanted. Was it too much to ask for? His eyes closed again, but the darkness behind them was no different to that when his eyes were open. He lay there, imagining thick, hot tomato soup. He could practically smell the heavy aroma penetrating his senses, making his mouth water. He parted his lips in painful anticipation of the abundant flavour he was about to receive, but none came. His incarceration caused him to dream so vividly of things that he had once taken for granted.

He tried to move by pulling his arms up so that he might wrap them around his small frame in an attempt to console himself, but he couldn't. His wrists and ankles were bound together with barbed wire. It dug into his flesh when he moved, sending piercing hot agony through his already tender flesh. He cried out, unable to stop himself, but his moans were soundless, his voice gone, his throat like sandpaper inside. Only his tattered teddy bear lay in his hands. He couldn't even bring himself to pull that closer for any semblance of comfort. He let his tired head lower once again, but everything ached. Every movement was another shot of pain through his body. He couldn't reach for the bear.

Bear? Stephen frowned. He didn't have a teddy bear.

His mind swayed inside his head, and he fought to stay with what he felt, rather than what he knew. He forced his arms and legs to move, forced his tired and beaten body to get up. He moved his hands cautiously, but the binds were gone. He crawled from where he had just been. Not his bed, as he had expected, but somewhere else—somewhere strange to him. As he crawled, the tiredness ebbed away until he could breathe again.

He turned and let himself sit for just a moment, his head spinning. There was a wall close-by, a puddle of water at its base. The musty smell of the room scratched at the back of Stephen's throat—he was in a cellar.

He rested his back against the bars. They hadn't been there before. Had he even got off the bus? He was sure he had. He reached out to trace his fingers along the dirty metal. "Hello?"

No answer.

A movement in the corner of the cell caught Stephen's attention. Tensing, ready to fight off any threat, he leaned forward slowly on his hands and knees.

On the ground, where he had just crawled from, lay the pitiful remnants of a small child. The tiny body lying in the dirt, dark curls of hair covering her dirt-smeared face. She could be no more than five. Her eyes were open, watching Stephen, every ounce of pain that she had endured reflected in them.

Her eyes stayed locked with his. Barb wire tangled around her small, thin wrists and ankles. Stephen rubbed at his own, the echo of the feeling from before alive on his skin. She didn't move. She did nothing. Not even cry. She just stared at him, her shallow breaths rattling through parted, chapped lips. Stephen edged closer to her; she made no attempt to move away, but her eyes followed his every move. He fumbled as he tried to untie her wrists without causing her any more undue pain. He undid the wire around her ankles, his teeth clenching in anger when he saw how the barbs had stuck in her flesh. They had been in there so long that the skin had begun to heal around them. Who the fuck had done this to a small, helpless child? When he tried to pull the wire away gently, some of the scabbed skin came with it, pulling a gooey infected mess out with it. He winced for her as he continued to remove it, but the little girl made no sounds. When she was free of all her binds, Stephen offered his hand out to her. She hesitated at first, looking too weary to move. But then, with a small, weak smile, she reached for him. Small fingers—feathers in the breeze—touched and then rested in his hand. He lifted her frail body onto his lap, taking pains not to touch any of her wounds or hurt her, and wrapped his arms protectively around her.

The frailty of her bones made him frown—there was no weight to her. She leaned her head against his shoulder, and he raised a hand to stroke her hair as he stared at the empty shell she had left on the floor in the corner—small and broken. She had no need for it any longer.

Stephen closed his eyes. It was her time. Her pain was gone. Her suffering was over. "It's okay," he whispered as he held her closer to him. "You can go now. I'm with you."

Her warm breath danced across his skin, and he felt her smile against his neck. Tears rolled down her pale cheeks, and he kissed one as he stroked gentle fingers along her arm.

"Thank you," she whispered.

***

Stephen's eyes snapped open, and he came around with gasping alertness as if waking from a nightmare. His heart hammered in his chest as he glanced around the dark woodlands ... Except, it was no longer dark; the sun had risen.

The woman from before stood over him, her beautiful, hazel eyes on his face, watching him. He frowned, dazed and confused. Breathing hard, as if he had just run a marathon, he offered the small ball back up to her. Maybe she wanted it back.

The woman shook her head, a sweet smile on her lips.

"She belongs to you now," she whispered softly.

Chapter Seven
Eden

"Are you really going to follow me the whole way?" Eden scowled at the dog. He sat on his haunches, tail wagging, tongue lolling out the side of his mouth. Eden could swear he was smiling. He'd followed her all the way since she'd left the man, his little paws scampering behind her, stopping when she did. "There's no more food if that's what you think. You took it all." He angled his head at her. Eden rested her hands on her hips and tilted her head in the same way, causing her earmuffs to slip sideways until they freed themselves from her head and tumbled to the ground.

Great.

The dog immediately trotted over to them, and Eden scooped them back up before they ended up in his mouth. "No," she admonished him. "These are mine." She gently pinched the tip of one of his scratty ears. "You don't even have the right ears for them."

The dog let out a slight huff, like an acknowledgment to what she was saying.

"You understand me, huh?" Eden snapped open her earmuffs and put them back onto her head, but as she did, the two ends came clean apart, one of them recoiling on itself and springing from her grasp. "Great. Just fucking great." She snatched up the one from the ground again and pushed them back together, but it didn't matter which way she twisted them or how close they got to her face for better inspection, they were not going to stick back together again. "Brilliant."

She let her hands drop and sighed, feeling defeated. The dog gave a bark, and she turned weary eyes on him.

"Don't even look at me like that." She stuffed the earmuffs into her bag. "Cold ears, empty stomach and thirsty." She pointed an accusing finger at him. Two of those are your fault, mister."

She fastened her bag back up and positioned it over her shoulder so that the strap crossed her chest. She pulled her useless, moth-eaten jacket around herself and clenched her jaw, trying not to shiver. The tip of her nose, and now her ears, tingled from the cold. She had no choice but to go in the same direction the man had taken. Of course, he'd be pissed at that, but she had been going that way first. She was heading to Fortvania, one of the small towns in Exile. Things would be different when she got there; she'd prove herself, get a job and a place to live … She just had to get there—but that wasn't going to be tonight.

Eden ducked when she heard the low hum of a vehicle approaching from behind. She lay a protective hand on the dog's head instinctively. "Shit. Sweepers," she said to him. That, or money hunters, and she didn't want to face either.

She scanned the area for places to hide—places they wouldn't bother to check without good reason. Lazy, detestable Humans. There was water close by. The scent of it wafted her way and called to her like a homing beacon. It created an indescribable hunger in her. She crouched lower, splaying her hands on the road and closing her eyes. The earth throbbed, its own pulse beating under her fingers, beating in time with her heart.

"This way," she said to the dog, rising up enough to move. Energy cursed through her in ways she had never felt before. Shit. It couldn't be? This wasn't just water near her, this was *the* water. The stream of all streams—pure water. "God, do you feel that? Can you?" she breathed in deeply, inhaling loudly and letting out a pleasant sigh as she slipped into the shade of the trees, the mongrel happily trotting beside her. Her bangles jangled as she broke into a run, her ankle boots thudding against the earth. The water's song called to her, urged her closer, pulling her to it—a mother with open arms.

Eden had known these streams existed, but she had never found one before. She now realised that she would have known if she had ever been this close to one. A pure stream. She could hardly contain her squeals of delight. She raced through the trees, possessed by a need to get to it, the ache in her legs invisible to her in that moment. The dog ran behind her, silent to her senses. She bounded over debris, over leaves and twigs, racing to get to the water. And suddenly, there it was.

Eden stopped dead in her tracks, heart pounding, eyes wide. Sheer awe wrapped itself around her as she stared. It shimmered with purity, shining in the moonlight that filtered in through the branches above.

"Have you ever seen anything so wonderful?" she breathed. She took tentative steps closer as if it would vanish if she moved too fast. Her hands shook with delight as she neared the water's edge. The bank was small, the water gently lapping up the sides. Heat rushed over her skin, each throb of her heart filling her body with energy like she had never known before—she was alive with it. It ran hot in her veins, liquid energy spreading through her. "Oh, my God," she called out softly.

She lowered herself onto the small part of the bed that was exposed—tiny stones crunching under her boots. It was the most amazing thing she had ever seen. Leaning down to the water, she hesitated with her hand above it. Did she dare to touch it? It could vanish in a moment, or she could spoil it.

What if touching damaged the purity of it, and then all the benefits that would come from it would be lost.

Shit. She snatched her hand back and pressed it into her lap as she sat back on her heels. She wanted to touch it so badly, but images of that kid who fell into the chocolate river and ruined it swam into her mind. Yeah. That would be her. Fall in, fuck it all up.

The dog sat himself next to her, eyes on her as she tapped her fingers trying to figure out what she should do. "What? You have any ideas?" He wagged his tail in answer, and she grimaced. "You're no help." She chewed on the inside of her lip, her mind ticking away. "Wait." She sat up straight. "Yes. Bottle …"

She twisted and tugged her bag over her head, pulling it open. She rummaged through its contents, knocking aside bits of junk, make-up, creams, pens. "Shit. Where is it?"

The bottle. Had she really forgotten it? Left it at the bridge? There was no going back for it now, that was for sure. Puffing out her cheeks, she shuffled back to sit down cross-legged. There had to be another way; she just had to think of it.

The dog moved to lie next to her, resting his head on his paws. Eden reached out absently and ran a hand through his scraggly fur. She froze when she caught sight of a figure just a little further down along the stream.

Sitting up straight in a panic, she breathed, "God, no."

It was the man from before—and he was kneeling over the water and scooping handfuls into his mouth. What the hell was he doing? "No. No … stop it."

She pushed herself up onto her knees, hand slapping over her mouth to silence her protests. He was damaging the water—contaminating it. She let out a shaky breath, blinking away the tears in her eyes from what he had done. Fucking shifters. Strong senses—all but the common one.

"Stop it. Please," she whimpered. She was crawling forward without realising she had started to move, sobs catching in her throat. He had to stop. He *needed* to. Before it was too late.

She reached the part of the stream where the bank was thicker and right in the water. A fallen tree lay in her way; the water having washed away the foundations where it had planted its roots. She crouched behind it, eyes on the man. He was sitting back now, leaning against the trunk of another tree. His head was back and it looked like he was talking to someone, but Eden couldn't see anyone around. She strained to hear what he was saying, but the words were muffled and spoken without any pause.

In the next minute, he was slamming his hand down with speed, grabbing something from the ground. Shadows danced across the water and the temperature dropped. The wind rose, whipping across the surface of the stream, spraying Eden and the dog lightly with its purity. The dog whimpered and backed away, tail between its legs, the hackles on its fur rising. "Hush …"

The man leaned forward, and for a moment, Eden was sure he'd see her. But he rose to his feet, oblivious to her presence … A chill ran up her spine.

She watched him rise to his feet … while his body continued to lie on the ground.

She swallowed hard, waiting wide-eyed, her breath coming out in soft, white puffs of air. She watched as the 'shadow' of the man, some kind of darkness, stood up, rising to a magnificent height; and while her senses told her it wasn't evil, evil lurked. It pressed against Eden's skin, chilling her. Unable to pull her eyes away, she watched as he turned to face the water, then ran and dived into it head first.

There were no splashes, no ripples. It was almost like he wasn't there at all. But she didn't doubt what she had just seen. Her eyes were *not* deceiving her. She turned her gaze back to the motionless body on the ground, wondering for a moment whether he was dead. The branches rocked with the wind, tossing leaves down. They floated into the water … but they didn't land on the surface. They soaked in, dissolving as the stream devoured each leaf in turn.

Oh, God.

It was there in her mind. All those fucking stories. *All* of them. She raced back to her bag, throwing it open and pulling out her belongings. Her book was at the bottom. She hadn't looked at it in such a long time, didn't even make sense why she kept it. Yet she carried it around with her always—her little comfort blanket of sorts. There was a name on the front, the name and address of a woman in Fortvania.

Eden plonked herself down in the dirt, the book on the ground between her knees as she leafed through the old, yellowed pages—pages that had been written long before she even existed. Pages with words she couldn't read and pictures that made no sense.

"Come on. I know it's in here." She flicked through it, a specific image in her mind. She had seen this before. She was sure of it. She reached the final page and let out an exasperated sigh. *Shit.* "It's not here."

Desperately, before the image in her mind vanished, Eden stretched to the edge and pulled out one of the roots of a tree that would soon follow the same fate as its fallen comrade. Snapping it off, she wiped away the dirt and brushed away the small stones stuck on it. Using the root like a pen, she drew the image in her mind in the mud and stones. She had seen this image before. She could still see the pages in her mind, so clear. A man. A tree ... *the* man and *the* tree. Her brow furrowed. What had been on the other side? A swan?

No.

She pressed her palms to her temples. "Think, Eden. Come on. You know this." A dog. No ... a cat. "A big fucking cat." She had seen it in the book when she was little; she had sat flicking through it at her grandmother's house—when she had thought that it was all nothing more than drivel.

Eden drew the cat with the swan, but the swan was bigger, different. As she rounded the last part, drew the tail on the cat, the water of the stream lapped against Eden's leg, startling her. "Shit." It filled in the lines she had made in the dirt and then swept them back. Eden scrambled away, expecting the water to come again, but it barely moved.

The image in front of her soaked into the water— soaked into the earth. With her heart pounding in her chest, she lay a tentative hand down across the top of it. To her surprise, she found it was warm. Breathing hard, she reached for her book again, turning each page slowly this time. She thumbed the corner of each page, making sure that none of them had stuck together ...

She gasped suddenly, anger surging through her. "That piece of shit." She stopped just over halfway, bending the book back on itself and running a finger down the centre ... along the rough edge. "He fucking took it. That *fucking* arsehole."

Eden slammed the book shut and pressed it to her chest. Slowly, almost fearfully, she let her gaze travel back over the trunk of the tree to the man.

He was awake again—*whole* again. He held something in his hand, holding it up to the moonlight.

Eden's hands shook, her body trembling.

It was *him*. It was really him.

Chapter Eight
Helena

Helena's clinic was in the centre of one of the many gated communities of Exile. *Humans* advertised these places as safe havens for *Others*, small villages where they could stay … which meant *not leave*, so that they didn't roam. They had every convenience they could want or need. *Others* saw them for what they were, though—an open prison, with their wired gates and fences stretching far and wide, and the curfew enforced by the sweepers that kept them in place. *Others* were not stupid, nor as blind as the *Humans* thought they were.

If it was real freedom, they would all be wandering around and hunting whatever the hell they wanted, *when* they wanted. This was just another way to segregate *Others*, to keep the numbers down and prevent the one thing *Humans* were afraid of—a mutiny. The day would come. One day. *Humans* would only have so much control before *Others* started to say *enough*.

Helena knew this. She embraced it. She embraced them—*all* of them. It was just after ten in the morning when she pulled into her parking slot outside of her clinic and home—she lived in the rooms above the place. It was convenient this way. There was always work to do, so she practically lived in her doctor's office. Her home was just somewhere to sleep really. There was always someone who needed her help … who needed medical attention. She would never turn them away.

Lee's car pulled in behind hers, and behind him, the van that contained Luke, the *Other* from the bus, arrived.

Helena allowed herself a moment to just sit—to calm her mind and her mood so that she could keep a lid on everything and hold a perfect smile in place when speaking to Lee. He only needed one excuse to get her to come and work at Norton labs, and she sure as hell wasn't going to give that to him. She gripped the steering wheel so hard that her knuckles turned white, but she kept her eyes on the rear-view mirror, waiting for Lee to get out so that she could slip her mask back on.

But he was on the phone.

The street that housed her clinic was normally full of people this time of day, but not at the moment. People would be hiding. From the house, next to Helena's, Benny peeked out between the blinds, small beady eyes meeting hers. How soon would the word have spread? Whispers that Helena was back, and that she was with other *Humans*, would have gained momentum like wildfire.

Humans thought they had control. They thought that they could see everything and knew everything; but the *Others* here, they had a system. Helena was sure this wasn't the only village to be this way. They'd have known the *Humans* were coming long before they actually arrived. They'd have run around, warning each other and closing down the hatches, literally pushing people inside and retaining an air of normality before the arrival of the real monsters.

Benny lived in the house next door to Helena. She had helped him move there when he had brought his crying grandson in for medical attention about three years ago. His old, mottled hands had shaken so badly when he had asked her to help him. He hadn't dared look her in the eyes. It tore at her heart right now, too, to see the fear there again; even from this distance. Benny wouldn't be long for this world—

not be long at all. Every time Helena saw them, she felt guilty. She hadn't been able to save the boy's leg. Benny and his grandson were necromancers. Not gifted with the healing powers of shifters, his small bones had shattered when he had been caught in a trap laid out by the *Humans*. It had nearly severed the leg itself from just under the knee.

Helena didn't wave at Benny as she got out of her car, but she offered a slight reassuring smile before breaking eye contact. Hopefully he would understand that this *invasion* was nothing to worry about.

No longer on the phone, Lee climbed out of his car as she did, pulling at his shirt cuffs and straightening his sleeves. He strode over to her, his gait exhibiting confidence and assurance. Everything about him emanated masculinity and perfection. If only the inside would match, then he would be truly beautiful. Helena wasn't sure exactly what it was about him, but there was something deep and dark lurking behind those sweet, blue eyes.

"This place is quiet today," he commented as he walked toward her.

"It always is," she lied. Of course, it never was. Children ran and played. People spoke to each other on the streets. There wasn't a *Human* place for miles from this village, and their system alerted them to any oncoming trouble. "They know the rules. *No fun. No life.*

"Indeed." Lee looked around him with a haughty expression on his face. "I wish you wouldn't insist on living here, Helena. It makes me worry about you."

She touched a hand to his arm gently and forced a saccharine smile to her face. "I never have anything to fear. You protect me well." Helena recoiled inwardly at this dance … Always this dance when Lee was around. She needed him not to question things so that she could stay here, in peace, and help *Others*.

Lee gestured to the two men in the van. *Bring the Other in.* His motion was that simple.

Helena dug into her shoulder bag for her keys. Not that she needed them—her assistant, Tracey, was in, but she needed the moment to gather her wits so that she could put a cap on that small rebellion that was bubbling inside her. It would do her, or the people here, no good if she were to speak out of turn to Lee. It had taken her years to build their trust, and if she let Lee ship her out, she'd be letting them down more than herself. It had taken her a lifetime not to be seen as the enemy. "Got them," she said with her fake smile in place. "Shall we get him inside?"

Helena's house was the old kind—Victorian and tall with steps that led up to the large main door. Standing on the steps, one could easily look down into the window of the floor beneath, but Helena had made sure it was protected by both a metal fence and a mesh so that no one fell down the drop—she'd learnt the hard way how easy it was for that to happen when a very sickly, and a very pregnant, woman had come to her door one night. Thank god, she had been a shifter, or she might not have healed from the fall.

Helena opened the large double doors to her clinic and made enough room for the men to roll the gurney with the *Fae* inside without chipping any of the paintwork. The ground floor was kept sterile—clean walls, clean floors—the scent of disinfectant and lemon creeping out. While many might be repulsed by the medicinal smell, it was more of a homely smell for Helena; the scent that let her know she was in her safe place. Yet today, she had brought the lion to the rabbit den. She gripped the door handle, steadying herself and her rapidly beating heart. The first room was a waiting room—small, standard and efficient. There was no one waiting today, thankfully. No one for Lee to mock and 'make plans' for. Behind that was Helena's consulting room, and beyond that was another room where she performed small surgeries.

Tracey, Helena's assistant and aide, was in the consulting room, cleaning the countertops. The clinic was closed when Helena was out on call, except for minor ailments—Tracey could deal with those. She beamed when she saw Helena, but the smile quickly vanished as Lee came in behind Helena.

"Can you get the plinth ready for me?" Helena said, face stern, words harder than she would use if they were alone. Saying please like she usually did would make Tracey equal—*Others* were not equals. At least not in Lee's eyes.

"You know that if you came and worked for my uncle, you'd not need one of these *things* working for you?"

"It keeps them out of trouble," Helena said quickly, throwing Tracey a furtive, apologetic look. "Besides, it's cheaper labour, and they can work longer hours. They're replaceable, too."

Lee chewed on that for a second as he regarded Helena. "Very true," he mused.

Of course, that would appeal to him. Although Helena did pay Tracey when she could, it wasn't a lot, but it was something. Tracey had two boys and a husband to care for. She did get an education from it, though. Someone who could help *Others* the same way that Helena did. Doctors were valuable, especially in this world.

In the very back room stood a plinth, the side of which was lined with hanging hooks. Helena didn't keep the straps attached to them; she didn't like to. How could you claim to be a friend—a doctor—when you had the very things that could hurt the patients on display. It didn't mean that she didn't need them. Shifters needed them. They were hard to anaesthetise, and when they were out of it, their animal sometimes tried to take over. The last thing she needed was a spontaneous shift in the middle of trying to stitch a wound.

The men loaded the *Fae* onto the plinth, and Tracy pulled the binds from the small cabinet.

"Iron," Lee said, making Helena wince internally. Iron would render the Fae's magic unusable. Not that he could use it now—his mind was shot. He still stared out vacantly, not seeming to register anything. Of course, there was always the slight chance that he actually could. Helena wouldn't know, however, without being able to image his brain, but she didn't have those facilities here. No, only Lee and Norton Industries had those, she thought balefully.

The men lifted the *Fae* onto the bed with ease, carelessly dumping him onto the firm surface. Luke Irving. Helena kept his name at the forefront of her mind—he was a person, and no matter his crimes, he still deserved to be treated with dignity.

The men shackled him, strapping his arms and his legs, as well as putting a strap around his throat and another across his chest. There was no way he was moving now, even if he did wake.

"I will leave one of these men with you," Lee said. "I don't want this thing waking up and harming you."

"He won't harm me." She trusted them, and none of the *Others* in the area would allow harm to come to her. Of course, she didn't say that part. "I know what I am doing."

"I don't trust their kind."

"I promise. I will be okay."

Lee's gaze fell onto Tracey, who was standing in the farthest corner, trying to make herself as small as possible.

She put a protective hand across her slightly swollen belly, her mother instinct to the fore. This one was a girl. They'd celebrated when they had found out, though Helena had warned her: no more babies after this one. Her body couldn't take it. Helena just hoped that she would make it to term. It had been hard enough with the last one.

"More vermin being bred, I see," Lee snarled. He strode over to her, and Helena took a small step forward before quickly stopping herself. Tracey shrank back, and Helena stiffened but said nothing. Her mind screamed at her to get Lee out of there. But she knew he was just showing off. Showing what a *man* he was. He didn't realise that this didn't impress Helena one bit. He grinned at the terrified girl, content with the fear he saw etched across her face. He stared at her for moment, and Helena's heart dropped to the pit of her stomach. After what seemed like an eternity, Lee ground out, "I would feel so much better if I had a way to protect you."

"You do protect me," Helena assured him sweetly, moving closer, desperate to get his attention off Tracey. "This man isn't going to wake up again."

Frowning, he turned to face Helena, turning his back on Tracey. Helena almost sagged with relief. "You should put him out while I am here. He is down for execution anyway."

Helena's gut twisted. "I do not wish to kill him."

"I can do it for you," Lee said, his eyes lighting up in eager anticipation.

"Really, there is no need." The *Fae* was going to die anyway; he was meant to die. He had been sentenced to death, and that was his fate ... but still. She wasn't going to be the one to do it. Maybe he wouldn't wake from whatever this trance was. Maybe he was already gone and his body

73

just needed to catch up. She would find out when she did more tests.

"If you remove all his blood, you would have a lot to synthesise."

"If I remove all of his blood, then he will die for sure."

Lee nodded coldly. He went to the cabinet above the computer, where she logged everything. Her hands balled into fists. He had the keys to it—that was part of the deal. He had keys to everything. He unlocked it and pulled out a small lock box.

"Lee …" Helena stepped forward, her stomach doing somersaults. He couldn't do this. "Please."

It is the only way I can feel safe," he said flatly. It was bullshit, she knew it, but she forced an acquiescing smile to her lips and held her shaking hands behind her back. Blood pumped through her veins so fast that it thumped loudly in her ears. *Please don't.* She didn't voice the words, they wouldn't matter. As far as Lee was concerned, this man was going to die anyway, so he could do whatever he wanted to.

He pulled out a vial, and Helena swallowed hard. She'd only had to use that twice. A combination of deadly herbs, it put the subject to sleep and then they never woke again. She used it when there was no hope and the only thing she had to offer was mercy. But even then, even though she used it in those desperate times, they had stolen a part of herself. It wasn't her place to play God. And it sure as hell wasn't Lee's, either.

Helena forced herself to watch, even though every part of her screamed at her to look away. But she owed it to the *Fae*. She owed it to herself. Looking away would show Lee that she was weak, and then he would insist that she work in his laboratories. He pushed the needle into the *Fae's* arm none too gently and pressed the plunger.

Exile

The *Fae* awoke, jolting against the straps, making Helena jump.

Luke … His name was Luke … *Luke* awoke. Eyes open, they looked straight at Helena before he sucked in a sharp breath and then slumped back heavily. Just like that, he was gone, the light fading from his eyes as they stayed on Helena.

Helena bit her trembling lip, her heart pounding inside her chest as she tried to get a grip.

"Now you can work on him," Lee said heartlessly, handing the syringe to Tracey.

Helena swallowed and forced back the lump in her throat. "Thank you," she said coolly, her mask impeccable.

Lee sidled up next to her, his warm hand taking hers and giving her cool fingers a light squeeze. "Dinner tonight? Instead of breakfast?"

She blinked away tears that threatened to rise and looked up at him. "Dinner would be great," she said, fighting to keep her hand and herself in place. Helena gaze met Tracey's, who was still standing behind Lee. She pressed the back of her hand to her mouth as they stared at each other, eyes brimming with tears. Helena tore her gaze away from Tracey and looked at Lee. "Thank you," she said quietly.

Chapter Nine
Stephen

The child had been real. Stephen knew she had. The impression of her against his skin was still alive—still warm. He could taste her tears against his lips, smell the dampness of the room. The echo of dripping water still resounded in his mind. It had *all* been real. He rolled the little ball in his hand as he sat back, unsure what this new form of insanity that had suddenly descended upon him was. Maybe it was nothing more than sleep deprivation and a lack of food. But everything he had felt was as real as the pain in his chest where his family resided. He rubbed at his eyes. *Fuck it.* Shit was playing havoc with his mind.

His gaze focused on the glass marble, watching as it rolled across his palm. A sudden flicker had him pausing midway a roll, frowning. The colour had changed. He held it between thumb and forefinger and squinted. There was something inside it. It appeared to be a lighter shade, bluer perhaps. He cast his eyes skywards and cursed at the dullness of the night—the moon above, not quite full, not quite giving enough light that he needed to see.

Stephen got up and held the marble towards nature's weak light, but it refused to give away its secrets. As he stared hard, a tiny picture—a minute display of some kind—started to take shape within its depths. Like the kind of thing one would see inside a child's key-chain. Staying focused, he finally started to make out a picture of a small girl and her teddy bear, lying there in the darkness. The girl—it was *the* girl.

For God's sake. He couldn't see into it properly. Maybe his mind was playing tricks on him. Without warning, he grew dizzy, his mind swimming as his body swayed. He reached out to catch himself, clenching the marble tightly in his hand. "Fuck," he breathed, fighting the pull of his mind to drag him under.

This was just exhaustion and shock. It had to be. The voices he had been plagued with all his life in his head had suddenly silenced—but now he had this to deal with. Whatever it was that was going on with him made no fucking sense at all. His mind hadn't had chance to catch up with one thing when the next problem arose.

What did the marble mean anyway? He had no idea. It didn't fucking matter; none of it did. He sat himself back down and tossed the ball into the bottom of his satchel. He rubbed his face–calming himself. His stomach rumbled, giving a not-too-friendly reminder that he hadn't eaten, and it wasn't happy. But he couldn't shift and hunt here. He didn't even know what *here* was, let alone the laws. He lay back, resting his head against his bag as he settled himself down onto the dirt and closed his eyes.

He had barely caught an hour of sleep when light started to stream through the canopy of dense foliage overhead. He cracked his eyes open, his senses instinctively reaching out to detect any possible threats. When he perceived nothing, he drew in a deep breath and closed his eyes briefly. Involuntarily, his thoughts flicked to his sister and best friend, and with that came the pang of longing. A fortnight ago, they had been the ones leaving, and whilst he hadn't wanted them to, he knew they had no other choice. He'd dreaded every moment of it–every day that had brought them closer to that portentous instance. Fate had been laughing at them, though—it was Stephen who eventually got to go, and they had got to stay. For that, at least, he was grateful, he mused. He would happily have exchanged places with them to save their baby and them from this fate.

However, being here alone, struggling for survival in this godforsaken place, seemed even harsher when everyone he had ever cared for thought he was dead. Somehow, the fact that no one knew he was alive made the feeling of loneliness in him even more profound.

Sunlight crept in through the edges where the trees thinned at the top. Its warm rays peeked through the woods, creating eerie beams of light that touched the surface of the water behind him. Stephen licked his dry lips and cleared his throat. His mind floated back to just a few hours before—maybe the water had made him crazy—some bug that had got into his system … But still, try as he might to convince himself of these things, his mind wasn't shifting. The image of the girl remained.

God, he needed to eat. He needed to fucking hunt and just be himself. He pushed himself up, eyes and ears still scanning the area. There was no movement, no sounds to be heard. No snapping twigs, no birds, nothing. His stomach rumbled once again, causing him to curse at the shoddy service as his stomach announced its annoyance at the lack of food over the last twenty-four hours. There was no way he could just sit there when he was so damn hungry. *Fuck*, even Cade's microwaved regurgitated rabbit seemed appealing now. Stephen rubbed the sleep from his eyes, stretched and yawned. His shirt lay on the ground, filthy and torn, but it was the only shirt he had. With a muttered curse, he pulled it on and fastened the laces of his boots.

Pulling the cord on his bag tight, he slung it over his shoulder and looked around him. There had to be something, and somewhere, he could hunt. Just a rabbit …

Exile

Even a fucking squirrel would do. It wouldn't really matter. Something to take the edge off.

Stephen climbed back up the slope, tracing his steps from the night before. He found the road with ease, but he wasn't going to walk along the edge of it. He wasn't just Stephen Davies any more. He was Nicholas Mason, escaped convict. They'd be looking for him. He followed the road, walking along the line of the trees instead, listening for oncoming vehicles or *Humans*—any kind of imminent danger.

Stephen wasn't exactly sure where he was going; he just walked. One foot in front of the other and no real destination in mind. His stomach distracted, and it was hard to keep focus or pay attention. Soon, if he didn't eat something, his *tiger* would start with his demands, and then he would really be screwed. He was control. He had been heir to the alpha, but even his *tiger* would only be pushed so far.

He walked along a path of sorts parallel to the main lane. It was one that had been used by countless others before him, and their footsteps had worked the land flat and compact. The grass had been killed off long ago. But there were no cameras here, nothing to watch and to alert the *Humans* that *Others* were loitering around. Maybe that was why this path was here. Back home, the *Humans* would have policed every area, ready to catch any *Other* who dared to be out and in areas prohibited to them. They would have been caught and passed over to their own kind so that punishment could be dealt accordingly— 'accordingly' meaning execution, of course.

Never was it enough to simply punish the *Others*; they found much more pleasure in handing them over to the Societies and the Councils, ensuring that punishment was dealt with there, because it was always harsher, always public. *Humans* had an odd desire for things that gave them a sadistic kick—always searching for reasons to execute them. They'd probably revelled in the day that Stephen was declared dead.

The path came out near the back of a store; right at the point where the *Humans* dumped their trash. It figured with the trodden-down path—trash—the discarded remnants of *Human* greed. It wasn't the store that was the destination; it was the bins and everything the *Humans* threw away. What kind of desperation would cause *Others* to have to rummage through the droppings of *Human waste*? Stephen's mouth twisted with disgust as he realised that the makeshift path was more well-used than the actual lane. He shook his head in disbelief, his mind imagining *Others* that had come before and after him to search for the scraps of humanity. *Humanity* … He scoffed at the word. Pathetic *Humans* wouldn't know what humanity was if it came and slapped them in the face.

So, this was Exile …

Exile with all its glorious trimmings. Oh, what wonderful things would be in store for him. Stephen let out an almost defeated sigh. Maybe some water would do him good now; clean, fresh water. Not the water of the stream that gave him weird dreams of small girls dying in damp cellars.

As Stephen emerged from the trees, he saw the bins. Someone had beaten him to it. Well, damn it, there went his dinner. He rolled his eyes at himself. A woman was bent over one of the metal bins, and as Stephen approached, she stood and spun on her heel so fast that Stephen was sure she might have twisted an ankle. He scowled when he saw who it was. As she held her hands out in front of her ready to cast her damn spells, his scowl deepened. What did she think he was going to do? Fight her for scraps?

"You again," he snarled.

"No, you mean *you* again. I wasn't following you this time."

The mongrel she had been companioning with bounded out from behind the bins suddenly and raced over to him. Stephen crouched down, eyes still on the witch as he stroked the dog's fur. "Hey, boy," he said, before addressing the witch once more. "I wasn't following you, either."

She lowered her hands a little, eyes squinting at him. He hadn't got a good look at her before in the dark. She was young—maybe early twenties. Her hair was tipped with purple, reminding him of a flower whose middle had faded from the sunlight. If Stephen was the caring kind of man, he might have felt a little sadness that such an attractive creature had been reduced to delving into the depths of *Human* waste for something to eat.

Luckily, he was not.

"You can put your hands down; you know? I'm not here for you." He gave the dog one last scratch behind the ears before rising again. He brushed himself off, brushing invisible fur from his clothes, while mildly registering the fruitlessness of such an act—they were dirty and ruined anyway. "The rubbish bin is all yours. I promise."

"I'm just looking for a water bottle. I'm going to Fortvania."

"That's very nice for you," Stephen said nonchalantly. Whatever Fortvania was, he hoped she had a dandy time. "I just want some water."

"You have money?" She still hadn't lowered her hands all the way, still ready and poised to attack. Fucking itchy trigger fingers. God, he hated witches.

"I'm not sure that is any of your business." Not that it mattered, the store behind her was closed—the shutters were down and their lack of clientele was also a good hint. Of course, the swinging board on the door stating 'Closed' should dispel any uncertainties if one were to have them ...

"You're going to buy water?"

Or maybe not.

"Maybe. I might. Are you going to let me get past you, witch? You can get back to your rubbish cans."

She kicked against some of the bits of rubbish she had flung to the ground in her efforts to locate a water bottle. It rolled towards Stephen, spilling out some of its sloppy orange coloured guts as it did. Whatever it was—or had been—was well beyond saving. Stephen caught it under the sole of his boot and grimaced.

"Too good for you?" she asked with a quirked brow.

"Of course it is," he said. "Do you not see all of my riches and gold and jewels, witch?" He held out his arms and moved full circle slowly. "Money drips from me, see?" Was he too good for it? Damn fucking right he was. He was the son of the alpha ... *dead* son, but son nonetheless. Pack *Others* did not rummage through the trash, no matter how desperate.

The witch uttered some half-coherent insult at him, and he walked toward her. He would take his chances with the little ice-tipped fingers. What could she actually do to him that was worse than anything he had already endured?

Tipping her head to the side, she watched him with curiosity. "How is your wrist?"

The wrist ... Of course. He had actually forgotten about that. He pushed his sleeve up and nodded. "Pretty good." The marks where the silver had bitten in were still there, but now, instead of angry red gashes, faint lines streaked his skin. In another hour or so, there would probably be no trace at all of the damage he had received.

The witch smiled. "Worked a treat, I see." She put her hands down, pulling her bag around to her front without taking her eyes off Stephen. She was a rabbit, watching, waiting—in front of a starving, ravenous *tiger*. "It's Eden, by the way."

"Eden?"

She nodded. "As opposed to 'witch'. My name ... It's Eden."

"Like the garden?"

She scowled at him. "Yes. Like the garden."

"Where Adam got screwed over?"

She glowered at him. "What bitch twisted your balls?" She shook her head then turned her back on him again, resuming her rummaging through the trash.

Stephen bit back a retort.

Fine ... Whatever. He just wanted a bottle of water.

Chapter Ten
Helena

Helena balled her fists at her side, taking in a short, sharp breath as she forced a smile to her lips. Lee got to his car, smiling across the roof at her before getting in. The life he had just taken meant nothing to him. How could he be so inhumane? Her heart hurt just at the thought of it, but she held it in—down in the depths of her soul. Luke would probably not enter his mind again. Did she envy him? No. She couldn't imagine being so cold.

Lee pulled away, glancing over his shoulder and waving at her one last time. She waved back, keeping the smile pasted on her face until he left the village and the entry gates closed behind him.

Tracey was standing behind her in the shadows of the entry hall, her expression reflecting the exact same feelings that weighed in Helena's chest. She had her hands clasped in front of her, her lip quivering and her eyes shimmering with unshed tears. Helena closed the door to her clinic, the soft click echoing loudly in the heavy silence. Resting her hand on the door sign, she was half-tempted to flip it to closed and just hide away for the rest of the day—but that would be a failure to others who came seeking her aid.

"I'm sorry," she whispered to the other woman. She wasn't just apologising for Lee and his actions, she was apologising for all of it. Apologising for her kind and the cruelty they bestowed upon *Others* every damn chance they got. Some of them, like Lee, positively thrived on it. The compassionate hand on her shoulder told Helena that Tracey was not blaming her for anything, but guilt at her inability to save a helpless being weighed heavily on her.

Exile

Helena squared her shoulders and stood up straight. He'd be back to pick her up at seven—and he would be punctual—and somehow, she would get ready mentally and physically, pulling herself together and doing what needed to be done.

Unable to look the other woman in the eye, she turned and walked back to the room where Luke was and paused at the door, heart thumping. Her mind yelled at her to stay out, not torture herself with the sight of his lifeless body lying there. She gripped the door handle, her palm sweaty. He was dead. *Dead*. She tried to tell herself that. Tried to tell herself that it didn't matter now what she did to him—he was gone. He wouldn't know, nor care, nor feel anything at all. But she did. That was the problem. She cared … a little too much, perhaps.

Setting her jaw in a determined line, she twisted the handle and pushed the door open. The air conditioning had come on and a cold blast of air hit her. Luke was just where they had left him, his lifeless eyes closed, his binds in place.

"Are you really going to drain him?" Tracey breathed from behind Helena, making her jump. She made way for Tracey to enter the room.

"I don't have any other choice." Not if she wanted to keep her office here and keep the distance between her and Norton industries. If she wound up working for them, she'd not be treating live *Others*, she'd be draining them, using their blood and body parts for medical experiments. "You don't have to be here." Normally, she would have asked Tracey to get the equipment ready and set up, but today it didn't matter. Not with this. Tracey was bringing new life into the world. It would not be right to ask her to aid in the draining of one that had just left. Helena had the machine for this. She'd jab the needle into the coronary artery and the machine would do the rest—pumping the blood like the heart would do, only it was actually syphoning it out into a large drum. "We have some sterilised tools in the machine?"

Tracey nodded.

"Want to deal with them?" It wasn't so much of a question, more of a command—a way out for Tracey so she didn't have to do this part or say anything. "Give me an hour in here?"

Tracey nodded again, but her eyes were fixed on Luke. After a long moment of Helena wondering if the other woman had understood what she had asked, she finally said, "Give me a shout if you need anything."

"I will," said Helena with a weak smile.

As soon as Tracey had left the room, Helena closed the door behind her then slumped heavily against it. She stood there for a moment, staring at the *Fae* on her table. She'd let him down. Whatever he had done, whatever his crimes were, as a doctor, she had broken her vows. She closed her eyes and covered her face with her hands.

With an abrupt movement, she stood up straight and took in a deep breath. He was dead. Nothing could change that now. No amount of self-berating would bring him back to life. "Just get it done," she said to herself as she tried to force down the mental shutters.

She plucked a pair of latex gloves from the box that hung by the door. She was about to handle sharp objects and blood, together. Not that *Fae* could transfer so much. They didn't have the same fluid transfer problem that shifters had, but it wasn't worth risking.

She started by unbuttoning his prison issue shirt. His skin was pale, like so many *Fae*—milky white that shone through their skin. Scars marred his chest, one right down the centre like someone had cut him to get access to his heart. It wouldn't be surgery. No one would do that for *Others*. They didn't care if an *Other* had a heart defect; they'd just be left to die in infancy. *Others* were rarely trained in this kind of thing—unless Luke had been Society. No sooner had the thought entered her mind than she dismissed it as ludicrous. Society members did not find themselves in Exile or prison.

With a deep breath, she picked up the large needle attached to a tube that would suck his blood out and deposit it into a drum. She placed a hand on Luke's chest—it was still warm from the life that had been there just moments before—then made the mistake of looking at his face. It was so gentle and young, the look of the kind of man who would protect another. Maybe that was what his crime had been. It was usually something like that, she thought sadly.

"I'm sorry," she whispered, stroking her thumb on his chest. She was sorry for a lot that day. But mostly, she was sorry for the *Humans* and what they were, what they did. She felt for a gap between his ribs so she could reach his heart with the needle, but his face kept drawing her gaze.

This would not work.

Focus, Helena. He's dead.

Biting her lip, she pushed the tip of the needle into his skin, then stole another glance at him. "This is wrong," she said, shaking her head. She pulled the needle out again, resting it on his bare stomach as she tried to gather her thoughts. She couldn't look at him while she did this ... There were blankets under the bed—fresh, folded ones for patients. She pulled one of those out and placed it over his face. She wouldn't need to stare at that face and know what she was doing.

Avoiding looking at his cloth-covered face, Helena focused solely on the spot she needed to on his chest—

anything that would take away the oppressing feelings of guilt and shame. She gripped the needle hard and positioned it over his chest again. Counting her breaths, she plunged the needle into his flesh. It was stiff to go in, but smooth. When it was all the way to the hilt, she pulled down the tape on it and secured it into place, pulling Luke's shirt closed over it so she wouldn't have to see it.

She was being a coward, but she didn't care.

The machine stood on a small table and it whirred to life with a deafening mechanical hum when she pressed the red switch. She watched as the first stream of blood emerged from Luke's chest and wound itself down through the pipes and to the machine.

Rubbing her hands over her face, she backed away until she reached the counter. With her head down, she made herself listen to the mechanic vampire draining Luke.

The slight knock on the door startled her from her thoughts. Tracey cracked the door open and said, "Benny is here."

"Benny?" It took her a moment to apprehend what her aide was saying. *Benny*. Of course "I'll be out in a second."

Tracey cast a glance at Luke before nodding and closed the door. Helena pinched the bridge of her nose and gave herself a moment before following her out.

Benny was standing in the hallway with his grandson. He had a stooped posture, and his hands trembled to a great degree. Some of it was due to what Helena believed to be Parkinson's disease, though so far, his tests had come back inconclusive. But today, his hands were shaking more than usual—nerves. She didn't need her medical degree to tell her that. "Morning, Benny," she smiled. "Kyle."

"I-I-I saw Mr Lee here," he said as he hobbled closer. "D-did … What did he want?"

Exile

Only a fool would underestimate Benny with his stammer and nerves. His mind was as sharp as a pin. *Mr Lee?* He didn't deserve that kind of respect. "Should we make tea?" Maybe something that would break up the sadness and the darkness pressing in against them all. The malevolent white elephant in the room that Helena wanted to avoid just for a few more minutes. She looked at her assistant. "Tracey?"

But Tracey was staring blankly in front of her, her eyes vacant.

"Trace?"

"Oh … *Oh* …" She seemed to abruptly snap back to full consciousness. "Sorry, I …."

"It's okay," Helena smiled gently. She knew where Tracey's mind was—in the exact same place Helena's was. With the poor *Fae* on the table in the back room. "Should we have tea?" She turned to the boy. "Kyle, would you like some juice?"

Kyle nodded enthusiastically. "I read the book you gave me, Miss Helena," he beamed.

"You did?" She gave him a wide-eyed look of wonder as she ushered him in the direction of the sitting room. These were her private quarters, a sitting room that doubled as a kitchen. "Come and tell me all about it."

Kyle wanted to be a doctor like Helena. He was smart enough for it, too. Unfortunately, it was hard for *Others* to get that kind of schooling, especially in Exile. But she didn't mind teaching him herself. One day she would need someone to take over her work. There would always be *Others* who needed care and didn't get it. And maybe she could capture this young mind before life turned his thoughts sour.

Benny knew where the sitting room was. Helena had

let him come and sit there many times. She often let *Others* in here when they needed to talk. They were just people, just like her. They were friends, and she treated them so. It had taken a long time for her *Human* status to become something in the background, though it never really went away. She helped Benny into the high-back chair, which he preferred. It was good support for him and easier to get out of.

Tracey filled the kettle and set it to boil. She didn't need to ask Benny what he wanted to drink—always the same, red tea, no milk, no sugar. He'd been back here enough times. At first, it was to watch Kyle when he was learning from Helena, but then she suspected that it had become more of a comfort thing for him. He'd sit in the chair, watching the television or snoozing. Sometimes, she'd make them some supper, and they'd all sit in her small kitchen in pleasant companionship.

Benny's wife and daughter had been killed when *Humans* had attacked their village seven years ago. They had believed the *Others* to be harbouring a criminal and had created carnage in their attempt to find the lawbreaker. They had burned down homes, killing dozens, and injuring young Kyle when a wooden beam had come crashing down from the ceiling, crushing his leg and leaving him with a limp to this day. Though he had only been three at the time, the boy had vivid memories of the event, but spoke little about it. Benny, however, loved to talk about his wife, often referring to her as if she were sitting right there or back home making his dinner. Then he would remember, and his eyes would grow dark, making Helena's heart break for him.

"I had work with Norton to do today," Helena said, taking the subject head on. "Police work. Lee was there. That was why he came today."

Exile

"Something happened?" Kyle asked with childish enthusiasm, all ready to hear the doom and gloom, but no real comprehension of what it meant.

"One of the prison buses got stopped, one that comes from the mainlands. It was transferring prisoners."

"Was?" Tracey asked, handing a mug to Benny and one to Helena. She gave Kyle a glass of fresh orange juice and water for herself.

"Thank you." Helena took the mug and rested it on the coffee table. "Was. Yes. It was stopped. I don't know what happened exactly. Something …" She paused, unsure what to say about it. The roof got peeled off like a sardine tin? Because that was what it had looked like. "Someone stopped it, and the guards were attacked."

"Like highway men?" Kyle cut in. "I was reading about them. How they used to stop people in the olden days. They'd take all the money and jewels."

"Kind of. I guess. We don't know."

"Was anyone hurt? What about the prisoners? This is why they called you?" Tracey fired off her questions.

"The prisoners," Helena started, "they were catatonic. I couldn't see why. That was why they called me."

Benny was listening, but his focus was on his tea, keeping his hands steady as he held the mug. He would ask if he wanted to know something. Benny was a watcher— silent. But it would be an idiot to think he wasn't processing everything. His body was old, his muscles failing him now, but his mind was still there. "They brought someone in?" he asked. He had seen the van, and he knew what was in it.

"For me to examine. To maybe try and determine what caused it."

Benny met Helena's eyes. He knew she was lying, but she wasn't about to tell him the truth of it. "There are no lives here," Benny said. He knew Luke was dead—he and Kyle were necromancers—so he could sense it. He could raise the dead, but not back to themselves. Dead was still dead, even when the bodies were reanimated. Kyle still struggled with his ability. When he was upset, which thankfully wasn't that often, he would raise anything that was dead and close to him—by accident. Helena had almost died of fright one night when she had first had Kyle at the clinic and found a half-decayed crow at her window, his missing eyes and maggot-eaten stomach spilling out all over the place as he tried to reach his summoner.

Chapter Eleven
Stephen

Clearly having decided that Stephen was no threat to her, Eden turned her back on him and resumed her bin diving. He watched her for a moment with an edge of curiosity as she muttered to herself, tossing out bits of garbage in a haphazard way. She tossed a half-eaten sandwich to the ground, and the dog leapt on it. He glanced at Eden first—as if asking permission to eat it—giving her a whole three seconds to voice any kind of protest before picking it up and carrying it off to a safe distance so that he could chomp on it.

Maybe Stephen should warn her how imprudent it was for her to turn her back, not just on him, but anyone. But the warning died on his lips as his mind disengaged to focus on the pleasing view in front of him—her perfectly formed backside.

The dog seemed to scowl at him from where he sat devouring his claimed meal, and Stephen shrugged at him. A man could look. He smiled at the mutt before turning and heading towards the shop, to what he needed to do—get water. He pressed himself against the wooden door to the back of the shop, shutting everything out of his mind and pushing away the sounds and smells of the real world. He listened for any sign of life in there. Just because the sign out front said closed, did not mean that all was vacant. After a couple of minutes, Stephen decided it was clear. If there was anyone inside, they were either asleep or dead. The latter would have been preferable for Stephen. The fewer *Humans* in the world, the better, in his opinion.

93

Stephen tried the handle. The lock was in place, but that was all. He stepped back to get a better look at the place. No cameras, no chains, no other locks on the outside. God, the *Humans* really thought they were above it all—even being broken into. It was laughable almost. Maybe they thought themselves above all of that, or maybe they were just being realistic. If someone wanted in, all that shit would not stop them, especially if they were *Other*.

Stephen wrapped strong fingers around the handle once more and forced it down, pushing the door as he did. It gave a satisfying crack as the lock broke under the brute force. Instinctively, he glanced behind him to see if he had gained anyone's attention, but both the mutt and Eden were too busy to notice. Obviously, he was no worry to either of them.

Stephen left them to it, pushing the door open with caution. Just because he had detected no one there, didn't mean he would not double-check. The door creaked on its hinges, motes of dust flying into the air and getting caught on the shaft of light streaming in through the half open door. The place was oddly empty. It wasn't just that there was a lack of scents, but there seemed to be a lack of … anything. Not even the faint lingering stench of *Humans*.

Outside, the scent of the earth was poignant, a sharp contrast to the bland odourlessness of the interior. "The door is open," he called to the witch. "There are plenty of water bottles in here."

"No, thank you," she shouted back, her voice muffled by the bin she was bent over.

"Suit yourself," he muttered more to himself than to her. Women … Witches and women—the worst combination. His brow knitted together as he pondered that. Actually, that was a lie. *Humans* and women—now that was the worst. God, what did it matter? He didn't like either of them, and neither one made any ounce of sense.

On the counter was a selection of magazines. Stephen ran a hand across the top of them before picking one up. He raised his eyebrows at the headline. *Pregnant with twins and still a virgin*. Okaaay then … *Ginny's husband will stand by her*. Stephen snorted. The guy was a fucking idiot. He leafed through the pages, finding the rather gormless image of Ginny's husband. *Husband, Jason, knows his wife would never be unfaithful. "It's a whole new world," he states. "God wants us to overpopulate the Others, so he gave us two babies for free."* Yep, definitely an idiot.

Stephen flung the magazine back onto the counter with a shake of his head. The level of stupidity in *Humans* just seemed to increase with each passing day.

There was a row of three refrigerators at the back of the shop. The middle one had no light on, while the light in the other two was dim. They held the usual bottles, carbonated garbage, vacuum-packed cheese and meats; things that Stephen would never have eaten back home, but right now, he'd fucking eat anything. His stomach had reached new levels of hunger, aching in its intensity. He grabbed a packet of pre-packed ham and beef and grimaced at the sight of it. Maybe he wasn't that hungry after all. Shrink-wrapped and sitting on the shelf of some corner store was not his idea of fresh. Still attached to the body, warm and wet with blood and saliva … Now that was fresh. This here? This was nothing short of sacrilege.

Stephen closed his eyes picturing the chase … the hunt. God, he missed it so much already. Having the animal in his sights as he hunkered down ready to pounce. It was so much better when they ran—more fulfilling when they were caught. The sitting part, after the animal was dead … that was just the contented sigh after the climax. Stephen tossed the meat back onto the shelf. He would starve to death. He was sure of it.

He turned to leave then stopped abruptly. On the wall, next to the last fridge, was a phone. It stared at Stephen. Given everything that had happened in the last day, he wouldn't have been surprised if the damn thing talked to him of its own accord. It could mock him and accuse him of all the shit he didn't want to hear from his own mind. The phone brought new possibilities with it, though. He bit the inside of his lip as he stared, the pangs of sadness jostling inside for the life he had left behind. Did his family even miss him? Were they upset about his death? How had his father broken it to them? He pictured his mother's distraught face, his sister's guilt, and his father … nothing. His expressionless face would have given nothing away. What about Cade and Phoenix? All those faces swam in his mind and tugged on his heart, causing his chest to tighten. Fucking *Humans*. They had done this. They had caused all of this. He wanted to turn his back on the phone, but he couldn't make his feet co-operate and walk him away from it. It pulled to him inside.

As if of its own accord, his hand reached out and picked up the receiver. It was probably dead anyway. To his surprise, the dial tone buzzed loud and clear in his ear. Before he could change his mind, he punched in the number he wanted and waited.

His father answered on the second ring. Stephen held his breath, his heart suddenly hammering in his chest with longing at the sound of his father's voice.

"Hello?"

He couldn't speak, couldn't say a damn thing. His words caught in his throat, and he had to swallow the lump that formed there.

There was a lengthy pause, then his father's quiet tone, "Stephen? Is that you?"

Stephen laid his forehead against the hard wall, fighting the deluge of emotions that threatened to overwhelm him. "Yes," he murmured.

Absolute silence followed his reply, then he heard his father's footsteps and a door closing. He could see it all in his mind like he was still there. His dad getting up from the desk, walking, shoulders back, head high as he took himself to the quiet room in the office. "You can't just call here." Stephen placed a hand on the wall next to the phone to steady himself.

"I'm sorry. I ..."

"It's dangerous, Stephen," his father cut in. "You can't call here again. You're ... dead to us here." A harsh intake of breath. "You have to be."

Stephen gripped the receiver hard. What could he say to that? Maybe he hadn't believed it before. It had all been such a rush, going from one moment to the next ... getting him out of there, faking his death. He wasn't meant to be a lone animal. He didn't work that way. If he could just feel them all close, just one more time.

"Goodbye, Stephen," his father said but hesitated. "Take ... care of yourself." Even as the click on the other end of the line resounded loudly in his head, Stephen kept the receiver to his ear. If he put it down, he would be disconnected, and that would be it. His life, his family—all of it—over. He wasn't ready for this. Not yet. He punched a fist into the wall next to the phone and resisted the urge to slam the receiver back into its cradle and break the fucking thing. Why did *this* have to be his life? Why? God damn fucking *Humans*. They had caused all this. Not him. *Humans* with their greed and their lies and secrets. He placed the receiver back, forcing himself not to slam it. What did it take for a father to tell his son he was dead to him?

After a moment, Stephen stood up straight, squared his shoulders and glared at the phone. *Fuck 'em*. If this was how it was, then this was how it was. He glanced around the shop, his eyes resting on the back door—suddenly he felt very claustrophobic. Four walls pressed in on him as his *tiger* fought for release. His jaw ached with the thought of the hunt, and he swapped his anger for the predatory hunger inside. His muscles clenched with the need for release.

The witch wanted a water bottle? Stephen couldn't stand there and wait for his mind to get over all of this shit. He snatched a bottle from the fridge and went to the door— save her routing through the trash at least.

But the witch wasn't there. The stench of *Humans* reeked outside. Had he really been in there so long? It had grown darker, and thick droplets of rain splattered the ground, hitting Stephen in the face as the grey clouds overhead shifted. But under the sound of the splatters of rain hitting the tin roof came the sound of metal grinding. Stephen inched himself back into the shop. There was no denying the sounds of the brake pads that needed replacing and their distinct screeching as metal ground against metal. He ducked out of sight and into the shop for what felt like the hundredth time that day.

He questioned his own bravery and the merit as a soldier with the amount of times he had cowered so far from confrontation. What kind of fighter did he make for his people? A living fighter was better than a dead one, he reassured himself. But that did nothing to ease the niggle at his pride.

Crouching, Stephen made his way to the large double doors at the front of the shop. There was only a small window. The other window was boarded up; it looked like someone had tried to kick it in, and whoever owned this place hadn't bothered to replace the glass. He tried the handle gently ... It opened.

He angled his head and stared at it. The door was open ... unlocked. That didn't make one ounce of sense. Outside, a large van stood ... a meat wagon. Only it wasn't carrying the one-natured animals for slaughter. It was for *Others*.

"Oh, for God's sake." Stephen cursed his own stupidity as the slow mental cogs of his mind whirred and clicked everything into place. The back door with no security. The unlocked front door ... even the unsecured rubbish outside. This was a fucking mouse trap, and Stephen and Eden had been the mice.

How could he have been so fucking stupid? He was better than this. At home, he'd have never got caught this way. But at home, he was in his territory. He knew everything and everyone. Any moment, these *Humans* would come crashing through the door. They were probably heading around the back already. He'd been set up. If it wouldn't make so much noise, Stephen would have slammed his fist into the wooden frame of the door. How delightfully simple, yet clever, of the *Humans* to trap him here. They bagged themselves a *tiger* and a witch in one easy sweep. Fucking great.

Holding the wooden frame with one hand while the other still clutched the bottle, he squinted through the small piece of glass. Sweepers—it had to be. Three *Humans* were standing outside, armed with what resembled foam guns. Stephen doubted that was what they contained. Two of them were trying to lift the witch into the back of the van as she kicked and thrashed in their grip, putting her feet against the barrier to stop them. *Shit*. They'd be coming in for him at any moment, and though he was physically faster and stronger than *Humans*, he was no match for their weapons. He couldn't fight those—no matter how fucking strong he was. They would be armed with silver. There was nothing he could do for the witch. Even if he had wanted to.

There had to at least be three *Humans*. Stephen couldn't hear any others as he made his way to the back door. Perhaps he could make a run for it while they were occupied with the witch. He couldn't help her now. He'd only end up shot himself and captured. Stephen crept across the shop, keeping his head down low.

He pulled the door open and poked his head out just enough to see that there was no one there. Maybe they hadn't yet realised there was someone inside. Keeping low, Stephen eased out of the back and then darted to the path. No one heard or saw him. As soon as the *Humans* were out of sight, he ran toward the main road.

The witch—she'd be punished. *Humans* always went for execution as punishment, but that wasn't punishment at all. That was final—game over. Kind of pointless, Stephen thought. If he were to punish someone, he would find a more satisfying way. Nail them to the wall and leave them there to die a slow, painful death. There was no sense of vengeance pushing the button that controlled the lethal injection. Punishment had to be something that counted. It had to matter.

Chapter Twelve
Helena

Red or black? Or even blue? Helena laid the three dresses out on her bed, but no matter which one she tried on, none of them seemed right. Of course, the problem wasn't the dress, it was the date itself—not that this was a date, she quickly reassured herself. It was dinner, with her boss. Plain and simple. Tracey leaned against the small vanity unit in front of the window, her hand on top of the slight swell of her belly. "Which one?" Helena asked, already sick of staring at them and ready to just scrap the lot. She picked up the black dress and drew her brows together. It was short, but not too much—just enough to show a little leg— and the neckline on it was decent enough, not too revealing. The red dress, though, was longer, but the plunge on it was certainly too much of an invite to any mating male. The blue dress was both the right length and had just the correct amount of plunge to keep her respectful, but … it just wasn't right.

"Depends on what message you're trying to give," said Tracey, pushing herself up and grabbing the black dress to hold it in front of Helena. She lined it nicely with Helena's curved figure. "This one says lady of the night. Someone who will stay out late … you know?" She gave Helena a wink before leaning over to grab the red one and hold that over the black.

"Lady of the night? Right." Helena took the red dress from Tracey and put the black one back on the bed. "So, lady of the night or the Scarlett Harlot?" she said, dropping the dress back down dejectedly.

Tracey smile. "Well, you could go with blue? Make him think he's out to dinner with his mama. Would keep his hands at bay." She took the red dress and swapped it for the blue. "Actually, yes. Blue. This one gets my vote."

"You want me to look like his mother?"

"I want you to look like someone he won't be interested in." Helena's eyes met hers in the mirror. "Sorry."

"It's okay," Helena sighed, standing in front of the mirror with the blue dress pressed against her body. She hooked her head through the loop between the dress and the hanger and let it hang down in front of her. "Maybe I should just go with jeans and a shirt? Put him off for sure." Tracey was right. She should go with the one that would get the least interest.

Tracey came to stand behind her. She reached up and wrapped her hands around Helena's long brown hair, pulling it back off her face and then twisting it into a light bun, softly feathering out the ends. "I think you could wear a bin bag, and Lee would still be sniffing around." The two women stared at each other for a moment, unspoken words passing between them. Tracey disapproved of Helena meeting Lee, but what choice did she have? If she didn't keep Lee on her side, he would make her life very difficult, and then where would that leave the *Others* whom she tried to help? This was about more than just her. This was about keeping harmony—keeping her office where she wanted it and where she could do the most work for their kind. "You'll be okay with him? I mean ..."

Helena turned and took Tracey's warm hand in hers. She'd never had female friends before—never really connected with any of them. They all seemed too blind and caught up with their hatred for *Others* that when Helena announced that she saw them as equal, she was shunned. It was only natural that the one female she managed to get close to, in some way, was *Other*. She leaned in and kissed Tracey on the cheek. "I'll be fine. Lee wouldn't hurt me." Even as she said it, she wasn't sure that that was totally true. He had killed the *Fae* in front of her, justified it as doing it for her own good—and maybe he believed that.

"How did you wind up with the lion falling for you?"

Helena widened her eyes a moment. "I haven't a clue," she said as she took the blue dress from around her neck. "I think the black one." She slipped off her work blouse and removed the slimline pencil skirt she had been wearing. Tracey bunched up the dress and pulled it down over Helena's head.

Helena turned, running her hand over her flat stomach and hips, and smoothing the material out along her body.

"You look stunning," Tracey said. "He'll be thinking his luck is in tonight."

Helena smiled. "Maybe." So much as Lee was an asshole, he truly believed in the *Human* cause, and that wasn't so much his fault, but his parents'. It was something that was instilled in all *Humans* from birth, and some, like Lee, believed it with fierce conviction. Could Helena really blame him for that? No, but she wished he would listen. Wished he would change his mind. He was dedicated and that made him blind to so many things. He was passionate. He followed through on what he said, and while his words might not have been the words people wanted to hear, he was a man of his word. He had Helena's respect for that, at least.

Helena stood closer to the mirror and pulled the skin under her eyes so that they widened. "I look like I haven't slept."

"That might be because you haven't," Tracey scowled. "You were gone long before I came into work."

Helena stifled a yawn. "I think I might have got an hour before the phone rang this morning. Maybe I'll fall asleep and bore Lee to death."

"We can hope," Tracey muttered. "Let's get your hair and face done before he comes. He'll be on time; you know it."

"Oh, I am sure of it." And she was. Lee would arrive at seven, to the very second.

Twenty minutes later and she was ready—hair done, make-up fixed and shoes chosen, rejected and re-chosen. She was good to go, and Lee, as expected, was on time. He didn't ring the bell, or knock on the door. Helena came down the stairs just as he walked into the clinic. He closed the door behind him and came to stand at the bottom of the stairs, his eyes locking on her.

"Ready?" he asked, a look of pure male appreciation on his face as his gaze travelled down her slim form.

"I just need to make sure that Tracey has everything she needs, then I am good to go."

Lee's smile was genuine—the man Helena knew was in there. He put his hands behind his back and clasped them together. He had put on a shirt with a tie, his neatly pressed trousers just seeming to make him stand taller. He really was an incredibly handsome man.

"I have the drum ready if you want it." The drum with the *Fae's* blood. The sooner that was out of the clinic, the better she would feel.

"I can pick it up after. Drop it at the lab on the way home if that's okay?"

"Sure. Give me a minute?" He inclined his head politely, and she left him standing there while she went to find Tracey. He was being the perfect gentleman tonight. She might have even fallen for the act if she didn't know him already, and who he could really be. But she did appreciate the effort. It had been a while since she had been anywhere, let alone some kind of date. Not that this was a date, she reminded herself—more like an obligation. But thinking like that caused guilt to settle heavily in her chest. No matter the person, it wasn't in her to treat them so coldly.

Tracey hadn't come down; she didn't want to see Lee again. Helena could understand that. It had taken her a long time to win the trust of *Others* here. Lee had done everything possible to show them the exact opposite.

"Are you sure you'll be okay?"

Tracey was just putting Helena's dresses back in the small old closet. "I'll be fine."

"It's been a long day."

She shrugged. "We're not busy. I can rest."

"Will you give Benny and Kyle some supper?"

"Of course. Then I was thinking of inviting a few friends and having a party." When Helena angled her head and placed her hands on her hips, Tracey gave a giggle. "I'm kidding." She leaned in close—the advantage with Lee was that he wasn't *Human* and that meant he had normal hearing. "You will be careful, right? If you need anything, you'll call?"

Helena wrapped her arms around Tracey, bringing her into a friendly, reassuring embrace. "I will," she whispered, but it was a lie. They both knew it. What could *Others* do if something bad happened? They would not challenge Lee Norton, not for anyone—especially not for a *Human*. It wouldn't matter that she was their friend or that they trusted her. They would not start a war over her. "Lock the door when I am gone."

The clinic closed its doors at night and became a place for emergency care. But Helena wasn't stupid enough to leave the locks open. There was a knocker on the front and a sign that welcomed people to still come by if they needed help, but there were no appointments. Tracey was staying over to keep an eye on anyone who needed anything. She would sleep in one of the patient rooms. They didn't have anyone in tonight except Luke—but he was dead.

Helena left Tracey in the bedroom, knowing she would only come down when she heard the car pull away. Lee was still standing at the bottom of the stairs where she had left him, reading something on his phone. He closed it and put it away when he saw her, turning a brilliant smile up at her.

"All sorted," she said.

"Good." He held his hand out to her when she reached the step before the bottom. She froze and stared at his outstretched hand. If this wasn't Lee, would she take his hand? Would she hesitate? Would accepting it give him all the wrong signals? He leaned in closer, smiling patiently. "It's just a hand, Helena. I'm not going to bite."

She gave a small, awkward smile. "I know. I'm sorry. It's just … I haven't done this kind of thing in a long time."

He turned his hand, palm up, showing her that he was completely sincere. She smiled, then took the last step and placed her hand in his. It was strong and warm as he enveloped her delicate fingers in his.

"I thought we might go to Livingston's," he announced.

"Isn't that out of town?"

He nodded. "Do you mind? I just wanted something different, away from home and work and everything else."

"Livingston's would be great."

Exile

He opened the car door for her and helped her in. His car was new, not the one he used for work, and she suspected that it was borrowed from his uncle. The scent of leather inside was thick and warm, offering comfort as she sat back.

Livingston's was about an hour away by car, maybe a little more. Helena enjoyed the time to let her mind wander. What a crazy day it had been for sure. "Has there been any luck in tracking down that missing prisoner?"

"Mason?"

"Yes."

Lee shook his head. "Nothing yet. But we will. He'll have to surface somewhere. Sweepers will catch him if we don't."

Yes, sweepers. God, how she loathed those. Why couldn't *Others* go out at night after hours? Why couldn't they be free to do as they chose the same way *Humans* were? The laws wouldn't stop the *Others* with ill intent, just as it wouldn't stop *Humans*. It was just another useless form of control.

Livingston's was one of those destination restaurants. Helena had never seen it before. When the grand building came into view, Helena's breath caught in her throat; it was magnificent, possessing all the grandeur of a castle. Bright lights shone out into the night, bringing life into the darkness. Valets stood out front, ready to open doors and park expensive cars. The place was absolutely bursting as Lee pulled in behind another car. It really was a place out of this world. "This looks amazing," she breathed. "It looks like something from a movie."

"Doesn't it just? I have never been here before."

Lee's announcement shocked her. "Never? Not once?"

"Nope."

She narrowed her eyes at him, trying to work out if he was just kidding. Lee was slick—slick meant liar. Did he tell all the women that to make them feel special? "Thank you for bringing me here."

When they reached the front of the line, attendants on both sides of the car opened the doors. Lee handed the one on his side the keys, and the one on Helena's side offered her a white gloved hand to help her out.

"Thank you," she said to the young *Human* man. She doubted that the *Humans* would employ *Others*, even if it was cheap labour.

Lee came around the car and offered her his arm.

"Mr Norton," the greeter said as they entered the restaurant. "I have your table ready."

"You booked?" Helena asked with raised brows. She was pleased and a little impressed. Outside of work, Lee was different.

"Of course," he grinned. "This isn't the kind of place you just show up to."

No. Of course it wasn't.

They were seated by the window that overlooked the waters. Her gaze fell on the mountains that lay just across. They rose high against the skyline, an impressive sight. Tonight, the sky was clear, blue almost, dotted with twinkling stars. "It's so beautiful." They looked so close from where they sat, yet Helena knew they were miles away. She had visited them on very rare occasions.

"Best seat in the house," Lee grinned.

"It's so amazing. Thank you."

The greeter handed them menus and took an order of drinks for while they browsed the menus. Whiskey for Lee, wine for Helena. She'd just have one—she wanted to have all her cognitive faculties in perfect working order.

Exile

Helena glanced down the menu—none of it had prices; everything sounded divine.

"Tell me about your work, Helena. What is it that intrigues you about *Others*?"

She paused in her reading, unsure how to answer him and not fall into some terrible hole with it. "I ... I don't know. They just do. They have so many differences."

"You don't think that it is against nature? Do you believe in God?"

"I do," she said tentatively.

"Then how can you agree to these ... things?"

"Well, God made them, too. Who am I to say whether it is wrong or right."

Lee smiled and nodded slowly. "Good point, I guess."

"I just think that there must be a reason."

"What reason?"

"Well, everything ..." Her words were cut off by a deafening boom. The glasses and cutlery on the table clattered and people around them screamed in alarm as the ground beneath them vibrated, shaking the building in thunderous applaud. The sky lit up, orange and yellows billowing into the air across the waters.

Lee and Helena shot out of their seats, their gazes on one of the mountains as plumes of dust and smoke rolled out.

The mountain just seemed to ... collapse.

Chapter Thirteen
Stephen

Stephen dragged his sorry ass back along the path. *Run away to Exile*, they had said. *It's freedom*, they had said. Like shit it was. It was starvation and tiredness. It was law and order of the worst kind. It was gun-trigger *Humans* with traps and nothing to stop them—no fear of what repercussions they would face for what they did to *Others*. So they did what they wanted, and no one gave a shit. What kind of world was this? Gemma and Cade had had a lucky escape. This would not have been the place to raise a child. Shit, they'd probably have got locked up on the first night, and then what? Their child would have been killed anyway. At least this way he was still alive—even if they thought he was dead. Another dismal attempt by the great Malcolm Davies to save his kin. He'd faked the death of his own grandchild, but so much as Stephen hated to see his sister in such pain, it was safer that way. Her baby was a true mix—a species not allowed in the eyes of the *Humans*. His power and abilities would be unmatched amongst *Others*. The *Humans* would have found him and killed him because of it.

It all made Stephen wonder what other secrets his father held, however. What else had he done for the good of the pack? Maybe it was better he didn't know.

Twigs snapped behind him, making him spin around abruptly and lower himself to the ground. Stephen tensed, ready to unleash his *tiger* on whatever idiot had followed him. It wasn't the witch, that was for sure. He growled low in his throat, a warning to whomever it was that it was dangerous to get any closer.

A soft whimper sounded in response, and suddenly, out of the darkness came the scratty mutt that had been with the witch.

"You," Stephen said, his relief at not needing to kill someone tangible. "I don't have anything for you." He had nothing for himself, either, and even if he did, what were the chances of him sharing?

The mutt scampered closer, unafraid of Stephen's *tiger*. Often, animals could sense the animal within the shifters and avoided them. Dogs in particular, but cats on occasion, too—though maybe cats were just antisocial, vindictive bastards. Tail wagging, the dog sniffed at Stephen's jeans until he bent down to pat his head. "I'd not sniff those, mate. Been days since I got changed.

The dog lifted a paw and dragged it down Stephen's leg.

"Okay, okay. Come along, but I haven't got food for you, and don't expect me to share. So feel free to bugger off when you realise that."

Stephen's vision swam a little and his skin prickled as he stood upright again. Soon the hunger would be so intense that he would not be able to control his *tiger*. He had to find something before the animal in him took over and hunted the first live thing in its path—which could prove fatal for the four-legged creature wagging its tail in front of him right now.

Maybe he could make it to daytime and then hitch a ride to some place where wildlife ran free—he had no bloody clue. But he needed to sleep again, while he could. He'd had maybe an hour total, and that sure as hell wasn't helping him to control his hunger.

As he headed towards the place he had slept the night before, the mutt trotted happily by his side—anyone looking

111

at them would think Stephen had owned this dog for years. No *Humans* or sweepers seemed to have been to this place in a long time. Perhaps he had managed to find himself a safe spot. A couple of hours of rest and then he would set off again.

Stephen dumped his bag on the ground in front of the fallen tree and dropped down next to it. His head was about ready to burst. The dog lay close to Stephen, quiet, watchful. Stephen didn't even have the energy to reach out and stroke his fur. His skin buzzed with need and his stomach rolled with hunger. If he could just sleep, he could find the strength to hunt later …

The sound of the dog's heartbeat echoed in Stephen's head. It would be pumping warm blood through his tiny body, keeping alive every appetising muscle and organ contained within his small form. It called to Stephen, a tormenting lunch bell in the middle of a famine-stricken town. Stephen clenched his fists, his nails biting into the palms of his hands.

Each breath came slow and laboured as Stephen tried to focus his mind elsewhere … anywhere. Anywhere that wasn't the ever-so-inviting *thump, thump* of the mongrel's heart.

Vampires often claimed drinking the blood of dogs was like a short sharp dose of cocaine. It numbed the senses and made everything shit in the world pale into some kind of oblivion, but then it came with payback—the feeling of shit when *Human* blood rejected the blood of the dog. Stephen would take their word on it. As hungry as he was, he wasn't about to start taking bites out of the dog.

He pushed the thoughts from his mind before they became too dangerous, and he actually let his desperation consider what was against his values. His *tiger* paced in the confines of himself, starving, demanding to be fed. Stephen inhaled deeply, pushing it down.

"One …"

Every muscle tensed. His nerves alive with unspent energy.

"Two …"

His breathing became loud and ragged as he forced his mind to focus on the slow and controlled rise of his own chest. New colours melded and shifted, the woodlands no longer earthy greens and browns, but vibrant shades that had come to life. The dog grew more appealing with every passing moment. Stephen didn't need a mirror to know his eyes had shifted. They would be blazing with gold and green, his hunger very much alive.

"Three …"

Every follicle on his body came to life. The itch peaked and spread across his skin, his flesh burning with the need to rip itself apart. His *tiger* paced and growled, but Stephen held himself together, refusing to let this happen.

"Exhale …"

He couldn't take it much longer. His own pulse echoed in his head at the speed of a freight train. Sweat trickled down the back of his neck, pooling against his shirt. The rumble in his gut rose as the *tiger* fought for freedom.

Stephen rolled onto his side, panting. He had no choice. He couldn't hold it any longer. His mind swam with everything that had happened so far. It didn't matter if there were sweepers out there or that he was an escaped convict. Nothing mattered right then. Balling his fists, he put his head to the ground and rolled onto his front. The trees spun as his canines pushed down and he started to shift. His jaw moved painfully out of place, clicking at the joint with a sickening crack.

Shit.

He pushed himself onto his hands and knees, his arms shaking from the effort of trying to hold himself up and from trying to hold his shift at bay. His mind grew heavy until he could hear nothing of the woods. Not even the soft sounds of the dog's gentle snores as he slept, oblivious to the monster that was fighting to come out just a few feet away from him.

Grunting, Stephen crawled away, putting as much distance between him and the dog as possible. He used a tree   to pull himself up onto wobbly legs, his entire body quaking from the effort. The bones in his face moved, a pressure under his skin, between his eyes. He pressed a hand to the bridge of his nose to reverse it.

Fuck it.

He launched himself into a tree, crashing against the trunk with a thud. His canines were fully extended now— there was no stopping this shift now. God help anyone who came into his path. Stephen stretched his jaw as he stumbled through the woods, making room for his teeth to completely shift and for his jaw to realign. He tore at his shirt and jeans, his hands half paws, his claws ripping through the fabrics as he pulled them from his body.

With a pain-filled growl, he dropped to the ground and let his body go, his bones and muscles spasming, his muscles ripping apart and reforming as his entire body restructured itself.

By sheer chance, the land across the water, in the opposite direction Stephen had come from, was occupied by farms—*Human*-owned farms. It appeared that the *Humans* used the woodlands and water as a natural border. Just to the side of that … *fucking good luck*—fresh meat. Stephen salivated, and all logic escaped him. Frantic, he tore across

114

the ground to find something he could sink his teeth into. It wouldn't matter what it was at this point—as long as it was living. He desperately needed to satisfy the hunger raging within his body. He leapt into a field, his paws slamming against the earth. Tonight, an unfortunate ewe had strayed from her flock. Her death was swift and efficient, like all Stephen's kills. He dragged her body out of the field to eat.

Nostalgia washed over him as he devoured his meal, a longing for home and his old life. It wasn't often that Stephen had got to do a real hunt alone. Not that he was incompetent—on the contrary. He had been quite the established hunter and provider of the pack at home, but pack runs and hunts were as vital to his kind as breathing. Alone, he had mostly caught rabbit in the wild, but in pack hunts, it was bigger game they hunted. His mind wandered to the races, the competitions, the flouncing about of *tigers* ... He gave an abrupt shake of his head. He had to stop thinking about these things. They were gone now. No longer his—just memories in his mind. And that was where they needed to stay. Buried deep in his mind.

With a heavy heart, he admitted to himself that what had happened had been for the best. What would have been the alternative? His father's death at the hands of the *Humans*? The discovery of Cade and Gemma's illegal baby? Surely that would have led to death, too. It didn't matter, though; even the pacifying thoughts were already becoming a little tiresome.

After he was done, he left the carcass just under the hedgerow and ambled back to his things, his stomach full and his mind calm once more. It would be days before she was discovered. No doubt the putrid stench of rot and decay would finally give her location away. If the weather didn't fare too well, maybe it would be sooner.

He allowed himself a moment to think of Gemma as he reached the water's edge. She would take his place now as second to their father. Maybe she would do a better job of it than he had. She had a smart mouth, and as long as she kept that in check, she would survive. But Stephen ... he'd always fought against being in that position. Argued that he had never wanted it in the first place and that just because he had been born into that role, didn't mean he had to accept ... Yet now, as he sat in the darkness, in this place known as Exile, away from everything and everyone he had ever known, he realised that maybe it wouldn't have been so bad.

As for the baby ... he lived. Unknown to his parents. Somewhere he was safe and well looked after, Stephen was sure, but how unjust it was that his parents and family, his rightful life, had already been taken from him—all because he had been born. In the eyes of the *Humans* and *Others* alike, his existence was illegal, but not through any reason other than fear of the unknown. If they found him, either side would butcher him and display his entrails for all to see. In truth, it was probably far more humane that he would never know the life of Society and law. If Stephen ever had reason to hate the *Humans* and their fears and *Others* for not standing up to them, this was it.

In his short twenty-five years of life, he had borne witness to far too many children being massacred. He couldn't endure another.

As he licked a paw then swiped it behind his ear, Stephen pushed thoughts of his old life from his mind. Usually it felt so good to sit after feeding, to cleanse himself and his mind, but so many things irritated him now. He licked his paws and then rubbed them over his face and ears. It was the first time in a long while he had fully cleaned himself.

Back home, they would normally lean over each other; bonding as they cleaned off the blood from the hunt.

He exhaled heavily as he finished his half-hearted attempt and let his eyes wander over to the sleeping dog across the water. Lucky little shit. Seems he had been spared from a very hungry *tiger* tonight, he thought wryly. A movement in the trees drew his gaze and he froze. A shadow moved through the gaps. The hackles of Stephen's fur spiked instantly. Someone was there, but there was no time to shift back. He leapt into the water, swimming furiously to get to the other side.

A woman was standing by the dog—the same ethereal woman from yesterday—her hand hovering just over its head. Stephen let out a warning growl and she glanced up at him, smiling as her warm hazel eyes met his. Soft waves of hair hung down, and she tucked a strand behind her ear. As she lowered her hand towards the dog once more, Stephen dragged himself out of the water and took a threatening step closer, baring his teeth in a snarl.

"I will not harm him," she said in a delicate voice, but he didn't back off.

She let her arm drop, realising that the *tiger* in front of her was not standing for her intrusions. She glided around the still sleeping dog, and Stephen waited, giving her room to leave. She came to stand in front of Stephen, though, bending down to place a folded note on the ground. She pushed it towards him, her face filled with sincerity rather than anything malicious. Stephen had a hard time holding onto his growl in her presence. People who mean harm give off a scent—that or fear—but she gave no such indication. If anything, her scent was vaguely familiar to him—and not because of their acquaintance the previous day. The slight waft of *tiger*, but nothing that said it was what she was.

117

"Take it," she said, nudging the paper closer to him and then rolling a marble across the ground to him; much the same as the day before. He trapped it under a paw with feline grace, and when he looked back up, she was gone.

Chapter Fourteen
Helena

Helena hadn't needed to ask for Lee to take her to the ... what? Crash site? Bomb site? Big hole inside of a damn mountain site? Whatever it was, and whatever its name was, didn't matter; what mattered was getting there and helping anyone who needed it. Lee knew Helena's skills were bound to be needed. If they'd not just been about to have dinner together, she'd already have got a call that an escort would be on their way to take her to the site. As it were, she now sat in the car next to a grim Lee, who was trying to quickly steer his way towards the pandemonium they would indubitably encounter.

Helena's mind instantly envisioned crushed bodies, people caught in the rubble ... mothers, wives, dads and uncles, all of them stuck and wanting help. Bloodied eyes and broken limbs. Most, if not all, of the mountains had been excavated in ways so that their insides were carved out jack-o'-lantern style. Inside were places of work—they varied with their functions. It was only the smaller mountains that didn't house man-made constructions, but those still had uses—good farming land for cattle, or even good land to build on.

As she got out of Lee's car, she was damn happy she'd chosen the flats over the heels. They had to park the car far back, because of all the rubble and fallen rocks obstructing their way. The air was still thick with dust—white plumes rolled out every time something new fell. Sirens and alarms rang out in the night chaotically. But the one thing that was missing, Helena realised, was the sound of cries ... screams.

"What was here?" she asked Lee as he shoved his door shut.

"Sweepers." He eyed her over the top of the car, as if sensing she needed more than that. "*Others*. But they were sweepers."

Well, shit. Others working as Sweepers were always odd to Helena. They worked for the very side they hated, catching their own kind and handing them over. All the money in the world wouldn't make Helena do that. She suspected that they used criminals for this—the lesser criminals at that. Ones that wouldn't care or have morals and all that would matter to them was what they would get in return. *Others* were no different to *Humans* in that respect; they were just as greedy, just as power hungry. It was a shame that either side didn't realise they were siblings, fighting each other for the same damn thing—control, to be the one in charge. One day, she hoped that they would somehow join forces rather than fight one another. So much blood had been shed on both sides, and neither one of them was giving in.

They would one day. Prophecy would see to that. Fate would bring in the natural order of things and something would happen. Maybe this was it, she mused as she stared out at the destruction. Old stories had told them of a man who would come one day. He would bring a joining of the two sides. He would wield a power like no other. It was both scary and exciting at the same time.

"Are we going to the site?"

"Yes. As soon as we find out what the hell is going on." Lee scowled as his glance raked over the masses. There were more clean-up guys here than there were medics—another sad truth of the world. They wouldn't be too concerned about tending to the *Others* here. They would just wait for them to die, ship them off and clean up.

Exile

"I wish I had my medical bag with me," Helena murmured as she carefully stepped over some rocks. God knows what they would find there.

"Someone will have one." The hard expression on his face softened for a moment. "You don't have to come if you don't want to." She threw him a quick glance. If she didn't know Lee better, she might actually have believed that he was concerned for her safety. But Helena knew the only concern he was likely feeling was that he had realised it was only *Others* who would be hurt or injured here, so Helena's medical expertise was unnecessary in his opinion. And to add to it, he now had her in tow when he'd rather be dealing with all this without her around.

"I want to come. I can help. There might be people hurt in there."

"Dead most likely."

"Not if these are *Others*. Especially if they're shifters."

A man came rushing toward them before Lee could reply. He was wearing a hat and some overalls—one of those suits that was all in one and zipped up at the front. "Mr Norton," he huffed, offering him a hand before glancing down at it and realising it was filthy. "Sorry," he quickly muttered, retracting it.

"Dobbs," Lee acknowledged him. "This is Dr Barnes, an associate of mine."

The man nodded at Helena, but his attention immediately returned to Lee. He squirmed, clearly uncomfortable—and Helena would bet not just because of the tragic incident. Lee Norton was a man that made most people break out in a nervous sweat. "It was a money hunter place," he informed him, keeping his eyes down and voice low as if Helena might not hear him. "The whole place has come down inside." He glanced at her briefly and she frowned. Was he worried what Helena thought of money hunters? If anything, she felt sorry for them. They were so down on their luck that they went out and caught their own kind for the sake of a few pounds. She had heard tales of money hunters raiding homes of *Others* and reporting that they were out after curfew. Of course, the laws would never believe the protesting *Other—Others* were all liars.

"Is anyone alive?"

"A couple. We pulled them out. And a woman. I don't know if she is … she won't make it."

Human doctors could do shit for *Others*. They bled out or healed way too fast and either the *Other* would be up and gone or dead before the *Human* medic could do anything about it. Doctors like Helena weren't rare as such, but usually their skills weren't so much for heal and repair, but top-down investigations. "Can I look at them?" she asked "Maybe I can help."

Lee's jaw clenched, his displeasure at her concern for *Others* evident. In spite of it, he made no comment but merely said, "Dr Barnes is specialised in medicine of the *Other* kind." Helena felt thankful that he wasn't making an issue out of her wanting to help, even if inwardly he was annoyed. He really was trying hard to win her affections, she realised. Whatever his reasons, she was gladly grabbing the opportunity being given to her.

Dobbs gave a solemn nod and started to lead them towards the cave-in. "They're just up ahead. You can't go to the site itself. It's not secure yet." He turned back to Lee. "Whole damn top looks like it's gonna come down. It's balancing on what's left inside. It's gonna drop."

Lee frowned. "What are they doing to deal with that?"

Helena followed quietly behind them as they walked, her gaze taking in the vastness of the destruction before them. It had taken long enough to drive there—it might have only been across the lake from the restaurant, but the road to there was one, long detour. And they really were parked miles away from the site. They had taken much too long to get there—lives might have been saved ...

As the mountain came into view, Helena realised that this was the Twins. Two mountains side by side, matching peaks out on the horizon, with a walkway connecting them. Only now, one of the mountains had gone. There was nothing but destruction that remained. This was two things in two nights, she mused. Yesterday, the bus, today this. Helena dared not even ask what tomorrow would bring.

The injured were laid on the ground near the bustle of people and vehicles. Not a single one of them was being tended to—not one had been given blankets or something to lie on. They were literally just laid out on the stones and mud. No one would touch them. The only other medics here would be for any *Humans* ... and from the way the woman in the red suit was knocking back a coffee and watching the show, Helena guessed there were no *Humans*.

Her blood boiled at the sight. What would it take to make the *Others* comfortable? To place something under their heads? Cover them with a blanket. This was the stuff that would forever leave that void between the two species. Neither one of the sides could see it.

They stopped suddenly, Lee having been given the whole rundown of things. Another man came over to join them—neatly-pressed suit, grey hair, receding hairline. He had a distinguished air about him, giving the impression of someone important.

As they shook hands, Helena grabbed the opportunity to make for the injured. "I'm just going to look at these people," she threw casually, already walking towards them.

Lee glanced at her, but was forced to merely nod at her in compliance as his companions drew him into a new discussion.

Helena gave an inward sigh of relief at having avoided any protests on Lee's part and walked over to the woman medic. Her flaming red head of curls was tied back in a ponytail, her face looking almost bored as she sat there sipping coffee. "Excuse me, do you have a bag I can borrow? Supplies. I'm Dr Barnes."

The woman ran her gaze over her dismissively. "There's no one here that needs tending to. It's just *Others*."

"I deal with *Others*," Helena said patiently, tamping down the urge to yell at her for her heartlessness. "They need tending to."

The woman scowled at the *Others* on the ground before zoning back in on Helena. "You're one of those?"

She narrowed her eyes at her. "*One of those*?"

"An *Other* whisperer," she scorned. "One of those hippie doctors that thinks all life is sacred."

Helena's eyes stayed level with hers. "I am a doctor. My job is to help people. Those are *people*."

The woman's lip curled derisively at that. "I don't have many supplies spare."

"You have an entire ambulance full," she said unwaveringly, spotting the racks in the back.

"I said *spare*."

Helena gritted her teeth and lifted her chin in determination. "Just give me what I need. I will see that you are reimbursed for whatever I use."

The woman glared at her. "I am not authorised for that."

Helena wasn't the violent type, but sometimes, with people like this woman, she really would love to be able to

124

enact the phrase *scratch her eyes out* and wipe that smug look off her face. Instead, very calmly, she said, "I am with Lee Norton. He will authorise you."

A flicker of unease crossed her expression before she quickly cleared her throat and said, "I have to hear that from him, then."

She hated to use Lee's name. She hated to need him in any way, but right now, lives were involved. From what she could see of the *Others* lying just a few metres from them, one was already dead, another was pretty near death, too, and the other had a damn good break in his leg. The first and the third could wait, but the one in the middle ... she could make a difference there. She could save him.

"I'll tell you what. I am going to get what I need, and if you have a problem with that, go and take it up with Mr Norton himself." She didn't wait for a reply as she stepped past the woman and climbed into the ambulance.

"You can't do that," the woman sputtered in indignation.

"Apparently, I can." Turning her back on the woman, she quickly grabbed the dressings and supplies she thought she'd need. Would Lee come and vouch for her? Possibly not. He liked Helena, she knew that, but did he like her enough to go against his beliefs with *Others*? Based on what he had done to Luke, she doubted that very much. But it was up to this medic to go running to Lee, and from what Helena could see, the other woman wasn't quite willing to go and confront the formidable Lee Norton.

With her provisions in hand, she swiftly made for the three lying side by side. The one with a broken leg was a young, skinny man—no wonder his bones were broken. There wouldn't be much she could do for him, except splint it up and send him back to her clinic for proper casting. She could x-ray it, too, but the bone was sticking out of his flesh, and it wouldn't need a whole load of machinery just to confirm the obvious to her.

"Don't worry," she said gently as she knelt down next to them. "I will get you to my clinic soon and take care of you."

He nodded but said nothing. He just stared out, silent and quiet, barely seeming to register Helena was there. She glanced over at the young, dead woman. It was difficult to see her face—it was crushed in, tangled, bloody blonde hair framing bones all smashed in. Despite there being no doubt about whether she was dead, Helena felt for a pulse just to make absolutely sure before turning her full attention onto the injured man in the middle.

He was large—the kind of large that held presence in a room no matter where he was. His chest rose and fell slowly, his breathing laboured as he struggled to draw in air. "My name is Helena," she said. "I am a doctor. I'm going to help you."

With great effort, he lifted up a weak arm. She caught his hand in hers and gently lowered it once more. "It's okay," she tried to soothe him. "Just try to relax. "His face was pretty bad—much like the girl's. His eyes were dark and swollen, but his left one was filled with blood and she had a horrible feeling that all that was left was an empty socket. Maybe his eye was in there, but she couldn't be sure. She'd have to wash it out and see. The bruising around the other eye was really bad, and Helena wondered if he might have lost his sight. On the side of his face where the socket seemed to be missing, the skin was torn and his cheek so swollen it looked like he was holding a golf ball in his mouth.

"Can you speak at all?" Helena asked, leaning closer. "I need to know what you are." Different *Others* meant different medicine. If he was a shifter, which she doubted, he would heal himself, but if he was something like a witch, then he would need something else.

His mouth moved slowly and incomprehensible gurgles escaped his throat.

"I didn't hear you," she said gently, leaning in more. She knew she shouldn't do that—lean in this close and make herself vulnerable to attack. What if he was faking it?

"*Fae*," he finally rasped.

Her stomach knotted at that, and Luke's face swam in front of her. She had let Lee kill him. Could she really lose another *Fae* in the same day? Not a chance.

She needed to know what kind of *Fae* he was; what his element was. Then she could help him to heal better. She ripped open his torn shirt as gently as was possible to reveal a chest dark with bruises. She pressed down gently with the tips of her fingers, hoping to God that he didn't have any internal bleeding.

"What is your name?" she urged.

He blindly lifted a hand up again, and she hastily took it.

"You're safe," she reassured him softly. "Tell me your name. I'm here to help you."

"X-Xander …" She barely caught the whispered reply.

"Okay, Xander. I want to take you to my clinic. You're hurt pretty bad."

He moved then—tried to at least—his face screwing up in pain.

"It'll be okay. I promise. I live in an *Other* community." She squeezed his hand tighter, trying to show him that he was safe, she wouldn't hurt him. *Shit*. She'd do everything she could to bring him back. One *Fae* for another. This was redemption. A chance to pay back the life she had let Lee take.

She would fix this—if only for her conscience.

Chapter Fifteen
Stephen

Stephen hadn't planned on going to sleep. Until he actually woke up, he hadn't realised that he had—although *woke up* was probably the wrong term, he thought as he rolled to his side choking and gasping for breath. His own damn fault. He had been holding his breath during his sleep, and the choking part was his body's way of saying, breathe or die. He coughed and wheezed as he sat up trying to compose himself. It had been a while since he had woken to one of these fits. It happened often those first few days after the cage. After … He pulled his thoughts away from that path.

He didn't want to think about that.

He never let himself think about that.

He gave another vicious cough then bolted up off the ground and stumbled to the other side of the fallen tree. He doubled over and retched, his big body heaving violently.

Good morning, Stephen Davies …

His brows drew together, and he mentally corrected himself. Stephen Davies no longer existed. It was *Nicholas Mason* now.

Bloody hell, he would never get used to his new name.

He sank down and leaned against the trunk, his body exhausted. His mind clambered desperately to gather itself. He had got stuck with his odd dream on repeat. God, he hated deep sleep. He hated dreaming even more. Dreams were cruel—wicked gifts from torturers sent to hunt unsuspecting victims in the night, giving people things they wanted, only to take them away again as soon as they woke.

Sometimes Stephen's dreams were so real, so vivid, that he woke gasping for air. He hated them and what they grabbed away from him. He'd give anything sometimes just to go back to sleep and stay in his dreams—the happier dreams. The ones that laughed and mocked him with what he didn't have. In his dreams, anything was possible. Things he never had the courage for. Things he wanted more than anything.

Now, there were new dreams. Dreams about people and places he didn't know—strangers, faces he had never seen. They took him on walks through his imagination to faraway places. New possibilities. These dreams were, perhaps, the worst … the most vivid of them all.

His mother had once told him that dreams were sometimes glimpses of the future. Maybe she was right, but that meant that free will and choices were nothing but well-placed illusions. She said the future was set, and it was just the path along the way that people got to choose. But all roads led to the same destination. He wondered if that was true. Would he have landed in Exile no matter what? Lying on the ground, homeless and vomiting his guts up? What if those dreams *were* snapshots into the future? If so, he didn't want them—any of them. Where was the fun and the adventure in knowing what was coming? He wanted the surprise of tomorrow, or to believe tomorrow still existed. Because for some, it wouldn't.

Stephen's sleep—filled mind tried to conjure the images that seemed to be hidden behind a veil in his mind. Had it all been just a dream?

A marble?

A note?

None of it made any sense, and yet, as he uncurled his fingers, a note stared back at him. His heart hammered at the sight of it. What the hell was going on? He tossed it to the ground, staring at this alien object that had come into his world ... somehow transported itself from his mind to his hand. The woman—the same woman—she had been in both his dreams. Who was she? He clutched his head, his stomach rolling with another wave of nausea. Was it possible he had reached a new level of insanity?

The crumpled note lay on the floor, still folded. He hadn't opened it last night, in his dream or real, or whatever the hell it was. He frowned. He didn't recall the moments after he had slammed his paw down on the paper. The next thing he knew, he was waking up, choking. With an oath, he grabbed the note and opened it.

55 Woodgrove Terrace.

That was it? A bloody address?

He closed his eyes for a second to regain a semblance of balance both inside and out. It was like a god damn bad hangover after a night spent lost in the twilight zone. Woodgrove Terrace? Where the hell was that? No indication of what it might mean. Was he supposed to go there? The address had to mean something, but his foggy mind couldn't process any of it.

As he used the tree to help push himself up onto shaky legs, the ground swayed and threatened to tip him over. Through the dizzying haze, he vaguely realised he was naked. Bewildered, he frowned. When had he shifted back?

Still clutching the rough wood of the tree for support, he lifted a weak head and took in his surroundings. No one else was around it seemed. Thank god for that, given his wardrobe situation.

He mentally put together what had happened the night before. He had sat down and waited for the dog to sleep. He had fought his hunger and then shifted. He had come back and seen the woman … He clamped his hand around the paper. There was something he was forgetting. He leaned heavily against the tree. Perhaps a dip in the water would help him wash away the cobwebs that hindered his memory of the last few hours.

Stuffing the paper down his bag, he glanced over at the dog that had just raised its sleepy head to look at him. "I'm going for a swim; you watch my shit." The dog gave a flip of its tail and put its head back down again in reply.

Stephen staggered down to the water's edge and walked into the water before his mind could tell him to stop. Icy coldness slammed against him, igniting every nerve fibre.

After scrubbing and rinsing away the dirt from his body, he climbed out of the chilliness, feeling refreshed, even if his memories hadn't come flooding back. Letting the morning sun soak away the water from his naked flesh, he ran his hands through his wet hair. His skin glistened as droplets ran a lazy path down his body, his shoulders starting to relax as the warmth of the sun seeped into his skin. He closed his eyes and turned his face towards the rays, inhaling deeply and breathing in the soothing smells of Mother Nature.

With a sigh, Stephen turned to reach for his clothes that lay in a neat pile near the dog and stopped short. He hadn't taken them off here. He hadn't folded them, either.

He froze, listening, searching with his senses for any presence close by. There was nothing; not one odd smell or sound to warn him of anyone else there. Still on alert, he picked up his shirt and held it out in front of him. He'd fucking ripped it right down the middle the night before— but as he stared at it now, there wasn't a single tear in it. The same went for his jeans. Although he had torn those off his body as well, they were completely whole now.

Exile

Stephen grabbed his clothes and pulled them on with an odd sense of déjà vu. He was positive that the blanks in his mind were nothing more than a blackout due to hunger. Blackouts weren't unfamiliar to him. Not since … the cage.

He paused, surprised at realising that his stomach felt sated. Had he fed? He couldn't remember doing so. Had his victim been *Human* or animal? He hoped for animal—but if it turned out to be *Human*, he hoped that he had at least concealed his crime with the efficiency he had been taught, he thought dispassionately.

The mutt growled suddenly, but it wasn't a warning to Stephen—it was something else. He almost seemed to be growling … *at* Stephen.

Stephen turned to face the trees, and … hunger and memories slammed into him. The sudden urge to run and hunt hit him with such force that he stumbled back.

"Shit."

As if unable to help himself, he began to run—like a shadow of himself from hours before, tracing the steps he had taken, each memory becoming more vivid with every step. Images flashed of him ripping his shirt off, shredding it in his need to shift.

He reached the middle of the woods, his memories a movie in his mind. This was where he had tossed his jeans onto the ground. Staring at the ground as if it would give him some kind of answers, he absently patted his jeans, looking for marks and tears. Not a single one anywhere. This was some creepy fucking shit.

As he patted his hand over his pocket, he felt the solid lump of a marble … which he hadn't put there. His heart lurched in his chest. Pulling the glass ball out, he held it up to the light. It wasn't like the others. There was no picture inside this one, just a drop of clear glass.

Without conscious thought of what he was doing, he headed through the trees once more at a run, emerging at a large patch of grass. Running barefoot along the path he had taken as his *tiger*, pictures revealed themselves in his mind as he went, a domino effect until he reached a hedgerow that separated the woodlands from farmland.

The chug of a tractor broke into the morning silence. In the distance, cattle and farms came to life for another day's work. Stephen walked along the edge until he came to where one field ended and another began.

Memory flooded him. He'd eaten a ewe. He remembered the hunt and the kill, how she had felt in his jaws as he had sunk his teeth into her flesh. *Shit*. He looked up and down the hedge. He had dragged her under one of them.

He jogged along the hedge, looking for a carcass. Nothing. No blood. No guts. Not even a discarded bone. She couldn't have been cleaned away already.

He fell to his knees on the ground. What the fuck was happening to him? He thumped the earth with his fist. Maybe he was wrong. Maybe it had all been a dream; either that or he really was insane.

Or maybe … maybe the ewe was just further along. Every hedge looked like the one before, and Stephen sure as fuck was no botanical expert. Frantic, he crawled along the base of the hedges like a madman searching for answers in a world that made little sense.

Lost in his frenzied searching, Stephen failed to notice how close he had got to the *Human* lands. Everything about him was off-kilter—even his valuable senses that had kept him safe all these years. With a surprised jolt, he stared at the *Human* boots that were suddenly in front of him, then slowly peered up, his gaze travelling along a pair of well-worn jeans until he was looking up into a *Human* face.

Before he could so much as blink, something cold and hard pressed against the base of his skull.

Fuck.

"Move and we kill you," said another *Human* behind him. "It's silver."

How gloriously fortuitous it was for the *Humans* this morning. Their catch had literally crawled right to their feet. The *Human* grinned down at him, and Stephen took a deep, long breath, closing his eyes in defeat

Bloody fantastic.

The man in front of him snapped a silver, spiked collar around his neck, one similar to that which his father had used for the cage. Stephen bit down on the panic rising in his chest at being bound that way again. It would do him no good to lose it now.

Stephen gritted his teeth as hundreds of tiny pins pierced his skin. His head became heavy and his vision blurred.

The *Human* behind him yanked his arms back and tied those together as well. Stephen's breathing grew shallow and weak, and everything around him started to fade. .

The world went black.

Chapter Sixteen
Helena

Helena spotted the small, blonde woman first. She hid behind a tree, watching Helena from the shadows. It took her a moment to make out the shape of a man standing right behind her. Two sets of glowing eyes trained on her, following her every move. They were no doubt *Other*, and she suspected Xander was their friend. No one else had seemed to notice them—but then everyone seemed to be too caught up with worrying about how much the collapse would cost Norton Industries.

Surprisingly, Helena felt no fear, nor did she feel threatened by the two onlookers. Maybe she should have, but her gut instinct told her they meant no harm. *Humans* would surely have told her she was being foolish. But *Others* weren't as the *Human* race wanted everyone to believe; they were not evil, hostile beings.

"You're going to be okay," she said, just loud enough so that their *Other* hearing would pick up what she was saying. "I'm going to have you taken to my clinic in Fortvania." She glanced up at them as she spoke, making sure they heard. That would help reassure them while, at the same time, letting them know where they could find their friend.

She made short work of letting Lee know she needed to get the two injured men to her clinic. Fortunately, Lee was obliged under Exile law to let these men get medical treatment. After informing Helena he would come by the clinic as soon as he had things under control, he instructed the woman medic—who tried very hard to hide her displeasure—to drive Helena and the two *Others* to Fortvania, and allocated a guard to accompany them.

Exile

As the ambulance rolled away, she glanced back at the trees, but her two spectators had vanished. She looked down at Xander and the man with the busted leg—he would be easy enough to tend to. Tracey could deal with him. The entire drive took place in silence, the medic's mouth set in a firm line as she transported her unwanted passengers. The silence was fine by Helena. At least she wasn't busting her arse about why helping *Others* was wrong.

When they reached Fortvania, Helena jumped out of the ambulance and punched the code into the box for access to the gate. Not many people knew that code—only the officials at the gate, her and a couple of other professionals who would need it. It wasn't so wise to let the residents have it. What if they became traitors? Not that that would stop anyone if they really wanted to get in, but it made the residents feel safe … as safe as could be. Of course, Lee had the code, but they didn't need to know that.

She got the gate open and waved the ambulance through.

"Where do you want it?" the woman said when she pulled up outside Helena's clinic.

"If you give me a moment, I will get my assistant."

"I don't have a minute," the woman cut in coldly. She got out of the ambulance and started to   lower the ramp with quick, abrupt movements. Was her distaste really so great that she would just dump *Others* like this?

She lowered the ramp with Xander on it, and Helena had to grab for him, sure that at that angle, he would slide from the bloody bed and land in a heap on the ground. The guard hastened to help her, probably worried about any bad feedback about him getting back to Lee. Whatever the reason, she was glad for the help.

The woman stood back, arms crossed over her chest, refusing to lift a finger to help.

"Just give me a minute," Helena panted and earned herself another glare from the woman. "I'll just be a second." She dashed up the steps to her clinic and hurriedly unlocked the door. "Trace. You here?" she shouted, racing through the front room. "Trace?"

"I'm here," came the sleepy reply from the sitting room. She yawned as she emerged. "Sorry. I dozed off."

"It's okay. We have two new patients coming in. One of them is *Fae*. He's hurt pretty bad. The other guy just has a busted leg."

All traces of sleep vanished from Tracey's face as she pulled the small jacket tight around herself, but it didn't cover her bump anymore. "What can I do?"

"Can you set up the exam room? We need to bring them in."

"Sure," she said, already heading that way.

Helena dashed back out to find the medic had the man with the broken leg sitting on the path and looked to be trying to roll Xander off the gurney and onto the ground.

"You're trying to just dump them here?" Helena asked in disbelief, grabbing the side of the gurney and stopping her from tilting it.

Benny's light had come on next door, and slowly, the lights in other houses started to flick on one by one. Inquisitive eyes stared out from behind curtained windows.

"Just get those things out of my ambulance," the woman snapped. "I have to get back to some *real* work."

So many words slammed through Helena's mind, but none she wished to say out loud. Not that they would bother the woman—her skin was probably as thick as her head. But they would bother Helena, so she kept her mouth shut and turned to the guard who stood there looking on awkwardly. "Could you please help me get him inside?"

As she helped him manoeuvre the gurney up the steps, Tracey appeared at the doorway. "Can you get that one in the back and fix up his leg?" she asked her, nodding towards the man still sitting on the path.

Tracey nodded and smiled, but her eyes were on the ambulance. Strange *Humans* coming into town never went down well, no matter the purpose.

Xander hissed in a pained breath as the gurney bumped up the steps. She placed a gentle hand on his chest—broken ribs for sure. God, she hoped that he wasn't bleeding into his lungs. She could not let this *Fae* die. "Hang in there for me, Xander."

He was running a fever. That intoxicating *Fae* scent was stronger now—rich and light, like the crisp air of a fresh morning. She had to hold her breath not to drown in it, or she'd be lost.

As soon as they had him on the examining table, Helena thanked the guard, who gave a curt nod and left without a word.

Tracey had already set everything up for her—a clean sheet on the bed and Helena's medical kit to the side. Everything was sterile and ready to go.

She must have been working on Xander for about an hour when the front door opened and she heard footsteps—heavy—male no doubt. She tensed. Only one man had the keys to her clinic.

"Everything okay here?" Lee asked as he came to stand in the doorway. His eyes fell on Xander, but she moved so that his view was blocked. For some reason, she didn't want anyone near him; felt some inexplicable protective pull toward him.

"Yes," Helena said. "Both of them will be fine." Tracey had already taken care of their patient with the injured leg. After a night's rest, he'd be set to go. "This one was hurt pretty bad, but he'll make it." Lee's gaze ran over her, and Helena was suddenly very aware of the state of her. She was covered in Xander's blood, pretty sure that she had smudges of it on her face and in her hair, too. There'd been no point in changing her clothes; her beautiful dress had long been ruined. She cleared her throat, uneasy under his thorough scrutiny. "There were others?"

His eyes met hers again. "The rest were dead."

Her heart fell at that, but she nodded sombrely. Although she had hoped for more survivors, she'd known it would be highly unlikely to find any. "Can you give me a moment? I'm pretty much done here. I just need to tie up a couple of loose ends. I'll meet you out back?"

Lee cast a last glance towards Xander before turning his gaze back to Helena. "Of course."

Lee was sitting at the small table she kept by the window. She used it to work, or to read while she was eating. He stood when she entered the room.

"You're covered in blood," he remarked, his face grim.

She had washed her hands and face, but her dress was still streaked with red. "It's not mine. It's the *Fae's*."

His eyebrows rose. "Another *Fae*?"

She shrank inwardly. "Yes."

A look of something Helena couldn't quite decipher crossed his face, but it was gone again almost immediately. It was probably disgust, she thought.

"I can put him out again, like the other?"

She caught herself before she could say or do anything that could prove disastrous for the *Fae*. "No. This one is okay," she said coolly. "He will live."

140

Exile

Lee's penetrating gaze bore into her. "He doesn't have to."

Panic set in, but Helena kept an impassive mask firmly in place on her face. Ignoring his remark, she quickly said, "What happened at the Mountain?"

He paused, then sighed. "Money hunters. They blew the damn place up. That *Fae* you have in there is one of them. Do you know how much money hunters cost us a month?"

"They're just making a living," she said carefully. Money hunters, people who worked for the sweepers; who caught *Others* and handed them over to *Human* authorities. Maybe Xander was one of them. Maybe he had his reasons for doing what he did, but that wasn't her business. Her business was to fix him, to make him well again.

"I don't like you working on them. It worries me." He went to her sink and took the wash cloth from the tap where it hung. He held it under running water, wringing it out before coming back over to her with it. "You have blood on your face." Her hands flew to her cheeks; she must have missed a spot. She went to take the cloth from him, but he dodged her hand. Gently, he cupped her chin and lifted her face, touching the warm cloth to a point just above her cheekbone and lightly wiping any remaining vestiges of blood away. "They're dangerous. Out for themselves. I can have him taken to our facility," he said softly. "We can treat him there."

And here was the real Lee she knew once again. It reminded her how she should never let his gentlemanly manners and charm fool her—they weren't real. Fighting the urge to pull her face from his grasp, she patiently waited for him to finish. "Thank you," she said steadily. "But he is okay. I can fix him."

141

His hand paused in its swabbing, then resumed again. "If he dies, you will drain him?"

"*If* he dies, I will," she said.

But she wasn't about to let that happen.

Not this time.

Chapter Seventeen
Stephen

Someone was going to die. He didn't know who, nor did he really care, but someone was going to get their very own, personal introduction to the reaper himself. Stephen's neck ached, his arms hurt and his wrists burned with a fire so deep that he was sure Satan himself had come to roast him alive. He tried to breathe, but something tight bound him in place, pressing against his chest. He blinked, once, twice, flashes of the world burning his eyes with the onslaught of the unwelcome brightness.

His blurred vision took its time to clear. Speckles of his mind fog clinging across his eyes as he tried to make out where he was. He wasn't dead yet ... That would be soon. It appeared that his worldly captors had a plan. His death was not going to be easy—if it wasn't for the fact that he was still alive, realising he was chained to an inverted cross above an altar was a pretty good indicator.

All he needed was a sign around his neck with the words,"The end is nigh", and the picture would be complete. He might have laughed at his predicament—if he wasn't sure he was about to die.

He twisted where he was but didn't manage to budge. He was surprised to find that he didn't have nails through the palms of his hands or feet. Did the *Humans* really not understand the concept of a good crucifixion? Perhaps they didn't realise that the cross they had strapped him to was the wrong way around, he thought wryly. One would think that in the house of God, they would have at least got that small detail right. Stephen was willing to offer lessons, if they let him down.

143

Mason Sabre

There were binds around his wrists, and beneath his feet was a small rest for him to stand on—that would have been handy if his cross had been hung the right way around, he mused. The chain around his chest went all the way to the beams above, holding Stephen in place and the cross up.

He rolled his eyes. Even in religious sacrifice, there were cost cutting measures.

The altar was typical, except for the blood stains on it. Maybe throat incision and blood draining were on today's agenda. He wasn't partial to watching someone bleed to death—even more so if it were him doing the bleeding.

Stephen angled his head as best he could to get a better view of his surroundings. From the corner of his peripheral vision, he realised that he wasn't alone. He strained to see the two unconscious people in the same predicament behind him.

"You've got to be kidding," he muttered as he caught sight of a shock of red hair. For all her talk about having almighty powers, the witch seemed unable to keep herself out of unpleasant situations. The other captive was female, too, but didn't appear to be a teenager quite yet—just a goddamned kid.

By the time the witch began to stir, he had lost feeling in both of his arms, his shoulders burned and though he could have done with a quick trip to the men's room, he didn't think that the *Humans* would let him down for necessities such as bathroom usage. And he had no doubt that it had been *Humans* who had put them there. His gut instinct told him they hadn't strapped them up and were just leaving them to die. They'd be showing up soon, of that he was sure.

He heard the witch tugging at her binds, huffing as she did. The chain around her rattled in the rafters above. The position of her cross was just behind Stephen's and a little to the side. Did that mean he had been considered as most important of the three? *Oh, to be the special one in the gang of the forsaken*.

He rolled his eyes as the frenzied clanging behind him continued. "You might as well give up. You won't get the ties unfastened."

For a moment, she ceased her futile struggle and Stephen twisted to watch her. She began speaking, but the language she spoke was unfamiliar to him.

"Speak English, for God's sake."

She paused in her inane babble. "I can't," she uttered, and then started again. Stephen banged his head on the wood behind him. Of course … Slow, drugged-up Stephen Davies. *Wiccans* … Did they ever learn? He'd been better off when she'd still been unconscious.

"I'm sure your witchery isn't going to work, either." The *Humans* knew what they were doing. They would have put something in place to stop her getting out so easily. Silver for him … For her?

"I'm not dying here," she retorted, trying to yank her wrists out with no luck. "Jesus fucking Christ," she yelled.

"It would appear that you don't really have a choice," Stephen drawled. "Maybe when our hosts return, you could put in a formal complaint?"

"Fuck you," she snapped, and Stephen laughed. That only ignited the witch's colourful language some more, making him laugh deeper.

He stopped when someone entered through the door at the back of all of the pews at the other end of the church—literally, *through* the closed door. It was a girl, her form faded, but clear enough to see; a weird form of

145

transparency. She stopped just in front of Stephen, her pale—no … *faded*—eyes staring up at him inquisitively.

"Who are you?" Stephen demanded, a strange disquiet coming over him as he frowned at her. She didn't reply, but rather offered a nod, and then she … *floated* … to the girl on the other side of Stephen.

Seconds later, the girl on the cross gasped and tugged at her chains in the same manner as the witch had just done. She pulled against everything, desperation in her attempt to get free. A vampire? A real god damn vampire? Stephen had heard that vampires kept a part of their souls when they were first turned and crossed over, he had read about how their souls came back to their bodies. Even seen pictures of it, but to actually witness it was something remarkable.

If the vampire was awake, then darkness must have fallen outside. Maybe the *Humans* who had incarcerated them would be visiting soon … Stephen hoped, at least. The young vampire started to weep; sobs of a child. Stephen's stomach knotted. God, this was worse than the witch chanting. He gritted his teeth. Her sobs might pull on people's heartstrings, but the sound grated against his nerves. If she was a vampire, then she was probably dozens, if not hundreds, of years old—not a little girl at all.

"Crying isn't going to fix it," he growled at her after a minute.

Blood trickled from her eyes as her eyes fluttered his way.

Eden gasped. "Show some compassion," she sputtered. "She's just a kid."

"Oh, I'm sorry," he said, turning back to the vampire. "There, there. I'm sure it will be quick. You're a vampire, after all. You're already dead."

Exile

Choking on her indignation, Eden could barely get her words out. "Y-You're such … such a … She's a child."

"She is a *vampire*," he snarled.

"Maybe, but she is just a girl."

Stephen scoffed. "She's probably been a child longer than you and I have been alive. She's probably older than the two of us put together."

Before she could reply, the doors opened, actually opened this time, and the vampire's crying ceased. Had it been for show? Did she think someone would fall for her childlike performance and come and rescue her?

Six *Humans* strode down the church aisle with purpose, an air of authority around them. But, even from here, Stephen could smell the fear in one of them. Whether the fear was of the people with him or of Stephen and his companions, he was not sure.

The man at the front was dressed in a cassock—the full kit. Stephen was impressed. They had gone to so much trouble to appear authentic. No one spoke as the priest, real or pretend, began to lay out his various items of religious paraphernalia on the altar. The other men stood in perfect formation around him. They were all wearing the exact same thing; the young, the old, it didn't matter—some weird Amish style community maybe?

The youngest member in their group watched curiously, his eyes darting from Stephen to the 'priest' as he set to work. Stephen seemed to be the whizzy new plaything that he had never seen before.

After the priest had laid out his belongings, he picked up the aspergillum and moved backwards, sprinkling Stephen. Stephen jerked his head to the side, blinking his eyes instinctively as the cold … *water* … hit him.

"What the fu—" He caught a scent as it landed on his face. "Holy water?"

Pretend priest scowled at Stephen and held his hand up to silence him before moving to Eden. She strained against her binds, twisting her head.

Stephen took in a deeper breath, trying to identify exactly what the smell was—this definitely wasn't holy water.

He moved on to the vampire and splattered her with the water before coming back to the altar. Laying out a bible, he began reciting his prayer. "St Michael, the archangel, defend us in battle," he began.

"You're reading a demonic prayer?" the vampire burst out, finding her voice and shocking Stephen. "You cannot exorcise our souls."

He turned his face in her direction, but didn't falter in his words. "Be our protector against the wickedness and snares of the devil …"

"It won't work if you're using petrol to burn us," she said.

Petrol. Of course. Why hadn't Stephen been able to tell what it was? What the hell was wrong with him … And petrol? Fucking *burning at the stake* kind of petrol? "Are you serious?" Stephen blurted. "Fucking petrol? If this was a real casting, water would do. If we were really demonic, you'd actually be able to do it, you stupid fucks."

Maybe. But *Humans* were idiotic enough to believe water could be given power to exorcise souls.

"Let me go," the vampire wailed suddenly.

One of the men who had stood at the back shot a look at the pretend priest and something passed between them— a hidden message that Stephen was sure wasn't anything good.

Exile

The priest nodded and the *Human* drew a long blade from a block. Without hesitation, he walked to the vampire, grabbed her hair and took off her head in one clean movement.

Eden gave a shocked cry, and Stephen froze, stunned.

Stephen decided maybe he needed to be quiet.

Chapter Eighteen
Stephen

Religion was an irregular oddity—kind of like an oxymoron, in some odd bent way. It seemed to be the basis of many lies and corruptions. It certainly gave the government conspiracies a run for their money. So many lives had been lost in the name of God. People died for religion … the very thing that was meant to be the good in their lives. They got murdered and slaughtered for it. Stephen would never understand killing in the name of God when God himself had apparently said, "Thou shalt not kill". He didn't remember the small print in his studies as a child—the small print that gave people exclusions from the rule if they were different. Maybe that was the lesson he had missed when he had been locked in his father's shed with Lacey Jefferson—bible reading, of course.

Lacey Jefferson …. He sighed. His mind digressed.

The majority of the time, religion was just an excuse. Especially with the *Humans,* who never had the courage of their convictions. Stephen prided himself in saying when he had ended the life of a *Human*. Not in the name of God, not for any cause worthy of mention, nor was it for fun. He wasn't a sociopath, or even a psychopath. He was, however, sworn to his kind. He would kill for his own, and he had. Many times.

Hello, my name is Stephen Davies, and I am a Human assassin. It has been three days since my last kill.

Stephen smirked, lost in his own thoughts for a while, only brought back around when pretend priest dropped the vampire's head into the bowl on the altar in front of him. She didn't burn or suddenly turn into a pile of ash. Fiction writers and Hollywood had a lot to answer for with that expectation.

The poor, unfortunate species had been *Human* once, some time, long ago. Stephen pitied vampires for that, but everyone had their faults, right? Hollywood had the soul part right. They soul did leave, kind of—most of it, anyway. But some part remained. It had to or the vampire would not retain any shred of humanity and become nothing but a blood-craving creature of the night. Almost like reanimated bodies.

Pretend priest poured some of the petrol onto the vampire's severed head while the *Human* who had taken her head lit a match and dropped it into her hair.

That was one way to make the vampire burn and turn into ash, Stephen supposed.

The church was as bog-standard as they came. Religious items and sculptures decorated the place, hymn books sat at the end of wooden pews. Large stained glass windows that prevented the light from entering the church cast eerie shadows, and as Stephen glanced around the sanctuary, ignoring the rising stench as the vampire's head burnt, one of the windows caught his attention. At first he couldn't make it out. Maybe he was just seeing shadows—it wouldn't surprise him if he were suffering some mental form of delirium at this point.

The shadow grew, flying past each window, and Stephen squinted, unsure what he was seeing exactly. A bat? No. He dismissed the idea of Bruce Wayne arriving as his saviour. Stephen caught glimpses of it until it reached the window above the main doors. It started pecking on the glass—a bird perhaps? —and his *Human* captors all paused to look up at the intrusion.

Once, twice, three times it took for its beak to peck through the glass and send shards crashing to the floor. A large, white feathered swan flew through the gap, fitting in with ease. Pretend priest turned back to Stephen, ignoring it; his chanting carried on, louder as if the volume would aid in the removal of the satanic entities.

The swan floated to the stone floor with grace, but it was not a swan who landed. Feet touched down in silence, and Stephen almost smiled as the wings folded back, the pure white feathers receding into the being of the girl from the bus.

His captors stopped and stared in stunned silence for a moment. The *Human* who had decapitated the vampire was the first to make a move ...

The fool.

He charged at her with the bloody blade in his hand raised in the air and ready to dive into her. The man looked like he was going to jump like a basketball player, launching himself up to sink the ball through a hoop, only it was a blade for her head. But the girl didn't move an inch, squaring her shoulders, ready for him. At the very last moment, she ducked and narrowly missed feeling the burn through her skull as he sliced her open. She raised her hand in slow motion, aiming it at him. The momentum of his jump thrust the man towards her, unable to stop himself—either that or she was pulling him by some unseen force. Her fingers latched around his throat, and she slammed him down onto the stones.

He didn't get up again.

Stephen would have thought that she would pick up the blade the *Human* had dropped on the ground—it was what he would have done—but she paid no mind to it. That, nor to the other *Humans* in the room. Instead, she spun around and went the other way. Stephen pulled against his binds, the chains rattling. She was leaving? He swallowed

152

down any protest on his lips—Stephen was not one to admit that he needed fucking help to get out of this mess. Ever.

A small boy entered the church and the girl stopped and stood next to him, waiting. Pretend priest took his cowardly stance between the other four *Humans*—a dance—the grand ball at the end of the year.

The hesitant young *Human* made a cautious move towards them. Maybe he knew he was going to die, yet he didn't want to seem weak in front of the others. He held his baseball bat up in trembling hands, ready. What was he planning to do with it? Stephen had no idea, but he could barely hold it still.

He didn't get close enough to the girl and boy before he was struck down. It was much the same with the *Human* on the bus. One moment he was standing there and the next he wasn't.

That left three …

They all charged at once. One of them managed to get a fist off in the boy's face, knocking him back, then he turned to run for it. But the boy was on his back in the manner of an extremely hot huggie blanket before he could exit the church. Stephen pressed back into the cross, and the witch gasped from behind him as the *Human* suddenly caught fire. The vampire might not have become a pile of ash, but the *Human* certainly did.

He rolled as the other two men headed towards them at the same time. The idiot priest had taken to chanting once again. All he needed was the damn witch to join him now. But pretend priest stood alone, and Stephen contemplated sympathy for him. He must have chanted St Michael's prayer at least a dozen times, and they were all still there. Apparently, he still had faith. He stood frozen when the kids reached him, chanting over and over, faster and faster. So lost in it was he that he didn't even seem to notice how close they had come.

As if aware he wasn't a threat, the girl walked right past him. He was just a man in a suit that he thought gave him power. He was a fool, a mere *Human*, nothing to her, his words useless. Why did he stay there? Why didn't he run? Get out of there and save himself. He kept his eyes on the girl as she passed him, turning so that he was facing her. His words were so loud now that St Michael himself might actually hear him.

The girl climbed up to the witch first and with no effort at all, she snapped open the binds that held her in place. Then she moved to Stephen. There was no point in taking down the vampire. She was dead.

Stephen dropped to the ground with a painful thud. He couldn't break his fall properly; having lost all feeling in his arms, they were nothing more than useless limbs.

Pretend priest ran then, his words dying on his lips, his eyes wide as he realised what a pile of fucking shit he was in. Stephen fixed his eyes on him as he rose and shook out his arms then rubbed them to get the feeling back. The sound of the priest's desperate footsteps echoed on the concrete floor as he ran down the centre aisle. One moment the girl was standing with Stephen, and the next she was airborne, her arms—*wings*— out, her speed like nothing he had ever seen before. She landed gracefully at the doors, making it impossible for the priest to halt in time. She grabbed his wrists as he slipped right into her path; he squealed like a fucking pig, trying to fight her off as she dragged him back towards the boy and Stephen.

The boy startled Stephen by grabbing his hand and pulling him forward. When the priest was close enough, he joined their hands and looked at him expectantly. Stephen scowled—he was in no mood for handshakes. His hand tingled as circulation returned to his arms, but just as he was about to snatch his hand away, vivid images flashed through his mind—memories. He saw himself leaving the altar and going to … a cell? He couldn't recall. His memory backtracked …

Realisation hit him. It wasn't his memory—it was the vampire's.

He reached a house, dark, dismal … No. No, it wasn't. It was a just a normal house, but its aura spilled sadness from its pores.

Screaming. Someone screamed out into the night. Why? Why were they screaming? Stephen's mind rollercoastered through the maze of someone else's memories. The scream got louder, a woman's scream, piercing. Faces … so many faces. Men, *Humans*, all of them faces that he knew. He matched them up to each man who had stood before him moments before. Those who were dead now. Even the young one. The scene slowed down, finally reaching the point that it wanted him to see. He could no longer hear the whimper of the priest or the way he fought to let go. He couldn't see the girl and how she held him down by pushing him to the ground by his shoulders.

The boy still clutched onto the priest and Stephen's arms, careful not to touch Stephen's skin, but making sure the two stayed connected. He didn't need to, though. Stephen had an iron grip on the priest, making the other man's flesh go white as his hand got crushed under the brute force. Sweat and tears ran down his face as he called out for him to let go.

Stephen heard none of it.

A woman stood on the step of the house, her hair in a neat bun, her apron around her waist. Her smile was fresh and pure. All lies. She stared along the street into the night. She was waiting. Waiting for something that Stephen couldn't see yet. He stood next to her, an eagerness nestling in his chest, not dread.

A girl wandered along the street in their direction. The woman's heart jumped in her chest, her pulse racing suddenly. The girl ... the vampire ... Stephen's gaze travelled slowly over the woman. This was her mother ...

His heart clenched.

The witch had been right. The vampire had been just a child, in years as well as appearance—the modern-day clothes, her mother still alive. This girl hadn't been a vampire for long. She stood at the gate at the bottom of the garden, reminding him so much of Phoenix that day when he had had to take him to see his father to get his closure. Was this what this was? Closure? But the woman smiled at her daughter and went down the front steps to greet her, unlike Phoenix's father.

At first, both women hesitated, staring at one another unsure what to say, and then the woman reached out and wrapped her arms around the girl, pulling her into a motherly embrace. The girl hugged her back tightly, her head resting on her mother's shoulder as her eyes welled with blood-stained tears.

Stephen could feel the relief. It was almost tangible.

"Do you want to come inside?"

The vampire gave a cautious look towards the house. How long had it been since she had been there? What was it that had made her into a vampire? The woman took her daughter's hand and smiled affectionately at her. Why couldn't Phoenix's father have been as accepting as this woman? At least she was trying.

Inside the house sat pretend priest on the sofa with a

deceitful smile upon his face. He stood when the vampire entered, making her come to an abrupt stop. The girl retreated till her back hit the door then looked toward her mother.

"It's for your own good," the woman whispered, tears in her eyes.

The vampire turned to flee, knowing that she had been set up, lured by her own mother. But the priest grabbed her before she could take more than a step and pushed her into the room, slamming her down onto a chair. Other men came in, and Stephen recognised all the faces of the men in the church. The vampire screamed and fought, pushing at them to escape.

The woman repeated her words to her like it would make it all okay. "It's for your own good." The girl screamed as they held her down, fighting against them as they bound her wrists. The priest backhanded her across the face to silence her, and then they dragged her out.

No *Other* was in the church when Stephen opened his eyes. The witch, the girl, the boy … They were all gone, leaving him alone with the priest. He was down on the floor, begging. "It was for her own good," he pleaded. His hand was sweaty in Stephen's grasp, and fear emanated from him in waves, an acrid scent. Stephen felt each ragged, gut-wrenching breath in his chest as he stared at the pathetic specimen of a *Human*. Vermin—a disease of society.

With new found strength, he tightened his grip on the *Human* and stood, not realising till that moment that they had both gone to the floor. He reached up for the cross that he had been attached to. Now that he didn't have silver restraining him, it was nothing for him to pull it down and spin it around. The priest pulled against his grip, his other hand rising protectively above him, but Stephen didn't let go.

He dragged him along, crushing the bones in his hand and going for his throat. But he didn't save him the way he had done to the others on the bus. He didn't rip his throat out and send him to the other side. That would be too easy. Instead, he lifted him with ease and put him on the cross, snapping the binds into place.

"Please, n-no …" he wailed. On the block of the altar were two blades. Stephen picked them up and drove each one into his wrists, pinning him to the cross. His screams fell on deaf ears as Stephen took the bowl with the vampire's ashes and placed it in front of the *Human*. He held his hand up between them and let his claws extend. Placing one claw under the priest's left ear, he slowly drew it down.

"Please …" The *Human's* eyes were wide with terror as he begged for mercy.

Stephen felt every grain of skin split into a wet, red marker. He traced his claw along his throat, zipping his flesh open. He choked and gurgled, opening his mouth to try to scream as his blood poured down into the bowl below him.

"That's how you perform a sacrifice," Stephen snarled.

Chapter Nineteen
Stephen

Every life was meant to be valuable. The good, the bad and even the absolute evil. This was the belief, at least. Not that Stephen followed it. He rebelled against his childhood teachings—the brainwashing that all life was sacred was nothing but bullshit. He had asked his father once, "Who decided that all life was sacred?"

His father had replied, "Who decides when it isn't?"

Stephen hadn't been able to answer that, either, but it didn't take away his wondering. There had to be a line. Did someone like pretend priest deserve to live? He'd killed a girl—vampire or not, she was still a girl—and yet because he was *Human*, his crime would have gone unpunished. He'd have been hailed the hero in his world, cheered on and put up on a fucking pedestal. He would have been seen as doing God's work.

Humans were so blind.

Once upon a time, everyone believed that the world was flat, that it was the centre of the universe. Those beliefs had eventually changed. So could this. Taking a life, one that deserved to be taken, always left Stephen with a fiery electricity in his gut. It surged through his veins and he was sure that if there was a pool of water close by, he'd be able to walk across it—he felt that good, that empowered. Every muscle in his body ached with victory, every nerve ending standing ready.

The media would call it murder. He called it justice. They would think nothing of the crimes pretend priest had committed against the girl. She was a vampire—an *Other*. She didn't have those rights. Oddly enough, she would have

159

paid taxes to the treasury. She would have had to abide by the rules set down by *Human* law. There was no equality unless it benefited the *Humans*.

There was no reason to the things the priest had done—other than his own sickness. The vampire's only crime had been that she had been different. As for his little group of followers, Stephen bet they didn't know why they didn't like her, other than it was what they had been taught all of their lives. Just because she was a vampire, it had been given as an excuse to indulge in their sick tendencies. She had not bitten the priest. She had not harmed his family or bore him any ill will. Yet he could violate her and slay her without reprimand. His kind would rejoice in the triumph over one of the damned.

When Stephen emerged from the church, the girl, the boy and the witch were all waiting for him outside the gate—a peculiar group, it occurred to him, as he looked at them, his eyes focusing on the girl and the boy and the memory of what they had just done. What were they? A fucking violent swan thing and a supernova kid? He thought to thank them for their help, but he didn't feel that gracious right then. What he really wanted to do was walk right by them and not say a god damn word. He was suddenly mad inside.

Just go for a run, Stephen.

Yeah, that was it. It was all he needed. Well, that and some fresh meat. He'd have given anything just then to be able to go run and hunt.

Of course, that was never going to happen.

"We parked the car outside of town," the boy said as Stephen got closer, making him stop. His mind saw two children standing in front of him, but his brain told him that they were way beyond their years.

He glanced over at Eden, who was quiet for a change.

"You know them?"

"No," she said with a small shake of her head. "I don't."

He turned back to the two children, frowning. "Who are you?"

"My name is Freya," the girl replied confidently. "This is Aiden."

"It's such an honour to meet you." Excitement bubbled from Aiden as he stuck out a small hand. Stephen scowled at it for a long moment before eventually taking it. This kid couldn't possibly know who he really was—Stephen Davies, son and *ex*-heir to the Society's alpha. Could he?

"Are you going to come with me this time, Nick?" Freya prompted. The use of his fake name resolved any misgivings about whether they knew who he was. So why was the boy so excited to meet him? All Nick Mason was in this place was an escaped convict.

"Come where?"

"Our house," Aiden said. "We're here to help you."

Stephen snorted. "You're *children*. Thanks, but I think I'll manage on my own."

"Well, they're hardly helpless, are they?" Eden scoffed, making Stephen glare at her.

"You can't leave yet," Aiden urged. "You need to go back and get Sarah."

"*Sarah*? Who the hell is Sarah?"

"The vampire," Eden said impatiently.

Well, hadn't they all made nice friends while he had been inside dealing with the vermin.

"She's dead," Stephen said flatly. "She has no head. What do I possibly need to go and get her for?"

"Do you have to argue every point?" Freya said, annoyance thick in her voice.

"Do you have to give half-arsed answers to every question?"

"Just go and get the vampire. It is your *duty*."

Stephen did not take kindly to being ordered about—and definitely not by a couple of children. And what the fuck did she mean by it being 'his duty'? The kid had to be delusional. He ground his teeth and crossed his arms over his chest.

"Please," Eden begged, realising he was on the verge of telling them all to go to hell. "They did just save our lives. Do it as a way to thank them, at least?"

He swore and rubbed a hand over his face as he debated what to do. His hand came away red, and he frowned as he stared at it. He touched his fingers to his nose—it was bleeding. "Shit." He didn't remember getting hit or injured. Without warning, like a dam suddenly bursting, blood gushed from his nostrils.

Eden rushed forward and quickly handed him a cloth from her bag. "Here, take this."

"You need to go and get Sarah," Aiden urged him. "Or the bleeding won't stop."

"What do you mean?" Stephen muttered as he tipped his head slightly forward and pinched his nose.

"There is no time to explain," Freya cut in. "Get the vampire and then we will tell you all you need to know; but right now, trust us. You need to get the girl before it is too late."

He glanced at them—his mind was yelling for him to get away from these idiots, but, incomprehensibly, his gut was telling him to go get the girl. And Stephen had always been a man who followed his gut instincts. What did it matter, anyway? So, even though his head said these were kids and talking some pile of bullshit that he didn't need to

162

be a part of, he found mumbling, "Fine." What Freya wanted with a dead, headless, girl, he had no idea, and it wasn't his place to judge apparently.

Her words 'your duty' bounced around in his head. His duty to do what? Clean up the shit. Did she want the head, too, or just the body? Well, she was going to fucking get them. Both parts. She could piece each bit of ash together.

He took in a deep, calming breath and inwardly repeated, "Thou shalt not harm one's rescuers and aid." But his patience only went so far. There was a limit. With another deep breath, he turned to walk up the steps to the church once more, like a good soldier.

Willpower—that was the key to all of this. That, and visualising his hands around Freya's throat as he throttled her ... just a little.

For whatever reason, he expected that one of them might come along to help him—at least to carry the body— but even the witch just stood there with her arms crossed over her chest, watching. Why was she suddenly part of this team? Maybe she was going to use some of her hocus pocus to bring the vampire back to life. Although he doubted that the cream she'd put on his wrist would work so well. There had to be limits to what that shit could do.

He stopped at the door at the top of the steps, reluctant to go in with everything swirling around in his head and not one piece of shit making sense. There was an odd sense of regret deep in his chest about the vampire and the fact that she had met her final death—not that it was his problem, but just for a moment, his thoughts had been no better than the *Humans* and he had judged her. He closed his eyes and let himself accept that and make peace with himself. His nose was bleeding again, and he wiped a hand across his top lip to clean away the blood.

When he opened his eyes, he was in the church. He frowned. He hadn't walked through the doors. He hadn't bloody moved. A veil of dread settled on his shoulders. Pretend priest lay dead exactly where he had left him, and his little group of merry men lay in their crumpled heaps on the floor. That ruled out zombie reanimation.

Maybe it was the witch who had got him inside? Little conundrum and ka-pow, he was in the building. But she didn't seem that powerful to him.

Lying near his feet was the *Human* Aiden had graced with a heated hug. He nudged the *Human* onto his back with the tip of his boot. He was dead alright.

A sound caught Stephen's attention, letting him know that he wasn't alone in the church. The weight of someone's stare pressed on him, and he glanced around, surveying each corner, every nook and cranny, slowly, watching for the tiniest of movements. Had they missed one of the *Humans*?

Something in the shadow near the priest moved.

He squinted against the dullness of the place, but saw nothing. "Hello?" he called as he walked towards where the priest lay. He had bled out more than Stephen expected. The bowl had overflowed and left a pool around the base at the altar. It was such a shame that the vampire was dead; there was fresh takeaway being served.

Something in his peripheral vision caught his attention, pulling his gaze away from the admiration of his sacrificial work. Turning slowly, he only managed to get so far before something smashed through him. Wind slammed against his chest, not stopping at the natural barrier that was his flesh, but going right through, creating a cold wave inside him and coming out on the other side. He reeled back, catching himself on the altar and sending everything flying.

Fuck.

164

Exile

What was that?

It felt like his soul had been whirled out of his body. He gasped without feeling breathless, his body thinking it should be winded. His heart thumped without racing. He wanted to pant, yet there was no need. She left him … empty.

She?

The heavy drapes at the back swayed gently in an echo of her passing as she moved to hide in the shadows. He heard her, but didn't want to get too close and scare her. Each step he took, he kept his eyes fixed on the abnormality he could see just inside the darkness.

It was the girl who had entered the church, he realised, perplexed. The one who had joined with the vampire's body. She was different than before, though. Solid. He could touch her if he reached a hand out, and it felt natural to try. He had an odd awareness of her—like he'd had with Anya. Something connecting them, some part inside him telling them that this was right.

"I'm not going to hurt you," he said gently as he stretched his hand out to her.

She cowered back into the cover of the drapes, and Stephen sighed. With shock, he realised no air came from his lungs to make a sound.

Something was very wrong here.

Another flutter of movement came from behind him, and he went perfectly still, his senses coming alive, combing the area around him. He slowly twisted around, turning his back on the girl and leaving her in the drapes. She might be dead already, but she was afraid of something.

Stephen grabbed the knife from the priest's table, and his gaze fell on a small lump lying on the floor in a pool of blood. It hadn't been there before. He would have seen it for sure. He picked it up and wiped it on his shirt.

Mason Sabre

Another marble.

Gripping the knife tighter, he glanced up. "Who's there?" His voice didn't echo off the stone walls. Strange. "If I have to come and …" He didn't get to finish the threat as nausea hit him like death in his stomach. He reached out to grab the altar to steady himself as dizziness stole his vision. Something loud popped within the confines of his eardrums and then, just like that, it was gone.

Stephen didn't dare move. There was no one else there. The girl still sat huddled in the corner, but he could see nothing else.

The marble was warm—not warmth from his hand, but its own body of heat pressing into his skin. He scrutinised the glass ball and noticed a mirror scene in its depths—a miniature photograph, three-dimensional model of the death he'd had the kindness to inflict upon the priest.

Wasn't this how it had been with Anya? With the fat man?

Setting his mouth in a firm line, he focused on the other bodies, striding towards the two that had got their heads slammed together by Aiden and Freya. He dropped down to the ground and plucked up another two balls— same as the priest's, in a swirl of colours and shapes, they each depicted the way they had died.

All thought was lost for a moment as Stephen darted from one body to the next, turning them over, searching. The concrete did not scrape or hurt his knees as he dropped carelessly to the ground next to each one. Every *Human* was just the same as the other—another ball, another scene, shades of blues and purples, all identical, as if the purpose was to document the deaths.

He held all the marbles together in his hand, small mysteries before him.

His head shot up, and he glanced towards the vampire's body. He strode to where she still hung and searched her.

Nothing.

He rifled through her clothes, her pockets, but there was no marble on her. A chill went up his spine as he remembered that he already had one ... in his pocket. *Shit*. Cursing at his own stupidity, he shoved his hands in and yanked it out.

The ball was clear.

The girl crept out from her hiding place and came to stand behind him, looking at pretend priest's corpse—she was crying, not blood this time, but tears.

"He's dead," Stephen said quietly. "He can't hurt you again."

She nodded slowly and seemed to pull her tears back in. He held his hand out to her as he had done before, and this time, she took it. Her hand was solid in his, warm. She was real now—more real than when he had seen her before. She wrapped her arms around his waist and laid her head against his hard chest. Stephen put his arms around her, as he had with Anya. They stayed liked that for a moment, Stephen seeking as much comfort from her as she was from him.

"No one can hurt you anymore," he whispered against her hair. Closing his eyes, sadness welled inside him, deep and thick, threating to choke him. He held the girl tighter, pulling her to him, every emotion she was feeling, as if he could literally take it from her. He pressed his face into her soft hair—it smelt like lemons and sunshine.

With a gasp, he fell back, the bright light in his eyes suddenly. He was outside the church again, kneeling on the steps by the door, his hand resting on the thick doors to support himself. A shiver shook him, his mind disorientated. He pushed himself up, but his legs were weak. He felt completely lost. The despair inside him in that moment glued him to the steps like a magnet, his limbs heavy as if they were filled with sand. Something inside him was missing. He doubled over and pressed his head to the cold ground.

Freya approached him holding two velvet pouches—one blue, the other silver—with gold and red strings around the tops. She took the marbles from his hands and placed them into the blue pouch.

Blood still dripped from his nose.

"Let her go, Nick," she whispered.

He looked up at her, disorientated. "Let her go?"

"Sarah. She's going to kill you." Freya held out the pouch. "Place her ball in the bag."

He had her ball between his thumb and forefinger. His mind was cluttered with so much sadness and despair that he had no real idea what he was doing or what he was thinking. Freya helped him, gently taking the tiny ball and placing it in the silver pouch.

Stephen collapsed.

Chapter Twenty
Helena

The rhythmic bleeping of the machine was comforting to Helena these last twenty-four hours. They had been the most critical—they always were with patients like Xander. Things could go one way or the other. If they made it a full day, chances were they were going to make it all the way. Of course, it didn't always pan out that way, but it did give hope.

Helena had the television on in the corner, but the sound was turned down to a soft murmur. Her eyes drooped as she sat there, her head tilting forward as she slowly started to nod off. After the third time of having her chin slip off her hand and jolting her awake again, she sat up straight and rubbed at her stinging eyes, yawning as she stretched her arms over her head. God, it felt like a lifetime ago since she had climbed into her bed and actually slept. That didn't seem to be changing any time soon, either. She was alone, having sent Tracey home to bed—it would do no good for her to be up all hours. When she came back in a few hours, then Helena could finally get some sleep.

Xander was asleep, a bandage over the eye she had been unable to save. She ran gentle fingers through his hair, offering him some peace—he seemed to respond to touch. It was doubtful he would have any sight in the eye that had been saved. It was pretty busted up. Maybe his own healing would fix it?

Xander and the one with the broken leg had been the only ones to make it out alive—according to Lee, anyway. He was damn lucky. His leg was broken, too, and he had a couple of cracked ribs, but so far, he was responding well to the treatment. It was all on him now, and how much he wanted to live.

The beeping on the machine spiked suddenly, making her sit upright. Xander groaned and tried to part his dry lips.

"Hi," Helena said, standing, and instantly pulling the pocket light from her shirt. He had pried his eye open as much as he could so she flashed the light into its depths without actually touching it—it was so swollen she'd only cause him more pain. The pupil was dark, the white all red and shot to hell. "Xander? Can you hear me?"

He swallowed carefully, then rasped, "Wa—"

She strained to hear him. "Water? You want a drink?" He couldn't answer but Helena was already getting a glass from the counter beside her and filling it with water. She added a straw and pushed the tip into his mouth. "Here," she said gently. It took a few attempts to drink as he struggled to sip the liquid and swallow. She couldn't help but watch him. Even with the eye missing and bruises, he truly was beautiful.

His throat moved as he began to gulp down the water, greedily. "Slow," she urged, trying to pull the straw from his mouth, but he bit into it and grabbed blindly at the hand holding the glass. He was unbelievably strong, despite his injuries. "Easy," she said. "You'll bring it all back up."

As if she hadn't spoken, he continued to suck the water down until it gurgled in the back of his throat and he started to cough. His grip slackened and Helena quickly yanked the glass away and rolled him onto his side. He vomited all the water he had just ingested—it landed on her jeans and shoes and splattered the lino floor around her. She winced—well, she'd been covered in worse, she thought resignedly. Muscles bunched under her hand as she rubbed his back while he continued to cough.

Exile

When his body finally relaxed, she rolled him back onto his back, and within seconds, he was asleep again. She stared at him, an inexplicable protectiveness overcoming her. He was young, couldn't be much over twenty. Not being able to help herself, she brushed his hair back from his face, again struck by how spellbindingly beautiful he was. But that was a trait of all *Fae*. Anyone would be hard-pressed to find an ugly one.

Pulling the blanket back over him, she stared down at the mess by her feet. God, she was too tired to care to clean that up, but it had to be done.

With a sigh, she got a bucket from under the sink and started to fill it with disinfectant and hot water. She cleaned the excess off her shoes and then started on the floor. Nothing smelt worse than vomit and lemon disinfectant. It reminded her of being a kid and always being sickly. One of those distinguishable scents that lasted a long time.

When she was done, she quickly raced up the stairs to change her clothes. She didn't want to leave Xander alone for any longer than was absolutely necessary. She stuffed her soiled jeans into the washing machine and dumped her shoes in a bucket to soak. They were medical ones, so they'd just wipe clean when they had been disinfected.

Just as she was pulling a fresh pair of pants up, the doorbell chimned. It only rang upstairs—downstairs, it would be a knock, one that wasn't loud enough to wake *Others*.

"Shit." She wriggled into her jeans, almost falling over in her haste to get them on. She raced barefooted down the stairs and peeked through the spyhole. A man and a woman stood on the other side of the door—neither looked hurt.

Charily, she unlocked the door, but left the hatch on. Not that it would stop anyone, but it would give her a bit of time to get away or call for help. She was alone and not

171

about to open the door to two strangers, no matter how harmless they might look. It was usually the people who seemed the most innocent that posed the highest risk. "Can I help you?"

"We're looking for our friend," the man said. Helena made him out to be in his early forties, while the woman looked a little younger—mid-thirties maybe. "I think he is here."

"What is his name?"

There was a small pause before the man replied in a quiet tone, as if worried someone might hear him. "Xander." Helena bit her lower lip and resisted the urge to cast a glance back towards where Xander was. Just because they said they knew him, didn't mean they did. Call her paranoid, but she was all for safety. She had learnt that lesson a long time ago—the hard way. Letting one of her patient's loving husbands in only for him to turn out not to be so loving after all. Her imprudence had been the reason for that woman to get killed.

"Visiting hours are ..." She stopped short. Shit, she didn't actually have any visiting hours. There was no visiting really—it wasn't something that was done here. Her mind raced over what to say. "Come back after ten." People would be around then, and her doors would be open.

"Please," the woman begged. "At least tell us that he is okay." A sudden flash of realisation hit her, and Helena was almost certain this was the couple that had been lurking in the trees at the accident site.

Deciding to trust her instincts, she opened the hatch but kept a firm grip on the lock. They'd struggle to get in if they tried. One good thing of having a clinic in the middle of a town of *Others* was that they helped protect the place from just about anything.

It had its limits, of course.

"He's okay," she offered cautiously. "Just sleeping."

The man's shoulders literally sagged in relief.

"Can we wait out here?" the woman asked, her own relief visibly noticeable.

Helena gave a small nod. "Sure."

Just as she was about to close the hatch, the man stopped her. "Please tell him that Nigel and Mel are here. Tell him—" he paused. "Tell him that we got out okay."

"I will." Helena said gently, then closed the hatch and leaned against the door for a moment. Her mind was debating just letting them in, but she was so tired, she couldn't completely trust that her instincts were reliable at that moment.

She peeked out again—they had sat down on the step, and the woman, Mel, leaned into him, taking comfort from each other. Helena decided it would be okay for them to wait there.

Xander was still in the same position she had left him. After she had checked his vitals for the hundredth time that day, she walked to the small kitchen area and put on the kettle to make some coffee. It would help keep her awake for a few more hours. She flicked on the small television that sat on the counter. The explosion was all over the news. No survivors, it said. Well, she knew that was lies—but then the news in Exile wasn't exactly trustworthy. Authorities showed what they wanted, how they wanted, and who knew how many fabrications and falsehoods had been presented as facts. There were two, maybe four, survivors—if she included the two people outside. She leaned against the counter with her mug in her hand, listening to the report. Gas explosion, the newsperson said.

Gas?

173

That didn't make any sense.

Walking over to the large, comfy chair in the corner, she dared to sit down for a moment ... just a moment. She needed to sit and rest. Her back ached, her whole body ached. Her eyes stung so badly that it was a fight to keep them open.

Just one moment wouldn't do any harm. The door was open; she would hear Xander if he needed anything. She could hear the machines beeping away, their tune comforting as she listened to them ...

***

"Helena ..." A voice called her name from a distance. "Helena, wake up."

"Wha—" She sat up with a jolt, her heart thumping wildly in her chest. Tracey was standing over her. "Shit. I nodded off."

"I can see that," her assistant smiled fondly.

"Xander ..." She sprang to her feet, her head still foggy and weighted down with sleep. She had been dreaming of something ... someone ...

A man.

"He's okay," Tracey reassured her. "His friends are with him. I found them sitting outside."

Helena's heart sped up and she rushed to Xander's room, stopping at the doorway to watch them. "Are they okay?" she whispered to Tracey, who had followed her there.

Tracey frowned at the odd question. "Well, Xander seemed to know them, so I guess so." She put a hand on Helena's shoulder and squeezed lightly. Go get yourself a shower, and some more sleep or something. I got this. No offence, but you look like hell."

"I feel it," Helena admitted. She didn't even know how long she had been awake for. *Too* long. "I'll give Xander one last check before I do, though."

"He's fine," Tracey said firmly, her voice stern, but Helena ignored her. She just needed to be sure, that was all.

The woman, Mel, was standing at the foot of the bed. Nigel was standing to the side, near Xander's head. "He needs a lot of healing," she said to them as she walked in. "But he should be okay. I'm Doctor Barnes." She offered her hand out to them. "I'm sorry about last night."

The man dismissed her with a wave of his hand. "It's fine. I get it. I appreciate you making sure he was safe from any threat." He stepped back so that she could see Xander, who was asleep once more. "His eye?"

Helena chewed on her lip. "Come out here with me." She didn't want to risk Xander hearing her. He didn't know yet, and she wasn't sure just how much he could hear even when he seemed to be sleeping. "I'm hoping he will regain full sight in the right eye," she said when they were outside the room, "but the left … it's gone. I had to remove it."

Nigel's jaw clenched, his head dropping as he ran a hand over the back of his neck.

"You're friends of his?" she asked softly.

"More like a brother," Nigel said. "He'll be okay?"

"I'm hoping so."

"Hoping?"

Helena blew out a deep breath. "It's on him now and how much he wants to recover. Medically, he will heal."

"The world has gone mad," Mel suddenly said from inside the room. At their quizzical looks, she pointed at the television. "The news."

Helena felt the earth disappear from under her feet. That was the man from her dream. She struggled to breathe as she stared at the handsome face on the screen. Dark hair, stubble covering a stubborn jaw. He looked older here, but those eyes ... She would know them anywhere. There was a fire in them, something that drew her.

The image on the screen flicked to a church. There were emergency services everywhere and in the corner of the screen, a photo of the man. *Escaped Convict, Nicholas Mason*. So, that was him—the missing convict from the bus. She reached over and turned the volume up.

"Mason, convicted killer sentenced to execution, escaped custody on Tuesday. Police warn that he is dangerous and anyone seeing him *must* call the number on the screen immediately."

Except, that number wasn't the police. That was Norton Industries. Mason was wanted for the killing of a priest and his attendees.

"Crazy is right," Helena mumbled, realising she must have dreamt of him because the television had been playing while she had dozed. She must have caught a glimpse of him on the news before she had nodded off, his image infiltrating her sleep-filled mind.

"That's the bus you got called to?" Tracey asked from behind them.

"Yeah."

"Must be the guy, right?" She leaned in to look at the screen better. "You'd think that he would lay low."

"I would if it were me," Mel agreed.

"Maybe he is just crazy after all?"

Time would tell, Helena guessed. Exile was a big place, but not so big that he wouldn't be found. If he kept killing *Humans,* though, even his own kind would hunt him down and turn him in. They'd not want to rock the boat with things.

"Blight," Xander murmured, causing them all to spin around.

"Xander?" Nigel was at his side in a matter of seconds. But Xander blinked, focusing his one good eye on the screen, his lips in a hard, firm line. "Blight," he rasped again, pointing at the man on the television. "Blight."

Helena had no idea what he was saying, but Mel and Nigel seemed to. They glanced at each other, their expressions one of shock—and maybe fear.

Blight.

What the hell did that mean?

Chapter Twenty-One
Helena

Such a beautiful face was beginning to emerge from underneath the blood and bruises. As each hour passed by, it seemed that Xander healed some more. He might not have had the healing powers of shifters, but he was certainly healing faster than any *Human* would have done. Helena wrung out her cloth in the bowl of water on the trolley by his head and cleaned his wounds once more. The water had been mixed with a special blend of herbs, something that Celby had shown her how to do—a witch's blend. Of course, Helena wasn't a witch, and she had pointed that out, but Celby had told her that there were so many powerful things out in the world. One did not need to be a witch to use them. It had seemed she had had a point.

Whatever it was, it stank to high heaven. Green and thick, but just one scoop—no more, no less. Celby's words echoed in her mind every time she used it. It appeared to literally *wipe* away Xander's bruises. She worked her way across his face, around his mouth. The cuts on his lips had all but gone now, leaving behind soft, full lips, the kind that she could imagine would hold a smile enough to steal anyone's heart. His entire face was in perfect alignment, his milky-coloured skin just adding to the flawlessness of his beauty.

She left his covered eye till last. No number of herbs or potions would bring that back.

Carefully, she peeled back the tape holding the dressing in place. Even though she knew what to expect, it still saddened her to see. His eye was completely gone. There had been no way to avoid a whole eye removal—the entire eyeball had burst, most likely from debris that had landed on that part of his face and squashed his eyeball into the socket. God, she couldn't imagine how that must have hurt.

The wound itself was healing nicely, no longer deep purple around the edges. She removed the dressing fully and reached for her other bowl. She always used fresh water and herbs when cleaning this eye, fearing that the other might cause him an infection. As she dipped a new cloth into the bowl and was busy squeezing out the excess water, something thick wrapped itself around her throat, asphyxiating her. She gasped for breath and tried to grab at what was choking her, but despite feeling the undeniable pressure of powerful fingers strangling her, there was nothing there. She started to panic, her nails clawing desperately at her own flesh.

She slid off her stool, the bowl clattering to the floor as her arms flailed and she fell back, taking the trolley with her. It slammed against the wall, sending utensils and bandages flying. She tried to scream, but she couldn't suck in any air.

The pressure on her throat grew, and she grabbed for the door, missing it and landing on the floor, her face smashing off the tile and shattering her cheek. Her foot thrashed out, kicking the stool and sending that crashing into the machine monitoring Xander.

The door burst open, and Tracey raced in, eyes wide. She fell to her knees next to her, calling out her name. Helena gouged at her throat, trying to pull away the invisible force that had her in its grip while Tracey looked on, panic-stricken.

Helena felt herself start to lose consciousness, darkness edging her vision. A blur of shapes filled the room as people piled in. She felt herself being lifted from the floor, and all at once, the pressure was gone. She wheezed and coughed, trying to suck in huge lungfuls of air.

"Breathe, Helena," a woman's voice said. Someone put a glass to her mouth and she tried to take a desperate sip of the water, only to end up in another fit of coughs, blades of fire searing her throat.

Mel had her arm around Helena's back, and she lifted her with ease, getting her to her feet and walking her to the office chair in the corner of the room. When her vision finally cleared, she was able to see Nigel standing next to Xander. Her patient was sitting up in the bed, vacant eye socket staring at her.

"I-I d-don't …" Her words came out as a hoarse whisper that scraped along her throat, her eyes watering from the effort of trying to swallow. She reached a hand out toward Xander, not knowing what she wanted or why.

"Here," Tracey said, handing Mel some of Helena's herbs. "Put that on her throat."

It was icy warm against her skin all at the same time, the cold chill of mint, the warmth of the oils, but it helped her muscles relax and she found herself able to breathe a little better.

"I'm sorry," she rasped. "I don't know what happened." Her eyes were on Xander. He looked even taller now that he was sitting up on the bed with Nigel's help—giant tall.

"It was Xander," Mel said gently.

Helena frowned. "No …" She shook her head slowly. "No, he was nowhere near me."

"He's *Air-Fae*," Nigel said. "His powers work like tel—"

"Telekinesis," Helena finished off. She hadn't come across one of them before, but she had heard they could move the air. It seemed they could move items and objects, but all they were really doing was manipulating the air around them. She had read about them.

"He did that to me once," Mel grimaced. "Feels like your head's going to pop right off."

Helena touched her own throat and looked at Xander. "Why?"

"Natural reaction," Nigel said. "What were you doing?"

"Cleaning his wound," she said, her voice sounding a little more like her own again. "I was cleaning and changing dressings."

"I'm sorry," Xander said hoarsely. "I didn't mean to." Before she could reply, he cocked his head to the side as if he were listening to something and went perfectly still. "Someone is coming."

"Who?" Mel asked.

"*Human*," he whispered, eyes fixed on the door.

Shit. It would be Lee coming to check. He was waiting for the *Fae* to die—hoping for it really. He couldn't kill this one, not without a legal reason. But he could sit and wait and come and claim his blood. "It'll be Lee," Helena said. "He said he would be back."

The bleeping of the monitor had become so natural that it had been nothing more than white noise till now, but as Xander's expression became one of alarm and he tried to move, the sounds spiked. He scrambled to get from the bed.

"Wait," Nigel said, grabbing him. "You can't move."

"It's Lee Norton," Xander ground out, gripping his friends arm. "I need to—"

"I know," Nigel said.

"What's wrong?" Helena asked. "He's just coming to check. It's okay."

181

"We need to get Xander out of here. Lee can't see him." He hurriedly helped Xander pull off the stickers that held the wires in place.

As he was about to yank out the IV of herbs and water attached to his arm, Helena stopped him. "Wait, leave that." She struggled to her feet. She wasn't sure what exactly was going on, but the urgency with which Nigel and Xander both looked at her told her that she couldn't let him see them. If Lee was on his way, then he would be coming in without waiting for an invitation. She wouldn't have the time to ask what he wanted with Xander.

The signalling beep that someone had just come in the front door sounded. Helena stood up straighter, her hand going to her throat. "Give me something to cover this," she said.

"Helena," Tracey said. "There's nothing there."

"What? How is that possible?"

"Air doesn't bruise," Xander muttered as he pushed himself off the bed.

Right. *God*. She turned to Tracey. "Take Xander to my living space, okay? I'll go and deal with Lee."

She squared her shoulders and walked out without waiting for a reply. She glanced at the mirror as she passed it, still shocked that her throat wasn't bruised. It should be marked, but there was nothing there, not even where she had scratched herself. Maybe the herbs had cleared that up, but right now, that's not what mattered.

Lee was standing at the front door when Helena came out. "Lee," she said, smiling. "Is everything okay?"

"Chaos," he said. "Did you hear about the church?"

"I did," she said. "It's terrible." She hoped her voice sounded normal once again. "Would you like a coffee? I was just getting one for myself." She coughed, her throat still feeling bruised and scratchy. "Sorry. Think I must be coming down with something."

"You need to take care of yourself," he said, his gaze studying her intently. "How is the *Fae*?"

"Come in the back, and I'll update you," she said nonchalantly.

But Lee seemed distracted. Which wasn't like him. He was always focused, dedicated to the cause, but right now, there was something off with him. "The *Fae* is improving?"

"He's doing better. Still not out of the woods yet. I couldn't save his eye, but he should be okay to see with the other one."

"He'll live then?"

Helena sensed his disappointment at that news, but that wasn't what was bothering him. "Yes, he should do."

"Maybe we can have him shipped to the lab? Free up your place here? Stop using up your resources?"

Helena tried not to show any panic at his seemingly harmless and considerate suggestion. "No, I don't mind," she said calmly. "Besides, he might be able to work or something afterwards." Often, those she treated stayed and worked where they could. Many of the people in the village had been her former patients. That was probably what helped with the trust issues.

Although not pleased with her response, Lee offered her a brisk nod and stiff smile.

"Is everything okay?"

"There was a problem this morning. Well, it happened last night. We don't know when exactly. An entire parish was slaughtered."

"Slaughtered?"

"Yep. We got there too late. They were all dead. Priest, too."

"Jesus. Who would do something like that?" she muttered, more to herself than to him.

"One of the choir boys had gone in to set things up for the day. He'd forgotten—you know how boys are. He saw the whole thing happen, hid till it was all over."

"Oh, my God. Do you know who?"

"Nicholas Mason. The missing convict from the bus." His jaw set in an angry line. "Monsters they are. All of them. We should have every last one of them killed at birth. You should have seen what he had done, Helena. Even killed one of his own kind. She was just a child. Took her head clean off."

Helena's hand flew to her mouth. "Oh God." There had to be some reason, she was sure, but she couldn't say that part to Lee. "What now?"

"We've got men looking. They can't have gone too far." Just then, his phone rang, and he plucked it out of his pocket. He gave a series of nods and encouraging noises to whomever was on the other end, then hung up.

"Everything okay?" Helena asked again.

"They've found him. Nicholas Mason. This bastard is mine," he ground out. "You're good here? Don't need anything?"

"No," she said with a small shake of her head, relieved he would be leaving. "You go."

He leaned in close suddenly, making her jump. He smelt like expensive cologne, and she found herself thinking how out of place that seemed at a time when people all around them seemed to be dying.

She tried not to cringe as he placed a kiss on the side of her cheek. "You call me if you need anything."

Chapter Twenty-Two
Stephen

Stephen was more than sure that someone was messing with him. He was going to wake up at any moment, and Gemma or Cade would be standing over him laughing their asses off. Or maybe he was tripping, because this sure as hell wasn't real.

Another damn house with mysterious secrets stood before him, but just a blink ago, he had been on his knees outside the church with blood pouring from his nose. How the hell had he got here? He reached up to feel for any blood still trickling down, but there was nothing there.

God damn it. What the hell was going on?

He was dreaming, he reasoned with himself. It was the only viable explanation for all this shit.

The house was cast in shadows, and he felt an inexplicably irresistible need to go in. Was he meant to? Did he even have a choice? He felt like he did, but perhaps he was nothing more than a fool dancing in the flames of his own anxiety with pacifying self-lies.

A slight movement at the side of the house caught his eye and he froze, his senses growing alert. He peered into the shadows then sucked in a sharp breath at the sight of the same woman from the woods standing there. Her stare pierced through him, and for a moment, he thought his feet would carry him to her of their own volition. He gave himself an inward shake and told himself to get a fucking grip. Beautiful as she was, he didn't want to speak to her—or play this damn game anymore.

Clenching his jaw in determination, and ignoring the overwhelming urge to head straight into the building, he turned his back to both the house and the woman and started to walk away—and fate, or whoever was running this fucking show, could sit and bitch about it. The woman was part of this game—someone's game—maybe even hers. But he refused to fucking play.

A thorn in everyone's sides—his purpose. It was where he was the happiest.

Six feet of mud surrounded the brown concrete in the unkempt garden; Stephen made sure to stay on the brown concrete, his boots crushing weeds peeking out between cracked flags. Gardener's day off, he thought sardonically.

He ignored the annoying tug in his chest that made him want to turn back, fighting the hard pull and the feeling that he was forgetting something back there.

Fuck off.

He gritted his teeth and continued to walk, determined to put as much distance between him and the house as possible, determined to get away from that woman playing havoc with his senses. Mind over matter. That was all.

Stephen strode past houses that reeked of money and *Humans* and when he rounded the corner of one of the streets, he almost walked straight into the woman from the house. She stood there with her head angled, hands on her hips. God damn it. He should have handed her a set of wire frame glasses and stuck her in front of a blackboard. She'd be set then.

"Detention for St—" He caught himself. "Nicholas Mason?"

She frowned at him, and he burst out laughing. He didn't know why he was laughing, but God, he just couldn't stop.

"You think this is all a joke?" Her voice rolled over him like silk.

"I don't even know what *this* is," he said, his laughter suddenly ceasing and turning to anger. "I don't know who the hell you are or what you're talking about."

"I'm *Helena*," she said, as if he were supposed to know this piece of information already, and as if she were baffled as to why he didn't.

"That's great," Stephen gushed mockingly, then strode right past her.

"You can walk past me and ignore me all you want, Nick. But this is meant to be, and it will find you one way or another."

He stopped without turning. What a shame such beauty was lost on an absolute nutcase, he thought to himself. "Not if I choose," he threw over his shoulder.

It was her turn to laugh, and he hated the way his body reacted to the velvet sound. "You might have been powerful once, but not now. Even *you*, Nicholas Mason, don't get to walk away from fate."

Stephen gave her a shrug. Who cared what she or fate thought? They could both get lost for all he cared. He started walking again—away from her and Freya and all the stupid things that no one would explain to him. He didn't understand, but he wasn't going to play any longer.

He was done.

She caught up with him as he walked, and despite his long strides, she managed to keep pace with him, no problem. He scowled. She wasn't overly tall, came to about his shoulder—she should have been almost running to keep up. Now he really knew it was all a dream. He picked up his pace and kept his mouth clamped shut. Dream or no dream, he didn't care to chat.

"Brisingamen is closer than you think," she said.

Mason Sabre

Despite his resolve not to talk to her, he found himself turning his head to look at her. "I have no fucking idea what you are talking about. What the hell is Bring—Brisinga—?"

"That isn't for me to say."

He swore. "Fate. Right." He shook his head and rolled his eyes.

She stopped suddenly, but Stephen didn't miss a step. "You must find Brisingamen," she called out as the distance between them grew longer. "You must do what is right."

"And you must kiss my ass," he muttered.

He blinked and when he opened his eyes again, he was no longer walking, or even outside. He shot up on the bed he was lying on.

What the f—

Sunlight filtered in around the edges of the drawn curtains; a bird sang its morning call, its cheerful *tweet, tweet* like nails down a chalkboard to Stephen's ears. A gun with pellets and an open window; that's all it needed.

How the hell had he got here now? He really wished he knew what the fuck was going on. He didn't recall getting into bed and yet, here he was. He didn't recall getting into a car and being brought to this house, yet he must have done that, too.

Aaaand … while he had been sleeping, someone had cut him open and filled him with bricks and sand. *Bloody hell.*

Groaning, he forced himself out of bed and landed on the floor with a thud. What a dignified way to get himself out of his pit.

He managed to drag himself from the room and out into the hallway. The place was in a worse state that Cade's dilapidated abode had been when he had first bought it. The walls were bare, there was no paint on the walls, no carpet on the floors, even the plaster was missing in places. Stephen

188

made his way down the not so sturdy looking stairs with shaky legs.

Boards covered the large window at the stairs, allowing a minimum of sunlight to creep in. Whoever was responsible for the upkeep of this place needed firing.

Stephen stopped at the bottom, listening. There were no sounds in the rooms around him. No movement, no creaking floorboards. He made his way down the stairs and opened a door that led to a room at the back of the house. Tacks stuck out where there had once been a carpet, bits of fluff and dirt clinging to them. Dust and litter collected in the corners of the completely bare room. There was no furniture at all, not even lighting. A few candles sat on the mantel of the fireplace, and from the accumulation of cold wax that hung down like icicles, it was clear that many candles had been burnt here.

He made his way across the room, ears and eyes listening and looking. This wasn't his house and he had no fucking clue how or why he was here. The door at the other side of the room led to a kitchen—two foldout Formica tables stood together in the centre of the room, one with a fruit bowl and little else on it. It reminded him of the kitchen they had when his sister, Gemma, was a baby—poor but functional. It even had one of those ovens with the rings that never lit the entire way around, that burnt more food than they would cook. Not that it had mattered to Stephen. He didn't need to cook. His food always came raw and dripping.

He opened the fridge in the hope of finding something that would sate his hunger a little. His senses were assaulted by the sudden blast of rot and decay, making him retch and quickly back away. The cupboards and drawers weren't any better; harbouring a few packets of cereal and a collection of tins, nothing that made Stephen want to eat any of it. No matter how hungry he was. Although judging from the condition of the fridge, he wasn't sure there would be much of anything he would have dared to eat anyway.

He snatched an apple from the bowl and bit into that. At least it was fresh, but biting into it was like sandpaper. He was a shifter. Fruit was like trying to quench a dire thirst with one raindrop at a time. His body craved meat—red, dripping and fresh from the kill kind of meat. The thought made him groan with hunger.

The apple reminded him of his mother and how she would offer him fruit to keep him quiet when he used to get boisterous at the thought of an impending hunt. He knew it was a joke, but each time he had been stubborn enough to eat it and grin at her with defiance. Each time he had munched down the tasteless apple or pear and thought how victorious he was. Perhaps he was the fool; after all, she had managed to calm him with scraps.

The sudden dawning on him of his mother's rather clever manipulations stung with the reminder that he would never be able to call her again. He would never be able to speak to her again. He sighed as he chewed and stared at the corkboard by the back door. There wasn't that much on it—dates on post-it notes. His gaze wandered idly over them until one caught his attention. "Bus service 12. 21:00. East Burlington Road. Third row. Left."

He stopped mid-chew and his heart lurched. His bus. His seat. All the details of his transfer. He snatched the note from the board and read it a third and fourth time, as if that might somehow help to make things clearer. He flicked through the other notes pinned to the board with little more than a passing scrutiny. A road map was pinned to the corner; nothing odd about that, save for the X marks the spot on the exact location where the girl had stopped the bus.

His rescue had not been some mere coincidence. He wasn't sure he liked that.

He took the note and sat down at the table. He flicked the note over between his fingers and then tossed it onto the table, but it slipped down to the partly lined floor. He grabbed it, and when he brought himself back up again, Helena was sitting next to him.

"You." He narrowed his gaze at her. "Who are you?"

"I told you," she said. "I am Helena."

"What do you want?"

"I cannot give you answers. You must discover that for yourself. If I told you, I would endanger your life and many others after that. Take you where your heart whispered."

He frowned. "I don't understand."

"You will," she said, and then stood. Stephen grabbed her wrist.

"Wait ..." He had questions. He had things that he wanted to ask. He couldn't remember what they were, though. If she just stayed a little longer, then maybe they would come to him.

"I can't." She pulled her hand away and Stephen was left clutching her bracelet as it came off her wrist. Before he could grab her again, she slammed her hand onto his chest and sent him flying backwards with the chair and hitting the wall. Fucking Alice in the rabbit hole kind of falling.

His eyes opened fast. He was in bed again.

God, he was growing tired of this.

He pulled his hand out in front of him—he still had hold of her bracelet, and he could still feel the impression of her hand against his chest, still warm and throbbing. She had to be real. If he had woken when he was holding her, would she be here now, too? His mind tried to spin off in many directions, but he caught it.

Her words still resonated around his head, bouncing like a ball in a pinball machine, hitting every other infuriating riddle. He struggled out of the bed and to his feet, forcing his so tired body into an upright position. His head argued with him, pain rocking it and threatening to take him out again.

It was the same room as before, same corridor he came to, same layout. Chatter travelled up the stairs from the kitchen, and though there seemed to be a multitude of voices—very *young* voices—the sound of Eden's giggle and the distinct tones of the kids who had saved his ass put him somewhat at ease. The door opposite his was open, and he caught sight of a shower—a bathroom, thank fuck.

He couldn't make sense of any of this, but right now, all he cared about was a hot shower. Not giving a shit if it was rude, or whether he was allowed to use it, he staggered to the bathroom, already dragging his clothes from his body.

Shutting the door, he threw his shirt onto the floor and slipped off his jeans before reaching in to turn on the taps. He couldn't contain the groan of pleasure that left his lips as he climbed under the hot spray and let it run down his tense body. He leaned his head against the wall and took a moment to enjoy the solace, for a moment letting himself forget where he was and what he had done. Sliding down the cold tiles, his eyes heavy, not with sleep, but exhaustion, he sighed and let the water pummel him.

Nothing was making any bit of sense. He had endured so much trauma in one week—almost as much as his sister had inflicted on him in her entire existence, he thought, a faint smile curving his lips. His heart ached at the thought of his family. God, he missed them all so much.

Exile

When he finished his dismal attempt at a shower, he went back to the room, a little refreshed, at least, and thinking more clearly. He hadn't yet acquired new clothing, he realised, and had no choice but to put on his old, dirty garments. If the police were to see him, they would be sure to enquire if he had committed murder.

Ah yes … He had.

This time when he wandered down the stairs, the children and Eden were in the kitchen, sitting around the tables and sharing breakfast. There were two more children—a small girl and a boy of maybe three. The boy sprang from his seat as soon as he saw Stephen enter and raced over to him. Stephen stepped back, hands up in surrender. He could face *Humans*. He could face war. He could kill them and wade through their blood and shit, and every damn grotesque atrocity that he had ever seen, but kids …? He was way out of his depth.

The little boy grinned up at Stephen and pointed proudly at the gap in his mouth where he had just lost a tooth. "Mummy calls the tooth fairy," he yelled excitedly.

The sincere innocence in the child's actions left Stephen at a loss. "Err … that's great," he finally managed to say, filling his voice with as much enthusiasm as he could muster and coming up short. He didn't do kids … had no idea how to handle them. Look at this one—he didn't know Stephen, yet anyone would think they were the best of friends.

Aiden came to the rescue, grabbing the small boy's hand and leading him back to the table. "Toke, breakfast" he said, ushering the boy back into his seat.

"I want my daddy," Toke whined, but no one really paid him any mind.

Mason Sabre

A hush had fallen over the room when he'd entered, and as Stephen looked up now, all pairs of eyes were on him—well, all apart from Freya, who was sitting at the table reading, her book propped up against the fruit bowl. The witch sat there, a half-eaten slice of toast in mid-air as she stared at him. A steaming cup of coffee sat on the table in front of her, making her look right at home. He glowered at her. Maybe she had left her broomstick at the church. He could offer to go and fetch it for her after his own coffee so she could be on her merry way. It was the polite thing to do, after all.

It took a moment for everyone to go back to their breakfast, as if this were just one big happy family having their morning breakfast together. "Toast?" Eden said, lifting a plate toward him. Stephen grimaced and walked to the counter to pour himself a mug of coffee. It wasn't hot, and it wasn't the best, but it would do.

As he was reaching for a cup from the shelf, he caught sight of the board he had seen in his dream—the one with his bus details on it. He paused and glanced over the papers pinned there, but the note was not there.

"How are you feeling?" the witch asked, turning in her seat.

"Like I was kidnapped, drugged and almost crucified. You?" he quipped, then turned to Freya without waiting for her to reply. "The witch is still here."

Freya peered over her book at him without actually raising her head. "As you can see," she said sarcastically.

"Why?"

Eden crossed her arms over her chest and stared at him in blatant affront. "You know, I'm right here."

He raised his eyebrows at her and took a sip of his coffee. "Yep. That is why I am asking. Aren't you listening?"

194

A very unladylike epithet left her lips, and by the way her fingers squeezed her mug spasmodically, he was almost certain she was debating throwing her mug at his head.

"She is here because she is supposed to be here," Freya cut in. "Just like you."

He narrowed his eyes at her. "And what exactly am I doing here?"

"You're *meant* to be here," Freya said again.

"What the hell does that mean?"

Aiden took out the pouch Freya had shown Stephen before from his pocket and held it out to him. "Take one," he said, offering the open pouch the way one might offer a crisp. "Put your hand in and choose one of the balls." Stephen was once again struck with the intense impression that Aiden and Freya were far older than they appeared.

Stephen hesitated at first, some part of him wanting to be defiant even on the simplest of things. But he did as he was asked, pulling out one of the balls. Aiden held out an open palm, and Stephen handed it over with a scowl. Aiden held it up so they could both view the content, and Stephen found himself leaning closer in curiosity. "This isn't a ball or a marble," Aiden said. "This is why you're sick. You're feeling the sickness contained within them. The evil that they hold."

"I don't understand," Stephen said, reaching for it. On closer scrutiny, he realised it held the young man's scene.

"You're a soul reaper, Nick. This is your purpose. You reap souls and then pass judgement on them."

Stephen's eyes flew to Aiden, then jerked to Freya. "Is this some kind of fucking joke? What the hell are you talking about?"

Freya set down her book and pinned him with a cool stare "You don't think all that's happened and everything

195

you've experienced these past few days is strange?" She nodded towards the marbles. "The things you've *seen*?"

Strange? Now there was one hell of an understatement.

"Have you ever asked yourself why you were always able to ... *read* ... people? Hear voices in your head?"

He frowned. He had always just thought he was crazy. He turned the ball over in the light cast from the kitchen window. Outrageous as all this sounded, he couldn't deny his past, or the things he'd seen recently. "You want me to believe I play God?"

"Kind of," Aiden said. "But it isn't blind judgement; you see their crimes and the suffering. You see the things that they have done. The secrets they have. Nothing can be hidden from you. You know that, don't you? You've seen it."

Stephen thought back to the fat man at the bus and the boy in the comer of the room; the priest and what he had done to the vampire. "Yeah, I saw their crimes," Stephen said with a clenched jaw.

"Tell me," Aiden said, nodding to the ball in Stephen's hand, "the man inside this one? Do you deem him worthy?"

Worthy? That was a question. Who the hell was he to decide if he was worthy? It seemed odd, that he held a man's soul in the palm of his hand, his to judge. The young *Human* had judged them all within minutes because it was the right thing for him to do. Would judging him make him no better than the *Humans* he supposedly held the souls of?

"He isn't worthless," Stephen said, looking up. "Misguided."

"He doesn't deserve to be damned?" asked Freya.

"A little harsh, don't you think?" He had been *Human*, and Stephen was very aware of how ironic his words were, but no matter his feelings, the hatred he felt for the *Humans*, he could not bring himself to cast judgement based on that. It wasn't right to damn them just because he could—though he had no doubt the *Humans* would not be so lenient.

Aiden took the ball back from Stephen and passed it to Eden. She held her hand out in front of them and rubbed the back in a circular motion, like grinding it to chalk; it fell away little by little until it was nothing more than dust.

Stephen gaped. "What did you do?" He grabbed her hand. All traces of the ball were gone.

"You gave his soul another chance," she replied. "It means that he goes back into the queue. He gets another chance. Does he choose damnation and suffering, or the path of righteousness? This time, he didn't pick either, so now he gets to try again. He has free will."

"What? Like reincarnation?" All of this was just too fucking crazy to process.

All three of them nodded. As long as none of them cheered, they'd do okay.

Aiden pulled another ball from the bag—the vampire this time. "This one is a little different, though," said Aiden. "She is vampire. If her soul was already reincarnated when she suffered her crossover, then that may need to be reaped, too. Maybe her reincarnation made a choice. You will know soon enough. She will find you."

Bloody hell. "What of the reincarnation?"

"Could be anyone," Freya said. "Could be *Human* or *Other*. We don't know. *Humans* have it down to cot death or sudden adult death syndrome. The new body will just die for no reason so that the soul can be reclaimed and made whole again."

"And if her soul wasn't reincarnated?"

"Then she will be made whole again now," said Eden.

"What about Anya?" asked Freya, taking the pouch from Aiden and pulling the young girl's ball out. The small child. "What do you think she deserves?"

Stephen studied the ball for a while. In truth, he didn't know what to choose for her.

As if she had read his mind, Freya said, "Trust your intuition."

His brow puckered, and he blinked over at her before focusing on the small ball once again. It didn't feel right to send her to Eden, but he wasn't clear on what choices she had made. She was just a child. In her short life, it felt like she was worthy, yet he wasn't sure why. Why not give her another chance? But then that felt so wrong to do.

"I'll keep hold of this one a while," he finally said, and put it back into the bag.

"What about this one?" said Aiden and showed him the ball that contained the pretend priest. Stephen scoffed automatically at the thought of sending him anywhere but fucking hell. Although it would be a shame. He could be reincarnated as *Other*. That would be poetic justice.

"He doesn't deserve a damn thing," Stephen said in the end.

Aiden already knew that answer. He had chosen these souls on purpose. He took the ball and held it in the palm of his hand, much like Eden had done. The skin underneath glowed just a little, and Stephen watched with fascination as the ball melted to nothing more than a pool of black tar.

The boy let the ashes fall from his hand to the floor— but they soaked through the air and were gone before they could land.

"You're one of Lucifer's oil burners?" Stephen said as he started to actually believe all this whacky talk… and began to understand the concept of what Aiden was.

Exile

Aiden shook his head. "I'm not Lucifer's anything. I'm yours."

Chapter Twenty-Three
Stephen

He'd slipped into another world—another dimension. That had to be what all of this was, because nothing else made any sense. He had his own pet demon? How did that work? Why? Was he meant to just take all of what these kids said as gospel? They were kids, for God's sake. Who was to say this wasn't some fucking fantasy shit they had dreamt up? Maybe the note on the board had been placed there afterwards to mess with his head? What did he do? Say 'Yes, thanks' and take people's souls? He needed to think and to just get away from them. Whatever these kids were playing, Stephen could leave them to it. They had the witch—they could fucking play with her.

"I should probably get my bag and get going," Stephen muttered before he had time to think about it. He drained the last of his coffee and set the mug on the counter. "Thank you for letting me stay here for the night."

"You're leaving?" Eden said, her chair scraping backwards as she stood abruptly. Aiden had jumped to his feet, too, though Freya hadn't batted an eyelid.

Aiden turned to Freya, desperation in his voice. "He can't leave, Freya. You said …"

"I have imposed enough," Stephen cut in, frowning at the outburst. "I do thank you all for your hospitality, though." He kept the sarcasm from his words as best he could. "Nice to see you again," he said to the witch. He was sure they would cross each other's paths another time. She seemed to be like a bad smell that he couldn't get rid of.

"Freya," the boy said again, more urgently now.

Exile

Unperturbed by Aiden's despondency, and ignoring Stephen's farewell, she got up and went to stir the porridge that was bubbling in a pan on the stove. Taking it off the hob, she leaned over it to blow across the top before moving to fill the five bowls on the table.

Annoyed at her total disregard of him, Stephen turned to leave. He wasn't about to sit and wait for her to acknowledge him.

"No, please, wait …" Aiden begged, making him pause. He darted around the table to Freya's side, expression frantic. "He can't leave."

She continued to calmly add a spoon to each bowl then pushed one towards Toke, the small boy, first, and then the girl. She glanced up at Stephen with a raised eyebrow as she reached for the next bowl.

Realising she was offering him some of the gruel, he frowned. "No, thank you." Was she ignoring him and the boy on purpose? He shifted from one foot to the other, becoming restless. The two small children had started to eat as if all was well, but Aiden stayed next to the stove, his eyes firmly fixed on Stephen, as if he might disappear at any minute.

"Okay, well … thank you for all your help, but I'll just be on my w—"

"You can't leave," Freya said, finally speaking and looking over at him. She might look young, but her eyes were 'old'. She had none of his youngest sister's teenage naivety about her.

"Why? You tell me all these crazy things and then just expect me to sit here and happily accept it all?" he asked derisively. "Look … You got me off the bus, and I thank you for that, but I'm not whatever it is you think I am. I am not who you are looking for."

Mason Sabre

"You have some other place to go?" Eden cut in.

He clenched his jaw and fixed a glare on her. They both knew he had nowhere to go.

"Then stay," she said, as if he had voiced that out loud. "It doesn't matter what we all believe, whether you are right or wrong, but at least you get somewhere to stay."

Stay? He had no reason to stay. Sure, it was a roof over his head, but he was Stephen Davies. He worked better alone, and he wasn't responsible for these kids. Nor did he want to be.

"The *Humans* will be looking for you," Eden said, adding weight to her argument. "You're an escaped convict."

"Perhaps that is a better reason I go; then you are all free from danger."

"You're meant to be here, Nick," Freya said coolly. She was sitting, eating her breakfast now, as calm as anything— unlike Aiden, and even Eden, who seemed to have an edge about her.

Nick—he would never get used to that name. It always startled him to hear it. Stephen. He was Stephen Davies. He grasped onto that thought now. He needed more than anything to remember who he was. Losing his name would be like losing himself. It would be accepting all of this, and he couldn't. He *wouldn't*. Because this was not his place. His place was next to the *Other* alpha. His job was to protect his people.

Freya pushed the bowl toward Aiden. "Come and eat." But he was watching Stephen, ready to pounce if he tried to leave.

"*Humans*." The little girl, who looked to be around the same age as Toke, suddenly bolted from her seat.

"Nakita?" Aiden said, coming closer.

"There are *Humans*," she repeated frenziedly.

202

Exile

"Where?"

"Outside. They're coming."

They all jumped from their seats at the same time. Toke stood up on his and raised his little arms towards Stephen, making Stephen freeze.

"Take the children and go," Freya said, turning to him.

"Go where?" Stephen asked, but she was already turning away from him, closing her eyes and standing absolutely still in the middle of the kitchen.

The air in the room cracked and grew heavier in an instant. Freya's lips began moving as she uttered silent words. She'd better not be a goddamn witch, Stephen thought disdainfully. He had had enough of those already. The scars down his arm began to throb and he clamped a hand over one of them. *What the h—*

He rubbed along his skin, suddenly remembering the pain that had put them there in the first place. Eden raced around the table and picked up Nakita, spiking the panic in the room. Stephen had fought wars, the moves usually strategic and planned, but sometimes he'd had to think on his feet—but right now, that all felt like an eternity ago. This was going to be different from any other fight he had done on the fly. *Humans* and *Others*. Life or Death. He could feel it in his gut.

Freya hadn't answered his damn question. *Fuck it.* He leaned over and picked up the boy, who immediately wrapped his small legs around his waist.

Freya's eyes flew open suddenly, glowing. The fabric at the back of her shirt began to bulge as her wings started to form. "Get out of here," she hollered.

Stephen had seen what she could do, what she was capable of. He knew that this was not a child, no matter what she looked like … But just leaving her there? It didn't feel right.

"Now," she yelled again.

"We need to go," Eden called to him from the door.

Stephen gritted his teeth, hesitating between getting these kids to safety and leaving one behind. "Are you coming?" he called to Freya.

"Don't worry about me," she said. "You need to go." And with that, she turned and headed deep into the house. Stephen swore, conflicted about whether he could leave a fourteen-year-old girl to fight a battle on her own. *She can take care of herself*, his mind told him. *Probably snap your neck with no effort at all*. She had pulled the roof off a bus, snapped metal binds from around his wrist. It wasn't her that what is danger, it was the *Humans*.

God damn it, he was going to miss the grand show, he realised. He did love a good slaughter.

With the boy in his arms, he ran after Eden and Aiden through the yard. The wall wasn't so hard. He was tall, and it was easy to lift Toke onto the top. He took Nakita from Eden and did the same, then bent down, clasping his hands together so that Eden could get a leg up. When he had helped her up, he turned to Aiden.

The boy took a step back and gestured for Stephen to go ahead without him.

"Aiden … come on …"

Aiden shook his head. "Go."

Stephen glared at him, fighting every fucking instinct inside of him because these were kids and this wasn't right.

"You need to go. Get them two out of here."

With a curse, Stephen turned and climbed the wall, scaling down the other side before helping Eden down.

Holding out his arms, he urged the children to jump. He caught Toke while Nakita jumped into Eden's arms.

Toke wrapped tight arms around Stephen's neck, almost cutting off his air supply. He pried them off a little before he passed out from asphyxiation—but when he turned around, he came face to face with a small group of *Humans*. God, he was an idiot. Of course, the *Humans* would have come around the back.

The amateur soldier-like geared *Humans* all stood there, guns aimed at Stephen and Eden. Just to the left, standing farther behind the armed men, were two other *Humans*, both dressed in suits. One was tall and athletic, while the older one had a slimmer build—obviously not the kind that worked out at all. Stephen pulled Toke close instinctively, an odd feeling of protectiveness suddenly coming over him.

Fuck.

He had to think. They were only *Humans*. Armed or not, they were weak and feeble and easy to break. But they were probably armed to the teeth—undoubtedly, their usual guns, wards, charms—anything they could get their sleazy hands on. They even had the side switching, deserting, backstabbing *Others,* who sold their uses for a meek existence in a cage and three square meals a day with satellite television.

"Give us the child and the necklace," one of the men ordered, aiming his gun at Stephen.

Stephen frowned. "Necklace? What fucking necklace?"

"The necklace," the *Human* repeated impatiently, because emphasizing the word was going to help to make things clearer.

One of the men swung a gun towards Aiden as he suddenly came around the side of the house. He followed

205

him with his weapon until he finally stopped next to Stephen.

"Ah … the more, the merrier," one of them sneered.

Stephen swore inwardly. Why hadn't the kid just stayed out of the damn way?

One of the *Humans* took a step toward Eden, but Aiden stepped in front of her, putting himself between them and the men. This was all so wrong. Stephen could never accept protection from a child … or a woman.

Without warning, the *Human* lunged, but Stephen had dropped Toke down next to Aiden and pushed himself in front of the children before he could reach them. The man stumbled to a stop and the other *Humans* all stepped backwards, guns raised and aimed at Stephen. He snarled at them, his *tiger* very much at the forefront as his eyes glimmered gold.

He eyed the enemy, taking in their weaknesses. One of them was overweight, his pudgy belly hanging down over his jeans. He would be slow, the easy one to take out. The one next to him was smaller than Stephen, not much muscle. Easy pickings, he thought as he assessed them quickly. The last one would be the sturdiest fighter—from the way his shirt strained over heavy muscle, his arms bulging, Stephen knew the man spent most of his life in the gym.

"Give us the children and the necklace, and we will leave you alone."

Did they really believe that Stephen was that gullible? "Come and get them if you want them," he said in a low voice.

None of them moved. The chubby man shifted nervously from one foot to the other.

Stephen smirked.

Exile

The older *Human* in the suit came closer, but not too close, his trusty sidekick shadowing him. He wasn't the physical type. His suit held no creases, his shoes highly polished and shining. He was so neatly tucked in around the edges that Stephen envisaged him getting manicures. Would be gratifying to cause him to break a nail or two ...

Stephen didn't know who these *Humans* were, what they wanted, or even whether they were important. Nor did he care. He let his jaw grow slack, unnoticed, allowing it to unclench so that his teeth could adjust in the confines of his mouth as he focused on the *Humans*. It was one thing to partially shift, but it was another to keep it hidden. The tips of his teeth began to pierce the inside of his bottom lip, and he opened his mouth just enough so that he didn't cut through his own flesh like an idiot.

"Give us what we want and no one gets hurt," the overweight *Human* said.

That was the problem with *Humans*. They didn't realise that what they said and how they smelt never matched.

The lies dripped from the man, the acrid scent of fear giving him away. He was so fucking nervous that Stephen was sure that if he took one step too close, he would piss his pants and probably end up shooting himself in the foot. Did the piece of shit really think that he would just hand over these kids?

"Not today," Stephen murmured. "Not today."

Chapter Twenty-Four
Stephen

The *Human* in front of him was eager and foolish, thinking he could hide behind his weapon and get what he wanted through force and threats. He had no idea who he was dealing with? He could change that.

Another brave *Human* crept up behind him.

Sneaking up on a tiger?

Not very smart.

Did he really think Stephen wouldn't sense him, or expect not to get bitten? Stephen didn't turn nor grace the new arrival with any form of acknowledgment. Instead, he closed his eyes and focused on pushing down all of the energy inside him—going into his arms, his fingertips, down to his very core, where his *tiger* listened and waited for the next command. They were in perfect sync. This was why he had been son to the alpha. This was why he was the heir. Controlling and reining in his animal took skill and dominance.

In a sequence of movements that no *Human* could have kept up with, Stephen shoved the children and Eden out of the way then swung his arm around and latched onto the pudgy *Human's* throat. The man had no speed, no chance to get away. He probably didn't even realise he was dead as he clutched at Stephen's arm.

Stephen angled his head and watched the life slowly ebb from his eyes. He gurgled, blood spilling down his chin like an infant with milk. Stephen clenched his fist and pulled, taking a handful of throat with it.

Exile

There were shouts, then the two *Humans* moved in perfect cowardly synchrony, the smaller of the two going for Toke and Nakita, while his gym buddy headed for Stephen.

Stephen made a grab for the smaller *Human*, knocking him off course to keep him from the children, but that gave the brawny *Human* an advantage. He flung Stephen to the ground, face first in the dirt. He pressed down between his shoulder blades with his boot, pushing harder when Stephen tried to move.

A foolish mistake.

No one messed with Stephen Davies.

The *Human* was going to die.

Stephen tried to move … but he couldn't get up from under the boot. He blinked in surprise. It should have been easy to push the man off him. With a grunt, he tried to push up again, but it felt as if he had a boulder pressing him down. He twisted to look at the children, hoping he had given them enough time to run away. His heart fell when he saw them standing in exactly the same position, watching as the *Human* in front of them slowly approached. Their expressions were filled with innocence and, oddly, a lack of fear.

"Leave them alone. I swear to fucking God, I'll …" The boot on his back dug down harder, the tip like a hot poker in Stephen's back. There was fucking silver on it—no wonder it had rendered him weak.

He clenched his jaw and pushed up, grinding his teeth against the pain. But his energy had been sapped from him— he might as well have been trying to move a tractor off him.

The man's eyes flicked from one child to the other, seeming unsure exactly as to what he was meant to be doing. *Idiot*. Stephen figured it hadn't been his job to do the grabbing—he had just been there to make up the numbers, but now he was stuck with the job.

Where the hell was Freya? She hadn't come out of the house yet.

The small *Human* suddenly gave a cry and leapt for the children, but Eden sprang in front of them, grabbing his wrist to spin him away; but the *Human* was stronger, and she landed on the ground with a thud, grunting as the back of her head slammed against the hard ground and knocked her out. Great.

"Not the fucking children," Stephen ground out. With renewed strength, he bucked under the weight on top of him and rolled himself over. The *Human* stumbled back, but quickly regained his balance. He went to kick Stephen, but he twisted and sunk a clawed paw into his muscled leg. The man screamed, and Stephen worked fast. He yanked at his leg, knocking him over. The *Human* gave a bellow and tried to catch himself, putting his arms out as he began to fall, but Stephen's mouth clamped down on his arm, his teeth digging into his flesh. Oh, how he loved partial shifting. He could open his jaw wider this way, and bite hard, pushing his teeth through the skin and flesh until he felt the bones beneath.

The *Human* pushed against Stephen, blood pouring down, his heart thumping so hard in his chest that it pumped fresh blood out of the wound. But Stephen clung on. His claws sinking deeper into the *Human's* skin. They rolled together, the man starting to cry like a fucking baby in the dirt. *Pathetic*.

Always take down the big one first.

Stephen was on top of him in seconds. He grabbed his head, about to put him out of his misery, but the look of sheer pain and suffering in the *Human's* eyes made Stephen stop. He hoped it hurt—a lot.

Exile

He pushed himself up, leaving the man there to suffer. It was what he deserved. But the *Human* vultures were on Stephen again, taking it in turns to attack. Even the blond-suited *Human* had moved his position, lining himself up. He tried to sneak run into Stephen, but he stepped away, keeping his balance, and turning to slam his hands between the *Human's* shoulder blades to knock him to the ground with his own momentum. His head smashed off the ground with a sickening wet thud. He lay unmoving in a pool of his own blood in the dirt. Stephen breathed heavily, a growl rumbling deep within his chest as his *tiger* reared up and demanded release, bringing with it a feeling of power that ran under Stephen's flesh, energising him. His eyes shifted, the world around him a mass of colour. He turned to the children, but before he could reach Aiden, the smell of fire wafted in the air, thick and acrid.

Stephen spun around, but nothing appeared to be burning—not close, anyway, as the scent would indicate. Aiden stood, trying to get the children away from the smaller *Human*. He grabbed Toke, but the *Human* grabbed the other side, holding the small boy between them like a rag doll. Toke tried to tug his arm away, but the man held on fast.

Aiden lunged, grabbing the Human by the wrist. "Leave him alone."

Nakita stepped back and away as Aiden held firm and began to shudder. The *Human's* eyes went wide, his head tilting back as he let out a silent scream. Stephen watched with fascination. He had never seen anything like it before. In all the wars he had fought, with so many different *Others* who had stood beside him, he had never witnessed one such as Aiden. Even the suited *Human* had the sense to stay out of the way with his side kick. They both stood frozen, watching, not even a small attempt being made to help one of their own.

They were a disgrace.

The smell of burning flesh filled Stephen's nostrils and burnt the tiny hairs in his airway, staining them with their vile scent. The *Human's* agonising screams pierced his eardrums as he watched smoke begin to pour from his pores—tiny grey worms slithering out into the air. The veins under his skin bulged and glowed in colours that matched Aiden's eyes. The tormented man fell to his knees, even as Toke and Aiden still held onto him. He vomited up blackened sludge that appeared to have once been an internal organ. Even Stephen grimaced and took a step back, watching with awe.

The *Human* was going to combust at any moment, he was sure of it. His eyes bulged as if they would burst clean from their sockets. His skin bubbled and blistered and began to fall away in red and black clumps, lava peeling from his skin. He took one last pleading look at Stephen before one of his eyeballs slid down and dribbled along his left check.

He fell to the ground, his lifeless corpse smoking.

Stephen swallowed hard as he stared at what was left of the *Human*. No one moved, the shock of what had just happened gluing them to the spot.

"We have to go," Aiden said to Stephen, dragging his mind from the fog.

Coughing from the stench and the sting at the back of his throat, Stephen moved towards them. Eden lay unconscious on the ground. None of the children seemed fazed by what they had just witnessed. He tried to not think about it as he stepped over the still bubbling *Human*.

Two more *Humans* suddenly arrived from the side of the house. It was reminiscent of some odd boxing match,

Stephen thought. Not that it was a fair fight. It never was with *Humans*. Heaven forbid they might actually lose and realise that they were the weaker species.

The suited *Human* and his sidekick came around the other side. Snakes. All four of them. Any moment one of them was going to lash out. The brave and foolish *Humans* moved toward Aiden and Stephen.

Stephen didn't have enough arms to go in all directions, but he went for the girl. Aiden swung an arm out and lifted Toke out of the *Human's* reach, running for the forest and the woodland border.

The older *Human* tried to grab him, but Aiden was too fast. He easily darted out of the way and avoided his capture, even with the small boy in his arms.

Never underestimate a small teenage boy, it would seem.

As the young *Human* turned, Nakita jumped back out of his reach, putting herself right into the arms of the *Human* closest to Stephen. He lifted her up victoriously, wrapping his arms around her chest with a grin on his face.

Stephen lunged for him, slid and landed on the ground just short of them. The suited *Human* moved out of the way and smirked. Nakita kicked against her captor. "Daddy," she yelled. Her wails only seemed to make the *Human* smirk more, a smirk Stephen would remove from his face at the first opportunity.

One of the *Humans* that had joined them lashed out with his boot, a silver plate across the front. It connected with Stephen's face, sending his vision into a swirl of darkness and light. The next thing he knew, the young *Human* was crouching down beside him. He was wearing a pair of black gloves threaded with silver.

These fuckers had thought of everything.

213

He clasped a hand around Stephen's throat. "The necklace," he said, angling his head at Stephen. "Give it to me."

If he could have spoken, Stephen would have told him that he didn't know what the hell he was talking about, but the silver burned his skin as the hand crushed his throat.

He tried to peel the *Human's* hand away, but the silver was draining him, making him tired and weaker than any *Human*.

Fucking thing.

The *Human* holding Nakita stayed behind them. She squirmed against him, but he held her tightly.

"We will get the boy and the necklace," young suit said. "We will meet again … though maybe next time, I won't leave you in such a good state."

He laughed, but Stephen's eyes were on Nakita's— small, green, and so full of determination.

Why hadn't he realised it before? These children were shifters. He focused his sights on her, envisioning what she needed to do to get free—head back, hard, slamming into the *Human's* nose. Once, twice, three times, in fast succession until the *Human* screamed and blood poured down from his face. Twist …

Stephen readied himself. While the suited *Human* continued blubbering away with his pathetic threats, Stephen let out a roar, launching himself up as Nakita did exactly what he had told her to do. She slammed her head back, making the *Human* scream.

Lunging for them, he knocked her free from the man's grip. He rolled with the *Human*, latching an arm around his throat from behind. "You will leave us now," Stephen said to the two suited *Humans*.

Exile

Nakita quickly scuffled to stand beside Stephen, her small hands clutching his jeaned leg.

"I could take you out right now," the older *Human* said.

"You could," Stephen agreed, "but you won't. You will leave, and I will let this one go."

The man glared at him, jaw clenching. "I will get what I want," he ground out. "I always do."

"Then we will meet again," Stephen said, smiling. "Now get the fuck out of here."

Chapter Twenty-Five
Stephen

Stephen's mind stuck itself somewhere between fantasies of the *Humans*—and the many ways they could die at his hands—and his own anger at his inability to protect these children. Yet, these were not his children ... not his responsibility. He repeated that in his mind, but it didn't sate the urge inside him—the *tiger's* need to go and mess the *Humans* up.

That was the one and only shot the suited *Human* and his sidekick would be getting at him. They wouldn't get a second chance.

He picked Nakita up and held her small body to him. They'd not get these kids. He'd kill them first.

He looked down near his feet, where the witch still lay out cold. He nudged her with his booted foot. "Witch," he said loudly, but she didn't move. "Oi. Wake up."

"Eden, wake up." Nakita wriggled in his arms and he let her slide down. She kneeled by Eden's motionless form and gave her a tentative shake. "Eden, wake up."

Eden's head rolled to one side as Nakita shook her, but that was it. She wasn't waking. She had a pretty nasty cut at the side of her forehead from what Stephen could see. He was going to have to carry her. He let out a frustrated breath as he crouched down next to Nakita. Where the hell was Freya? He looked around, looking back at the house—ignoring the melted *Human*.

Nothing.

Shit.

The *Humans* had run off with their tails between their legs, but the man Stephen had caught was lying unconscious

216

against the wall. He would wake soon—maybe—then he could go back to them all in one piece.

"If I carry Eden, you'll walk close to me?" he said to Nakita. She looked at him with big eyes and nodded in earnest.

With a scowl, he wondered why it was he was bothered with saving a witch's arse. They were one of the most despicable species in his books—deceitful and conniving.

He leaned down and scooped her up in his arms easily—she was light, thinner than she looked. Stephen stood, his head throbbing like a hangover without the pleasure of having got himself inebriated the night before. Where was the fun in that?

He glanced both ways—go back to the house and find Freya, or head for the woods to Aiden? Both seemed to be able to handle their own, but both of them were kids.

Kids … The word didn't match what he knew they could do. His *tiger* coiled inside him—the need of the would-be alpha to protect the young. But what they could do went against so many things that it created nothing but confusion in his head.

What if Freya did need his help? But shit, he couldn't fucking do anything with Nakita and Eden with him. They'd distract him, and maybe he would even make things worse.

He chewed on the inside of his lip. Take Nakita and the witch to Aiden, make sure they're safe, and then come back, alone, for Freya. It was about the only plan his *tiger* was going to accept, though even with that, it wasn't happy about it. A rock and a hard place—right now, he'd happily thump whoever it was that had invented that term.

Nakita grabbed the side of Stephen's jeans as he walked, making him stagger for a moment, but he didn't want to shake her off. As they headed in the direction Aiden had taken, Stephen tried to ignore the pounding of his head.

Aiden wasn't difficult to locate once Stephen reached the border of the trees—he was not the quietest of children.

He found him and Toke sitting against the base of a tree. Toke was seemingly unaffected by everything that had just gone on. He sat quietly next to Aiden, in his own world, playing with a twig in the dirt. To be that young again and not worry about a damn thing, Stephen thought nostalgically.

Toke glanced up at him, his expression unafraid, and then smiled before going back to what he was doing.

"Where is Freya?" Stephen asked, Nakita still stuck on Stephen. He half hoped that she had somehow made it here ahead of him and that was why all was quiet at the house.

As he kneeled and placed Eden on the ground, Aiden scrambled over with the jacket he had been sitting on and pushed it under her head. "She'll come. She's safe. You don't need to worry," he said.

Stephen wasn't worried. He had seen what she could do. That shit was impressive and maybe a little frightening, especially for the *Humans*. But it just didn't sit right with him to leave her out there. It was how he was built and trained. He was the … *had been*, he corrected himself, the second to the alpha. He had been there to protect his father. It was what he did and what his purpose was.

He watched these children now. Why did they not seem to react to anything? To things that Stephen himself found urgent. The *Humans* had attacked them, but Aiden wasn't panicking. Instead, he spoke of Freya, who they couldn't be certain was still alive, like everything was fine. Even Nakita had let go of Stephen and had gone to sit with Toke and watch him play. "I'll go and find her," he said.

"No, you don't need to," Aiden said. "Stay here with us. She'll come."

"And if she doesn't?"

"Freya will make it," he said more determined. "I promise, Nick. She will be okay."

Stephen glanced back over his shoulder, fighting with his natural instincts telling him to go back. "If she isn't back in thirty minutes, I am going to go and find her."

"She'll come."

"How can you be sure that she is okay?"

Aiden stared him square in the eyes, his face serious. "Because you're still alive, that's how."

"What's that supposed to mean?"

Aiden got to his feet slowly, using the trunk of the tree to help himself up. He wheezed, and Stephen stood and caught him under the arm.

"What's wrong?"

"I'm okay," he said, breathing hard. "Doing what I did takes all my energy, that's all." He went to Eden and crouched down beside her. Stephen watched in fascination as he muttered something in a strange language and then leaned in and breathed on her.

Her eyes fluttered open a second later. "See," he said, as Eden sat herself up. "Everything is fine. We just have to wait."

Stephen clenched his jaw. Sitting and waiting was not his strong suit. He needed to do something, and it didn't matter what that something was … just anything that didn't involve inaction.

"Freya will come," Aiden repeated, sensing Stephen's unease.

With barely contained frustration, he sat down opposite them, leaning against a tree. Every few minutes,

Toke and Nakita would glance his way as they played, as if checking he was still there. The poor kids probably felt safer with an adult presence, he mused.

"My head hurts like a bitch in heat," Eden said, rubbing at the back of her head.

"Maybe because you got yourself knocked out," Stephen said drily. "I had to carry you all the way here. Lay off the cakes and chocolate, would you?"

She scowled at him. "You're a real charming shit, aren't you?"

"You're a witch. Not worth wasting my charm on you."

She rolled her eyes at him and shook her head.

"Why do the *Humans* want the kids?" he asked after a moment of sitting with the events going over in his head. And what necklace had they been talking about? One that he was apparently meant to have. "Why did they come for them? It doesn't make sense. They're just shifters."

A faint rustle from the trees had Stephen jumping to his feet, his *tiger* soaring to the surface, ready to attack. It backed down again as Freya emerged from the depths of the woodlands rather than the direction of the house. Not a single mark or scratch on her. "We can't go back to the house," she said as she joined them and threw down a bag. "I got as much as I could, but we have to go elsewhere now."

"We're hiding from the *Humans*?" Stephen growled, not making any effort to mask the disgust in his voice. "We don't let them run us out. We fight together."

"And how do you intend to do that?" Freya shot. "You have seen for yourself that not even you, the marvellous Nicholas Mason, is capable of fighting them off."

"They are weak." He refused to believe anything else. It was only because they were armed—with silver no less—and the kids were there. Had he been on his own, he would have ripped shit out of the lot of them, no matter what weapons they had. "They're only *Human*."

"Underestimating your enemy is what almost got Nakita taken," Freya said as she leaned down to rummage in one of the bags. "Norton …"

Any anger that was riding inside him at the way Freya dared to speak to him was shot down with the sound of that name. He frowned. "Norton?" The name rang a million fucking alarm bells in his mind. "The *Human* I just acquainted myself with was Norton?"

"He isn't all that he seems," she said. "He is dangerous."

"He isn't *Human*?"

"Oh, he is, but he is on the top of the *Human* food chain. He's relentless. Powerful."

"So am I," Stephen shot back. His mind was working overtime. Did the *Humans* think that Stephen was weak? That he was nothing? They were in for a shock if that were true. He'd show them. Maybe Freya didn't know who he really was or why he was there. All that spiel she gave him, but *Others* weren't weak nothings. Had she forgotten that, too? He had been next in line for Alpha. Aiden was some kind of supernovae, and Freya was … well, he didn't know what the hell she was, but she had some pretty fucking awesome powers. The witch, too. They could fight.

"Not here you're not. Norton is after you. He let you go today for a reason."

"He wanted the children."

She glanced over her shoulder, eyeing Stephen up. "Like I said, Nick, do not underestimate him and what he appears to be. What he wants, and what he shows you, are two different things."

She pulled out a dressing and handed it to the witch.

"Thank you," she muttered, lifting it to the back of her head. She was bleeding—maybe why she was so damn quiet.

Freya pulled out another dressing and a small first aid kit and kneeled behind Eden. Nakita shuffled closer to Stephen, and he felt an unfamiliar urge to lift her up and ensure that she was okay. He wasn't used to small children, but Nakita didn't irritate him the way other kids normally did. Maybe there was hope for Stephen yet.

Working in silence, Freya cleaned Eden's wound. The *Humans* knew what—or maybe whom—they were hunting. He was just sorry that Eden had taken the hit, even if she was a witch. Freya reached into the other bag—the Exile survival kit, it would seem—and pulled out some wraps. She cleaned the wound and put a stitch in it before covering it up.

"So you're just going to leave the house because you're afraid?" Stephen said, digging because he couldn't let this shit go.

She turned a cool stare onto Stephen, her face serious as if he had just laughed at the wrong time in the middle of a funeral. "What do you propose we do, Nick?"

He shrugged. "I don't know. This isn't my fucking adventure." He leaned forward. "Why did you get me off the bus?"

"Because it was meant."

"Meant for what?

Instead of answering him, she started to pack the bag away, infuriating him even further. She handed Eden a bottle of water and then took another and cleaned her hands with it. When she sat down, Toke immediately climbed onto her lap and began to suck on his thumb, his eyes watching Stephen. Freya ran an absent hand through his hair. "There's a warrant out for your execution. We knew where you would be and when. Once an execution is carried out and completed, they file it. We found it."

"Carried out and completed?"

"Yes," she said. "As in done."

"I wasn't executed," he snorted. "Obviously."

"Really?" She raised questioning eyebrows at him. "Then tell me, Nick Mason, what exactly does it state on your warrant?" She leaned around the boy to her bag of tricks and pulled out his papers. He wasn't sure if he should be annoyed that she had just taken his things. Perhaps a discussion on personal space and privacy was needed.

She tossed them across to him, and he unfolded them with a scowl. He stared at the stamp across his name then blinked to make sure he was reading it right.

'Executed', it wrote.

Date of death was completed three days ago.

"What the …?"

Could somebody please tell him what the hell was going on?

He wasn't dead.

He would damn well know if he was …

Chapter Twenty-Six
Stephen

Stephen knew he wasn't dead, or, at the very least, he was pretty sure he wasn't dead. He flexed his fingers, splaying them in an attempt to feel something. Yep, he was alive. His fingers were cold, his arms aching. The other clue to his mortality was the numbness in his backside and the pins and needles in the tops of his legs signifying he was still among the living.

If he had died, though, he was sure he would remember his death. What cruelty it would be to take the final voyage and then have missed it. Like all the thrusting and then ... nothing. No orgasmic boom to thrust into one last time. Bugger to that.

He was alive.

Maybe if he had died for real, his father would have grieved in front of everyone for a change. Would he act as if he had just lost the heir to his throne? Maybe he'd have had a royal send off. Maybe it would have been good to stay around for a week. He could have gone to his own funeral—alive. He could have seen which miserable bastards bothered to turn up.

Oh, the fun he could have coming back from the dead.

His father's words rang out in his mind, chasing away any fantasies he might have. He was dead to him. Dead and gone. Just like that. It would appear that he didn't care.

Stephen knew there would have been no royal procession for his death. God forbid they pay respects to the heir who dishonoured his people, his name and his father. No, Stephen was sure that his send-off would be nothing more than the shadow of a weeping woman, one who resembled his mother. His father would have stood there, his face cold and hard, unmoving … unloving. His best deception was the expression he never pulled. The poker face he had down to such a fine art that his name was probably on the patent for it.

Of his sisters, he knew that Gemma's days would be torn with guilt and grief for the death of her brother, but more importantly, the death of her son. Stephen's heart twisted at the thought of her. For all his life, he would never be able to remove the gut-wrenching images of his sister and his best friend when they received the news of their newborn's death. What they must be going through. He shook his head, trying to remove his own heavy guilt. He'd give anything to be able to be there and help her and Cade through their loss—although there was probably nothing he could do other than just be Stephen. There would be no funeral for the baby, either. Not even a box. No markers, no certificates.

The baby's only crime was his creation.

Evie, Stephen's youngest sister, would weep, though. She would cry for months about it. God, he missed them all so much. If he could just see them one last time ...

Maybe being dead was the better option, after all.

As Stephen leaned back and observed his surroundings and its occupants, he realised that Freya reminded him of his mother. Not in how she looked, obviously—she was much too young for that—but she had that air about her. The manner in which she spoke, even though she was young in body, held authority, without being loud or cruel. She was calm and said nothing, but always thinking and listening, and just when you thought you knew it all, she had a knack of smacking you right between the eyes. He had hated when his mother did that to him. Like she waited for the moment where she could say, "Ha." But he respected her for it, too. It couldn't be easy being married to the great Malcolm Davies ... even harder to raise his son and heir.

Freya didn't offer anything else. She said little at all, really. Her eyes were so different. They had seen things. A pool of knowledge resided in them. Stephen knew eyes and knew when they were scared or wise from the life they had led. Freya's were definitely the latter kind.

The eyes gave everything away. A person could tell all the lies they wanted, but eyes never lied. They held all the secrets, all the pain, the laughter—an entire life living in them. Just like the eyes of these children. They showed bravery.

"This warrant is fake," Stephen said to Freya. "Obviously, I'm not dead."

She glanced up to him and nodded with a smile.

"Are you going to answer my question?" he asked.

"Why you?" She raised her brow at him, and there it was again, that flash of wisdom in her expression. "Why not? You're a warrior, Nick. Why should I not have chosen you?" She tilted her head at him, a slight smile turning up the edges of her lips, but her eyes stayed fierce.

"I am no warrior."

Toke was dozing on her lap, his blinking gradually becoming slower until eventually he just closed his eyes and went off to sleep with the motion of Freya's fingers combing through his hair. She gazed down at him and sighed the way a mother would when she was filled with love. "Did you not fight wars? Did you not battle for your people and for those less able than you?" she asked without raising her head. "Do you not fight for what is true to your heart?"

"I did as I was ordered," he said without thinking about it. "That doesn't make me a warrior. It makes me obedient."

"Anya, the child you saw first ... Do you think she was a warrior?"

"She was just a child," he said as he cast his mind back to the cellar, the resounding drip, drip of the pipe near her still clear in his head. "She was a victim of something. I don't know what."

"Anya was a child, you are right there. That doesn't mean she wasn't strong or that she didn't fight. She had been in the dirt for over thirty days before you found her. Every moment, she had fought just to live. It was a futile fight, which is why you were sent there." She stopped stroking Toke's hair, but he stayed fast asleep. "I know you don't understand, but you will. Anya would have never found her way if you had not told her." Freya fixed Stephen with a glare. "Does that not make her a warrior? Someone who fought for what she believed in. That she had faith enough not to give up and die, even when every odd was against her?"

Stephen folded his arms across his chest. Maybe it did. For Anya, at least. "That does not make me a warrior, though. I have not done anything so valiant."

"Then tell me," she said, angling her head at him. "What is the real crime that led you to execution? Tell me it wasn't noble." She gave him a look that was so sure of herself, certain she was correct in her assumptions. She was wrong, but she wasn't going to listen, and she wouldn't understand. He didn't expect her to, either. He was a coward, and he had disgraced himself. What he had done was out of fear of losing his father, not out of bravery. It did not deserve honour.

"You've told me about me. Now tell me about the children," he said, nodding towards Toke and Nakita and changing the focus of the topic. "Why does Norton want

227

them? Why are they here?"

Freya leaned back and crossed her legs at the ankles as best she could without disturbing Toke. She nodded toward Nakita. "She has special capabilities. She can take your abilities from you and then give them to someone else."

"What do you mean?" he asked, visions of his *tiger* being removed coming to mind. How would that be possible?

"Exactly what I said."

Stephen mentally scratched his head and tried to understand what she had just told him in the literal sense. Because it made not one shred of sense. Take his abilities? Make him *Human*?

"She can take your ability to shift from man to *tiger*," interrupted Aiden. Stephen had almost forgotten he was there. He was so quiet. "Just one touch long enough, and she could take it from you and give it to someone else."

"And me? What would happen?"

"If you survived," he said, "then you would be *Human*."

His words were a blow to Stephen's brain. It exploded with possibilities of what he could do with that information. The ways that could be used were beyond belief.

It was instinct for him to still think of himself as his father's second. His mind had not caught up with the fact he had been stripped of the title and position, and for a brief moment, he forgot that he was no longer next in line for alpha.

He made himself snap back to the reality of his situation and scowled as he tried to crush the idiotic plans his royal brain was attempting to hatch.

Oh yes, the mighty had fallen, and then suddenly remembered, he hadn't yet got back up.

"If she gave my power to you," he asked Aiden, "what

then? Could you keep it?"

Aiden gave a shrug and a nod and then took a bite of some dreadful looking food Freya had given him. His stomach recoiled from the mere imaginings of what he was eating.

"It would depend," Aiden said after swallowing. "If the recipient were *Human*, maybe they wouldn't be able to handle the power. They would either die or go insane. There would be a good chance that an *Other* could stand it—but they are stronger. Imagine the possibilities."

Oh, he had. His mind had run off with so many possibilities that he was struggling to call it home again.

Eden was awake, Stephen noticed. She was watching them, listening, but he turned back to Freya, his mind working overtime with this new information. "Toke is the same? That's why they want them together. They're brother and sister, right?"

"Yes," said Freya. "They are twins. They nestled together in the womb. They are two halves of the same being. Join them, and they become one powerful entity. They aren't even grown yet."

"Toke can do something different?" He couldn't help but watch them—especially the girl. He had smelt shifter on them, but maybe he had been wrong. It had been faint. Stephen could normally scent another shifter a mile away.

"In a way," Freya said.

He waited for her to add something else, anything else, but she was back to not divulging anything more than asked.

"Toke can strengthen your powers," added Aiden. "If he touches you, your powers grow stronger. He can do it just by being close, but the result isn't as efficient. The *Human* ... the one I ..."

"Melted?" Stephen thought back to the puddle on the

ground. Aiden had been holding onto Toke when he had turned that *Human* into nothing more than charred sludge.

He nodded. "I'm not really that powerful."

Stephen leaned back, contemplative. He understood not only what they were telling him, but what it meant, too—the bigger picture. It would seem that even in the world of *Others*, there were things—beings—that even he didn't know about. He wasn't sure what he wanted to know next. It would appear that Freya wasn't so forthcoming with the information, although she wasn't stopping Aiden from filling him in. He should at least ask more questions while he had the chance. Who knew when Freya would decide that he knew too much and that Aiden should be quiet?

"So, they want Toke? Why?" The moment the question left his lips, he realised the answer. Same reason he would want both of them. So many things slotted into place within his small mind. "He can make his sister's power stronger, can't he?"

"Yes."

Eden pushed herself up, edging closer to them. "She'd be able to take *Other's* abilities from them ..." Freya handed her some shrink-wrapped— Stephen would have said food, but that was not food. It was shit ... shit on a damn sandwich. She took it without hesitation.

"Without even touching them," Aiden said, finishing Eden's sentence.

Shit. That was fucking bad. They were like a gold mine of *Others*. The cogs of his imagination all clicked into place as it occurred to him just what the *Humans* could do if they had Toke and Nakita together. *Others* could be eviscerated. "And the laws governing this?"

"We are insignificant here," said Freya. "The *Humans* dislike *Others* and do not adhere to the same laws you are accustomed to. They aren't enforced here, and we don't have a ruling government established. The *Others* who are in a position to fight for our rights, our union, would seem to be easily swayed."

"Greed is an insatiable beast," Stephen offered nonchalantly.

"Indeed, it is."

It was difficult to reconcile what the *Humans* could do. Just when it was seen that they might be at their limit, they did something more. Taking these two children ... God, they'd be fucking unstoppable. "With Toke and Nakita together, they could hunt every *Other*. They would steal our gifts and use them against us as they pleased. They could make their armies better, their soldiers faster with no fear of death. They would be immortal exterminators."

"Imagine yourself *Human*, Nick. What would you do with these children if you had them?"

He didn't need to imagine what it would be like to be *Human*. He had already imagined what it would be like to have both kids in his father's pack, and his reasons were not anywhere near as self-motivated as the *Human*'s. He saw the potential in having these children within their ranks. They would be useful tools to any species. It was just unfortunate that the *Humans* knew about them.

His mind raced with thoughts of the children, but his body started to rage with thoughts of food. His clothes chafed against his skin, even more so as his mind grew excited with this information. It felt like each fibre of cotton had been shaved to sharp points and aimed at his damp flesh. He had more questions about Toke and Nakita, but they would have to wait for now. He just hoped Freya would be as amenable next time.

He had to eat.

Mason Sabre

Soon.

Chapter Twenty-Seven
Stephen

In all his worlds, all his hopes and dreams, and maybe even his nightmares, Stephen never imagined that he would be holed up, practically hiding, from the *Humans*. And not only that, but that his companions would be a witch, a demon, two super children and a ... *something*. He could just leave. They weren't his problem. He tapped his fingers against his thigh. They didn't matter to him. They were nothing and no one. Just rejects the same way he was. And life was hard—so fucking hard. Maybe they would learn that lesson themselves. Life wasn't all things pretty. The sooner they learned that, the better.

Toke was sleeping, but Nakita ... she was the curious one of the two. She was sitting with her back to a tree—like she already knew that rule. Never turn your back to wide open space. She was too young to have learned that, though. But Stephen couldn't deny that she had a position where she could see all around them and run if she needed to; it had to be more than just chance. Either that, or Stephen was just looking too much into it. Perhaps her parents had shown her. It would be something he would teach his children very early in their lives—if he ever had any. She reminded him a little of a young Gemma, the way she watched all around her but remained silent. The way she seemed to take everything in even though she was occupied with something else. She even leaned forward and held her tongue in the corner of her mouth the same way that Gemma did. It brought a bittersweet smile to Stephen's lips. His mind always seemed to want to go down this pity party path. He couldn't allow it; it would do him no good. Shit was done now, and he had to

233

move on and accept it all. He ground his teeth, exhaling heavily.

Get a grip, Stephen.

He stared out into the vast woodlands. It would have been great to just run and get lost in them. To be free. They appeared to be undisturbed—no path, no direction—much like him right now. Would be possible for a man to walk the entire earth in his lifetime? Always moving, never stopping. He imagined where he would go.

How big was Exile anyway? He knew it was more than one island. He knew so much of it was inhabited by *Humans* so they could control the *Others* who lived here—because these *Others* had no choice. It was runaway land. But it was free land, too. Maybe he could get a boat to another place and just become a faceless nobody. He really could be Nick Mason, leaving behind Stephen Davies … just the shadow of a shifter who once killed a bunch of people. But so much as he had lost, he knew he would do it all again. In a heartbeat. For protecting his family, his father and alpha, his sister, he would do what needed to be done, no matter the consequences.

A tap on his shoulder brought Stephen around from his thoughts and he jumped, cursing himself for letting his guard down enough so that even a child could sneak up on him. "Can you tie my shoe?" Nakita said, standing next to him and lifting one small foot. She was just over head height as he sat there. He looked down at the white laces that had come undone on one of her little red trainers.

"Sure," he said, but as he leaned down to fasten it for her, she turned and plonked herself down on his lap. He stiffened, but she leaned into him, her back pressed to his chest, as if it were the most natural thing in the world. He had to put his arms around her to reach for her foot, and as

234

he tentatively did so, he breathed her in. She had a comforting scent—shifter and something else. It soothed something inside him … the delicate stroke that his *tiger* needed to calm himself.

"There," he said when he was done, pulling it into a double knot so it didn't come undone again. He opened his arms so that she could get back up, but she stayed where she was, turning in his lap so she was snuggled up to him on her side. Stephen hesitated, his arms out, not touching her. Aside from his sisters, he hadn't really been around small children before—and when they were little, especially Gemma, he had been a kid himself.

He rested an awkward hand on her hip, which made her snuggle closer. Maybe she needed that comfort, too. Maybe she felt his *tiger* in there—although she wouldn't have had her first shift yet. That usually started when their bodies were ready for it … when they had learned the ways of their packs. He leaned back, forcing himself to relax and let Nakita nestle against his chest, her head under his chin.

He scowled when he realised Eden and Freya had been watching the whole exchange with interest, averting their gazes when he looked up.

"Where will you all go now," he asked after ten minutes of nothing. He worded it purposefully, in a way that didn't commit him to going with them. He glanced over at Freya, but it was Eden who answered.

"I'm going to Fortvania," she said. "There is a coven there—a grand witch."

"Fortvania?" The word made the hairs on the back of his neck stand up.

"You know it?" Aiden asked him.

The question rolled around in his mind. "No," he said after a moment, "I don't." He relaxed his shoulders, running an absent hand over Nakita's side. Only she would have been able to hear the thumping of his heart.

"You seem to," said Freya, observing him from the side. "The look on your face just then."

"I've heard it before, that's all."

"Where?" Aiden leaned closer.

The thought of the note in his pocket flashed through his mind, and he knew how stupid it would sound to say it out loud. "Someone mentioned it."

"Who?" Freya demanded.

"Just a woman I met."

"Where?"

Stephen frowned at why it would matter. He rolled slightly to one side, holding Nakita in place against him. She wrapped a small arm around his ribs, holding herself in place as he reached into his jean pocket and pulled out the piece of paper. He tossed it across to Freya.

"Who gave you this?" she said after she had opened it and read it. He noted the edge that had suddenly crept into her voice. "And when?"

"I don't know." Her interest in it told him she knew something, and that it was important. Yet, he couldn't tell her about the dream he had had. It sounded idiotic even to him. The random babbling of a madman. "Someone ... A woman. I was hunting, and when I got back, I found her standing by my things. She said her name was Helena."

Aiden's eyes went wide, and Freya and Eden glanced at each other, alarm across their faces.

Freya held Toke tight as she shuffled closer to Stephen. "Are you sure she said Helena?"

His brow furrowed at their reaction to the name. "That's what she said."

"What did she look like?" Aiden chipped in.

236

Stephen shrugged. "I don't know. Young. My age. Long brown hair, pretty, slim."

Eden was staring at Freya with a look of … fright … confusion. Whatever was going on, Stephen wanted in on the secret. He tried to move, but Nakita had got herself comfortable, clinging to him and restricting his movements.

"What is it?" he asked when he had enough of their secret stares.

"Are you sure she said Helena?" Freya asked.

Stephen let out a frustrated breath. "Does it matter? She gave me an address to go to. I was going to go there. Probably be some dead end," he muttered, "It's in Fortvania."

"We should go," Freya said. "Before the hours go, and we lose the daylight."

She cast her eyes skywards as if she was reading the way the sun moved or gaging that it would soon be dark. Which it wouldn't—it was still morning—but it made Stephen wonder just how far away Fortvania was.

***

Very far, it turned out. Freya got her old, battered car, which, quite shockingly, was running. Its engine, though, sounded more like the angry roar of a monster that didn't want disturbing rather than a gentle growl.

Stephen tapped his fingers on the roof. "I'll drive," he said to Freya. It was better he did the driving, perhaps—the more experienced one of the bunch. Besides, he only ever trusted his life in his own hands.

"Do you know where you are going?"

"No … just …" Just that she looked too young and … and he always drove.

"Get in the car, Nick. I won't kill you." She got into the driver's seat and the others squeezed into the back—except Nakita. She ran around to the passenger side and climbed onto a grumpy Stephen's lap without question.

Great. He had acquired some kind of mini magnet.

***

"This is Fortvania?" Stephen asked when Freya turned the car off the road and onto what was a small lane—kind of like the path near the store. It was usage made, just like the path near the store.

She let the car idle to a stop then turned the engine off and took out the keys. "The car should be okay to leave here."

His brows rose mockingly. "Because someone might want to steal this?" The damn thing was a death trap. One jolt and the dial on the dash would be firmly implanted into someone's head. The dials themselves were all gone. What was left were spikes sticking out. He had tried to turn one of them to get the heater from damn near freezing to something warmer—or off would have done—but the metal pin had just bent in his grasp, and he had given up, hoping that the journey wouldn't be too long and that he wouldn't freeze to death along the way.

"Because the sweepers might find it," she remarked with annoyance.

They bundled out of the car, and Nakita clung onto Stephen. Did she not realise that he repelled children? Maybe that radar in her was defective. Every other child he had ever come across had more sense and would either give him a wide berth or cry. But not this one. She wrapped her little arm around his leg as if it could stop him from leaving.

238

Exile

"If this is Fortvania, I see no houses." He looked around at the vast emptiness. Just fields and grass and more trees.

"Fortvania is a mile away." Freya nodded in a direction to the north.

"Maybe we can send the witch ahead of us."

Eden glared at him as she climbed out of the car. "You're an asshole, you know that?"

"So they tell me," he said wryly. "But you were already heading there, alone. What does it matter to go by yourself now?"

"Yes, b-but now ..."

"What's different?" he drawled. "We have two kids here that the *Humans* have already tried to take." He held out his arm, showing his prison issue tattoo to her. "I might also be a *little* wanted by the law. It makes sense."

He had been joking. It had been a good hour since he had poked at the witch, but as he said it, the more he realised it actually did make sense. But then, Stephen would never let a woman go into danger before him—even if she was a damn witch.

"Are you serious?" Her incredulous expression warned him she was about to blow up on him. He smirked. God, he got such pleasure from riling witches up.

"It isn't a bad idea" Aiden said suddenly. "If there are *Humans* there ..."

"No," Stephen cut him off. "I was kidding."

***

Fortvania was more than a mile away from the car, and with the drive and the walk, it was near dark when the gates finally came into view.

Stephen's gait slowed as they got closer. He was still carrying Nakita, her little arms wound around his neck as she stared at the looming gates. Eden carried Toke on her back—it was a long walk and as small as the kids were, it would be a strain.

"Do we knock?" Stephen asked, eyeing the locked gate and the guard sitting reading in a small gatehouse to the side. He had never seen a gated community like this before.

"I don't know," Eden said. She let Toke down and grabbed his hand as she marched over to the man in the booth. She tapped the glass, but he ignored her. "Hey," she called, knocking harder. Stephen stayed in the shadows as she banged on the glass, not wanting to risk being recognised. The gatekeeper shot her a sideways glance then turned the page over in his book. "We've come here to see someone."

The man looked at her with an aggravated expression and then pointed. With a frown, she turned to look at the sign he was pointing at: *Ring for attention*.

"Are you kidding me?" She pushed the small button under the sign with a curse then turned back to the man with a glare. Stephen was ready to thump him if he didn't let them in.

He put his book down and pushed the small window open. "Yes?" He was *Other*. Stephen caught the scent of him immediately. Another witch. God, this place was rampant with them.

"I am here to see Celby Hampson," Eden said, pulling out a card and handing it to the man.

"Do you have an appointment?"

"She asked us to come," Aiden lied.

"Just a moment." He closed the window and picked up the phone, watching them as he dialled a number. A moment later, the window opened once more. "She says you can go through." His gaze roamed over them all. "You're all together?"

"This is my husband and our children," Eden offered.

Sneaky witch, Stephen mused. Brownie points to her.

The man nodded, reached down and opened the gate to allow them access.

The place was like one of those old towns in the movies, where everyone was probably inbred, and the kids didn't know their aunts from their uncles, and their parents. The houses were old, weathered. They may have been impressive once upon a time—and the small maze of streets picturesque—but now they were shabby, boarded up in places.

They walked along the path, and Stephen felt the weight of eyes on him. Lights were on in houses, and no cars moved along the streets.

The house listed on his paper was at the end of the block. It was an old, tall, three-storied Victorian style house with steps leading up to the front door.

The curtain at the front window of the small house next door twitched, and Stephen knew someone was watching them.

Stephen put Nakita down on the bottom step and strode up to the door. A sign saying *Open* hung there, but he didn't go in. He knocked lightly and waited.

The clipping of shoes on a tiled floor got closer, and he waited expectantly, curious to see where the dream woman had sent him.

The door opened, and Stephen's eyes widened in shock.

No. It was impossible.

"Wh—How—" He found himself struggling to think, words refusing to form into coherent sentences. "You?" he finally whispered.

"Can I help you?" the woman from his dreams said, a worried expression on her face. "Are you hurt?"

"I know you," Stephen murmured as he stared at her, dumbfounded.

The woman stepped out onto the top step with him, pulling her white jacket closed around her middle. "You need a doctor?"

Chapter Twenty-Eight
Stephen

Stephen took a step back, grabbing the handrail for support before he took all leave of himself and turned around. "Who are you?" he growled.

"I am Dr Barnes," she said, grabbing onto the door, keeping herself half in and half out of the building. "Do you need medical attention?"

Stephen's heart pounded in his chest. loud enough that he was sure she would hear it. His eyes roved over her … every perfect curve. God, she was even more stunning in real life. She smiled nervously at him and pushed a strand of hair behind her ear. He wasn't sure what captivated him more— the sheer beauty of her or the utter femininity she exuded. His *tiger* rose to the surface, prowling, demanding he go to her, the dominance in him seeing something it wanted.

Possess. Take her.

His body reacted violently, a hungry need like nothing he had ever felt before pounding through him. He balled his hands into fists to keep from reaching out and touching her. He took a deep, shaky breath, the scent of her thick and inviting and …

He froze.

"You're *Human*?" He snapped himself back, mentally and physically, forcing his *tiger* down. He gripped the handrail until his knuckles were white. His *tiger* smashed into him inside, demanding, pushing him closer, deepening his voice with male dominance, but Stephen fought him.

This was not going to happen.

Ever.

"I am," she said, her voice rolling over him like silk. He

closed his eyes for a moment, resisting this inexplicable hold she had on him.

Shit. This was not … How was this possible? Someone was messing with his head. A *Human.* Why was his *tiger* reacting this way to a fucking *Human*? Even as the thought passed through his mind, a wave of deep-seated longing pierced him.

Get a fucking grip, Davies.

He ran a hand across the back of his neck, raised his head and met her eyes with his. "This is *Other* community," he snarled at her, accusingly. The scent of *Others* was thick in the air, but he could scent Helena above them all. Such an intoxicating aroma that had him reeling and his mind taking exit.

"I am part of the Humane Equals," she said, lifting her chin, as if that would explain everything.

He narrowed his eyes at her. "I've never heard of them."

"I work for *Others*. I am a doctor."

"You're a traitor to your own kind?" Stephen couldn't stop the hostility from creeping into his words. She was a god damn *Human*. And both man and *tiger* in him were screaming to make her his. No fucking way.

She stiffened, and the expression of hurt that flitted over her features was like a stab to the heart. God, what was wrong with him? She was *Human*. Who cared if he hurt her feelings?

"That's part of the problem," she said sadly. "The reason our kind and your kind can never be equal. People like you who believe it wrong to help the other side."

Stephen felt like he had been slapped, hearing his own words thrown back at him from the other side. He clenched his jaw. "It isn't wrong."

Exile

He couldn't take his eyes off her.

"What do you want?" She had put up a mental wall, and that disappointed Stephen. His *tiger* flexed inside, brushing inside his skin.

"You told me to come here," he said. "You gave me this address and told me to come." He fished a shaking hand into his pocket for the note. God, he needed to pull himself together. He needed to shift and sort himself out, that's what this was. Not enough hunting. Not enough shifting. It was sending his brain to think things he would never dream of. He patted his jeans. "I can't find it."

He turned back, suddenly remembering the others. He had almost forgotten they were there. They were watching him like he had gone mad suddenly. Maybe he had. "Freya … I gave it to you."

Freya came up the steps and rested a reassuring hand on his arm. "It's okay, Nick," she said.

"No," he said, shaking his head. "It isn't okay." He turned back to Helena, an angry finger pointed at her. "You told me to come here. You gave me the note. I even got your bracelet. Remember?"

Helena glanced at her wrist; a small bracelet hung there. "My bracelet?"

Stephen's hand shot out and grabbed her arm, pulling it to him. Such a mistake. The contact was like touching a live wire. The force of her mind smashed into his, easing in like fine wine he needed to sip. He held onto her, his eyes boring into the liquid depths of her own. They sparkled with every autumn colour … "I—"

Helena snatched her arm back, snapping his mind from hers. She rubbed at her wrist, her breathing uneven. "Don't," she said, her eyes fierce.

"You don't understand."

245

Helena backed away from him. "If you don't have any medical problems, then I need to ask you to leave." She pulled her sleeve over her wrist, covering her bracelet. "I don't know you. I have never met you before, much less told you or asked you to do anything."

He shook his head to clear it, hardly understanding it all himself. He dreamt her, he was sure, but how could he have when he had a note and a bracelet telling him it was all real? "You did. You told me to come ..."

"I can assure you, I did not. I have never seen you before."

Her words were like a dagger in his chest, and he didn't know why it was there or how to pull it out. She was *Human,* for God's sake—one of the vermin—but his mind kept forgetting it.

Stephen backed away from her, pressing the heel of his palms into his eyes. But she was there, in his mind. Helena. The beautiful woman with the flowing dress—the way she moved, shimmering in the darkness of his mind.

"Excuse me, I have patients to attend to," Helena said, breaking into his thoughts. "Have a good day." She pushed the door to close it, but Stephen moved fast, wedging his foot in the doorway.

"Wait," he said.

"I need to get back to work."

His heart beat wildly in his chest. The world around them was vanishing.

She swallowed. "I don't know you," she said with less resolve.

"I saw you ..." he rasped.

"It wasn't me."

He gripped onto the door, not wanting her to close it, but mostly, not wanting her to go. "You were by my clothes

... I was hunting ..." He dropped his bag from his shoulder. "Don't close the door." He pulled the zip down and fished inside, pulling her bracelet out. "See," he said, holding it out. "It's yours."

Helena stared down at the bracelet that was identical to the one she was wearing. Delicately, she picked it up and laid it across her fingers. Pushing her sleeve back up, she compared the two. "It is the same," she said, meeting Stephen's eyes again, "but it isn't mine."

She offered it back to him, their fingers brushing as he took it, sending another jolt of electricity down his spine. "Did you have two?"

"No ..." She cast a glance over her shoulder and back into the clinic. " I'm sorry, I really must get back to work. Maybe it was someone else who asked you to come here. But it wasn't me." She tried to push the door closed again, but his foot stayed firmly lodged in the doorway. She was no match for the sheer strength of him.

"We have travelled a long way to get here. We don't have a place to go."

She bit her lower lip before saying, "I'm sorry, I can't help you. This isn't a refuge. It's a clinic … and you aren't sick."

"I have children with me ..."

"I'm sorry. I ..."

He pointed at Eden, frantic. "This witch is hurt. She cut her head." He darted down the steps and grabbed Eden, shoving her toward Helena. "We tried to stitch it for her, but it might get infected." He pushed a flabbergasted Eden's head down for Helena to see.

She pushed Eden's hair out of the way. "Okay," she said on a slow exhalation. "But you all stay in the waiting room while I look at this."

Stephen stayed back, his eyes fixed on Helena as the others filed in first. Her eyes darted from the kids to Stephen like a magnet. What kind of game was this? If this was someone messing with his mind, they could pack the hell in.

Helena stepped back to let him pass when he moved forward, but her scent was everywhere. Thick, intoxicating, even above the sharp stench of antiseptic and disinfectant. His *tiger* roared to life once more. *Fuck*. He wouldn't last five minutes in there.

He jerked back, startling her, and with a quiet curse, jogged back down the steps.

"Is everything okay?" she called down after him.

"I think I need to run," he muttered, avoiding looking at her.

"Like ... *shift*?"

"Yes."

She clasped her hands together, a small gesture, but one which betrayed her own nervousness under the cool façade. "There are woods not far from here," she said. "If you carry on to the left when you leave here, you'll see them. I will be awhile fixing your friend up."

He lifted his eyes to hers, and he had to tamp down the desire that flared as his gaze roved over her once more. "You really haven't seen me before ... have you?"

She shook her head slowly, the soft curls of her hair gently bobbing around her face. "No, I'm sorry. I have never seen you before."

He ran an agitated hand through his hair. "I need to run," he grated, already turning away from this *Human* woman who seemed to be playing havoc with his senses.

Chapter Twenty-Nine
Helena

Helena closed the door and sagged against it, not yet ready to deal with the *Other*s in her clinic who needed attendance. Her heart hammered in her chest, her thoughts scattered. She felt like a schoolgirl, all giddy and dizzy with excitement, her hormones raging after the brief encounter with probably the most attractive man she had ever laid eyes on.

She let out the breath she hadn't realised she had been holding. She couldn't take the picture of him from her mind—tall, muscled, masculine, he was the epitome of male perfection. Someone had placed emeralds in his eyes and framed them with thick dark lashes, setting them in shimmering liquid she could have drowned in.

She'd barely stopped herself from reaching out to trace her fingers along the stubble of his exquisitely formed jaw. She bit down on her lip and pressed a hand to her chest, steadying herself. It had been a long time since a man had had such an effect on her—in fact, she didn't ever remember being this affected. Suddenly the girl inside her had come to life with just the stroke of his voice along her body. And God, when he had touched her …

She stroked the skin on her wrist where he had held her as if she'd been burnt—it had felt like an electric current had passed through her. One small tug and she didn't know if she'd have been able to resist falling in his arms.

"Get a grip, Helena."

This was what years of staying away from men did to her. It made her desperate for the first outrageously handsome man that came along. Yes, Lee was handsome, stunning some might even suggest, just as capable of making any woman quake at the knees, yet he didn't cause this kind of havoc inside her. Both men looked equally dangerous, equally powerful, but the man she had just met oozed dominance, the very feline way he moved warning of the animal he harboured inside.

Lee had control. He had authority. But it was the kind of power that came from being a cunning businessman—clever, calculated and demanding. That man—*Nick* she thought the girl had called him—his presence alone was a force to be reckoned with.

Helena slid around so she could rest her forehead against the cool door, her hands flat against the wood. She slid a fist down and gripped the handle. She could feel him out there. Some strange force seemed to be connecting them, making her want to pull open the door and ... what? Call him back? Watch him?

She drew in a deep breath and counted to ten. She needed to see to her patients. Xander needed his dressing fixed again, the young witch needed that nasty gash tended to, and the children probably needed something to eat and a good clean up. Would she really send them on their way again? Did they have anywhere to stay? Were these young little babes being well cared for or were they living in the rough?

All she knew was that she just couldn't have that man in her clinic. It wasn't safe. Not that she feared him, more herself. He was *Other*. She'd get herself executed with the thoughts her mind was having about him.

It didn't take x-ray vision to see the shapes of his well-defined body, the way his shirt hugged all the right places. The thick, hard muscle of his chest, the bulging arms, the flat, tight stomach ... She splayed her fingers out on the door, wondering what his skin would feel like under her fingertips. The taste of him on her lips ...

"Ten, Helena. Count to ten ..."

"I want my mummy," called a small voice, growing louder. Helena spun around at the sound of a young girl's voice, her eyes going wide. Freya? Was that her name? She stood holding the small girl's hand, both of them watching her. She flushed bright pink. They couldn't possibly know what she'd been thinking. "C-Can I get you anything? Juice?"

The small girl fussed, wriggling herself, but the older girl held her tight. "Remember what I told you," Freya said, restraining the small girl. "The two little ones could do with something to eat and drink. If you can spare it."

"Of course." Children had that knack where you felt they saw everything. Or was it simply that everything adults knew was reflected in the innocence of the young. Helena stared at Freya, swallowing hard because she was sure, right then, that these girls could see right through her. Flustered, as if she had been caught doing something terrible, she pushed herself from the door and quickly made her way towards the kitchen.

The witch's wound could wait—it hadn't been anything life-threatening as far as she could tell. "I'll get you all something to eat and drink."

Freya nodded. "Thank you." Her smile, the light curve of her lips, said she knew way more than she was letting on. She was an observer.

She went over to the sink and filled a jug with water and dilatable juice. She'd make them a sandwich or something, too. Outside, she could see the heads of the trees where she had sent him to run. Was he there now? Shifting, standing naked in the shade, his muscles flexing and moving ... Helena gripped the handle of the jug, her breathing hitching up a notch. She was losing her professional demeanour, and what for? Some strange man who had turned up at her door and claimed he knew her? He'd even become insulting when he'd realised she was *Human*.

She wasn't that damn crazy and desperate she would fall over him like a drooling schoolgirl.

Helena shut off the tap and yelped as she turned around. The smallest girl was standing at the door again, silently watching her. "Oh my, you gave me a fright," she smiled at her. "I made you some juice. Do you want some?"

"Did you put cranberries in it?"

"Cranberries? How did you ..." Helena's mother used to add fruit to juice, usually cranberries because that was what they could get hold of easily. It was a way to get more goodness into the kids. Helena hadn't minded. When they had sat in the juice for so long, she had liked to take the fruit and suck on their sweetness. "I don't think I have any," she said with regret.

"It's okay," the little girl said. The older boy knocked lightly on the door and then pushed it open.

"Stop wandering off, Nakita," he said.

"She wasn't doing any harm," Helena said to him, setting the jug down. "Would you all like a drink?"

"Yes, please," he said. "I'm Aiden." He offered a small hand out to her, a very grown-up gesture.

"Pleased to meet you, Aiden," she said warmly. "Your dad went to run."

"Oh, he's not my dad. He—" He stopped short, seeming to reconsider what he was about to say. Curious as she was, she didn't press him for any further information.

"Thank you," he said instead when Helena gave them all a glass each and sat the children at the table in her back room. Setting down some ham and cheese sandwiches in front of them, which she was pleased to see they immediately attacked, she said, "Are you all okay here while I tend to your ..."

"Friend," Freya finished for her. "Yes, we are."

Helena's face flushed at the way the smallest girl was staring at her. Her eyes bore into her like she knew things. It was madness of course. The girl was so young. Helena put her at five at most, based on the level of speech she had.

Eden was waiting for her in the small examining room, so Helena decided to pop her head in to see Xander first. He was sitting on his bed, listening to the television, his friends having left for a bit. They needed to make arrangements to care for him ... and face the possibility that he might not get his sight back. Helena nodded at him. "I'm just seeing to another patient."

Xander only smiled in response—not even a proper smile, more a twitch of his lips. But that was as much acknowledgement as she would get. Whether it was because she was *Human,* or because he was upset about his sight—or maybe both—she wasn't sure. She shut the door gently and then knocked before entering the room where Eden was.

"Am I okay to come in and look at that now?"

"Sure," Eden said, sucking in a breath and twisting in her seat. Helena had made her a cold compress to help with the swelling a little. It would be easy enough to fix then if it needed it—although whoever had stitched it, from what she could see, had done a nearly decent job.

After having a closer look at the wound, Helena realised Eden hadn't really needed her help at all. She had a compound paste of herbs and plants in her bag that she told Helena she had used on the gash. The way the wound was already healing was amazing. She had never known anything like it before.

"May I?" she asked, pointing at the tub Eden had taken out.

"Of course." She held it out to her, and Helena took it and sniffed. It was rich, spicy with the hint of something she wasn't sure about. "That's cloves you're detecting," Eden said.

"That's the hit?"

"Yep. Clove oil. It's great for anything you need to take a little pain away."

"Where do you get clove oil?"

Clove oil was a rare thing in these parts. Mostly it was kept to those who dealt with dentistry. It was good for mouth infections, but it was expensive to come by, and the authorities, for whatever reason, didn't like it being used.

"Do you mind applying some more on my wound?"

"Of course." Since this cream seemed to be doing wonders, Helena wasn't in the least bit hesitant in using it. She had seen some amazing concoctions put together by witches here in Exile, and this was no different.

She pulled a glove from her pocket and then dipped her finger into the cream. "Is ... Nick ... your boyfriend?" she asked as she applied it to Eden's bowed head, then quickly added, "Sorry. None of my business." She pursed her lips. What an idiot. She sounded like a desperate school kid asking if the popular boy was taken.

Eden snorted. "Nope, he isn't. He's a rude son of a bitch is what he is."

"Oh?" She was surprised by the intense relief she felt.

Eden put her head back, her eyes watering as the cream soaked into the wound. It smarted. "Yep. If we didn't need him, I'd drop a house on him." She laughed to herself. "Sorry. Witch humour. His bark is worse than his bite. From what I have seen anyways."

"You've just met?"

"Yeah ..."

Helena wanted to push more, but it wasn't her place. She capped the tub again and handed it back to Eden. "I'd love to get the recipe for that. I am always on the hunt for new remedies. Sometimes the herbs just don't do it, you know?"

"I sure do. Do you know Celby Hampson?" she asked. "I believe she lives here."

"Celby? Oh, I do." The smile that had spread across Eden's face disappeared again when Helena added, "She doesn't accept visitors, though. It is through appointment, and you have to know her. Keeps herself to herself."

"She won't see me if I just turn up?"

"Afraid not. She isn't the ..." Helena paused, trying to think of the right word. 'Paranoid' just seemed too cruel to say. "She doesn't trust people. Let's put it that way."

The disappointment was clear on Eden's face. She had probably come here to see her, like many witches did. They all wanted part of the weird and wonderful coven. Helena knew little about them. They lived at the top of the hill, around the back, ran their own farm and traded in herbs and things. Mostly cast offs they didn't want.

"I can call her tomorrow if you like. But I can't promise anything."

"You would do that?"

"Sure." Helena didn't hold out much hope. They'd be lucky if Celby even answered the phone, but then maybe if they were waiting on the call, she'd have them stay a little longer. They needed a place to go, hadn't he said that?

But ... could she keep her cool around him?

Chapter Thirty
Stephen

As he heard the door shut behind him, an inexplicably profound sense of loss settled deep in the pit of Stephen's stomach. An overwhelming urge to run back to Helena, claim her as his, had him stopping abruptly and balling his hands into fists as he fought the compulsion. She was a goddamn *Human*. Why was his bloody *tiger* demanding to possess her? She was just another pretty face. He'd been around countless beautiful *Human* women in his lifetime—had had no trouble bedding them—but they'd never been anything more than a one-night stand. Why was his *tiger* feeling differently towards this woman now?

But even as he tried to talk sense into himself, he found his body turning as if of its own volition and running back to the house. He was standing at the door once more before he had really had time to think about what he was doing. It was impossible to calm the raging need pumping through his veins. Man and beast clashed, one wanting to be logical, and the other wanting to throw caution out of the window and claim what he wanted.

Stephen wasn't exactly sure which part of him was fighting which battle.

Suddenly, he froze. He could *feel* her standing on the other side of the door. His entire body went rigid.

He swallowed hard and gripped the door frame, trying to steady himself. A growl rumbled low in his throat as his *tiger* made his demands.

Possess her. Take her. She's yours.

He unclenched a trembling hand and softly pressed it to the wood separating them.

Exile

Helena.

He closed his eyes and sucked in a calming breath, his open palm slowly clenching into a fist once more as he struggled to keep from tearing through the door to get to her.

She's lying to you. She's a fucking Human. She's messing with your head. He repeated the words to himself over and over again, willing them to sink in.

First, they fuck with him and his life, and now this last kick—fucking with the parts inside him he couldn't control.

He was done with it all. He wanted to find the tour guide of this weird and wonderful journey he was on and inform them he had had enough and needed to go home. He didn't want a refund. He didn't care about the wondrous sights he was about to miss. What he wanted was the normalcy of his life back.

"Fuck this shit."

He pushed away from the door and shot back down the steps, away from the clinic and the good doctor. He got himself to the path and ignored the urge to look back.

With each step toward the gate, he picked up speed. The gatekeeper saw him coming and pushed the button to let him out. Stephen snorted. Did they really think that if he wanted out, a gate would stop him? Stephen had got into more secure places than this.

He headed out toward the woodlands, almost salivating at the thought of the hunt. Adrenaline pumped through his veins, urging him on, ripping a growl from his throat as he found the solitary darkness where he could shift. He didn't care if at any moment, he would happen upon a *Human*. Let them come. He was sure they would be as pleased to see him as he would be to see them, he sneered. He was hungry, and right in that moment, not fucking fussy. One dead *Human* was as good as the next.

He stopped in the cover of the trees and stripped off his clothes, stuffing them in an alcove at the bottom of a tree before dropping to the ground. Relieved at every bone popping part of his shift, he stretched his paws out when he finally stood there as *tiger*. He backed up, paws down, tail up, eyes on his target—a tree. With a growl, he launched himself into the air, sinking his claws into its tough flesh. Fuck, this was what he needed.

He pulled himself up in delight, climbing way up onto one of the thick limbs overhead. Crouching low, his sharp eyes swept the area, his senses alert. A poor, unsuspecting deer ambled into his line of vision, and Stephen thrilled at the thought of the impending chase.

Till now, everything seemed to be straight out of a badly made movie, where the plot was so lame they'd be lucky if people didn't walk out of the cinema before the end. At least this would make up slightly for the hell he'd been through so far.

His quarry moved closer until he was right under him. She had no idea what was waiting above her in the tree. He didn't move. One wrong move and she would be gone, and he'd have to find another deer and start all over again. His frustration was already at an all-time high.

The deer moved again, just a bit more, and she was almost in the right spot. Perhaps he should have drawn X marks on the spot on the ground with chalk so she might know where to stand. He would get her in one hit.

He ran his tongue across his teeth. The anticipation grew wilder along his spine as the deer's front hoof stepped into Stephen's invisible marker. Had he been able to talk, he thought, he might have cheered her on, telling her she was doing great. Just one more step and nothing would matter.

Exile

In less than ten minutes, *nothing* in the deer's life would matter ever again. Stephen was doing her a favour.

One step ... two steps ... like a bad nursery rhyme. Just one more, like a teddy bear. He leaned forward and stretched out on part of the tree, clutching the branch between his paws as he tilted his head down to watch her. She was totally unaware of what was lurking in the darkness.

As she took that final step, he leapt, landing on her back, his paws going around her neck. She stumbled from the shock and the weight of him, no time to even squeal as he sank his teeth into the delicious flesh of her throat.

Her death was swift beneath his jaws, her body giving the occasional twitch as the last of her life ebbed out of her body. Blood poured from her throat, dripping from between Stephen's jaws and landing on the ground and down his fur.

On occasion, when Stephen was hunting and killing an animal with his jaws, he wished he could do the same to *Human*s. Not eat them but just to end their miserable, wasted lives. Although their deaths would not be so fast, he would hunt them and trap them beneath his paws like a cat with a mouse. He'd make sure they lived as long as possible while in his company, pulling each limb from their bodies. He would relish in every moment. *Human*s did much worse to *Others*. Stephen had seen it. He had seen the devastation and suffering they caused in the name of equality.

The mere thought of inflicting pain and death on *Human*s was enough to calm his mind from the day's events. Just enough that his mind cleared, putting him back to the place where his mind could plan.

His mind flicked to the *Human* who was wreaking havoc on his mind at the moment—Helena. The real one and the not so real one. Her expression had told him she honestly hadn't known who he was. And his instincts told him it wasn't an act. So how the hell did he explain all this?

Stephen paused mid chew, his eyes catching sight of his wrist where the silver had sunk in. His fur was brighter there, newer. It was like it healed at his normal *tiger* rate and not the rate of a shifter touching silver. Things suddenly slotted into place. The witch, she had put the cream on his wrist and it was after that he had seen the woman.

He desperately mapped his memories back to that point, his mind racing, putting flashes of information before him. *Shit*. Was it her? It had been her who had wanted to go to Fortvania.

Stephen's stomach dropped. This was her plan. She had probably used her witchery magic shit to make herself look like Helena …

Fuck. How could he have been so blind?

With a growl, he chewed down the last of what he was eating, tearing away ribbons of bright flesh and then swallowing it. The fucking witch. His meal had tasted so damn good, but now …

He pushed the deer back against the base of a tree. He would come back for her. Finish her. Another satisfying meal for him. He gripped her by the small head and pulled her body along. But his mind wouldn't stop tossing thoughts of everything that had transpired with the witch over and over in his head. He heard a crunch of gravel near him, the sound of tyres on the road. Instinctively, he crouched down. Dropping the deer, he slunk toward the sound. It was far away, but close enough sohe could hear it. He padded gently towards the sounds, head ready, nose sniffing for any *Human*s who might walk by.

He crept all the way along until he came to water. It wasn't deep, but it looked like some kind of river and then a drop. A car drove along, and Stephen dug his claws into the earth beneath him when he saw the driver.

Fucking young suit from the house.

Coincidence?

The events clicked in Stephen's feline mind, the predator in him realising many things at once. God, he really had lost his brain since landing in Exile. God damn witch.

It had been her by the water; it had to be. She would have followed him, placed the note there. *Shit.* It was probably her who had put the bracelet in his hand while he was out of it, too. She knew Helena. Somehow. Maybe they all fucking did. They hadn't been surprised by any of the goings-on. The man at the gate had let her in no problem, too.

They hadn't killed her at the house, either No, they'd fucking knocked her out and left her. How very convenient. Now look. The *tiger* was out of the house, and the *Human*s were heading to the town in a convoy.

Another thought had the hackles on his fur rising. *Oh God ... the kids*. He snarled, his top lip peeling back as he watched another *Human* vehicle and then another appear.

Shit, shit and triple fucking shit.

Stephen spun around, forgetting the deer as he raced back through the trees, heading back to his clothes. His chest swelled so hard from the effort. He had to beat those cars.

He raced like his tail was on fire.

Bloody witch.

How could he have been so stupid?

Chapter Thirty-One
Stephen

Stephen threw the deadbolt into place. No fucker was getting in—or out—without his say-so. Not until this shit was sorted out. He was breathing hard from the running to the clinic—that and scaling the fences at the back to get back into the community without explaining himself. Kind of made the gate pointless, in his opinion, but if it made them feel safer …

His clothes were a mishap of a madman who had dressed as he ran. He held his shoes in his hand, his feet covered in mud.

He didn't have to have super hearing to hear where everyone was—Nakita's laughter and shrieks of childish delight rang out from the back room where Xander was. As he charged in, he came face to face with two things—a baseball bat aimed right at his head, and a picture of his face—older-looking, yet still adorable—on the television screen with the word 'Wanted' penned across his throat on the bulletin: 'Mason. N. Prisoner 932416. Wanted for murder.'

Well, wasn't this just bloody fantastic?

Everyone jumped to their feet as he entered, all eyes on him. "Stop right there," warned Helena as she lifted the bat up higher in the air, ready to take a swing. His jaw tightened on noticing that the bat was silver-tipped—a good reminder that Helena was *Human* and, hence, the enemy.

He dragged his gaze from hers and his eyes locked on Eden. "You," he said, backing away from Helena's bat. "I'll just take the kids and go. You can stay here."

She frowned at him. "Nick …"

Exile

He narrowed his eyes at her, his hearing focused and his nose on her scent, looking for the lies that would drip from her in a moment. "You set this up, didn't you? It was your plan to turn us over, to have the *Humans* come to the house. You work for them. Fucking witches. Always the same."

Her expression turned to one of shock. "No …" She shook her head, but her voice had grown weaker. "I don't know what you're talking about."

"She didn't," Aiden said, stepping forward and standing next to Helena.

"There are *Humans* coming. The same one with the suit from the house. How do they know we were here?"

"They're looking for you," Helena said, nodding to the television screen.

"That wasn't me. It's bullshit." He stared at her dead in the eyes. His stupid fucking *tiger* heart. What had he been thinking? This was a *Human*—as beautiful as she was, she was one of them, and she would hand his arse in, in a heartbeat. "Give me the kids, and then I'll go."

Helena aimed the bat at Stephen, silver tip first, toward his chest, making him back away. His eyes blazed at her. What the hell did she think she would do? Drive him out? Every sense in his body was alive—listening, feeling, expecting. It would take one nudge, and the *tiger* would come raging out.

"Are you really going to hit me with that bat?"

"If I have to," she said, her fingers uncurling and then moving along the shaft for a better grip. His body reacted and his mind was sent wandering to places he didn't want to go.

"You're a doctor," he snarled. "You're supposed to fix people, not cause them harm."

Mason Sabre

"And you're in my house … yelling …" She jabbed the bat his way, threatening him with the silver tip. He growled and moved back, and she repeated the action, making him completely back out of the room. As soon as she was through the door, she shut it behind her.

"What now? Turn me in?" He narrowed his eyes at her, catching the slight shake in her hand.

"I—"

His hand snapped out, and he grabbed the bat in its centre, ignoring the searing agony that shot into his hand. He yanked it, pulling Helena forward and swinging her around so that she slammed into his chest, her back to him. "Now what?" he whispered into her ear, pleased at the way her breath hitched.

She held onto the bat, pressed to her chest, even though Stephen still gripped it tight. "W—" She swallowed hard, her heart pounding in her chest. "What are you going to do?"

"I want the children," he growled. "*Humans* are coming. I did not do what they are saying I did."

There was a pause. "Maybe you did …"

He snatched the bat away from her and placed his other hand on her chest, over her thumping heart. She sucked in a sharp breath. "It's not fear that speeds this up," he murmured in her ear, his lip grazing the tip of her ear. He fought his body's reaction at being this close to her and gripped the bat tight, sending the pain into his hand to remind him … to pull him back in his mind. "You know in here that I didn't do what they say, don't you? If you thought it were true, you would have turned me in while I was running."

She placed her hand on top of his, instinctively, and that simple touch sent his mind into a frenzy—not in the way

264

it did with others. Not in the way his mind entered theirs and tapped into their innermost secrets. Instead, it found a little peace—peace and madness that clashed into one inside his head and shook him down to his core.

His *tiger* paced inside, wanting, demanding. He inhaled deeply, taking in the scent of her. She responded to him, titling her head back, leaning on his shoulder, as if in a daze. She turned her head, eyes closed, so that her mouth brushed lightly across his stubble. She seemed to be just as affected by him, and the thought gave him incredible satisfaction.

Stephen was used to women responding to him physically—had used it to his advantage more times than he could remember—but it had never been anything more than sexual for him. He wouldn't have cared had they not been interested. But right now, he realised, he would have been bothered by an indifferent Helena. He would have … *cared*.

The thought was deeply unsettling.

Her body trembled slightly in his arms, and her breathing grew ragged, bringing images to his mind of very different ways he'd like to be making her tremble.

With an inward groan, he pressed her closer, pulling the length of her into him, giving himself a moment to enjoy the feel of her in his arms. Jesus fucking Christ, maybe he'd just gone too long without a woman, and his body and mind were going haywire.

"The *Humans* are coming," he said in a thick voice. "You need to let me take the kids."

"Y—You stand a better chance without them," she murmured.

"It isn't me they want …"

Her heart jumped then, a sudden bang against her chest that seemed to jar her out of her trance-like state.

"You're *Human*. You know the lies they will tell to get

what they want."

She tried to turn, but his arm was a steel band around her, keeping her exactly where she was.

"Aiden told me ..."

There was a knock on the front door, and someone tried the handle. Stephen gripped Helena tighter, his entire body encompassing hers. Her legs pressed against his, her very fine backside pressing into the male hardness of him.

"You need to go," she gulped. "I will keep the children safe."

"I can't leave them with you."

"You have to," she urged. "I have a place, but you need to get out of here." She dropped her hand from his, leaving him feeling empty and bereft. "Trust me."

He scowled at that. "You're *Human*." The words helped shake some of his own erotic haze and remind him what she really was.

"You can stand here if you want and argue with me about what species I am," she said in her most chastising tone, "but you're the one making this an issue. You need to go. I'll keep the children safe."

Stephen lingered for a moment, inexplicably reluctant to let go. He needed to, but his *tiger* was fucking strong and determined—and god damn blind.

She was *Human*.

She was the enemy.

"Do not let them take the children," he snarled.

She seemed to let out a relieved breath. "I won't," she promised. He released her and took a step back. She turned, bat still in hand, and stared at him for a minute, looking as bewildered and as disconcerted as he felt. She half-lifted a hand towards him, before snatching it back again. The rapping on the door came again, louder this time.

Exile

"Just a second," she yelled. Her eyes locked with Stephen's. "You need to run." She took steps backwards, going to the door where the children were. "Stay safe, Nick Mason," she murmured before opening the door.

Stephen bolted to the back of the clinic, bursting out into what must have been the area where the good doctor spent her rest time.

The back door was open, and it led down to a garden filled with flowers and herbs. At the side were small greenhouses—perhaps she grew her cures there. His mother would have loved this place, he thought absently.

There was a fence at the bottom—not too tall that he couldn't get over it. He bounded down the steps at the back, his heart somewhere behind him, his *tiger* growling inside for release. He leapt for the built-in grill when he reached the bottom, landing on the grate with a clank and then pushing himself up and over. More gardens greeted him as he raced away—garden after garden of something out of a *Real homes* television show. When he had reached the last one, he opened a gate that led to the road and … came face to face with three *Humans*.

He gave a feral grin.

"Greetings," he crooned. "Could one of you nice gentlemen please point me toward the nearest exit? I appear to have got myself a little lost."

Three *Humans*—bacteria in a Petri dish under a microscope as they multiplied—became six. Three more joined making it nine. It was a neat trick, Stephen admitted to himself. Just a shame he couldn't do the same and even the odds.

However, he had ten claws—one for each of them and one spare. He could use that to pick the remnants of dead *Human* flesh from his teeth. It was a perfect plan.

In theory, at least.

Stephen moved so that the *Humans* created a wall around him. This was how goldfish felt when being stared at by the big bulging eyes of a cat … except *he* was the cat. One would think these *Humans* had never seen a shifter before. Maybe they needed a live and in person demonstration. His eyes flickered with gold, yellows and the greens of his *tiger*—emerald fire.

He focused for a microsecond and knew his eyes had shifted when the *Humans* took an uneasy step backwards. Cowards. Maybe they liked that little trick … or maybe not.

"Are you going to arrest me? Or is this instant judgment day?" He needed to know what he was dealing with. Would he be fighting to keep his wrists out of silver chains, or would he be fighting to keep his head on his shoulders? Neither sounded appealing. The *Humans'* lives were the better option, but he wasn't optimistic in his chances.

"You took the life of over twenty *Humans*. You already made the judgment yourself," one *Human* spat.

"Over twenty?" Stephen arched a brow. Either his counting skills were off, or he had been killing in his sleep. What a shame that would be, missing it all. By his count, it had been seven since his arrival … well, actually they hadn't been his kills. Only two had died at his hands. Perhaps the *Humans* had looked further back … Maybe it had been the fat man's size—he counted for two, at least.

"You have been sentenced for the murders of the *Human* family outside of Ashdale two weeks ago."

What the fuck were they talking about? "I wasn't here two weeks ago ..."

But they weren't listening.

"The guards on the bus make twelve. There's another

six we suspect at the church in Marsden, and a further three some nights ago, in Cedar."

"You're accusing me of crimes that are not mine. Who is my accuser?"

The *Human* gave a nonchalant shrug. "That is not my concern. Maybe you can take it up with your maker when we send you back to him."

"Is that supposed to scare me?" Stephen scoffed. "My maker? I am not a vampire, mother fucker. My maker is the same as yours."

The man set his jaw in an angry line at Stephen's disparaging comments. "Your crimes have been listed, and you have been charged. There are no grounds for you to appeal. The decision is final."

"By whom?"

"It is not your concern."

Stephen moved closer, and they all took a nervous step back. "Humour me. By whose orders am I to be punished?"

"Councillor Benjamin Norton signed the death warrant two weeks past."

Two weeks? "This is bullshit." These men weren't even police. Stephen wasn't sure who they were, but he was certain asking for identification would not get him anywhere. Except maybe a little closer to them.

One of the *Humans* on his right side took a cautious step closer, and Stephen almost laughed. Oh, how brave he was. As they spread around him, he considered leaning in and shouting *boo*—they would probably shit themselves and run.

Maybe it was worth a go.

The *Humans* made a solid line—like the idiots they were. Doing only what they had been ordered to do and about to die because of it. The way Stephen saw it, he had

269

two options. He could attempt to run through them—though that was possibly a little suicidal—or he could take the route back over the fences, make his way to the street and run. Whichever he chose, it would hurt, and he suspected that there were more *Humans* out front. Bacteria was like that—it spread everywhere.

The man to Stephen's right made the first move and took any decision-making from him. He hesitated as he got near enough to make a grab for Stephen—and that was his mistake. Fear. The *Human* reached out, and Stephen turned, shifting his fingers to a half paw as he did. The man tried to move back, but he didn't estimate Stephen's next move properly. His claws pierced both the man's eyes with speed, earning a guttural scream as his hands clasped at Stephen's arm, nails digging into hard muscle and half furred paws. Had he succeeded, he might have pulled his own eyeballs out. Stephen poked his fingers and index finger into the man's cheeks and his thumb into his mouth, bringing his claws together inside the *Human's* flesh. The man's scream changed to gagging as he fought until Stephen slammed his head down to the ground—a *Human* bowling ball.

He thrust his other hand into the man's abdomen, clawing his way in until he found the bottom of his ribcage. He hooked his claw under and back through the skin to use it like the handle of a bag and launched him at the horrified others, who had stood there looking on till now, frozen.

The remaining eight *Humans* moved at once, and Stephen charged, teeth bared, claws out, not giving one shit which one of them he hit or where. They could add this to his list of crimes.

A siren rang out somewhere in the distance, the screeching sound a piercing shrill to Stephen's sensitive ears. With a roar, he clutched his head and stumbled forward, smashing though the *Humans,* knocking them over like bowling pins.

Loud shouts surrounded him, radios blaring, cries and screams and yells. He was sure there were more than just eight *Humans* on his tail now.

He raced around to the street, bursting out onto the road. As he ran, headlights lit his path as a car came up from behind him. Someone called his name—it sounded like Aiden—and Stephen faltered. He turned, the bright lights almost blinding him. He couldn't stop with the force of his own momentum as the car ploughed right into him, rolling him over the bonnet. Pain exploded in his hip and side as he landed on the road with a thud, grazing his skin along the surface. Despite the pain, he staggered to his feet, his eyes seeing nothing but spinning stars.

As the world spun, he thudded back onto the ground once again. Two sets of thick heavy boots filled his vision, and Stephen scented shifters.

"We need to get him out of here fast, Nigel," he heard a woman say.

A man offered a hand out, but Stephen couldn't seem to grasp onto it.

"Shit, Mel, get the door …" The man bent down and picked Stephen up, pulling him to his feet and taking his heavy weight.

But as he slowly started to get his bearings again, he realised they were outside the clinic. Aiden ran out of the open door … but the suited *Human* behind him grabbed him, lifting him off the ground.

Stephen shouted out, his legs buckling as he tried to run, but the large shifter held him tight.

Aiden's eyes glowed red—there was a loud yell, the man's skin searing under the heated grasp of Aiden's hands.

271

"No …." Stephen yelled as the *Human* drew out a blade and plunged it into Aiden's back and out of his midsection. The boy's eyes went wide, his eyes locked with Stephen's as the *Human* pulled the blade back out.

Helena raced down the steps. "Lee …." she screamed, her cries tearing through the air. She raced to Aiden, catching him as he fell.

"We have to go," the man said to Stephen, trying to pull him back to the car. Stephen pushed forward, but the man's hand on his chest stopped him. "You can't help him now," he gritted out.

"Let fucking go of me."

"No way in hell."

With a helpless roar, he stared as Helena cradled Aiden, falling to her knees with the child in her arms. Her agonised gaze met his, and Stephen glared at her. She had promised to keep the kids safe.

What an idiot he had been, trusting a fucking *Human*.

The man's eyes were filled with a fire of their own as he cradled his burnt arm, hatred blazing in their depths as they stayed glued on Stephen.

"Come on," the shifter yelled at Stephen as he and the woman shoved him backwards and bundled him into their car.

Chapter Thirty-Two
Helena

Helena scooped Aiden up and cradled him to her, stifling her sobs as she raced through the clinic with him. "Tracey," she yelled as she kicked the doors to the operating room open and placed him on her table, her heart torn in two. "I've got you, I've got you," she cried out in panic-stricken sobs, blinking away her tears. She was a doctor, for God's sake. She was supposed to be a professional and keep her cool, but right now, she was finding it completely impossible to do. "Trace, I need you."

Aiden shook in her arms, not making a sound. It was her own tears that wet his face, but it was his blood she was covered in—down her arms, her clothes, even on her face where she had held him close. "Hold on, Aiden."

Nick's shocked, distraught expression seared itself in Helena's mind ... the image of him as he watched Lee stab Aiden. She'd failed him—failed them both. She could hardly breathe or contain her weeping as she pulled back Aiden's clothing, cutting it away to get to his wound. Blood pooled under his body, running down the sides of his ribs. Her hands shook as she grabbed gauze and covered it. "I'm so sorry."

Tracey rushed in, eyes on Aiden. "Oh, God."

"Help me," Helena said in desperation.

Tracey threw her a pair of gloves and pulled her own on.

"Where are the others?"

"Eden has them. They're okay ... under Benny's."

Helena gave a relieved nod. *Just stay safe.* The hiding place that Helena had was an underground walkway with pockets to hide. It ran from under her house to under

273

Benny's. She had just been getting the others in there when Aiden had run out, and she hadn't been able to stop him. She should have been able to. She was the adult here. She was the one in charge …

But she got the little ones in the safe spot first and when she turned her back, Aiden was out of the door. *Stupid*. She was so fucking stupid.

Blood continued to seep out onto the blue parchment sheet under Aiden, soaking it. *Fuck*. Tracey had grabbed all the tools Helena would need and filled a tray with gauze and herbs to pack his wound.

"Stay with me," she demanded as Aiden's eyes drooped. She cupped his face, turning him to her, making him look her in the eyes. "Don't you dare close your eyes; do you hear me? Talk to me, Aiden. Tell me something." She wracked her brains for the things she would say to kids. It was easy when she was helping them, taking their minds off broken bones, cut knees. Nothing like this, though. "What's your favourite food, Aiden? What do you like to eat?" Her gaze flicked from his face to his wounds as she worked to pack them. Stop the bleeding first. That was the most important. "What do you eat?"

He didn't answer.

"*Aiden.*"

"T-toast," he stammered out, his jaw shaking as he shivered. "W-W-ith ch-cheese."

"Toast with cheese? I love toast with cheese."

Tracey smoothed a hand over his silky hair. "Maybe we can have some later," she smiled at him, and his eyes darted up to hers. "We'll make a big plate of it. We can all sit and eat it together. What do you say?"

He nodded weakly.

Exile

Helena took Aiden's small hand in hers, holding it still so she could insert a catheter. "Just a pinch." She pushed the needle in just as the door flew open, startling them.

Helena instinctively pressed a protective hand over Aiden as Lee charged in and stalked over to her. He grabbed her arm, digging his fingers in painfully, and yanked her to the other side of the room. Tracey stepped out of his way, her eyes wide, but her hand didn't leave Aiden's.

Lee's face blazed with anger as he fixed Helena with a glare. She scrambled to stay on her feet as he launched her against the counter. The edge slammed into her hip, and she bit down a yelp. He thrust his burnt arm at her. "Fix this first." His suit had been burned away, his skin red and blistered.

God, she hated him so much right this minute. She met his stare head-on. "I have to fix Aiden first. He …"

"No," he barked. "I am *Human*." His face was flushed with anger, his eyes wild. "*Humans* first."

She gritted her teeth. Fuck him. "The boy needs me. He'll not make it—" How dare he storm into her clinic like this … her *home*. "You can wait." She pushed to get past him, but he grabbed her and before she had time to voice any more protests, he jabbed her in the gut with a fist, sending her stumbling backwards and doubling over as all the breath was knocked from her in one swoop.

She staggered, trying to retain her balance, her vision waning. Wheezing, she tried to suck air back into her lungs.

His face was twisted with so much hate, so much anger. The charming, cordial façade he had been putting on for her had fallen away, and the real Lee was now showing his true colours. In a way, she was glad of the reminder of what he truly was. "The fucking kid waits or I end him myself right here, right *now*. Now deal with my god damn arm."

Mason Sabre

Helena met Tracey's frightened gaze, but Lee grabbed her jaw, yanking her head around so she had to look at him. "You kept him here, didn't you? A fucking convict," he spat. "All this time Nick Mason was here. How far have you gone to the other side, Helena? Now you harbour murderers in your clinic? You've made a mockery of me. You made a mockery of my name. Such a fool I am to think you were one of us. *Human* by nature, but you're just one of them."

Of course. It was all about Lee's pride being hurt.

"I didn't know who he was," she breathed, still winded from his painful blow. She felt a pang of guilt as she uttered the lie—like she was selling Nick out and saving her own skin. But she was trying to save Aiden.

"Ignorance is not an excuse," he snarled. Lee shot Aiden a hateful glance. "Fix my fucking arm before I get infected with his shit."

Helena didn't know how anyone could hate another in such a way, especially a child. It was beyond reason. Yet, seeing Aiden in the state he was in did nothing to Lee, made no pull on his conscience whatsoever. There was a frighteningly complete lack of compassion. Maybe Helena had given Lee too much credit. She threw Tracey a quick, pleading look to take care of Aiden as best as she could while she dealt with Lee, her heart breaking for the small boy who was being left to die. Tracey was a brilliant assistant, but she did not have the necessary skills needed to deal with this kind of wound.

Tracey gave her a reassuring nod behind Lee's back, and despite her fear for the child, the slightest flicker of hope ignited within her. She wiped away a stray tear from her eye and cleared her throat, glaring at Lee. "Let me take you to another room."

"No. We do it here."

Exile

"I have clean equipment there. This is compromised," she said quickly. She wanted him away from Aiden, but even more, she wanted herself away from Aiden and the temptation to help him and render them all dead. "I need to use sterilised tools."

Irritation flashed over his features. "Fine." He grabbed her arm, almost lifting her from the floor as he pushed her ahead of him. "We'll take this room," he said, choosing the one opposite—and the one that had the best view of the exit. "Do you know that … that *thing* you helped? He has kids with him. Innocent children. He has stolen them. It will be on your head if they die."

Helena clenched her jaw. He was lying. If he was concerned about the children, he would have known that Aiden was one of them. "He didn't have any children with him when he came."

"He's probably butchered them and left their bodies somewhere. He is a very dangerous man."

She nodded tightly, washing her hands at the sink, washing away Aiden's blood from her skin and trying her damned hardest to hold in the sob that had lodged itself in her throat.

The front door to the clinic opened, the door bouncing off the wall as one of Lee's men barged in with Eden in tow. "Sir, we found this outside." The man wore a Norton uniform and badge, sleek blue, and easily confused as a police officer—but more malicious.

"That's one of my patients," Helena said evenly as he shoved Eden into the room. She congratulated herself inwardly on how cool and composed she managed to sound. "She is resting … or *was*. I had stitched a gash up."

She felt Lee's assessing gaze on her as she carried on about her work calmly, setting his arm across a tray and cutting away bits of his sleeve that had fused with his skin where Aiden had burnt him. That gave her a little peace inside. At least Aiden had marked him.

Lee raised his head and pinned Eden with a cold stare. Guess he wasn't about to take Helena's word. "You were with Mason?"

"She was here before he arrived," Helena answered before Eden could drop herself in it, meeting her gaze briefly with a warning.

"I …" Eden frowned. "Who?"

Helena breathed a silent sigh of relief.

Lee narrowed his eyes at her. "What were you doing outside?" He didn't even flinch as Helena tweezed away the bits of charred flesh and fabric. Anyone would think she was working on a prosthetic the way he sat there unmoving.

"I was grabbing a smoke," she said, pulling a packet from her pocket with a guilty grin, feigning a smoker who had promised to give up and had now been caught red-handed. She nodded to Lee's arm. "I can heal that. I have potions and stuff. Make it so you can get on with your day."

Lee glowered at her. "Keep your filthy hocus-pocus shit away from me."

"Maybe she can help the boy," Helena said quickly.

Lee's lip quirked into an evil smile. "You think potions can fix that?" he sneered, and Helena thought she couldn't hate him more than she did right now. He watched her carry on tending to his arm for a moment then turned to the witch again.

She had to give Eden credit. No one would guess the panic and dread she must be feeling for the little boy in the other room as she stood there with an air of insouciance around her.

After a heart-stopping moment, Lee snorted. "Be my guest. *If* he is still alive."

Eden looked at her expectantly, and that's when Helena glimpsed the utter desperation and fear lurking beneath the calm exterior.

"He's in the other room," Helena said hastily. Witches could heal. They had to be strong to do it, but they could. Maybe Eden was strong enough—Helena prayed she was. Lee could scoff all he liked, but he didn't realise she was using her own potions, a mixture of herbs and distilled water to clean out the wound and prevent infection.

"You do know your little clinic is finished after this, don't you?" he sneered when Eden left the room.

Helena set her mouth in a firm line, refusing to give anything to him. She was not satisfying him with this shit. But he damn well wouldn't take her clinic from her. She'd see to that. She would run before that happened. She'd been in the Benjamin Norton clutches before and vowed he would never have that kind of hold on her again. She'd die first.

Another of Norton's men came in before Lee could say more. "We can't find them," he panted. "We searched everywhere. Neighbours said there were no kids with him."

Helena's worried heart jumped and dared to hope that everyone was covering for them—for *her*. They'd not be able to find them. They wouldn't even find the door—Xander had crafted an illusion, bending the air around it. So long as no one patted down the wall looking for a hidden way in, the door would stay invisible.

"They have to be somewhere." Lee twisted so he could face the man, but keep his arm where Helena could work on it. She was covering it in a cream—ironically, one that Eden had given to her. It worked better than so many *Human* concoctions she had to work with. "And Mason?"

The man shook his head, regret on his face. "Nothing."

"He'll be somewhere. Those kids will be somewhere. Have you searched every house?"

"Yes, sir."

Lee's lips pressed into a thin line. "Fine. Clear everyone out."

"What about you, Mr Norton?"

"I have my car. I'll meet you back at the block." The block, as Lee so nicely referred to it, was a square building built by someone who had totally lacked imagination—or who had thought something so bland was the new art.

The man nodded to Lee and threw a cursory glance over Helena before disappearing with the other guard.

Having soaked a piece of fabric in a mixture of Eden's cream and a solution of her own making, she covered Lee's wound and then placed a bandage over it. His arm would heal, maybe it would scar, but that was nothing compared to what he had done to Aiden. Lee flexed his hand and turned his arm over to examine it when she was done. "You know, when the demon dies, call me. We could do with his blood, too."

"He won't die," said Helena with determination. Not on her watch.

"Maybe," Lee said, standing and glaring down his nose at her. "If Mason comes back, I trust you to let me know. If you see the children, it will be in your own interest to tell me that, too. You do not understand what you're dealing with here, Helena." He bent down, palms on the table, and fixed her with a stare. "If you know where the children are, now would be a good time for you to tell me."

"I don't know what you're talking about," she said evenly, meeting his gaze and refusing to be intimidated.

Looking at her hard for another long moment, he eventually pushed himself up and stalked out. Helena couldn't get to the other room fast enough. Her heart squeezed painfully in her chest as she burst in and saw him lying there helpless with a tube down his throat, the rhythmic beeping of the machine a portentous sound in the room.

She walked to him on stiff legs, taking in every detail as she got closer. She had seen a hundred people like this, had treated adults and children alike in critical condition …

But this was different.

She leaned over Aiden, running a hand through his hair. "Oh, Aiden."

"I've got him packed up," Eden said. She was at the sink washing out small tubs and then placing them on the drainer.

Helena frowned. "What do you mean?"

"Have you ever cracked an egg into your car radiator when it has a leak?"

"No." Helena shook her head, frowning, trying to grasp onto the analogy and what it meant.

"I have," Tracey said. "When the radiator on a car fractures, you get it hot, and then you crack an egg inside it. The egg finds the holes and fills them. Fixes the radiator."

"Exactly," said Eden. She offered two tubs to Helena, one of them holding a jelly-like substance and the other a liquid. "This is what these both do. It will work on his body." She came to Aiden and peeled back the dressing on his wound. It had what seemed like a ball of glue balancing on top of it. Helena reached out to touch it, poking it with a finger. She was shocked to find that it was sleek, like varnish. Hard and smooth.

"That is what this is?"

281

Eden nodded. "It will work inside his body. It works its way in, forms tissue that will hold everything in place while his body fixes the tears. It stops the bleeding."

Helena pressed the surrounding skin. It was hard, like there was something inside there, just under his skin. "I feel there is a 'but' coming." There was something in the air that told her they were holding back.

Eden's eyes flicked to Tracey, who was standing at the head of the operating table where Aiden was lying.

"What is it?"

Eden rubbed at her arms as if she were cold then wrapped them around herself. The sight made Helena's stomach clench.

"Tell me."

Tracey tilted Aiden's head. They had put dressing over his ears. Helena didn't remember him being hurt there. "This," Tracey said, peeling one of them back. His ear was bleeding—just a small dribble. "Both of them. His nose and his eyes, too."

"We don't know what it is," Eden said softly. "I think he is ... Maybe this is how demons go?"

"No." Helena shook her head. She wouldn't allow that. "He can't die." She sucked in a quivering breath. "I was meant to be watching him. I was meant to keep him safe."

"There was no stopping Aiden," Eden said. "He wanted to get to Nick. He'd have burnt his way through the walls if he had to."

Helena watched Aiden, her lips parting to let out a shuddering breath. The slow beeping of the machine told them he was still alive—still in there. "Do you think Nick will come back for him?"

"Oh, I know he will," Eden replied. "He will come."

Chapter Thirty-Three
Stephen

Stephen let out an almighty roar, pulling against the bonds that held him in place. His fierce growl shook the ground around him.

"Let me the fuck up." He jerked at the belts strapped around his ankles and wrists. He bellowed when he realised some very brave bastard had strapped his head down. "I swear to fucking God ... let me up ... right now." He thrust every ounce of strength he had into pulling his arms free. That's all he needed. One arm. The bind dug into his flesh as he pulled and yanked, a barrage of cursing pouring from him with every tug. He slammed his head back the half an inch he could manage to move. "Get me off this fucking thing."

Panting, he blinked, trying to focus, but it didn't make a difference—the room was dark. Fucking pitch black. An infuriating *drip, drip, drip*, sounded close to his head, making him grit his teeth.

A door opened somewhere near the head of whatever he was strapped to, letting a slight breeze blow across his skin, cooling it and bringing out goose bumps. They clicked a switch and a light above Stephen flickered on, humming to life and breaking rudely through the darkness. Stephen clenched his eyes shut against the stinging brightness.

"You're awake," drawled a familiar voice. Stephen peered through half-closed lids, trying to clear the spots from his eyes as a man leaned over him.

"I am now. Get me off this bed." Stephen yanked again against the straps across his wrist. It wasn't silver, so it made no sense why he couldn't   break free. He frowned. "I know you?" he said when his vision cleared and he could see the man's face. "You … you hit me with your fucking car."

"That was an accident." The man shuffled so he was looking down at Stephen from a better angle.

"Great. Now let me up. I need to get back." The vision of Aiden slammed into Stephen's mind, and his stomach twisted at the memory of the fear in the boy's eyes. Fucking *Humans*. The arsehole who had stabbed him would wish he had never met Stephen Davies when he got hold of him. Stephen pulled again against what was holding his arms in place.

"We will …"

"*Now*."

Fuck, if he knew he wouldn't tear his shoulders in two, he would have shifted and got himself free.

"Hold still." The voice belonged to the woman from the car. She pulled at the tape above Stephen's head. Ripping it back, tearing a sudden pain into his skin.

"Let me up," he growled. "I need to get to the boy."

"You can't go back there."

"Like fuck I can't." The woman came to stand on the other side and Stephen twisted his head to look at her— blonde, older, pretty. He had seen her before—not just when they had hit him with the damn car. "Who are you?"

"My name is Mel. This is Nigel … I'm sorry about the car. We didn't mean to hit you. We needed to get you out of there."

The clinic … yes, that's where he had seen her.

Stephen didn't give a shit about these people— whoever they were. He just needed to get back to Aiden. He lowered his tone, holding back the fury that burned inside him and trying for a calmer demeanour. "Look, I really need to get back to the boy."

284

Exile

"The boy is fine," Mel said. "He is with the doctor."

Stephen clenched his teeth. *Yeah, fat lot of good that did him last time*.

"You need to trust us. We're trying to help you."

"If you were trying to help me, you wouldn't have me tied to this damn bed. I need to get back. The *Humans* will find the kids."

"The *Humans* are all gone," said Mel.

"Gone?" Just like that? Stephen didn't believe it. Back home, the *Humans* wouldn't have simply *gone*. No, they'd have fucking waited. But then maybe they were smarter *Humans*. "If they are gone, then I can get back to the boy."

"Not yet," Nigel said.

Stephen bit back a curse. They were shifters themselves, for God's sake. They must be able to understand the need to protect the young ... "Are you going to at least let me up? Why am I even tied down?"

"Because you tried to rip shit out of us both," Mel said, "and we needed to help you." She fiddled with the binds around his wrist, and a moment later, his arm was free. Nigel stepped back, watchful, arms across his chest. "You lost your top, and your jeans were pretty torn up. We thought you might have wanted fresh clothes," she said as she went around the other side of him to free that hand too.

Stephen rubbed at his wrists as he sat up, and Mel's gaze raked over the intricate tattoo on his arm—it always drew people's attention. He leaned over to unfasten his ankles himself. "Where the hell am I?"

The room was dismal, no windows, the light over him the only bright thing in there. The walls were grey, peeling with age and neglect. Cabinets covered the side, caked with a thick layer of dust.

"Norton's men want you. Why?" There was no beating around the bush with Nigel—succinct and straightforward, he said exactly what was on his mind. It was a trait deeply ingrained in Stephen, and one he appreciated in other men as well.

"Does it matter?" Stephen jumped off the table, landing on shaky legs. "How long have I been out of it?"

As he grabbed the clean shirt Mel gave him and pulled it over his head, he glimpsed his reflection in a mirror over what he assumed had once been a sink.

He looked like shit.

"Quite a while," Mel said. "Your face is on every poster, every wall and lamppost this side of Exile."

Stephen shrugged. "Maybe I am just photogenic. How far away are we from the clinic?"

"Norton is after you," Nigel pushed, and Stephen weighed him up. He smelt of snow leopard, but not part of a pack. There was that musty smell that came from living away from his own kind. He was taller than Stephen, surprisingly—not many men were—thinner though. He could take him.

"Probably my endearing personality," Stephen ground out, tired of this. "I need to get to the clinic. I need to get to Aiden. You both either need to take me there or move out of my way."

"Norton has a price on your head."

Stephen sighed inwardly and crossed his arms across his chest. There were two doors he could see ... the one they had come through and another one that was nothing more than wood. That would be the one he would use. "You want to turn me in? That is what this is about?"

"Norton has our friend's kid brother." There was sadness in Mel's eyes as she spoke.

286

"You want to swap me for him?" Stephen snorted. "If that's your idea, you're a pair of idiots."

"Xander, our friend, you saw him at the clinic." When Stephen gave no sign of recognition, he added, "He has an eye missing."

It vaguely rang a bell. "So?"

"He is wanted by Norton, too. He has a price on his head."

"Well, aren't we the band of merry men," Stephen drawled. "And you thought maybe you could exchange me for what? Them to lift it? Give his brother back?"

"You're the one," Nigel said. "We aren't turning you in, but we need your help."

Stephen rubbed a hand over his stubbled chin. "Look, you've got the wrong man. I need to get to the clinic, and you are both wasting my time. Will you show me, or do I go myself? Either way, I am leaving."

***

The *Humans* had left. Mel and Nigel had been telling the truth about that, at least, although Stephen wasn't sure about everything else ... The whole story about their friend and his brother—something just wasn't sitting right. And one thing he knew for sure was that what his gut told him was usually right.

Nigel pulled the car to a stop just before they reached the town. It would be too risky to be that close. They walked the short way to the gates, keeping themselves out of sight and off the road. Not that anyone came this way. They stopped when Fortvania came into view, its tall stone walls wedged oddly in the middle of nowhere, sticking out like an ugly sore. Stephen watched from a concealed spot. There were two *Humans* on the gate, both armed with what seemed to be rifles. They each held a short piece on their hip, trying to appear bad-ass, but the way one of them hugged his gun like a fucking security blanket told him they were anything but that.

Stephen slipped around the side of the main wall. The advantage of a gated community like this was that it had walls—and he had claws …

If the *Humans* had any sense, they would look higher to find him. But they thought of shifters as *Human* with a deformity, rather than people with abilities.

Stephen climbed over one wall, the same way he had done before to get to Helena's clinic. Really, they needed to just give him his own key. It was that fucking easy to get in. Even the guards on the gate … what was the point in them? They had them there to secure the place in case Stephen came back, as if they expected him to just try to walk through the gates.

The back door to the clinic was unlocked—again. Stephen gritted his teeth. Helena had no idea about security … and he'd blindly trusted her with the children's lives.

But as he slipped into Helena's silent living quarters, he realised perhaps this was on purpose. She would have known he would come back. She had to know. Maybe she wasn't just a pretty face, after all.

Nigel and Mel crept in behind Stephen. He focused on his surroundings—machines … the buzz of the electronics. He could sense the essence of life, but he couldn't hear anyone. No noise like one would expect in a medical centre.

The door that led into the clinic itself opened, and Helena stood there, Nakita in her arms. Her eyes locked with his, and despite his anger at her, his heart skipped a beat at the sight of her.

Before he could say anything, Nakita spotted him, her eyes going wide with delight. "Daddy," she shouted, wriggling free of Helena's hold and racing over. He frowned but didn't correct her. Maybe she was missing her real daddy and had the need to pretend. Little kids loved to play make-believe.

It might also be for the best if Helena believed these were his children. Maybe thinking he had a family made her stay away from him and made things easier for him.

"Aiden's sick," Nakita announced matter-of-factly as she held up her arms to him. He picked her up without hesitation, plonking her on his hip. Her little legs wrapped around his waist, her head coming to rest on his shoulder, bringing with it an instant calm as she connected with him on the level that only shifters could. Breathing in the shifter scent, he selfishly let his *tiger* take comfort in the shifter that would one day emerge in her. Only a true shifter could really give that kind of comfort. That was why they lived in packs. They needed the connection—even the ones who were solitary animals. Mixed with man, the shifter craved a slice of home.

As Nakita locked her arms around his neck, he instinctively ran a hand up her back, soothing her, but his eyes remained on Helena. Her face was red, the rims of her eyes tinged dark pink—she had been crying. She pressed her lips together as if keeping in what she wanted to say.

But the expression on her was what tore him to the core. He knew it well ... He'd worn it himself so many fucking times. It was the expression one saw in war—the one that said you were about to hear the worst news.

He inhaled deeply and squared his shoulders. "Is he ...?"

"Not yet," she whispered. "But there is nothing more I can do." She hugged herself, rubbing her arms as if she were cold. "I'm so sorry."

He tightened his hold on Nakita, closing his eyes briefly and then pinning her with a hard stare. "You promised to protect them."

Her bottom lip trembled and a tear rolled down her cheek. "Oh God, I'm so sorry ... I-I couldn't stop him. He—" Her voice hitched and she stopped.

He clenched his jaw, hating himself for the intense need inside to go to her and comfort her. He wanted to stay angry at her, to hate her.

She had betrayed his trust.

God damn it, she was *Human*—the enemy.

Hardening himself to her hurt, he finally grated, "Can I see him?"

Helena nodded quickly and swiped away at a tear. "Of course." She held out her arms and stepped closer. "I'll take Nakita for you."

The overwhelming urge to say no to her had him rooted to the spot. He made no move to pass Nakita over, and Helena's arms slowly withdrew, hurt flashing in her eyes. She knew what he was thinking. He didn't trust her with the child.

But then, it would not be good for Nakita to see or remember Aiden like this.

With great reluctance, he stepped closer and leaned down to hand the child over. But when Helena's arm touched his chest as she slid her arms around Nikita's waist, he froze. She might as well have branded him with a hot iron, the impact was so devastating. His instincts took over and he bent toward her, brushing his cheek gently against hers.

She sucked in a sharp breath and turned her head in surprise, her breath dancing across his lips.

Human.

Exile

Wake up, he scolded himself, snapping out of his sudden stupor before it took him for another ride.

He pulled back, mentally and physically. He had to fight with everything he had not to fall into this … this … whatever the hell it was. Damn his fucking *tiger* and its one-track mind. Helena was *Human*.

As if sensing Stephen's mental fight, Helena stepped away from him, creating a distance big enough that Stephen could think a little clearer. "Aiden is just in the room opposite the reception."

***

Stephen cracked open the door to Aiden's room, unsure what to expect, but fearing the worst. Freya was sitting with him, her dainty form resting on a stool beside the bed. For the first time, she looked caring. Aiden was lying on the bed, a sheet draped over him, and she was mopping a wet cloth across his face. He had wires coming from so many places, hooked up to a machine, and a tube down his throat.

Fucking Norton.

Stephen's chest tightened at the sight, his fury rising in both man and *tiger.* He made a promise to himself at that moment that he would find Lee Norton if it was the last thing he ever did. He'd make him pay. He'd give him so much fucking pain he would beg to die.

Blood trickled from Aiden's nose, and Freya immediately wiped it away with an already red-stained cloth. "He keeps bleeding," she said in a quiet voice. "We can't make it stop. I don't even know what it is."

"What about where Lee got him?" Stephen laid a gentle hand across Aiden's stomach, just under where the dressing was taped down. The dressing looked clean, white still, the blood not having soaked through yet. Had Helena managed to stop the bleeding?

"Eden patched him up."

The machine next to Stephen gave a louder bleep, faster. Aiden moved his head, trying to speak but hindered by the pipe in his throat. He raised his hand to pull at it.

"Just a second," Stephen said, shoving a hand under Aiden's chin and pushing his head back to peel away the tape that held the tube in Aiden's mouth. The boy's eyes fluttered open, and Stephen carefully pulled the pipe out. "Don't try to talk."

Aiden lifted his hand toward him, and Stephen grabbed it. Careful not to dislodge the catheter in his skin, he stared down at their joined hands. Small, delicate fingers in such a large hand ...

"I'll leave you in peace." Freya placed the bloodied cloth onto the side with three others. "Shout if you need anything."

"I'm sorry," Aiden said. "I—"

"It's okay," Stephen smiled. Blood spilled from the corner of Aiden's mouth, and Stephen grabbed a fresh cloth from the pile Freya had been using to wipe away the slow dribble.

Helena came in soon after had Freya left the room, and Stephen tensed. "Nakita—"

"Don't worry," she reassured him. "Freya has her." Going to stand on the other side of Aiden, she did a quick check of his vitals. Stephen tried his damndest not to stare at the perfect perfection of her face as she focused on her task. "We don't know what the bleeding is," she murmured, her brow furrowed. "I can't find a reason for it."

Stephen knew. He had seen it before. Not with demons, though, but with creatures of the underworld— they tended to bleed until they were dead. Like their body had to die to release the soul that was encapsulated inside it.

Exile

There was no way to stop this.

Warm, honey-coloured eyes lifted to his. "Do you need me to call someone? His mother?"

"No." She obviously assumed that Stephen was the father. And even as she stood there waiting for him to say more, he didn't correct her. It felt too odd, too cruel, to say otherwise. Like saying Aiden wasn't good enough to be his son. But Stephen also didn't understand why there was no mother or father. Why a child had been left here, in such a strange place, surrounded by even stranger people, to take his last breath alone.

Each time Aiden blinked, it was long and slow, but his eyes stayed firmly fixed on Stephen. He wondered if the boy had any idea what was happening—if he knew this was it. Stephen wiped away more blood, this time from the corner of his eyes. He coughed, and his entire little body shook. A rasp came from him as he opened his mouth to speak, but all he managed was to splutter out more blood. He whispered something, but even with Stephen's hearing, he couldn't make out what it was. "Shh," Stephen said. "Don't try to talk."

Helena stepped back discreetly, giving them some space to talk.

"I c-came for you," Aiden said eventually, his words weak. "Re-Remember ... don't open the do—" His words were cut off as another series of coughs wracked his small frame.

Helena quickly handed Stephen a glass with a straw, and he put it to Aiden's dry, cracked lips. "I'm right here, buddy."

"D-Don't open t-the door ... Please ..." The words were forced out, his face scrunching up through the pain in his chest, his eyes pleading. "Don't ... open the door ..."

Stephen frowned. *Don't open the door?* What was he talking about? Maybe it was the delirium talking …

Not wanting to upset him, though, he murmured, "I won't."

Aiden nodded weakly, then closed his eyes before making a frustrated sound deep in his throat. "The house—"

Stephen's brows knitted together. "Where we just were?"

"No …" Aiden swallowed and licked his lips, and Stephen offered him some more water. "The house."

"The house?"

"Yes." He sucked in a wheezing breath. "Come and g-get me … like you always do. You told me … to tell you … I didn't forget … just like I promised …" His little hand gripped Stephen's harder. "Not even now … I told you like I said I would—"

Helena reached a hand out towards Stephen then seemed to regret it, letting it fall back to her side. "He has had a lot of medication," she said softly.

He gave a curt nod. He got it. It was probably making Aiden talk garbage. But he was saying it with such conviction that Stephen wasn't so sure that it was all rubbish.

His eyes were now a mixture of blood and tears, his face twisting with the pain. "I promised … you told me to …"

"Aiden—"

"Promise," he panted. "Promise you come to find me … like you said …"

"Shh, just rest now—"

"Promise …" he said more forcefully, his eyes fighting to roll back. "*Please.*"

Stephen pressed Aiden's hand to his lips, uncaring now about the catheter there. "I promise. Okay?"

His breaths laboured, Aiden nodded, relieved. "Okay …"

He let his eyes close.

Stephen held his breath, watching, waiting, listening to the beep of the machine. Aiden lay still, his face peaceful, his chest moving slowly. He sat down on the side of the bed, his chest torn in two. If he could make him live by will alone, he fucking would have. Moving carefully, he lay down next to Aiden, his big body making the child's seem even more frail and small.

Helena came closer, and after a moment's hesitation, he felt a soft hand on his shoulder. He would normally have shaken her off, but he welcomed the touch of her. It comforted him.

He closed his eyes …

Chapter Thirty-Four
Stephen

Stephen knew he was dreaming the moment his eyes opened and he found himself standing in the middle of the room. There was something in the way the air moved around him—or rather, didn't, as was the case—that let him know he was in a different place. Not that this was dreaming exactly, or even that he was asleep, but it was hard to describe any other way. How did he explain being in a place that seemed liked another dimension while retaining the ability to think and not be at the mercy of his subconscious?

A sudden shiver ran up his spine, and he tensed. "I know you're there," he rasped. He could feel her behind him. Helena—the shadow of his waking nightmares on this magical mystery tour that was fast becoming his life. He wasn't sure he could face her. Not in any calm manner.

His mind replayed the scene of Aiden getting stabbed, stuck on a loop, and always ending with Helena's eyes …

She had failed him.

It took a moment to realise Aiden was no longer lying on the bed. The machines lay silent, just a decoration of this alternate world. He placed his palms down on the bed, feeling the emptiness that lay there instead of the child he had come to know.

"He's outside," Helena said softly. "You should go to him."

He didn't want to go. He didn't want to do any of this. "Why?" His voice was a hoarse whisper.

"Because you need to."

"Because it is my job?" he sneered.

Exile

There was a pause, then, "Because he is waiting for you."

A heavy dread settled in the pit of his stomach. He thought about all the times they had lost children in wars. The younger the victim, the harder it was to accept the loss. He had failed Aiden, too. He'd been seconds away from him and not been able to save him.

Stephen smoothed his hands across the flatness of the bed, delaying going outside. He knew what awaited him there—*who* awaited him—and he knew what he had to do. But he damn sure didn't want to do it.

He let his eyes close for just a moment. Why couldn't God give this burden to someone else? Not to someone who had sworn his life to protecting others.

"Nick." She laid a gentle hand on his back.

He stiffened then swung around to face her. "Why is this my bloody job? Why do I have to do this and not someone else?"

Sorrow crossed her beautiful features. "Because it is meant."

Stephen let out a derisive laugh. It seemed to be the mantra of the new world. "And you? Are you *meant*?" he said through clenched teeth. "What *are* you?"

"I'm here to help," she said quietly, then turned and walked out of the room.

***

Stephen found Aiden sitting at the bottom of the garden. It dawned on him that this wasn't the same garden as outside the clinic; not that he had paid much attention to it, but this was certainly different—a long stretch of grass, flowerbeds to the side of the large, dark red panels. The grass stretched out farther than he could see, and though he knew what this was, it didn't make it any easier. Actually, this being Aiden, it probably made it harder.

He hesitated before moving, staring down at the boy. This wasn't like Sarah or Anya; it felt different. Not just because it was Aiden, but that there was something else. Something he couldn't quite put his finger on. But somehow, he knew that, after this, lots of things would be different.

Loath to approach him, Stephen stood there stiffly, wanting to keep Aiden there for just a bit longer. Maybe it was selfish, but he wasn't ready to let him go yet. He knew it didn't make sense ... he didn't know this boy, didn't owe him a damn thing. Yet, for the sorrow he felt in that moment, he might as well have been losing a close family member. It wasn't right that the light of a child, whose life had barely begun, was being snuffed out so soon. This was wrong ... so very fucking wrong.

Aiden watched Stephen, his young eyes seeming old and wise despite his age. Sucking in a deep breath, he took heavy steps towards him, his mind screaming at him to turn back, but his heart knowing he had to do this. He'd end up leaving Aiden stuck between worlds, and that would be much worse than anything any *Human* could ever do.

"I'm not sorry for what I chose," Aiden said as Stephen reached him, his head craning up at his towering frame. "I will make the same choice every single time."

Stephen stared down at the boy, his own sorrow threatening to crush his heart. Even now, Aiden's words made no sense to him. "I don't know what you're talking about."

Aiden nodded lightly, a contented smile on his face, and got up to sit on a bench that was suddenly behind him— Stephen didn't remember that being there just a minute before.

He struggled to find the right words, but he felt that anything he said would be useless. But he needed to say something. He needed to find a way to lift the heavy weight from his shoulders.

"Remember to teach me Trentwich," Aiden said suddenly, bright eyes staring up at him. "Promise me."

Stephen knelt down on one knee, the way one might do to honour another. He honoured Aiden. "Trentwich," he repeated, testing the odd word on his tongue.

Aiden's eyes brimmed with sincerity. "When you see me ... teach it to me."

"I don't understand," Stephen whispered, wanting to promise the boy what he wanted but not having a bloody clue what it all meant. "What is Trentwich?" He'd never even heard the word before, much less knew what it was or even how he was to teach it to anyone.

Aiden shifted closer on the seat, letting his feet sit flat on the ground. His form was more solid than Sarah's had been, his demeanour stronger than Anya's. "Just teach it to me."

Stephen sighed heavily. "Aiden—"

He pushed forward on the bench, shoulders bunched. "You have to find me and tell it to me. You promised." Aiden's voice filled with the urgency of a frantic child. "You have to. You have to say it to me."

Shit, what did it matter to promise him what he wanted to hear? He'd leave this world happy. "Okay," he quietened him. "When do I say it?"

His face lit up. "When you find me ..." The statement was made so simply, so matter-of-factly, that he wondered if the boy comprehended exactly what was going on here. Did he realise he had just died? That they would never be seeing each other again?

"You promise me?" The innocence in that vivid green gaze made Stephen's breath catch. It was an innocence that was so trusting. He had trusted them all to keep him alive.

The image of Lee in Stephen's mind brought with it a fresh wave of anger. He balled his fists at his side, dreaming once again about how much he was going to make him pay for this. "Okay," Stephen said after a pause. He stared at his hand resting on the bench next to Aiden, not wanting to touch him yet and send him to wherever it was they went. He looked back up at him with a smile. "When I find you, I will say it. Okay?"

Aiden nodded with an answering smile and reached out to press a small, hot hand against Stephen's stubbled cheek. He comforted him in a way an adult should with a child, not the other way around. "And don't open the door ..."

"I won't open the door," Stephen repeated, feeling like a fraud, making promises he did not understand and had no way of keeping.

Aiden sighed and gazed out towards the end of the garden ... out into the long path of nothingness. "I have to go now," he said. "And you have to go back."

A tight fist squeezed his heart. He didn't fucking want to do this. He gripped the edge of the bench, the wood threatening to give way under his hold. He wasn't sure how much more loss his heart could take. How much more pain at seeing those too young be taken to the other side like this. He bowed his head and rubbed a hand across his forehead.

The light touch of a hand on his back made Stephen jump. Aiden stood at his side now. He hadn't even realised he had moved.

"I'm not sorry, okay? I'd pick you again. When you are sad, remember that."

Exile

Before Stephen could respond in any way to the obscure words, Aiden threw his arms around his neck and hugged him tight, burying his face in Stephen's shoulder.

Something inside of him broke, and he wrapped big arms around the child, holding him in a strong embrace.

"You're the best father I could have asked for."

The muffled words tore at him. Just like Nakita, he thought sadly, Aiden, too, had had the need for a father. He briefly wondered what kind of unfeeling bastard had abandoned his children this way.

Well, if he wanted to pretend that Stephen had been his father, then so be it. He'd consider himself lucky to have a son as brave as Aiden one day.

Aiden lifted his head. "I have to go now." He smiled as Stephen continued to hold on tight. "You have to let me go."

"I know," he murmured, making no effort to relinquish his hold on him. His heart filled with a heaviness that threatened to drag him down. In moments like these, he couldn't understand why the world was so fucking ugly. Why everyone had to hurt each other.

He was going to fucking crush Lee Norton. He'd pay for this.

"I don't regret it," Aiden said as if he could hear what Stephen was thinking. "I did it for you." He gave him one last hug.

Grief settled deep within him, not just for Aiden, but for all of it. The grief for his father, for his old life, for his sister and his friend, for the baby that no one knew existed. He ached for it all, so much in his chest that he wasn't sure he could hold it in much longer.

"I love you, Stephen," Aiden whispered. "Thank you."

***

When Stephen opened his eyes again, he found himself lying on the bed once more, his head on the pillow, and Aiden's limp hand in his. His face was damp, but as his mind jolted back to the present, he forced himself to clamp everything shut inside and pull every ounce of pain back into himself.

Helena was sitting in a chair on the opposite side of the bed, her own face damp with her tears. He pushed himself off the bed and fixed her with a cold glare. With slow movements, she reached up and turned the machine off, silencing the single dull tone that rang out. Her eyes met his again. "I'm sorry," she whispered, her voice cracking. "I didn't mean—"

He didn't want to hear it. He didn't want to hear the hurt in her voice because it pulled at him. It yanked at his fucking idiot *tiger* who wanted to seek comfort and offer it all at the same time.

But this was all on her. Aiden was dead because of her.

"Don't," he grated. "Just don't."

She nodded tearfully and swallowed. "Do you need me to call someone?"

He gritted his teeth. "There is no one." He pierced her with his stare, his accusations unspoken but heavy in the air. He used them like armour … a big fucking metal shutter he used to slam down in his mind and keep Helena out.

He had trusted a *Human*. Fucking idiot.

With a violent curse, he shoved back the chair next to him, the metal legs scraping along the floor with a loud screech. Helena cringed, her lip quivering as she watched him stalk out of the room.

Stephen ran out of the clinic and down into the main street. Fuck if the *Humans* saw him. He'd fucking show

302

them–he'd deal back what they had done to Aiden tenfold. They'd pay. All of them.

The road was empty, though. All the bloody cowardly *Others* hiding in their homes. They let these monsters ransack the place because of fear.

It was time to get rid of that fear.

It was time to show the *Humans* just exactly what they were dealing with.

Stephen refused to ever take it from them again. It was their time now.

No more.

He charged over to the monument in the centre of the town and sank to his knees in front of it. All towns had one of these, even back home—a large monument with the names of *Humans* on them. *Humans* who had fought and killed *Others*. This represented death to his kind … a list of murderers, not heroes.

He grabbed one of the rocks from the large pile at its base and smashed it against the stone, against the plaque welded to it. It didn't belong there. It mocked *Others* every single day.

He slammed the rock into it over and over again, rupturing the corner. Ripping it from the statue, he twisted it in his hands with hatred.

It ended now.

"Nick—"

Stephen ignored Nigel, who had coming running up to him. He bent the plaque one way and then the other, determined to snap the damn thing in half.

"Nick, you need to stop—"

Sweat ran down Stephen's temples. He'd stop when the fucking thing had completely broken. "Why?" Stephen snarled just as Mel and Xander joined Nigel. "Because the

Humans say we can't? Because we are cowards?" He waved the deformed plaque at the three of them. "Why do these names deserve to be on here? Why do we honour these people? If they were here, you would all be dead. *We* would all be dead."

"We know you're upset—" Mel started.

"*Upset*?" He let out a bark of laughter. "Of course I'm upset. A fucking child just died, and we stood around like cowards." Leaping to his feet, he came to stand face to face with Nigel. "You ran," he growled. "Both of you."

A small group formed around Stephen as Freya, Helena and Eden came running. He avoided looking at Helena, not wanting the turmoil she tended to evoke in him clouding his mind at that moment.

"You bring war upon us," Xander said, leaning on a crutch as he squinted through what was left of his better eye.

"War is already upon us," Stephen shot back. "We have always surrendered. How much more do we let them take before we say it is enough?" He glared at them. "I say it is enough." The plaque snapped in his hand, creating a sharp edge to it where the metal had bent in the middle. He tossed one half at Nigel's feet. "You want help with your friend's brother? Then stop being such a coward." He turned back to the monument, where the plaque had just been, and used the edge of the metal to carve into the stone. He wrote Aiden first, then Sarah, then Anya. All three of them deserved this spot. All three of them deserved to be honoured and remembered.

When he was done, he pushed through the small group and stormed back to the clinic. Eyes watched him. He could feel them as they peered at him from behind closed doors and windows. More cowards. More *Others* that lay down to take the shit that *Humans* laid on them.

But it was enough.

He would see to Aiden first. He would find the burning stone and do it himself. Even in death, *Others* were robbed of their rights. Their bodies had to be burned because *Humans* worried that *Others* could come back. Aiden would have the right send off. He'd see to it himself.

He shoved the door to the clinic open and was greeted by Nakita and Toke hovering around Helena's assistant. Nakita's eyes lit up as usual, a wide, childish grin spreading across her face as she raced to him. "Daddy," she squealed, but he was in no mood for it now.

"I'm not your daddy," he snarled at her, grabbing her little shoulders and stopping her. "Stop calling me that."

Her bottom lip quivered, hurt filling her young green eyes … but also defiance. "You're my daddy," she shouted at him.

"No, I'm not. You are not my daughter, and I'm not your daddy. Now back off, kid." He moved her to the side firmly, ignoring the guilt that lanced through him at her crestfallen expression. He watched her run to Freya, who had followed him back to the clinic and was watching them from the doorway.

She picked up the tearful Nakita and met Stephen's gaze. "Actually, Nick, she is."

Stephen blinked, not sure at first if he had heard her right. "I do not have children." Were they all crazy around here? "I sure as hell would know if I had had any." *Wouldn't I?* he thought to himself desperately. Was it possible he had got some woman pregnant, and the kids had somehow ended up in Exile? He had always been so damn careful to use protection ... for this exact reason.

Toke sidled up to Freya, staring at him with wide, frightened eyes. As he stared back at him, then Nakita, he realised how similar both their green eyes were to his. How much they both looked like him, in fact.

Stephen's heart pounded with unbelievable fury. Why right now? With all this fucking shit. With Aiden dying. He was so sick of all these bloody games.

The scent of *tiger* was suddenly so strong in the air … and so familiar. His *tiger* lurched as Stephen breathed in deep, sensing its own kin and pack.

"No," he grated, shaking his head and backing away. It was all crap. They were fucking with his mind again.

These were not his children.

It was too impossible.

Chapter Thirty-Five
Stephen

Stephen didn't think as he stormed out of the clinic, the onslaught of confusion and frustration battering his brain. All the fucking shit and games. This was low, even for Freya …

And he wasn't about to stand there and listen to it.

What was she trying to do? Hoping that he would fall to his knees and take those children as his own? Be the father they were obviously so very much yearning for? God, she couldn't have chosen a worst candidate for the job anyway. If there was one thing that Stephen was not, it was father material.

The man at the gate spotted him as he approached. He stepped out of his little box as if planning to stop him. Stephen almost wished it. It would be someone to unleash his pent-up emotions on. But the man took one long look at Stephen and stepped back inside his box, fumbling for the button that opened the gate.

As Stephen strode out, then fell into a jog, a security guard, who must have been patrolling the area, emerged from around the side. The man stopped, startled, then shouted, "Stop!"

Stephen didn't give him any acknowledgement, continuing blindly down the path. The *Human* spoke into a radio, the crackle of it soon fading out behind Stephen.

By the time anyone came, Stephen would be long gone.

His chest ached as he ran, his skin burning with fury. He ran along the road until he realised that it opened to a wider space. But he wanted confinement and quiet. He wanted to get away from all of them. But most of all, he wanted to make sure that Freya wouldn't find him.

The dense trees along the road created a thick shade, offering peace that Stephen welcomed. Twigs and debris cracked under his feet as he turned off the road and headed into the heart of the woods. The scent of salt was in the air, thick and clean. There was water close by. Stephen sucked in a great refreshing lungful as his pace slowed.

He came to a stop when he reached what had once been a wall—now nothing more than tumbling rubble. He had no idea how long he had been running for, but there was a satisfying ache in his muscles that managed to ease his mind a little and silenced the rage inside. Rolling his shoulders, he arched his back, trying to relieve the tension there. He ran his hands over his face, trying to dispel the faces that swam in front of him as his mind tried to piece together the last few hours—from Aiden to Nakita's unnervingly familiar green eyes.

They were not his children.

Stephen's hands shook as he turned and leaned against the wall. Nothing made sense ever since the moment he had got onto that damn bus. He grabbed a rock from the broken wall and launched it toward what seemed like a now dilapidated house. The old building was abandoned, its dark stone weathered and grey. Ivy grew up the sides, poking in between the stones—Mother Nature claiming it as hers.

As he stood there, trying to get his mind around things, he dimly realised that this wasn't just a house. There was another behind it and another to the side of that—this looked like it had once been a town. He frowned and let his mind take a moment from the madness of everything to step over the wall and into the overgrown garden.

A distant rustle brought him to an abrupt halt. He

froze, focusing his hearing as his eyes scanned the area. He caught the scent of *Human* in the air, distant yet discernible.

He hunkered down, placing himself behind the tallest part of the broken wall. The *Human* had either followed Stephen, or he was just damn unlucky.

Run away, little bastard. Fucking run. Stephen's nostrils flared, adrenaline pumping through him with the anticipation. His teeth lowered, man and *tiger* occupying the same space.

He was in no mood to face a *Human*, much less in a mood to grant them mercy if they got too close. If he was seen, he knew they would scream and try alert anyone near that there was an *Other* hiding in the woods—but they wouldn't scream for long.

He flexed his fingers out in the dirt, ready to pounce.

The scent grew stronger, thicker. Stephen pressed close to the ground, slinking sideways. His *tiger* was eager, pushing to break free, his fur just under the skin. Stephen's nostrils flared, and he sucked in a satisfying breath of the scent of *Human*.

His target was coming in at the opposite side, and although Stephen didn't know the area, he had a good idea of how it went. This was why he had been one of his father's best fighters—he was a quick thinker. He could make decisions, plans, without seeing what was ahead of him.

The *Human* came into view, his grey pants muddied at the bottom, his once shiny shoes now scuffed and dirty.

Stephen froze.

He had seen those shoes before.

Could he be so fucking lucky?

Lee Norton—the goddamn one and only—was being handed to him on a fucking platter … the finest steak a man could serve.

Oh, thank you God.

Stephen pushed down his fury and the primal urge to attack and tear the bastard to pieces. His *tiger* knew how to deal with targeted prey. The man in him knew how to deal vengeance.

Grabbing a small stone, he threw it in the direction he had come from. It echoed as it bounced on the ground, hitting against the solid mass of a tree. Lee spun around, bracing himself, a gun in one gloved hand. Stephen could almost hear Lee's heart racing.

He launched himself into the air, a growl tearing from his throat as he directed himself towards the merciless *Human*. Lee whirled around, his gun aimed in Stephen's direction.

Stephen twisted as he fired, rolling his shoulder back, but the bullet caught him just across the top. Lee stepped back and cocked the gun again …

It would take more than a fucking gun and silver to stop Stephen Davies. He lunged for Lee as he went to take aim once again, but Stephen was on him in a heartbeat. His balled fist landed in Lee's gut, bringing a satisfying *umph* from his lips and sending him flailing backwards.

Without shifting, he strode toward him, his gait purposeful. No claws, no *tiger*—this was the time for fists. A way to feel the rage surge through his body. He wanted to feel every fucking bone in Lee Norton's body snap one by one, and he would do it with his bare hands.

"You're one fucking stupid *Human*," Stephen snarled, grabbing him by the shirt.

Lee swung a fist at Stephen, smashing it into his temple and making him drop him. Lee scrambled on his knees to where he had dropped his gun. He was strong—stronger than any *Human* Stephen had come across. It was almost like he possessed the power of the *Others* without actually being *Other*.

"Oh no, you fucking don't." Stephen kicked the gun away and then grabbed handfuls of Lee's blond hair, pulling his head back and making Lee look up at him.

He curled his lip at Stephen, nothing but pure hate in his sadistic eyes. He spat at Stephen, blood mixed with saliva. "Do you really think you can beat your way out of this? My men will be here soon."

Stephen pushed his face into Lee's. "Well, we can have fun before they arrive, can't we?"

Unexpected pain exploded in Stephen's side and he arched his back, roaring as fire seeped into his skin. He tossed Lee away and clutched at his side. The piece of shit had stuck a knife into Stephen's side. Gritting his teeth, he pulled the blade out, growling in agony as his hands touched silver. He forced himself to grip it, defying the pain he was feeling. "Is this all you have?" he snorted. "Your pathetic kind need weapons for control, but you're going to need more than this after what you did."

Lee righted himself and wiped the blood from his mouth. "I did nothing," he said, pulling his jacket off and tossing it to the side.

"You killed a child today."

"That was not a child," Lee snarled. "He was a demon." His words dripped with nothing but hatred. "Another one less in the world, the better."

"He was a kid." Stephen grabbed Lee by the collar, but he twisted and jammed his gloved hand into Stephen's side where he had caught him. He dug his thumb in, silver on silver, bringing another growl from Stephen.

Eyes blazing, he backhanded Lee across the face, sending blood and spit flying. As he was knocked back, he

Mason Sabre

spat out the fragments of what had been a tooth.

"You killed a kid," Stephen roared again, advancing yet again.

Lee scurried backwards, pushing himself towards the stone wall. He hurled a rock at Stephen then grabbed another one. Stephen managed to dodge the first, but the second one slammed into his hip, momentarily stalling him.

Before Lee could throw anything else, Stephen was on him, gripping his shirt and lifting him so that the tips of his toes barely touched the ground. He ground his jaw, then launched Lee backwards, sending him flying. Lee landed with a thud, shaking his head as his dazed expression fixated on Stephen. Blood poured from a gash on the side of his face, but it wasn't enough—nothing would be enough.

As Stephen approached again, Lee put his hands up in a futile effort to stop him.

"Tick tock, little *tiger*," he mocked as Stephen grabbed him. "Time is running out. You know, you could have killed me already …"

"Death would be too easy," Stephen growled, slamming Lee down onto the ground again, every ounce of pain inside pouring into his movements.

Lee groaned and groped for the gun nearby. Stephen leapt at him, his hand gripping Lee's as he got hold of the weapon. His other hand went to Lee's throat, squeezing his windpipe. Lee wheezed, his face twisted in hatred. Rage and anger burned in Stephen, his *tiger* pacing inside, ready to take this life and roar in victory.

But it would not bring Aiden back. Nothing would.

As he stared down at Lee's exposed throat, his teeth elongated, the urge to go for his death tear, the one that he had used countless times, overwhelming. It was quick and easy … but too easy for Lee Norton.

Slamming Lee's arm against the ground, he shook the gun from his grasp, hitting it out of reach. With his hand pulling Lee's hair, he grated, "I should fucking kill you."

"Yes," Lee ground out, just as he brought his hand up suddenly and slammed silver into Stephen's face. "You should have."

Pain and fire exploded across his skin like he had just had acid poured into his eye. He reeled back, giving Lee a moment to gain advantage on him.

He snatched the gun up again and fell onto Stephen.

Stephen grabbed his arm as he tried to level the gun at him, and with his other hand, punched him in the face, knocking his head back.

"Maybe later," he sneered.

Lee stared at Stephen before his eyes rolled backwards, his consciousness slipping away slowly. He slumped to the side, falling with a hard thump and lying limp on the ground.

Panting, Stephen stared at Lee's motionless form. "Well, that was kind of disappointing."

Chapter Thirty-Six
Stephen

Stephen discovered that the larger building with the old crumbling wall had actually once been a school. It was small and quaint and perhaps had only held a few pupils in its time, but there were boards on the walls in the rooms, and torn, old and weathered posters depicting the alphabet and the times-tables. Nature had long since come in and made this place home, but the memories of a school remained.

At the very back of the school he had located what he assumed had been the nurse's office, or some kind of medical facility. Perhaps this was their version of a clinic. Maybe the school was a one-place-does-all kind of set up. In the back room was a chair—the kind of chair that one would expect to find in dentistry. It reclined with the use of an electronic foot device, but that had given up its life to damp and perhaps the occasional flood.

Stephen had strapped Lee to the chair—leaving him only in his underwear. He had found all kinds of things that worked as rope—bits of old wire and cables, a children's skipping rope ... shit, he had even pulled the cord from one of the old blinds down. They all did the job. He had tied one around Lee's throat, securing him there. He could move if he fancied choking himself to death. He had used the others to secure Lee's elbows and wrists, and his knees and ankles.

In the bathroom, the smashed glass of a shattered mirror lay splayed across the floor. Birds had taken residence in the old-fashioned cisterns stuck up high on the wall—he'd not seen one of those since Cade had bought his house ... and that rundown thing hadn't had a resident since the seventies.

He attached a shard to the end of a broom. At least he thought it might have been a broom once. Lee was right—he would not kill him. But there was a lot worse one could survive. Stephen rubbed at his arm at that very thought, his memories threatening to strike again as he traced the old scars under his tattoo.

Some of the lights still worked in this place. About three out of the five still had bulbs that illuminated the place, casting odd shadows along the walls.

But he only needed one ...

"What are you doing?" Lee mumbled when he came around.

"Having a sleepover," Stephen drawled. He bent down so they were face to face. "You're the guest of honour."

Lee pulled against the bonds that held him in place, unspoken fury flashing in his eyes. It satisfied him more than any cuts or bruises ever could.

"I wouldn't waste my energy if I were you," Stephen mocked. He inhaled long and deep—the smell of sweet revenge. "I got the prize catch, didn't I?"

Lee's jaw tightened. "If you kill me ..."

"I'm not going to kill you."

"You bring war on yourselves."

"Maybe. But it was you who brought it ... the moment you stabbed a child and let him die."

"I would have thought you were above torture."

He was fishing. "Torture?" Stephen straightened, picking up one of the blunt-tipped tools he had lined up on the tray next to Lee, and pressing it to his finger. "If you mean the act by which severe pain and suffering, whether physical or mental, is intentionally inflicted upon another, for purposes such as obtaining information, a confession or a punishment ..." Stephen met Lee's eyes. "Then no, I am not above torture. Not when someone deserves it."

"I am Lee Norton," he ground out, pulling against his bonds again.

Stephen leaned back down, face close, his voice a deadly growl. "I know exactly who you are." When Lee said nothing, he pulled up a nearby stool and sat so that he was close to Lee's head. "Ready?"

"You're going to fucking ..." He didn't get to finish his sentence. Stephen slapped a hand over his mouth and gripped his nose, making Lee buck and twist his head to the side as he tried to breathe. Stephen watched him, calm, unruffled, taking delight in the way the fucking worm wriggled desperately in his grasp.

This is for Aiden.

Lee's face grew red the more he fought, a muffled yell exploding under Stephen's hand. He pinched his nose harder, and only when Lee's eyes rolled back did he let up.

Lee gasped and sucked in huge lungfuls of air through hoarse coughs. There was nothing like facing the promise of death to weaken a man's spirit. Stephen had seen it. He'd experienced it first fucking hand.

Panting, he watched Stephen roll up his sleeve and tie a band around his arm. He had found a good few medical tools hiding in the cabinets in the room. Lee blinked long and hard and it was a wonder if he knew what he was watching as Stephen pushed a needle into his own arm and extracted a vial of blood.

Not changing the needle—what was the point?—he pushed the tip into Lee's arm and smiled as he emptied the vial.

"What ... wh—"

Stephen stared at the necklace he had conveniently left

316

nestling on Lee's naked chest, just under his arrogant jaw. *Silver* ... His blood pumped through Lee's body, the cells like warriors, defeating territories until the country that was *Human* was totally defeated.

It would not be long before Lee felt the bite of the silver on his skin. It would burn like fire until bleeding welts formed along his skin.

The wheels on the stool allowed him to move around Lee with not much effort at all. He swivelled so that his long legs rested under Lee's head and he could look down at him at an upside-down angle. A nice sense of calm filled him. He should thank Lee, really, for following and getting himself caught. For the moment, he had taken his mind off all the madness that had been surrounding him.

Lee jerked, his mind seeming to slip in and out. "What the fuck?" As if realisation had suddenly dawned on him, he began to pull against the bonds with renewed effort.

"Are you ready?" Stephen asked again.

"You—" he spluttered. "You'll fucking die for this."

"Oh, promises." Stephen leaned in closer, inhaling the sweet scent of Lee's fear. He'd never admit it, of course, but it was there, even in a man such as Lee. "You smell so divine. You know, I could take you out and parade you in front of all your people. Your *Humans*. What would they think of you now?"

Stephen knew what they would think. His friend, Cade, had found a turned shifter, and *Humans* and *Others* alike had tried to kill him, both sides fearing him and what he could do. Stephen wasn't about to make it that easy for Lee, though. Death would not come and save him from this.

"If you kill me, they will hunt you down. You will not get to live very long."

"Oh, I'm not going to kill you. Where would the fun in

317

that be?" He grabbed the tray, pulling it closer and shuffling the items on it around until he got what he wanted. "You know, you should thank me. I've just cured you of the *Human* condition."

"Fuck you," Lee spat.

"Indeed." He grabbed a small knife from the tray and held it up in front of Lee's face. "Don't you think that pain is one of those peculiar issues? A person can lose limbs, fingers, toes, and quite simply not feel it. I heard a story once about a butcher. He hadn't realised that he was leaning against the meat slicer, and it wasn't until a woman screamed that he actually felt the pain himself, realising that he had just served up slices of his arm along with her honey-glazed ham. It's like, if you don't see it, the brain doesn't register it, and then it doesn't hurt." He adjusted the mirror above Lee. "I think you should see this, don't you?"

"You're fucking insane."

"That's debatable." He slid a hand around his jaw, and Lee tried to jerk his head away. With no effort at all, Stephen locked his head into place, wedging the top of Lee's head against his shoulder.

Lee strained against him, growling out in frustration as he pushed against him. Stephen positioned the blade at the soft tissue under his eye. Lee froze, his breathing hitching as Stephen pushed the tip into the delicate skin and drew it outwards, bringing with it angry grunts and breaths from Lee.

With a steady hand, he drew an almost perfect line then nodded in appreciation of it. "Perfect." He hadn't gone too deep, just enough so he could split the top layer of skin. He swapped hands so he could get the other side and create perfect symmetry.

"I'll fucking kill you myself," Lee spat at him. "You and

that fucking bitch doctor. I'll kill the rest of the kids and make you watch."

Stephen let out a deep, bellowing laugh. "Perhaps." He pressed the blade in on the other side, cutting Lee's tirade of curses off and turning them into an agonised groan. Lowering the blade just about half a centimetre under the first cut, he cut again, cutting both sides, alternating, lost in his work and oblivious to Lee's protests. He cut until there were six equal lines, three a side, and then put the blade down to admire his work.

He used a piece of wet rag, part of Lee's shirt, to wipe the blood off his face. Lee's breaths came quick and fast, panting through clenched teeth, his eyes red and watering with each new cut. Soon he would beg for death.

Blood trickled from the cuts under Lee's eyes. Stephen tapped his finger on the blade. "I need something to get the bleeding to stop," he said to himself rather than Lee. "Just wait here a moment, won't you?"

He winked as he got up from the stool and pushed his tray out of the way. Opening each cabinet in the room, he searched through them one by one. The door of one of the cabinets came off its rusted hinges when he tried it, sending the panel crashing to the floor. "Oops." He leaned down to the cupboard under the sink and stared at the bottles. "Salt … Yep, that's what I need." It would clean the wound and, hopefully, stem the bleeding a little. He grabbed each bottle, making out their labels as best he could—most were so old and faded that it was almost impossible. He brought one of the bottles he opened to his nose and sniffed, jerking back with a curse at the sudden blast of foul smelling toxins. "Fucking hell, that's strong."

A pack of salt crystal cleaner, with added lemon—this would have to do. He filled a small bowl with water. "Now this might sting a little," he said as he approached Lee, bowl in hand.

"Fuck off—"

"Oh, I do love our little chats," Stephen said as he sprinkled the cleaner onto a bit of cloth and pressed it onto the first cut. Lee screamed, loud enough to have brought anyone close by running. But there was no one near.

What a shame for Lee.

He scoffed inwardly at Lee's earlier bluff that he was not alone and that others were on their way. Had he really believed Stephen would buy that crap? He was son of an alpha, and he knew that the alpha never went into battle first. He was the one to be protected. The *Humans* would never have allowed Lee to hunt Stephen alone.

He cleaned each wound first, pressing the cloth and the salt to the wound, and when Lee's screams silenced, he cleansed it with the water.

"Get me out of this fucking chair," Lee ground out as he cleaned the last cut. "I swear to God, when I get out of here—"

"When? There is no when." Stephen dabbed the cloth one last time and then swapped the cloth for the blade and positioned himself at Lee's side. He pressed his fingers into Lee's arm, measuring the distance and ensuring that he could keep consistency. This was a work of art, and although art was better when it was imperfect, Stephen wanted this right. . "Once, long ago," Stephen began, ignoring Lee, "there was a story my mother used to tell my sister and me. It was about an old *tiger*—Caspian, just like me." Stephen leaned over, pulling Lee's face toward him. "Did you know I was a Caspian *tiger*?" The way Lee breathed and his heart rate spiked told Stephen that he did.

Caspian *tigers* were rare. They weren't a race of *tigers*

like they used to be, but an oddity born into a family. That was what Stephen was ... the oddity. Of course, it wasn't until that witch ... Stephen gave an abrupt shake of his head. *No*. He wasn't going there ... wasn't remembering that night ... The scars under his tattoo throbbed at the memory of it.

"He was one of the first," Stephen carried on, clearing his throat. "Centuries ago, man found that he struggled to hunt. He would go for days stalking the same prey and, when the moment came to pounce, he would often miss, his body not as dexterous as that of a true hunter ... an animal. However, man was stupid and so he learned skills from watching animals. He sought the wolves and the tigers and watched how they hunted, because it was rare for them to fail. At first, man thought he would take one of those wild animals for his own and keep it for himself ... a lot like a slave.

"One man, he hunted with his tiger and happened upon an elderly woman. Although she was aged, her lands were full, bursting with cattle and so much food that the man and tiger knew they would never consume it all. It was more than they had ever seen. The greedy man decided she was old, though; he would use his tiger to end her days and claim the land and the livestock for his own. But the woman ..." Stephen chuckled as he cut line after line in a straining Lee's arm, "the woman was actually one of the old witches. So she cursed him. He could only watch as she waved her hands in the air, helpless to stop her as she made the man and tiger one. Of course, she didn't stop there. The curse permeated through his tribe, combining every man to his animal."

Lee panted, sweat running down his face and naked torso as Stephen worked on him, but his cursing had stopped. It didn't take long for him to give in to the pain.

321

"Unfortunately, the animals didn't like to cohabit. Each of them wanted to be the one ... the alpha. So, they fought. Some fled, taking refuge in *Human* towns, hiding their two-natured existences from the world, but when hunger struck, they could not fight it, and the kind people of the towns often perished. Those who did not die once bitten, became the *were* species—the curse ran through their veins.

"The first of my kind, a *tiger*—although his fur was not yellow and gold, his stripes not black—it was like sunset. His stripes were said to be that of blood. When he was a man, he bore the claw marks with pride across his bare skin. His pack copied him. Often, they used the blood of their catch to mark their bodies and honour the old one. He gave them courage and strength in return to use against their enemies.

"Eventually, as the generations continued, the *tiger's* fur grew lighter, gold and yellows flecked our coats. The red dissipated until now, it is only visible in our faces." Stephen sighed. "It is a shame that we lost our true colours. There is a belief that if a man is turned into a *tiger* ... if he is given the gift of a second nature and then his stripes are given to him by the one who created him, he will bear the true colours of our kind. He will rise and take his gift to his people ... starting the cycle once more." By now, he had reached Lee's hand. Leaning over him, their faces the right way this time, he murmured, "You, my friend, are being given a very special gift indeed."

When both of Lee's arms held their marks, Stephen stood, wiping his hand on a cloth while admiring his handywork. It was beauty in blood.

He didn't know what had triggered the story in his mind. He rubbed at the marks on his arm ... his own stripes ... cut into him *that* night. What he had bargained with ...

Don't go down that path, Stephen, he warned himself.

322

Exile

Lee was the focus now as Stephen's blood surged through his body, small warriors defeating each *Human* blood cell and making them better, stronger, infusing them with such a gift, giving them a life they never knew until every cell in his body altered.

He would be something new.

Something better.

And Stephen's to control.

Picking up the blade once more, he got into position again; there was work to do still. This line was crossed now and he could not go back—not even for his family. He had made this choice. He had made it for Aiden, and Toke and Nakita. A new world had to come for them. Times had to change.

Stephen pressed his blade into the skin on Lee's chest, working on him to construct perfect *tiger* stripes. Lee floated in and out of consciousness now, the pain so intense that he wasn't feeling it any longer. He couldn't deny the distinct scent of urine, though. He wasn't sure when that had happened. He had been too lost in the art he was making.

Lee opened his eyes again, but Stephen didn't stop working as he attempted to lift his head. He was lost in time as he sculpted the stripes into his skin. Lee became feverish and drifted off again, and Stephen took his time to glide the blade through his flesh, keeping his hands steady and slow so he did not tear the edges. He didn't want them becoming jagged. Lee had to be perfect—a living sculpture.

When his chest was done, he unfastened him and flipped him over onto his front. Whether he was awake or not, it didn't matter. He didn't fight nor protest as Stephen secured him once more and started on his back.

Lee would not be pleased with the gift that had been bestowed upon him—nor would he have any comprehension of the honour it held—but Stephen was not worried. He knew if he called, Lee would come.

He closed his eyes and sent his mind into that place where man and *tiger* lived, searching, pulling the new *tiger* to him and locking onto his mind.

He would fucking own him now.

Stephen couldn't help the wry smile that curled the corners of his mouth as he found Lee's slowly forming *tiger* huddled in the corner of his mind. He slammed mental cuffs on him. "One day, you will beg me to kill you."

***

Stephen rinsed his hands off in the sink. Fuck, he felt so good—the retributive itch inside him sated for a moment. He leaned on the edge, fingers grasping the cool porcelain, and let his eyes close and his mind settle. He could almost sort his thoughts in his mind as if it were all in a cabinet, one after the other, shelving this current one with Lee under great accomplishments. He opened his eyes and stared out of the window, but it wasn't woodlands he saw, or the fields beyond. In his mind's eye, what he saw was Aiden, his eyes wide as Lee stabbed him. *He will pay for a long time for what he did to you. I swear it.*

Nostrils flaring, breathing ragged, he pushed back, keeping his hands on the sink and letting his back stretch out. He had been carving stripes into Lee for hours.

His thoughts flicked to Helena and Freya and Eden … What would they be doing right now? Maybe they had incinerated Aiden by now. Maybe Toke and Nakita would be crying … but, for some reason, he didn't think that Nakita would. There was something in her … something that saw the world as it was, not with the childish innocence her brother had. She had strength. She was stubborn.

Shit. She reminded him of him.

Exile

Freya's bullshit made no sense, though. Those children weren't his. Maybe she had been talking in the general sense … because they were *tiger*? Maybe she meant in the pack kind of way. His father certainly considered all the pack members family, and the children were to be treated as the alpha's own. And while Stephen had undoubtedly stumbled upon an odd pack, he was not their alpha.

He wasn't their anything.

He dumped his tools into the sink and let the water run over them. Enough with the thoughts that could drive any man insane. He was done with them. Done with it all … except Lee …

The other man was quiet, unmoving, save for the slow rise and fall of his chest as his body kept him unconscious. He would crave fresh meat when he woke. For a moment, Stephen thought about the possibility of not feeding him. But then a hungry shifter was a shifter that wasn't thinking. He needed Lee to think. He needed him to think and wallow in the pit of fucking misery he had now found himself. It was a shame he didn't have the deer from earlier with him. It would have made a perfect snack for Lee to wake up to. He'd just have to find him something. Surely there would be some hare or rabbit in the area.

Making sure that Lee was tied up once again should he wake, Stephen left him in the room and secured the door, wrapping bits of fabric around the handle and latching it to the handle of the room next to it. If Lee got free, he would no doubt get it open, but this would delay him at least, and he'd make enough noise that Stephen would hear him.

Outside, he sniffed at the air, taking it in deep. *Rabbit.* Trusty fucking rabbits. They were close. He slid down the couple of steps and went around the side and into the tall grass, moving with feline dexterity as he slunk through the

325

overgrowth. But it wasn't rabbit he saw—it was rat. He smirked to himself. *Big fat delicious rats.* There was a nest of them burrowing into the side of a bin. Lightning fast, Stephen snatched one, grabbing it by its fat body and twisting the creature's neck before it even knew what was happening. He gathered another four of them—that should be enough to keep Lee sated a little.

When he got back to the room, he found Lee hadn't moved at all. Hadn't even opened his eyes yet.

Pity.

It would have been nice to come back to a fighting, screaming Lee Norton. He tossed the rats' bodies on the counter and then sat on the floor in the corner. He was tired, so fucking tired his mind and body ached. He'd need a whole month of sleep to recover from this.

He let out a sigh and closed his eyes for a moment. There was nothing more he needed to do for Lee.

Nothing more than wait, at least.

***

Stephen should have realised that even in sleep, he would not escape the twisted nightmare that had become his life. The cogs of his mind clearly hadn't been working. These people would hunt him down until his last breath was relinquished to them. Even then they would probably resuscitate him just because they could.

"You're kidding, right?" Stephen stared at Helena in disbelief.

"There are no jokes here. Just things that are destiny."

"Riiight." He shook his head. "And I thought you said there were no jokes. This whole thing is a fucking joke. Whatever it is you have come to tell me this time, save it. I am not interested."

He stormed away from her, walking around Lee and

326

out of the room. He didn't need to worry about Lee escaping. In his mind, he knew this was a dream. He just didn't know how to get himself back out of it.

"You have to do what is meant of you. You can't just walk away," she called, following him along the corridor.

He stopped abruptly and turned, stalking back over to her. She was dressed so differently from the other Helena. Something about her *looked* different. Older perhaps. "Of course I can," he growled. "I can choose."

She didn't back away as he approached. She wasn't afraid of him, and that worked to his advantage, because she didn't realise that he was a big fucking cat stalking his prey right now.

She yelped when he leapt, trying to back up, but she was too late, and he was too fast for her. He slammed her into the wall, her head banging off the stone. She didn't wince, though—dream women obviously couldn't get hurt, he thought derisively. "I have had enough," he ground out. "Okay? I don't know what this shit is. I don't know who you are or what you want. But I am tired of it. Do you hear me? You need to stop. All of you. You all need to leave me alone." Freya and her obscure accusations of parenthood as well.

"It is already chosen for you," she said steadily.

"Bullshit." He slammed his hand onto the wall next to her head. "I do have a choice, and this is me making that choice. Leave me alone. Do you hear me? Do you even understand?"

"People will die if you give up."

Stephen gave a bark of laughter before releasing her and backing away—from her and her madness. "Do not lay that at my feet. I am only responsible for myself. No one else. If people die, it is their own doing."

"Souls will be lost," she insisted.

"Then let them be lost."

"Valkyrie will not let you go."

Valkyrie? Stephen frowned, images of warriors and wars coming to his mind. "You talk in riddles. Valkyrie?" he scoffed. "A bunch of mythical ..."

Realisation slammed into him with a violence.

"Freya ..." he whispered in disbelief. "You're talking about Freya?" He glared at Helena, angry enough to make her press herself into the wall.

"You have the key, Stephen. You and your children. You're all meant to be."

"No." He shook his head, determined. "They are not my children." He would not listen to this. He would not take any more. Grabbing Helena by the arm, he yanked her to him.

"What are you doing?" she gasped.

"Testing a theory." He turned and ran, easily dragging Helena with him.

"Stephen ..." His name fell from her lips in a desperate plea as she realised what he was planning to do. It vaguely registered that she was using his real name. "Stop. Please." She tried to pry his fingers from her, but they were like steel bands around her flesh. "Please don't do this."

But he wasn't listening anymore. One more piece of information in this glorious fucked up riddle was one piece too much.

He raced down the steps with her.

Enough was enough.

She stumbled as she dug her heels into the earth to stop them—but to no avail.

With fierce determination, he rammed into a tree, smashing his body against the trunk of it, shouting at himself to wake up, his roar shaking the very earth they stood on.

328

Exile

Gasping, he came to, surging up and blinking as he took in his surroundings. He was back in the room … and lying on the floor beside him was the body of a woman. Long hair covered her face as she lay there absolutely motionless.

Panting, he stared at her in disbelief.

He had done it. He had fucking done it.

He had pulled her through.

Chapter Thirty-Seven

Stephen

His hazy brain didn't want to work, crashing into the walls of his skull and making his head sway. The woman on the floor stirred and he dragged his gaze back to her.

Fuck. What had he done? Crawling over to her, he rolled her over onto her back. "Helena?" he said, putting his fingers on the pulse in her neck. *Still alive.*

Sweat trickled down the nape of his neck and bile rose in his throat when he realised he may have seriously harmed her. He swallowed hard and did a quick check for any visible signs of damage.

"I'm sorry," he whispered. "I didn't—" His words trailed off. Any kind of apology suddenly seemed futile.

Her eyes remained closed, but she was breathing. Barely.

"I'll get you some help," he rasped, but as he started to get to his feet, she grabbed his arm with weak fingers.

"No ... stay ..." Her voice was a barely audible whisper.

"You need a doctor ..." His brow knitted in consternation. *Did she?* She was something he had dragged back to reality with him from in his dreams. He had no idea what exactly she was or what she needed.

She shook her head slowly. "No one can help." She coughed, reminding him of Aiden. Stephen was like a child trying to fit a square through a round hole in his puzzle toy— it just didn't fit.

"You have to follow what is meant. It is your destiny," she repeated the madness from before. "You feel it inside."

He scowled. "No." But he did. He felt so much inside that he tried to bury it and the fuckers just wouldn't stay down.

"Go back to your children ... Nakita ... Toke ... They are yours."

He gripped her hand tightly—surprised to find that he had been holding it—fighting the urge to shake her and make her stop this lunacy. His breathing came out harsh as he tried to control himself. "More riddles?"

Her eyes fluttered open with difficulty, a slight frown on her perfect brow. He didn't have the time nor patience for any more conundrums— he wanted honesty. It seemed that was a rare commodity these days. "You have to believe it," she rasped, her tone frantic. "Freya was telling you the truth."

"How do you know what Freya said?" he demanded.

Helena winced as she curled her legs up and rolled to the side. "I just know," she wheezed. "It is the truth. You must take your place."

He rubbed at his face, letting out a frustrated breath. "Would *you* believe it, Helena? If someone suddenly came to you with these kids, and said hey, guess what, they're yours?"

As her eyes met his, he noticed that they differed from the real-life Helena's. Older, and a different shade.

"Would you believe you could pull a woman from your dream?" she asked softly.

A week ago, he wouldn't have. But it seemed the world was so fucking mad these days. Everyone had gone insane. "It still doesn't explain things. What do I say now? Oh, okay, it all makes sense? Because it doesn't. There are two of you, and I can't work out what is going on. I feel like I am living outside of normality."

"It's too hard to explain—"

"Try," he gritted out, "because you aren't making one ounce of sense. And if you don't talk now, I will walk away from everyone." The more he lost it, the more Helena seemed to gain strength. He leaned forward, a growl low in his throat. "Please explain."

She didn't, though. She just stared back at him like he was a madman. Her gaze searched his as if she was seeking answers and reassurances … but there were none. They had the wrong man.

As he let go of her, coughs wracked his body, shaking him to the very core. He rolled onto his front, coughing until he vomited violently. With a curse, he wiped his mouth with the back of his hand and pushed himself up, forcing himself to move against the agonising pain in his head.

"Fine. If you're not going to tell me, I am done with it," he ground out.

Unable to keep himself up, like the very earth was pulling him down, he dropped back down to the floor. As soon as he did, Helena grabbed for him. It was her that held onto his arm this time. Maybe she would give him some answers that would make sense this time. Maybe she would wake him up and this would all be one big, fat, crazy dream.

When she said nothing, though, he clenched his jaw and tried to pull away from her. But she clutched his hand tighter, and for the first time, he saw real emotion on his face as tears filled her eyes. "I'm telling you the truth. You have to understand."

"I have asked to understand a hundred times, but no one is listening. I have asked questions, queried things. I have done as everyone has asked me to do and still all of you have shrugged me away. You placate me with answers that mean nothing. I get told that those children are mine, yet there is no way it is possible. Why should I believe you?"

"Because I am telling the truth."

"Prove it," he said. "Prove to me that I fathered those children."

She had less than one minute to talk. He wasn't feeling in a patient mood. If she didn't come up with something, he would find a way to get himself up. She wasn't giving him anything to help put things together in his mind—just small bits of information that made no sense on their own. But he could not do anything with them because he was missing the bigger picture, and he had no idea what it looked like.

"Your real name is Stephen Davies. You were born 17th November. You are the eldest child of Malcolm and Emily Davies," she began.

"Is that supposed to prove it? That's all you have? So, you recognised me from something? It isn't hard to do. Forget it, Helena. Nice try." He pried her fingers open and freed his arm. He was weaker than her in that moment, his final ounce of energy completely sapped, but he was fucked if that would stop him leaving.

"You have two sisters," she said, desperation making her voice louder. "Your father is the alpha to your pack and alpha to your community—both titles you were heir to."

He gritted his teeth and waited for more, staring straight ahead. "You could have read that anywhere, too."

"Your sister broke the first law of procreation," she said, making him snap his head around.

That was not public knowledge. They had done everything in their power to hide the pregnancy. How the hell could she know that?

"You helped her to cover it," she continued. "You helped her and your friend try to get away. But the baby … it
333

was a hybrid ... and he died ... That's what your sister believes, anyway. But he isn't dead."

"How do you know this?" Stephen growled, grabbing her arm with the little energy he had left. He'd not told anyone about the baby being alive. Not even Gemma or Cade.

"This world is not the world you think it is, Stephen. Things are *meant*."

"Why didn't you just tell me before? Why didn't Freya ... when she met me on the bus?"

"Would you have believed it more then than you do now?"

No, he wouldn't. He'd probably not have followed them anywhere, or stayed with them for even a minute ... told them all they were fucking nuts. "And Aiden? Is he mine, too?" He realised how absurd the fact was that he was actually entertaining the idea they might be his kids. And the notion that one of his children might have died generated a barrage of emotions in him.

"It's complicated."

He scoffed. "Yeah, because this is a fucking walk in the park, right?"

"You will get the answers. I promise. Just please ... don't walk away."

Even if he wanted to believe her, what she was telling him was unfathomable. She was talking of things that were impossible. They lay outside the abilities of any *Other* he knew. But as he watched her, he realised that she truly believed what she was telling him with all her heart. He recognised liars—and she was not lying.

In some inexplicable odd role reversal, he found that it was him now stretched out on the floor as she knelt by him. He felt close to death, and his own stupidity had perhaps done Norton's job for him. "And now that I pulled you from my sleep … what happens?"

"This …" With a hand on his chest, she leaned down, bringing her face close to his. His breath caught in his throat.

With gentle fingers, she took one of his hands and turned it over, placing a ball in his palm—a soul ball.

"I can't take my own soul," Stephen said in ragged breaths.

"It's not for you," she whispered.

His heart missed a beat as he realised what she was saying. "No …"

"Promise me Trentwich."

The name jarred against Stephen, making his mind stall. Trentwich. Again. "I don't know what that means." Frustration and despondency warred inside him.

"Just promise."

It was like Déjà Vu. Aiden all over again, except Helena was crying. The tears rolled down her face, but nothing fell on him. She lowered her face to his and pressed her lips softly against his—it was like having life breathed into him. He should have felt the wetness from her cheeks, but there was nothing.

She smiled down at him as she pulled away.

Then she collapsed.

Chapter Thirty-Eight
Stephen

Clenching his fist around the soul ball, Stephen leaned his heavy head back against the cold wall. The warmth of Helena's lips lingered on his. Was that how she would taste in real life?

Stop thinking about her, he chastised himself.

But she was intoxicating. Images of her flashed in his mind, and he was at a loss to stop them. It was a ghost of this moment that his *tiger* held onto. If he closed his eyes, he was certain that he would feel everything as if she were still there—the gentleness of a mouth that hinted at more ... the soft way her breath danced across his skin ...

What the fuck was wrong with him?

Lee murmured unintelligibly from the table, pulling at his bonds again. It was awake, Stephen thought derisively.

"What the fuck have you done?" Lee roared, but Stephen ignored him, his attention on the glossy whiteness of the empty soul ball in his hand. He rolled it around in his palm, feeling the weight of what it meant ... *who* it meant. Would this be for the real Helena? Dream Helena was gone. No body, no person ... nothing. Had she really been here at all? If it wasn't for the ball he was staring at, he would have decided with one hundred percent certainty that it had been nothing more than the crazy dream of a very tired man.

Lee growled as he tugged and pulled, breaking into his thoughts once again. "Let me up," he demanded, glaring at Stephen. "You're going to fucking die for this." His face flushed red with his rage inside. Oh, Stephen hoped that anger stayed with him. He hoped that he would forever remember these moments.

Exile

Pushing the ball into his jean pocket, Stephen pushed himself up. He would deal with who it belonged to later.

Standing over Lee, he grabbed his head and held him in place, forcing Lee's eyes wide open. His heart leapt with what he saw. His eyes were like Phoenix's, but where a bright blue circle surrounded Phoenix's irises, Lee's was lava red around the rims, as alive as real fire within.

"Stop bloody growling."

As he stared up at Stephen, his growl petered out. Lee still had his *Human* teeth, but his gesture was very much feline and it pleased Stephen no end.

"Maybe it is time for a little snack? You must be starving. I am a terrible host." Lee's eyes stayed on him as he moved around him, his growl a low rumble in his throat. "I am going to untie you a little, and you will not move. Do you hear me?"

Lee nodded.

"Good." He cut the wires from around Lee's legs and ankles, and suddenly the tension in Lee vanished, making the air around them lighter. Stephen searched mentally for him, going to that white space to locate him, and making sure that this wasn't Lee getting ready to pounce at the last moment. But the *tiger* inside was resting, his eyes open, but calm …

On the outside, Lee was watching Stephen, though, his nervousness palpable, lightning dancing on the edges of the air mixed with the sweet scent of fear.

Stephen worked his way along Lee's body, freeing him of each tie, making sure that none of his wounds had fused with the wires or cables. When he got to the wire holding down his arm, Stephen focused on Lee. "If I unfasten here, you'd better not try anything stupid." He leaned over him so that their faces were close. "I will put you down if I have to. You are mine to control."

Lee said nothing, not even a flicker of fear in his eyes. Stephen studied his marked face, unsure whether Lee was even awake in there. When Stephen snipped open the wires at his arm, Lee continued to simply stare at him. But Stephen wasn't a fool. If this was an act, he was ready.

When both of his arms were free, Lee sat up, affording Stephen a satisfying view of his handywork. He imagined walking into his father's office with Lee … imagined the shocked and disapproving expression on his face. His rebellious character relished the thought. On the other hand, maybe eventually his father would have seen the true magnificence of it.

He noticed that Lee had focused on something in the far corner of the room—the dead rats on the counter. *Fuck.* He was actually drooling.

"Want one?" he sneered.

He gave a vain attempt at snarling at Stephen, pulling a laugh from Stephen. Oh, this was fucking beautiful. The almighty Lee Norton, ardent *Other* hater, drooling for rats.

"Go to fucking hell—" Lee's voice trailed off into the low rumble of his *tiger*, his mind and body confused with where or what he was. Stephen adjusted the seat so that the back was upright and the leg support was down, allowing Lee easier movement if he decided to take it.

"Move, and I will kill you," Stephen warned.

Lee panted through gritted teeth, as if Stephen's words immediately placed invisible restraints on him. Man and *tiger* battled inside him, man wanting to rebel while his *tiger* his maker's to control.

"Now stand up."

Exile

Stephen grabbed him under the jaw and tilted his head back, wondering how much *Human* was left inside his creation as he studied him. He wasn't fighting. He hadn't jumped up biting and slashing.

"Step forward with your left foot."

When Lee did, Stephen grinned. Oh, this was fucking amazing.

"Now your right," he said, and Lee blindly obeyed.

A slow smile spread across Stephen's face. He couldn't have wished for this to go better. He stared right at Lee. "I do hope you're in there, Norton. I hope you're in there and can feel how helpless you truly are."

He ushered him to the door and down to a basement, where the boiler and the generator resided—he had discovered it when he had been exploring the building before. There was an old well, too. It was covered with a large, metal grate, and the sound of the water lapping down at the bottom echoed through the room, bringing with it a cold, salty breeze. Around the thick grey walls was a line of green moss and a lighter shade in the brickwork. This room obviously flooded sometimes—maybe in the winter when the storms were bad and the sea would rise. If it was anything like home, then the rains were sometimes relentless. The basement was a mirror image of the rooms above … walls and doorways in the same place. At the very back, Stephen had found what looked like cells. What kind of school was this where they had a dungeon at the bottom of it? But then, if this was an *Other* community and there had been shifters here, then only a fool would not have had a cage of some kind to keep the wild ones in when they were out of control.

Lee came to an abrupt halt, causing Stephen to almost slam into the back of him and knock him down the steps. He

339

had caught sight of the rats again. "You want to eat, you move first," Stephen whispered in Lee's ear. "Down."

Lee turned at an odd angle as Stephen pushed him forward, making him knock his head off the wall.

"Oops," Stephen said, pushing him down again. What was a little bang here and there?

Frowning, Stephen clicked on the light when they reached the bottom. Who made a basement and put the bloody light switch at the bottom of the stairs?

As they reached the well, he ordered Lee to sit leaning against the wall of the cell at the back. He was well behaved, Stephen thought sardonically. But just to be sure … it would be a fool who would skip the security steps in the name of overconfidence. He secured the extra ties he had down there around Lee's wrists and legs. "You are forbidden from removing these," Stephen said to him, both out loud and in their minds. "Do you understand?"

Lee nodded impassively.

"Good. I will be back in a moment with your food."

He secured the door in place—it worked with a lever to the side that pushed all the locks into place. Lee held the bars, his eyes wide, an infant taking in new surroundings. What was it like with them when their eyes shifted? The colours of the world shifted when Stephen's eyes did, like the artist had suddenly added more colour to the picture. Maybe it was like that for Lee now.

He quickly grabbed the pile of rats and went back down to Lee. The bars rattled as Stephen got closer, and he realised that Lee had made his appearance in the creature he had created.

"I see you're awake."

"Let me out of this fucking cage, asshole."

Exile

"Now, now." Stephen couldn't keep the sneer from his face as he got closer, anticipation overflowing in him for what was next. Lee had survived ... this far. There had to be a certain quality a *Human* possessed that meant they survived. Whatever it was, Phoenix had had it, and it seemed that maybe Lee did, too. He hoped so.

"If you're expecting me to eat that, you can forget it. I'll fucking starve if I have to."

"These?" Stephen held up the rats, stopping just a few feet from the front of the cell. "You don't want any? I got them just for you," Stephen said in mock offense.

Maybe this would work like Phoenix. The boy hybrid had superb strength and abilities. Phoenix was a smart kid, he had caught on quite fast that the reason half-breeds were killed was due to fear. But it was amazing to see what Phoenix could do.

Lee was different—he had a maker, someone to control him ...

Poor Lee.

"Fuck off," Lee spat.

Stephen threw his head back and laughed. "Oh man, you do amuse me. Almost as funny as when you pissed your pants in the chair." He held out a rat again. "Are you sure you don't want one?"

He took a bite out of the fattest rat. He never was one for eating rats. Rats seemed to be more of a food source for the foxes, even the wolves. It was a strange, peculiar taste, almost as if the meat was infused with perfume. Chewy, though.

"Mmm mmm mmm ..." Stephen closed his eyes and shook his head in approval. "So good."

"I'm not eating it."

Stephen shrugged. "If the hunger doesn't get you, the shift will for sure, especially doing it unfed. Makes not an ounce of difference to me." He took another big bite of the rat and watched as Lee's eyes focused on the juicy morsel, his pupils dilating.

He threw what was left of the body on the ground in front of Lee's cage. His resolve would falter ... eventually. Stephen had no doubt about that.

"Now, I want to know some things."

"I'm not telling you a damn fucking thing." Lee stepped back from the bars, arms folded over his chest in dogged refusal, but his eyes kept darting back to the half-eaten rat. The cuts across Lee's arms had stretched and bulged with the muscle in his arms. He would make a powerful shifter for sure, and probably a good fighter on the ranks—although Stephen had the inkling that Lee would turn down the offer to fight ...

"You know, if you're not going to tell me things, then I have no use for you."

"Kill me then," Lee gritted out. "I've met bullies like you before."

"Bullies like me?" He gave a snort of derisive laughter. "Who was following whom?"

He kicked at the lever holding Lee's cage closed, unhooking the bar. For a second, fear flashed across Lee's expression, and the glow around his pupils grew stronger.

Interesting.

"What are you going to do?"

"Nothing," Stephen said as he advanced. "Now, how shall we play this?"

"Play this any way you fucking want. I don't care."

Stephen inhaled long and deep, bringing his shoulders and head back. "Oh, but you do care. I can smell it in the air. So rich I can almost taste it."

Lee glared at him, unmoving. There was nowhere for him to go, and Stephen bet that it would be a long while before Lee would stoop to getting on his knees and begging. Lee might have been *Human*, but he had bountiful pride.

In a swift move, Stephen leapt at him, gripping the back of his neck and pushing him down with not much effort at all. It didn't matter to him right then if he broke his neck or *accidently* decapitated him. Stephen had not turned Lee so that his *Human* side could refuse things ... antagonise him.

No. He had purpose.

Lee pushed back, twisting his head to get away, but the way Stephen had got hold of him made it difficult for him to do much without hurting himself in the process.

Grabbing a rat, he put it under Lee's nose. "Eat it."

"*No* ..."

Stephen pushed harder, getting Lee's face a mere inch from the rat.

Lee stiffened his back, all the power and energy he had going into not being forced to move. Any other day, Stephen would have been impressed. But he had little time and little patience for that right now.

"The *Humans* at the town alerted you to my presence?"

No answer.

Stephen pushed harder.

"Did they?" he growled.

Seeming to struggle with breathing with the rat so close, Lee finally snarled, "Yes ..."

"And your purpose was to catch me?"

Lee gritted his teeth, as if fighting with himself not to answer. "You have the necklace and the children—"

A hand shot around Lee's throat, lifting him to his feet and forcing his head back. "Those are *my* fucking children."

"No," the other man wheezed, "they belong to me."

"Eat the fucking rat." Stephen grabbed it off the floor once again and slapped it against Lee's mouth, pushing it between his tight lips. "Open your mouth," he bellowed.

Lee kept his lips firmly closed.

Focusing, he reached out to Lee in their minds where they were now linked.

"Open it or I ram it through your head."

Lee shook from the effort of holding himself still and his mouth shut as Stephen forced his head back, but he was at all the wrong angles to fight him off. *Shame for him*, Stephen thought scathingly as he rammed the flesh into his mouth, keeping his hand over it so he couldn't spit it back out.

He choked and gagged as the rat went in. He had two choices, really—eat and breathe, or die. Either way worked for Stephen.

Survival. The utmost and yet most basic instinct, Stephen mused. Be it *Human*, animal, mammal or *Other*, it was there. The deep-seated impetus driving every last creature on this earth.

As Lee sucked in a deep breath, his *Human* side seemed to vanish, the animal coming to the front with a vengeance. He had taken his first breath of new life ... hand fed his first mouthful of *Other* nourishment by the one who had created him.

With a groan, he grabbed onto Stephen's arms for support—giving over to him—as he devoured the rodent.

344

Exile

Stephen shoved him away so he was leaning against the wall with his snack.

Cocky demeanour now gone, Lee wolfed down his meal, his *Human* teeth retracting and much sharper teeth descending through the cavities for the first time.

Stephen had never witnessed a shift from such a front and centre seat before. It was fascinating.

The cuts that he had drawn into his flesh began to split, like worms under the skin. Small points of fur began to emerge from the wounds—the pain that he would feel when his shift began gave Stephen a great sense of satisfaction.

He backed away slowly, eyes never leaving Lee. Newly shifted first time half-breeds were not things to be near when they were crazed with a hunger that they didn't understand.

Once he shifted, he would be in pure survival mode.

Lee rolled onto his stomach, like a newborn foal trying to stand for the very first time. As he pushed off the ground onto his knees, his legs shook until one buckled and his arms gave way, and he was face down on the ground again. Ripples and bumps moved under his skin as the shifter inside him pushed to emerge. Bones moved and clicked out of place, muscles changing shape. He opened his mouth, trying to yell as his face painfully reformed itself into something different.

Stephen's pulse sped up as he watched red stripes emerge through the gashes. It was the only fur he had—his skin stayed bare, but his body was almost *tiger*.

Suddenly aware of Stephen, Lee snarled, his lip pulling back as his eyes locked onto him.

Stephen barely managed to twist out of the way and shoot out of the cage before Lee leapt. Slamming the door shut and in place, he backed away from the bars just as Lee careened into them, ramming clawed paws through the bars, catching Stephen.

As one caught Stephen across the shoulder, he let out a violent curse. Blood poured down his arm as he grabbed the lever and yanked it into place, locking Lee where he was.

Fuck.

That wasn't meant to happen.

Grimacing, he slapped a hand over the gashes to stem the flow.

Stupid. Fucking stupid.

Lee slammed against the bars, snarling, spittle dripping from his mouth. Stephen stared at the bald, deformed creature in front of him. He had never seen anything as ugly as this—a being stuck in the transition between *tiger* and man. A *tiger* with *Human* skin mostly.

Something had gone terribly wrong.

It was something out of the Madam Tussaud's Chamber of Horrors.

When Lee's shift seemed to stop, he stood there breathing hard, his eyes riveted on the rats on the floor.

Stephen frowned. His needs should have come in at full force. He shouldn't be able to hold back. It was almost as if the *Human* side of him still retained a little control. Ordinarily, the first feed could be a month-old rotten corpse riddled with maggots and a new shifter would demolish it.

Stephen's shoulder wasn't healing, either, and it should have been by now. He clenched his jaw. All of this was a disaster ... one major fuck up.

Growling, Lee picked up a rat—like a man would, not an animal—and bit into it, blood oozing down his chin.

Stephen dropped to his knees, clutching at his aching shoulder, his blood pulsing under his skin.

Something was wrong ... very, very wrong.

Chapter Thirty-Nine
Stephen

"For fuck's sake—" Stephen snatched the mirror that he had fixed above the chair and held it in the air, twisting so that he could get a view of his back and shoulder. He was a fucking mess. Warm blood ran down his back, and his shirt stuck to him like a second skin ...

It wasn't even healing—not like he was used to. The time it took to secure Lee, lock the doors, and get his arse into this room was enough time that his injury should appear to have healed for a good week.

There was no silver in it to justify it—silver always made healing longer. And Lee ...even wounds from a shifter healed fast ... so it didn't make any sense.

What the hell was going on?

Fuck it. He'd have to get to Helena's clinic before he bled to death ... Now that would be great, wouldn't it? Finally completed one of life's most valuable pieces of art only to go and die.

Wiping his bloodied hands on the remainder of Lee's shredded shirt, he checked the door to the basement, listening for Lee. Absolute quiet greeted him. With any luck, he would be sleeping. Phoenix had slept for days after his transition—especially after his first feed. Maybe that first feed was what actually made them full shifters ... He made a mental note to find out at some point.

Lee would be okay for a little while, and well ... if any unfortunate *Human* came looking for him, they'd be damn fucking sorry. He could already imagine the news headlines: *Lee Norton goes wild ... slaughters all his men.*

Walking back to the town took a good hour. He didn't realise he had managed to run so far. Damn, he had been in a frenzy.

The high walls of the gated community came into view, and he slowed, stopping just short of the place. Now that he was here, he couldn't seem to make himself go back in.

He wasn't quite sure how he would feel looking at those children after everything he had been told. He still didn't believe they were his, and yet he felt nervous about being around them.

But most of all, he was uneasy about seeing Helena again. She played havoc with his senses, and he just didn't trust himself around her. The image of her floated around in his mind, and he swallowed hard as his body instantly responded.

No ...

Bloody no ...

Resisting turning tail and getting his arse back to Lee and his experiment, he forced himself to move forward on leaden legs. "Just call me Frankenstein," he muttered to himself. Frankenstein did not have children ... real made, genetic children ... or did he?"

The tension in Stephen grew, and his senses went on high alert as he got closer. Cars and vans littered the area in the distance. He kept close to the undergrowth, making sure to keep himself out of sight.

Getting a firm foothold in a small recess in the trunk of one of the nearby trees, Stephen hauled himself up until he was perched on the highest branches, hidden by the thick foliage. He counted. Three—no, four—*Humans* ... Trigger-happy fingers clutched their rifles—loaded with silver no doubt. Kevlar covered their chests while their eyes constantly scanned the area.

Exile

Unlucky for them, their sight was that of mere *Humans*, he thought with derision.

After he had scrutinised their every move and noted any weaknesses and blind spots, he climbed back down and made his way through the forest with predatory dexterity. He had already walked the perimeter outside the community, knew how wide it was and where each building stood. Being a hunter had the advantage of giving *Others* invaluable skills and sense of direction.

He followed the boundary until he reached the fence behind Helena's clinic. It was just a quick jump from one yard to another and then he would be there.

Six *Humans* in total so far—the four at the front and two of them behind. They walked from front to back, passing each other in the middle. One of the guards went by, his concentration straight ahead of him.

Stephen seized the opportunity to creep forward and scale the first fence, once again thinking how very inept *Humans* were. One thing any *Other* knew was that your senses stayed alert, your focus all around, not only in front of you.

He eased himself into the garden of the house backing Helena's clinic, keeping low as he streaked through.

The acrid smell of fire stung his nostrils as he raced through the garden. Something was very wrong. And it wasn't just because of the *Humans* around the outside. Dread churned inside him, the hairs on the back of his neck rising.

Ears and eyes trained on his surroundings, he deftly climbed over Helena's back wall and landed on quiet feet. Keeping low, he darted for the house.

He noticed the smashed glass panel of the open door before he reached it. Swearing inwardly, he carefully stepped over the shards on the ground and kept his ears open for any *Humans* on the inside.

As he slipped into Helena's back room, he took in the coffee table that had been pushed to the side and the glass and blood that decorated the main hallway that led to the door.

He broke out in a cold sweat.

There was so much blood. It trailed across the tiles to the room Stephen knew was Helena's reception.

Careful not to make a sound, he crept through the clinic and towards the reception area. As he neared, soft whimpering caught his attention and made his blood run cold. Heart thumping in his chest, he cautiously rounded the corner, eyes scanning every nook and cranny in the room.

Tracey, Helena's assistant, lay half slumped against the wall under the front window. Her face was dark and bruised, her lip split open. She had a slash across her cheek and blood dribbled from her nose. Her hands clutched her belly, blood pooling on the floor between her legs.

"Shit." He scrambled to her, falling to his knees next to her. Taking great pains not to hurt her any further, he pushed the hair back from her face with gentle fingers, lifting her face to his. "Shhh, it's okay," he whispered. "Are there any other *Humans* inside the clinic?" He kept his voice low. He needed to know there was no imminent threat from within the building before he found out exactly what had happened.

She shook her head slowly, turning her tear-streaked face into the palm of his hand in search of comfort as only an *Other* would do.

Gently stroking her cheek and giving her the solace she sought for a moment, he lifted her head back up to his.

"Tell me what happened?"

350

Exile

"*H...Humans*," she sobbed. "They came for—for— I don't know," she broke off crying, still holding a protective hand over her stomach.

"It's okay," he murmured. "Where—" Shouts and bangs echoed through the air outside, cutting Stephen off. He lifted his head to carefully peer outside the window.

There were three *Humans* in the distance—three fucking big *Humans*. A man was being forced to his knees with a gun aimed at his head while a sobbing woman was being held back. He could hear her crying and pleading for the man's life.

"Why should we let you live? Why should we let any of you live? You are given goodness. You are given food and shelter. And you repay us by lying. By harbouring a criminal. Tell us where he is," one of the *Humans* yelled. "Tell us now or this man dies."

Another loud crash sounded as *Humans* dragged an old man out of the house beside the clinic. He staggered as he tried to keep up, his leg twisted in a way that wasn't natural. The *Humans* threw him onto the ground next to the other man. It went against everything Stephen knew not to go out and fight, but even with his strength and speed, he'd be able to dodge a few bullets, maybe before one of them finally got him. And riddled with silver, there would be little he could do to help the two old men outside—or himself.

Stephen turned back to Tracey with urgency. "Where is Helena? The kids?"

"The kids ..." She looked at him with dazed eyes. "They're ... they are in the basement," she said in a hoarse whisper. "The safe hole."

"And Helena?" He held his breath.

Tracey curled over suddenly, sobbing with pain. "I don't know," she wailed.

351

Shit.

He couldn't help Tracey right now. Lying still was the best chance she had. He certainly didn't know anything about saving her baby. Fighting was what he was trained in. That was what he knew. "I'll come back for you."

"Wait—" She grabbed onto him, fear in her eyes.

"I'll be back, I promise." He gave her a forced smile and a gentle squeeze of the hand. "I need to get Helena. She will help you."

She let go of him reluctantly and he slipped away from her, backing out of the room and ducking under any windows.

He checked the rooms one by one, his heart dropping when emptiness greeted him each time. The floor was covered in medical tools and smashed pieces of glass and dishes. The last room he got to was Aiden's. He held his breath and pushed the door open. The bed Aiden had lain in just hours ago, was torn to shreds, the entire room in as much of a mess as the others.

He had no time to analyse the relief that surged through him when he saw Helena hovering by the window, her eyes on the goings-on outside.

She slapped a hand across her mouth as she watched the *Human* slam the butt of the gun into the back of the old man's head. "Benny ..." she whimpered as he slumped to the ground.

"Oh God," she cried then turned and ran straight into Stephen, who had come to stand behind her. He put a hand over her mouth as she screamed, muffling the sound.

"Shh, Helena," he said gruffly. "It's me." She stopped struggling, wide eyes looking up at him, and he slowly removed his hand. "Don't scream, okay?"

She nodded briskly then breathed a quick, "Yes. Please let go."

He frowned, annoyed at how reluctant he was to do so. As soon as he did, though, she launched herself toward the door.

Stephen's arm shot out, grabbing her around the waist and picking her up off the floor so that she was flush against him once more.

She struggled, trying to get loose. "They're going to kill him," she sobbed quietly.

"Going out there won't save him," he rasped.

Helena continued to fight him, tears tumbling from her eyes and down her cheeks. With a soft curse, he swung her around and pulled her to him, holding her tight against his chest.

"Helena, if you go out there, they'll just kill you, too," he murmured against her hair. She quietened, clinging to Stephen as she heaved with sobs.

He turned her away from the window just as one of the *Humans* kicked at the man's head, snapping it back on his neck. He clenched his jaw. *Fuckers*. People screamed, some charging for the *Humans*, but one by one they all dropped from silver bullets. He held Helena closer as she jumped with each shot fired.

God damn it. How could *Others,* who were so much more powerful than *Humans*, be in such an inferior position, could get slaughtered so easily?

"We have to go," Stephen said thickly. "Where are the children?

When he got no reply, he pushed her back a little so he could look down at her. "Helena ... Where are the kids?"

"Safe hole," she finally whispered, sniffing.

She turned her head and tried to look outside, but he gripped her chin and kept her eyes on his. "Don't. Don't look at that," he said firmly. "You don't need to see that shit."

Tears rolled down her cheeks anew, but she nodded obediently.

Swallowing hard, he fought the primitive emotions raging inside him to hold her close once more and keep her safe from everyone and everything. "Tracey needs your help, but we have to get out of here. Okay?"

She nodded again.

This was all such a fuck up—and all his fault. Whatever they were looking for, be it Lee, the kids or him, he was connected to them all in some way.

He peered out of the window one last time. People hovered, keeping back, fear in their stance.

What the fuck? Why didn't they fight? Even with a few losses, they could easily take the guards. Why did they submit? If everyone just took a stand, the *Humans* would stand hardly any chance at all. Yes, they'd get some shots off at the first *Others* coming their way, but that would be it. *Sacrifice the few to save the masses* ... His father's words echoed in his mind. Malcolm had known this shit all along.

Gemma would argue that that was the reason no one stood up. They didn't want to sacrifice anyone. But doing nothing led to the very same thing ... *Others* dead and slaughtered at the hands of the *Humans*. Only it didn't stop the *Humans*. The *Humans* thought they would get away with it ... and they did, the whole fucking time.

"Come on." He grabbed Helena's hand, telling himself the contact was more for her—not for him. Not because he was loath to let go of her. She needed him. She'd never make it out alone.

354

Exile

"Keep your head down," he said roughly, pulling her behind him.

When they reached the reception area, Tracey had managed to sit herself upright. Her legs were stretched out in front of her, knees slightly bent to the side, and her hands still on her belly.

Helena gasped and let go of Stephen's hand to run to her.

"I think I lost the baby," she whispered tearfully as Helena dropped to her knees next to her and pulled the weeping woman into her arms.

"Oh Trace ..."

"You didn't," Stephen said, he had come to crouch on the other side of her. He placed a hand on her stomach and gave her an encouraging smile. "He's still alive in there. I can feel him."

Tracey looked to Helena for her to confirm what he was saying.

"I—" She gave Stephen a bewildered look, no doubt wondering how the hell he would know that, or why he would give a woman such hope when it might turn out to be wrong. "Let's see, shall we?" she said, giving her shoulder a gentle squeeze.

She got up and grabbed a blanket from a cupboard in a corner, and quickly wrapped it around Tracey.

"We need to get her and all the others out of here. I know a place."

"Where?"

"I found somewhere. In the woodlands. Old. Backs onto the sea."

"Baxter's," Tracey said.

"It's haunted."

Stephen scoffed. "A few ghosts or those arseholes outside? We need to go. Right now. Can you get the kids?"

Helena nodded. "They're hidden."

"Where are Nigel and Mel … and their friend."

Helena struggled to meet Stephen's eyes. "They took Aiden …"

Stephen knew what that meant. Aiden's body had been cremated. "They'll turn up. We have to get out of here."

"The children are safe," said Helena.

"Don't think those *Humans* won't burn these places down if they have to, to find what they want. We need to get the kids out. Hidden or not, it isn't safe." He turned to Tracey. "I'm going to lift you up, okay? Hook your arm around my neck." He slid his arm around her back and the other under her legs, grimacing as the movement sent pain shooting through his shoulder as the wound tore open. "Go," he gritted out to Helena.

He followed her out of the door and into the back room. She went to the corner and pushed against the wall. There was a click and then it swung open.

Clever. Beyond the wall were steps. He followed Helena into the darkness then listened to a series of clicks and bolts and then a 'whoosh', followed by a scurry of feet as Eden, Toke and Nakita came running up the steps.

Stephen frowned "Where's Freya?"

"Here." Helena came out last with a slumped Freya leaning against her.

"She's sick, Nick," Eden said. "Like something … inside."

"We'll talk about it later. We have to get out of here. Can you can bring the kids?"

"Yes."

He pushed out of the house, his shoulder straining under the weight. He kept his ears open and his eyes peeled.

356

God, he wished he could do this as his *tiger*. His *tiger* had such better senses than he did.

He got to the end of the garden and lowered Tracey to the ground. "Just give me a second. He peered over the top of the wall, making sure it was all clear.

Picking up Tracey once more, he carried her to the gate at the side. Eden went through first with the little ones, followed by Helena and Freya, and then him. He would rather he was at the back of them. That way anyone coming up would get him first. That was the theory anyway. "Go into that yard there." He gestured to the garden he had come through that led to the main outer wall. "We're gonna have to scale the back, but we can do it."

Standing at the back wall to the main outer area, Eden placed her hands on her hips and stared at it. "How the shit are we going to get Freya and Tracey over this?"

"You and Helena go over. I can lift them up. You help them down."

She looked at Helena, eyes wide.

"Might work," Helena added.

"Has to work," Stephen said. "It's this, or we walk out the front gates, and I am not so sure that is going to happen."

"Right."

"Eden first."

"Me?" She placed her hand on her chest. "Why me?"

"Because you have magic. There is a *Human* patrol that comes around. I need you to knock one out with your witchy stuff."

"Wait …" She wagged a finger at him. "No one mentioned me doing any witchery shit to anyone here. Just …"

"Want to try the front gate?" Stephen ground out.

357

"Okay ... I'll do it. I have something."

She stuck her hand in her bag that rested across her chest—her little bag of tricks. She never let go of the damn thing. Probably be buried with it one day, he thought wryly. "Got it," she said, pulling out a tub. "This'll roofie the guy."

"You often *roofie* guys?"

"Ha." She squeezed some of it into her hands and rubbed them together.

"There are two of them," Stephen warned. "They meet in the middle and then pass. We can take them both out, or we can try and do a full cycle. If you get over the wall and race ahead, there is a little car that you can drop behind. Just pounce when he comes and let us know."

"Battle with them both?"

Stephen shrugged. "We can get over between them."

Putting Tracey down once again, he grabbed Eden around her tiny waist and picked her up, the pain in his shoulder burning down along his back, bringing an irrepressible groan from his throat.

"I am not that heavy," Eden shot down to him.

"Might disagree with that." She grabbed the wall, lifting herself the rest of the way.

"No one here."

"Good. Jump down," Stephen instructed.

There were a few cars behind her—old things that no one had used in a while. She just had to hide behind one of those. *Humans* couldn't sniff her out.

It didn't take long; less than a minute and suddenly there was a sound. Body on body. The odd 'humph', a groan and then, "He's down."

"Good. Helena next."

"Nick ... I—"

"You can do this. I promise. But you've got to go now."

358

He wished he was as certain as he tried to sound. "Ready?"

Without waiting for her to answer, he spun her around and gripped her waist. God, she felt so good under his hands. When she leaned her head back to look up, he breathed in the intoxicating smell of her hair. He was pretty sure it had nothing to do with which shampoo she used, and everything to do with the fact that it was Helena.

He gripped tight, fingers digging into her flesh as he held himself still for just long enough to calm himself and push his *tiger* back down. The urge to protect and to claim roared inside him with the force of a hurricane.

"You can do this, okay?" he said hoarsely. He quickly cleared his throat and hauled her up before he did anything to embarrass himself—like bend down and nuzzle her neck.

He felt a deep sense of pride at how quickly she managed to grab onto the ledge and climb over. She was over the wall and had dropped down onto the other side in seconds. They didn't have very long before the other *Human* came back this way.

Next, Stephen lifted Toke and then Nakita. He couldn't help but play dream Helena's words over in his mind again and again as he did. His children ...

The sudden fierce need to protect them sent his mind spinning, threatening to knock him off his feet.

Pulling himself together, he turned to Freya. "Your turn now."

Freya was light, small. The hard one was going to be Tracey. Sweat beaded on Stephen's forehead, the pain in his shoulder throbbing. Lifting everyone had been an effort, even though none had been heavy, and he would ordinarily not have even broken a sweat over it. Tracey was two people and in a mess. "We're gonna do this, okay?" He put his arm around her. "We can get over this."

The words were spoken as much for himself as they were for her. Yeah, he was a shifter and fucking strong ... and any other day, no problem. But his shoulder felt like it was literally splitting in two. Blood poured down his back, and his head was in such a spin that it was just about giving him motion sickness.

It was impossible for Tracey to pull herself up over the wall the last part, and no matter how strong he was, suddenly growing taller to be able to push her that far was most likely unfeasible.

He stared up at the wall. "This isn't going to work."

He picked up the sound of the approaching footsteps, and he swore silently. "Someone is coming," Stephen called over to them. "You all need to get out of there.

"We're not leaving you," Eden called back in a loud whisper.

"You have to. Get to the road."

"I know where Baxter's is," Helena said.

"Head there then." The footsteps were closer. "Go. You need to go now."

"Leave me here," Tracey said.

"And just where would that get me?"

"You could help the others."

"I am not leaving you. Just stay there."

He helped Tracey to the ground, letting her lean against the wall. Her pants were soaked with blood, and it was only because he could still hear the gentle heartbeat of her unborn baby that he wasn't worried. It was nice and steady. Despite the huge blood loss, the baby was holding on. Strong.

Exile

Stephen searched the garden and found a small shed to the side. When he opened the doors to it, he almost laughed.

"Ladders. Thank fuck." A break. He grabbed them and ran back to Tracey, a big fucking grin on his face like he had just found a lottery ticket. "Told you we can do it. We're gonna climb to the top, sit on the wall, and then I'll put this down the other side. Okay?"

He held his hand out to her, and she grabbed it. "Let's get our arses out of here Before any more *Humans* show up."

Tracey needed help, each step harder than the one before, but he pushed behind her, guiding her, giving her as much power as she needed. The *Human* patrol had passed without a word, not having realised that he hadn't crossed paths with his counterpart.

Yet.

Once Tracey was safely at the bottom, Stephen jumped down and pushed the ladder up and back over the wall.

"Let's find the others," Stephen winked at Tracey as he picked her up yet again. "Hold on."

Chapter Forty
Stephen

By the time Stephen got to the Baxter's with Tracey, he resembled something out of an apocalyptic zombie film. Blood soaked the back of his shirt from his wound. With each move he made, the slowly healing flesh was torn open again, and keeping as still as possible while he carried Tracey had been impossible.

The front of his shirt was covered with Tracey's blood, too, making his hold on her slippery and a constant battle not to drop her.

It was a relief when the first building came into view. There were more buildings in the distance that surrounded the one where he was keeping Lee. He sniffed the air, Helena's scent jarring him to a halt. His *tiger* sat up, a soft growl of anticipation coming from him as he headed towards an old, dilapidated house. Part of the roof was missing on the lower side where he imagined there might have been an extension building. Piles of old red brick littered the path to the door … but they were in there. *She* was in there. Stephen could feel her like a homing beacon to his *tiger*.

Tightening his hold on Tracey, he climbed the steps and pushed the old creaking door open with the toe of his boot. Inside, the building was dark, musty smelling. Wallpaper peeled off the wall to the side, giving way to the spots of black mould that was growing there. Once, this would have been a nice family home. Now it was empty … the heart of it dead.

"Helena … Eden?" Stephen called into the darkness, eyes and ears scanning all around him. The first room had no door, but it was obvious it had once been a lounge. A sofa and a coffee table stood in the middle of the room facing a smashed television screen. On the walls were pictures, the glass covered in dust, obscuring the smiling faces that looked down at them.

Feeling somewhat like an intruder in someone else's home, he walked to the sofa and gently lowered Tracey onto it. "I'm just going to set you down here, okay?" From what he could tell, the bleeding had stopped, and he sent up a silent prayer of thanks.

"Are they here?"

"I think so." He kept his ears open, alert. His *tiger* radar sensed movement in the next room and upstairs. A floorboard creaked overhead and dust trickled through a crack in the ceiling. "Freya?" he called out.

There was a moment's hesitation, then the sound of little running feet on the boards above them.

Tracey gripped his hand, and he answered with a reassuring squeeze.

"Nakita—" Eden yelled from somewhere above as feet bounded down the stairs. The next minute, Nakita was charging into the room, grinding to a halt as soon as she laid eyes on him. Her face lit up, but she stood there unsure, her big, green eyes watching him with caution.

"Daddy," she whispered.

Stephen felt plagued with sudden guilt from his harsh words to her before. Whether she knew what she was really saying, or if this was just a happy make-believe game to her, she was still just a little kid. It didn't matter if she wanted to pretend, or that he was surrounded by delusional people supporting her fantasy notion. But even as he thought all this, unease ran up his spine as he found himself staring at an expression on her small delicate face that was all too familiar …

Mason Sabre

He moved restlessly from one foot to the other. "Where is everyone else?"

"Did you hurt yourself?" She edged closer, her young eyes on his clothes.

He glanced down at his blood-stained shirt then gave a terse shake of his head. "No, I'm fine." Clearing his throat, he met her gaze. "Are you okay?"

"Nakita—" Eden scolded as she hurried into the room behind the child. She crouched down and took hold of her arms, turning her to face her. "You can't run off like that. It's dangerous."

"It was my Daddy," the little girl pouted.

Eden's tone remained stern. "It might not have been."

"She's right," Stephen said, nodding toward Eden. "It might not have been me. You could have got into trouble. You shouldn't run off like that."

"But I smelled you," she said stubbornly. She was too young to have her senses at peak, though, and much too young to have them trained at identifiable sources. Shifters really didn't come into their powers fully until puberty hit and even then, it was hit and miss. The only way a child would come into their powers early would be if they had been bitten—and Nakita wasn't bitten.

"You smelled me?"

"Yes."

He wanted to tell her it was impossible, but something in him told him that wasn't the case.

"Eden, do you have ..." Helena's voice tapered off as she rounded the corner and saw Stephen. "You're here," she said breathlessly, before her eyes fell to Tracey.

"I can still feel the heart beating," he said as she rushed over to the other woman. The scent of her permeated his senses as she hurried past him, sending his *tiger* crazy. He

364

clenched his fists and tried to focus.

She gave a grim nod then murmured, "That's good." As she took note of Tracey's vitals, she offered him a quick smile. "Shifter hearing is something I will forever be envious of."

It wasn't really the heart he could feel—it was the mind. He could read it the same way a person knew what the time of day it was just by how they felt. But it was easier to just say he could feel the heart beating. He didn't have a bloody clue how to explain it otherwise. He was shifter— Helena could understand him feeling a heartbeat. And the last thing he wanted was her thinking of him as some kind of freak.

It vaguely registered that Nakita had sidled up to him and slipped her hand in his. "Where's Freya?" he asked as the little girl leaned comfortably against his leg.

Helena shifted her gaze back to Stephen, her mouth opening then promptly closing again.

He scowled. "Helena?"

"She's in the back room."

Brows furrowed at her hesitancy to tell him Freya's whereabouts, he lifted Nakita into his arms without thinking. Her little arms went around his neck unprotestingly. "Where is Toke? Nigel?"

"Toke's in the back room," Eden said. "Nigel and the others haven't come yet. They might not be able to find us now."

Helena looked up from Tracey. "Maybe they didn't get out?"

Nigel didn't seem the kind of man who would lie down and take shit. He was a fighter—a survivor. Stephen had seen enough of them in his lifetime to recognise one when he saw them. But he hadn't seen nor scented him back at the clinic.

Nigel was a shifter, though. So was Mel. They needed to be around pack, and in the middle of all this chaos, that was what most of them were in this house … an odd mix yes, but pack nonetheless.

"They'll come," he said grimly as he handed Nakita to Eden.

***

Freya was sitting in an armchair by what would have been a fire. There was a table in the middle layered with dust and bits of rubble that had fallen from the ceiling. Her eyes were closed, and it struck Stephen that she looked … different. There were lines and wrinkles that shouldn't be marring such a young face.

"Freya?"

Her eyes cracked opened at the sound of Stephen's voice, and he blinked in surprise at the different colours shimmering there.

"What's wrong? Are you ill?"

Her breaths came in shallow gasps. "Brisingamen," she whispered the familiar word weakly. "You need to …"—she swallowed—"find it."

He grabbed the glass of water sitting on the small table beside her and handed it to her.

"I know who you are," he said tightly as she sipped water though dry, cracked lips. "I just don't understand everything else."

"You know?" she whispered.

"You need to explain it all to me. Make me understand it."

She gave a small nod then grimaced in pain. After a moment, she rasped, "Brising … it means fire."

His brows drew together. "Like Aiden?"

She nodded slowly, trying to sit up. Her head fell

366

forward, and Stephen caught her as she slumped and slid down in the chair. A weak hand rubbed over her face. "Find it. It isn't meant to be here. *I* am not meant to be here."

"What does that mean?" *Hell*. The more he asked, the more riddles he was given. "How can I find something when I don't have a clue where to start? When I don't even know what it means. *Explain* it to me."

"Aiden ... he told you ..." she wheezed, her eyes closing as if it was impossible to keep them open any longer. How was this the great and powerful Freya when she couldn't even sit up properly?

Her breathing grew slow, and he knew without checking that she had passed out. God damn it. She had told him nothing really.

There was a soft knock on the door, then Eden tentatively peered around it. "The children are hungry," she murmured. "It's been a long time since they have eaten anything." When Stephen stared at her without a word, she said, "I can go and ..."

"No." He exhaled heavily and took one last long look at Freya. He'd not get answers from her. "I'll catch something." After a moment's pause, he pulled the blanket over Freya and draped it over her legs as she slept. Everyone seemed to be depending on him, yet he was lost in the fucking dark without a clue as to why or what he was supposed to be doing. Food he could do—that didn't require much thought and was not as demanding on the mind.

"I found some tinned things. They'll do for tonight, but anything else in this house ceased to be edible a decade ago. The only other thing I managed to do was get the water working. There's an old water wheel at the back. Seems it's been working this whole time. The water is pretty clean."

Stephen ushered Eden out of the room, letting the

door close behind him with a quiet click. Maybe Freya just needed some rest.

"There will be some rabbit around here." Or rat, he thought to himself. If they needed food, fucking rat would have to do.

"I can cook it. I'll make a fire out back."

He rubbed at his temple. He was so damn tired. Not just physically, either. "That would be like a smoke signal." A fucking beacon. "These children are shifters ... they can eat it raw."

Eden screwed up her face. "And everyone else who isn't a heathen?"

"I'll find you some apples or some shit ... but no fires," he warned. "Feed them what you have so far."

***

Including the house they were in, and the building where he was, there were six buildings in total, all of them hidden from view of the main road.

Clever. They had probably been built this way on purpose. But even so, now they were nothing, empty and riddled with age and decay. Perhaps there was food in one of them—even if it was just old tins of peaches. It was better than nothing at all.

"You're hurt." Helena's voice came from behind him in the small kitchen where he stood staring out the window. He'd smelt her before she spoke, and he had to brace himself before he could turn around and face her.

He clenched his jaw and stuffed his hands into his pockets so that he wouldn't reach for her. "I'm okay," he bit out.

She took a step towards him. "Let me look at it."

"It's fine," he said curtly, jerking away from her. "It'll heal." One fucking touch from her and he would be lost.

Hurt flashed in her eyes, and her hand dropped back to her side. He cursed inwardly, hating the way his *tiger* snarled at him for putting that look on her face. "It's bleeding," she said stiffly.

Stephen reached behind him, bringing back a wet hand. "It doesn't seem to want to stop. Like bloody silver," he muttered.

She dared to take another step closer to him. "But it wasn't silver?"

He could lie ... he *should* lie ... "It's from a bite. An animal bite. I was ..." His voice trailed off as she took another step and came to stand right in front of him, invading all his senses. His mouth went dry and his brain stopped working properly. "I need to get some food," he said in a hoarse voice. "Eden asked—" But he stayed rooted to the spot, eyes fixed on Helena.

"Can I fix this up first?" She reached up and touched his shoulder lightly. Electricity shot through him and he stumbled backwards.

"No—" He couldn't think with her this close. She was like a drug he craved, and as much as he wanted to walk away from it, he just couldn't. "Maybe after ..." He walked backwards toward the door, banging into the table as he did. He needed to put space between them. "Is Tracey okay? The baby?" he babbled.

Beautiful brown eyes followed his retreat, her perfect brow knitting in consternation. "They're okay," she said after a moment. "She just needs to rest."

Stephen nodded his head, but he couldn't really focus on what she was saying. He was too busy imagining what it would feel like to run his fingers through her silky hair. His *tiger* prowled to the surface, fangs baring as he demanded to claim her as his own.

With a quiet curse, Stephen spun away. "I should go ... "Need to get food ..."

Chapter Forty-One
Stephen

Stephen sucked in a deep breath, filling his lungs with the crisp, clean evening air. He needed to clear his head. A yearning that would only get bigger with time pervaded his every cell. Her scent was strong to him—odd since she was *Human*—but it stayed with him as he followed the moss-covered path leading away from the house, wrapping itself delicately around him and closing him in ...

This was the calling card of a female. When a *tiger* found its mate, the scent was like no other—the beacon that said they were in the right place, with the right shifter.

But Helena wasn't *tiger*. She wasn't even *Other*. So none of this made any sense.

His *tiger* needed a bloody head check. It had the wrong species.

Stephen rubbed a weary hand over his face. He needed something ... something to take his mind off Helena.

She was so beautiful, her body, her face, her mind, so cruelly perfect. His *tiger* wanted to possess every part of her. If she had been *tiger*, he would have already made her his. No other male would have been able to get close ... no other male would have dared. She was like fine wine he needed to savour, one sip at a time.

But it was madness. How could his *tiger* have chosen a *Human*? If Eden had been a stronger witch, he might have blamed her for this lunacy inside his mind. It would make more sense than this.

"Nick ..." Helena's voice slammed into him with the force of a steam engine as she came running up behind him. "Please stop."

He came to an abrupt halt but kept his back to her. He was too close to the edge to face her right now. He concentrated on his breathing, trying to ignore the snarling of his *tiger* as he made his demands. She needed to go back inside and get the hell away from him—he was a ticking time bomb.

"What's wrong, Nick?" she said from behind him, worry leaking through her voice.

The sound was a sweet song that sang to his heart and called to his *tiger*. His eyes focused on the path ahead and not the ever-growing need inside him.

"Nick?"

"What?" he snapped, whirling around. He hadn't meant to be so abrupt, but it infuriated him that he had no control over what she was doing to him. She was so damn close, eyes wide as she stared at him, startled. "Look, I can't …"

She waited for him to finish, but his gaze had locked onto her mouth. Confusion marred her smooth features. "Can't?"

As he continued to stare at her mouth, her lips parted, her breathing growing shallow under his intense scrutiny. Fuck, he could sense her arousal … and that was his undoing.

Before he knew what he was doing, his hand had shot around the back of her neck, dragging her to him. His mouth slammed down onto hers, swallowing her gasp of surprise and devouring what he had been craving for so long. Her sweet taste was an aphrodisiac to his senses, making him want more. He growled against her lips as his *tiger* leapt in his chest, the fierce need to claim turning into an inferno now that it had had its first taste of her.

When he released her mouth, she was breathless, eyes closed and fingers clutching his shirt. The look of total surrender on her face had him imagining what she would look like under him, his body thrusting deep inside hers, claiming her. With a groan, he bent his head and took her mouth in a passionate kiss once more, his tongue sweeping in to taste the sweet recesses within. His need hitched up a notch when he felt her nails digging into his shoulders, desire shooting straight to his groin. He snaked an arm around her waist and brought her flush against him, nearly lifting her off the ground. She moaned into his mouth at the intimate contact, and Stephen's erection strained between them, the feel of her lush breasts pressed against his hard chest making him lose the last vestiges of control. All logic thought fled.

With a soft oath, he dragged his mouth away and trailed his lips and teeth along her jawline, hooking a big hand under one of her silky thighs and lifting it to his hip. He couldn't get enough of her. Her taste was so rich ... so addictive. He nipped the soft flesh at the side of her neck, and she whimpered, leaning closer into him. When her hands slipped around his waist and raked down his back, he thought he'd explode. *Take her. She's yours*. The words echoed loudly in his head, making him oblivious to everything else around them.

Desperate to be inside her, he lifted his head, panting, ready to lower her to the ground and bury himself between her legs. His eyes fell on the house in the distance and he froze.

He wrenched away from her, making her stumble and stare up at him with dazed, lust-filled eyes. God, he had to look away from her before he did exactly as he wanted—and whoever could see them be damned.

Hands raised, he backed up, still breathing hard. "I'm sorry. I shouldn't have done that."

Confused and furious at himself, he turned without

waiting for her to reply and fell into a run. He badly needed distance between them.

He raced across the uneven paths toward the cliff edge. When he reached the building where he was keeping Lee, he pushed down the bar over the big door in case any of them came to look for him. He didn't want anyone walking in on his little project. He imagined that they—especially Helena—might not be best pleased with his extracurricular activities.

Lee was lying in the corner, curled on his side like an animal. His cuts were still raw, much Like Stephen's shoulder—they should have healed by now.

His eyes fixed on Stephen as he approached. "Let me out of this fucking cage."

Stephen knelt by the cage and gripped one of the bars. "Your good buddies just tore up the town, you know." His voice was deceptively calm. "They killed innocent people."

Lee pushed himself up, leaning back against the wall, leg bent at the knee. "Innocent?" His lip curled in a sneer.

A tick worked along Stephen's jaw. "They had done nothing to you."

"They were *Other*."

He cocked his head to the side. "Like you now?"

He watched as Lee balled his hands into fists. "Fuck you. I'll never be *Other*. Whatever the fuck you've done to me, it won't last."

"Oh?" He raised an eyebrow at him. "How so? You have some magic trick that can reverse this?"

"Silver …"

He narrowed his eyes at him. "Silver?"

An evil smile broke over Lee's face before he crawled towards him. Much as Stephen despised to, he had no choice but to move back. It made him look weak, which he wasn't.

But he just wasn't giving Lee the opportunity to get the drop on him.

"Yep ... silver. Vaccines," he hissed. "Had all my shots." He wiped the wound on his arm, coming away with a hand smeared with wet blood. "My body isn't accepting your ... *disease*. We're all vaccinated against you filthy shifters."

Stephen's blood ran cold. *Fuck*. Who would have imagined that the *Humans* would go even this far? But it explained why the hell his wound wasn't healing.

"Your plan is fucked, isn't it?" Lee sneered, that malicious grin still in place.

Stephen smiled, unfazed, making the grin on Lee's face waver. "Maybe I have my own magic juice."

He grabbed a rat he had left just out of reach and tossed it into the cage. "I'll be back soon" he said coolly. "Keep yourself fed, arsehole."

"You're a fucking piece of shit," Lee called after him as he eyed the rat, defiance etched on his face.

He could hold back as much as he wanted, but the hunger would eventually take over, and he would eat this rodent just like he had eaten the others

Chapter Forty-Two
Helena

Helena sat at the counter on one of the tall stools they had found in the kitchen. It had been a nice kitchen once; she imagined. Something someone had probably taken pride in. A place for a family … somewhere to cook dinner parties and hold children's birthday gatherings. She held her hands clasped in front of her face, chewing on her thumb nail.

"Penny for them," Eden said as she came in and went to the sink to fill up a glass with water.

"I don't think you've got that much money," Helena joked with a sigh and a smile that didn't quite reach her eyes.

He'd kissed her. Full on and forceful. She could still feel his lips on hers. Even now. The graze of the stubble around his mouth, the musky scent of him that was all man and all shifter.

He'd kissed her …

And what a kiss it had been.

Her insides tightened with the memory. Nick Mason was a master of seduction, she had no doubt.

Then he had pushed her away like he'd done the most disgusting thing possible. The expression of revulsion on his face had seared itself into her mind forever. He had probably run to find somewhere to wash his mouth out. So much time had passed, and he still hadn't come back.

Eden leaned on the counter opposite Helena, glass to the side. "Everything will be okay, you'll see," she said with a warm smile.

Eden was one of those people who were always happy, Helena decided. Even now, in the midst of all this, her hair was like a bright flower, her face the centre that always smiled.

"Do you believe that?"

She shrugged lightly. "We have to. There has to be faith."

"How do you keep hold of it?" Helena sighed.

"Because if we didn't, we'd drive ourselves insane with all the thoughts of what if this, or what if that. How could you have peace inside?"

That was true. She'd already driven herself to the brink of insanity with all the *what if* thoughts. What if Nick didn't come back? What if Lee and his men found them? What if she were cast out from both sides? What if Nick really did find her disgusting because she was *Human*?

"Do you think Nick will come back? *Here*, I mean?"

Eden smiled, making her oddly shaded eyes sparkle. "Yeah, I do. Don't you worry about that."

"It's been hours." He could be so far away by now. He could leave and never come back —just like her father had. But then, his children were here, she reminded herself. He'd not leave them. "I feel like I am going crazy, you know?"

Eden laughed. "He has that effect on people." She gave Helena's hand a quick squeeze for reassurance before straightening again. "He'll be back. I promise."

Helena wanted to believe her. And part of her trusted it even … But the doubt of a very young Helena made her want to hide from fear. The chance that he might not come back created a gaping hole inside her chest.

Touching her fingers to her lips, she brought to mind the feel of his lingering kiss. It was complete madness. No man had ever had such a profound effect on her. There was something different about him. A feral quality that did strange things to her senses. It awakened parts of herself she thought she had forgotten. "Please come back," she whispered to herself. "Please."

With a heavy heart, she pushed herself off the stool. She had a house full of patients who needed tending to. Sitting there dwelling on that shit would not help her or anyone else.

Eden had given Freya the glass of water and settled her into the back room. Helena had never seen another like Freya, still not sure what species she was—and Freya wasn't saying. She hadn't wanted her sitting in the back room, but the girl had insisted. She had said she wanted to be alone and did not let Helena examine her, either, saying it was nothing and that once they got her necklace back, she would be okay. So they had let her rest on one of the large armchairs, her legs draped over the side and a blanket covering her—they had found some clothes and blankets earlier when scavenging around the houses, along with some other little bits they could use, like shampoo and tins of food. For now, they hadn't explored the school, which backed onto the edge of the cliff, the pathway of which had crumbled.

She checked on Tracey, who had been settled in the lounge, with Nakita and Toke curled up together in a sleeping bag on the floor near her. She was sleeping soundly, and Helena was relieved to see the bleeding had stopped. The poor woman's placenta had been low down, and Helena had reassured her that was all it was—so she hoped, at least. She couldn't know for sure without being able to use an ultrasound, but these things happened. As far as she could tell, the baby was fine, though … for now.

They had chosen to make the floor of the lounge into a giant bed, despite the fact that there were bedrooms upstairs with actual beds in them. She didn't want to leave Tracey and Freya downstairs alone and couldn't risk getting

Tracey up the stairs. The idea of putting Toke and Nakita to bed up there by themselves was also out of the question. It was safer for everyone this way ….

Helena shuffled onto the floor near Tracey and the children. The yellow glow from the risen moon streamed in through the grimy window, illuminating the stark lounge and giving it a semblance of warmth. She sent up a small prayer that it would light the way for creatures such as Nick. Did *tigers* respond to the full moon the same way wolves did? Helena wondered. The moon wasn't full tonight, but it was close to it, the edge tinged with the shadow of the earth.

She knew shifters had to shift every few days, but would an almost full moon compel him to?

Realising her thoughts were being consumed by Nick again, she sighed and rolled onto her side, tucking one hand under her ear and the other between her thighs. It felt like a lifetime had passed since Nick had shown up on her doorstep with the kids and Eden. So much had happened in such a short space of time. And the undeniable attraction she felt for Nick scared her to death. Never before had a male had such an effect on her—and she wasn't quite sure how to deal with it. There was an animalistic magnetism about Nick that turned her mind to mush and had her looking like a babbling schoolgirl every time she was around him. She tried not to think about the incredible kiss they had shared earlier, or the way he had run from her right after it. Right now, all she wished was that he would walk back through the door any minute.

Forcing her mind away from him, she wondered if Nigel and Mel and Xander were okay. She hoped they hadn't been found or captured and that wherever they were, they were safe.

Her own kind had killed innocent people, attacked and committed atrocities she hated to remember ... it made her ashamed to be *Human*. That was what Nick saw. That was why he wouldn't come back. He was disgusted with himself for having touched her.

With dread clenching her stomach, she let her eyes close and pulled the blanket more tightly around herself. She needed sleep to stop her mind going over all this madness.

***

It was still dark outside when Helena opened her eyes again. She blinked to clear the sleep from her eyes, and yawning, she propped herself up on an elbow. Toke and Nakita were curled up together in the corner, and Tracey was still sleeping. But the spot where Eden had settled down for the night was empty.

"Eden?" she whispered, not wanting to wake the others. She could hear muffled voices from somewhere at the back of the house, and her first thought was that maybe Freya had woken and needed something ... But at the deep sound of a male voice, her stomach flipped.

Heart in her mouth, she tiptoed out of the room and crept into the darkness of the hallway. The dusty wood creaked under her bare feet as she quietly made her way toward the kitchen.

The voices hushed as she reached the half-closed door and then carefully pushed it open. Her insides tightened at the sight of Nick's tall frame filling the small kitchen. God, he was so very beautifully masculine.

She flushed as his gaze swept over her bare legs, and she was suddenly very aware of her semi state of dress. Swallowing nervously, she pulled the over-sized shirt more tightly around her and watched as his jaw tightened. Her heart dropped. He was probably revolted just at the mere sight of her, she thought miserably.

"Sorry, didn't mean to wake you," Eden said as she pulled the door open a little wider.

"It's okay." She squirmed nervously and wished she had thought about wrapping the blanket around her first. "Is everything okay?"

"I found food," Nick said tightly, indicating a small bag on the counter. "Some apples too. I found a couple of trees not so far away."

Eden's eyes moved from one to the other, her sharp gaze not missing a thing. "Nick was asking for some of my creams," she said, holding out one of her pots. "To draw the silver out."

Helena frowned, the doctor in her instantly coming to the foreground. "Your bite? I thought it was an animal bite. I thought there was no silver."

"Me too," he muttered, but moved back when she took a step to have a closer look. Her heart fell at his blatant rejection, but she pushed down her embarrassment and focused on the fact he needed medical help.

She tried to assure herself his problem was her species, not her personally. But *Human* or not, she was a doctor, and right now, he needed her—even if he wanted to be a stubborn jackass about it. "I just want to take a look at it. I'm a doctor. Perhaps I can help."

He scowled and grabbed the cream from Eden. "I'll just use this. It'll take the silver out and then it will heal."

Helena stiffened, fighting down the hurt from his constant rebuff. Eden shot her a sympathetic look, probably thinking how pathetic she looked. "Okay," she said stiffly. "We found some clothes for you ... They're upstairs. They should fit ..."

381

He gave a curt nod of thanks.

Feeling like a spare part at a party she hadn't been invited to, she hugged herself and took a step back. "I'll go back to bed. You can come and get me if you need anything."

"Well, he'll probably need you to put the cream on for him," Eden said, jumping down off her stool. "I am going back to bed."

"You're not doing it?" The underlying current of panic in his voice would have been comical if Helena hadn't been the source of it.

"Nope. I am going to get some sleep. I'm dead tired." As she sauntered past a stiff Helena, she grabbed her hand and gave it a light squeeze. "See you in a few."

Helena returned her smile, unsure whether she should feel grateful or not at her leaving. Nick did not seem pleased at all.

As soon as Eden had left, he turned his back on her and went to the sink. Without a word, he turned the tap on and washed mud, and God knows what else, from his hands. Then he ripped his shirt down the front, popping open the buttons and letting it slide down his broad back, revealing rippling muscles under tanned, silky smooth skin. Helena gulped and tried not to salivate. Her eyes were instantly drawn to the tattoo that ran up his arm and across his shoulder. The intricate pattern was impressive, and it only served to magnify the perfection of his already beautiful form.

As he shoved the shirt under running water and used it to clean the blood from his shoulder, she mentally chastised herself and forced herself to stay focused on his wound. Dark, deep gouges marred his beautiful skin, the area around it an angry red colour, which showed an infection.

"Let me to help with that," she urged, as she watched him struggling to twist the right way to get to it. Water ran down his back, pooling at the top of his jeans and belt.

"I can manage," he muttered gruffly, angling himself so he could see his reflection in the window above the sink.

"I don't think—"

"It's fine." His eyes met Helena's in the glass, sending her pulse up a notch with his hot gaze. She swallowed hard, her body reacting in ways that were far from professional.

"D-Do you want me to grab the clean clothes for you?" She retreated, desperately needing an excuse to get out of the kitchen and put her shamed self back to bed in the dark where no one would see her.

He hesitated, his gaze scorching her. "I'll get them. Upstairs, right?"

She nodded, unable to speak for a moment. "Yes. There are three bedrooms up there. I put them in the first."

He gave her a curt nod.

"I'll leave you to it then." Even as she spoke the words, she was wishing he would stop her and tell her to stay.

When he said nothing, she turned to leave, but stopped at the door. "Do you not like me because I'm *Human*?"

He paused with the wet cloth pressed to his shoulder, that feral gaze locked on her once again and making it hard for her to think. He was quiet for so long she started to think he wasn't going to give her an answer. "I like you," he said eventually, his voice hoarse.

Surprise, and idiotic joy, shot through her. "You seem to want me to leave. It is because I am *Human*?"

Another long pause. "No."

"What then?" She couldn't keep the anger from her tone, the pent-up frustration of him having disappeared and leaving her after that devastating kiss leaking out. "Where did you go all night? What if Norton and his men came and found us?"

"Norton won't be finding you," he said with confidence. "You don't need to worry about that."

She frowned, wondering how he could be so sure.

"I was here."

Her challenging gaze met his straight on. "Avoiding me?"

"No."

"Prove it then," she demanded, stepping back into the room and closing the door behind her. "Let me tend to your wounds. I am a doctor, and you're bleeding."

He put the cloth down slowly, then turned, revealing every gorgeous inch of his torso to her. She tried to put herself in doctor mode and think of him clinically. *It's just a male body, for God's sake*, she scolded herself. *Yes, but it's a gorgeous male body*, her subconscious taunted her.

As she approached, she half-expected him to barge past her and leave. But with a soft oath, he grabbed the stool Eden had just vacated and sat down.

Tossing her the cream, he raised an eyebrow at her. "Fix it then, if you think you can."

She caught the tub with a small feeling of victory inside her.

As she inspected the wound, she realised he had actually done a pretty good job at cleaning it himself. "I just need to pat it dry," she said, grabbing a cloth from the side.

He sat with his hands flat on the counter, perfectly still. When she pressed delicate fingers near the wound to get a better look, he stiffened. She pursed her lips. Did he really hate her touching him so much? "It looks infected," she said evenly. "As soon as the silver is removed, I imagine the infection will heal itself."

She pressed the cloth to the wound, soaking up the water and a little of the blood where it still bled.

"You just rub it in," he said hoarsely, and she wondered if she was causing him that much pain. "That's all Eden did."

"Okay." She cracked the lid open, grimacing at the foul-smelling balm. "Jesus." It was colder than she expected as she scooped some out and pressed it onto his wound. He arched his back, gritting his teeth as his hands gripped the sides of the counter.

Hating that she was hurting him, but knowing this had to be done, she took another scoop of cream and pressed it firmly to his skin. He was burning up, so hot to the touch. Growling deep in his throat, his muscles bunched as the wound blistered like it was on fire. Silver bubbled out of it, sliding down his back, and Helena hastily wiped it off.

More oozed out, and she grabbed his wet shirt to catch the rest. Sweat ran down his back and despite the fact it must have felt like being branded, he stood perfectly still.

God, there was so much of it.

He was panting when the silver finally stopped seeping out and his skin started to knit itself together. It was amazing how it did that—no matter how many times she saw it, it always left her in awe. Pink flesh rose, closing, piecing his skin together perfectly where the tattoo blackened his skin.

"Thank you," he breathed, leaning heavily on the counter. His skin was soaked in perspiration.

"I can't believe how much it's healed," she said, then noticed the skin under his tattoo. She touched the black pattern where it ran onto his arm without thinking. "It's scarred?"

He snatched her hand away, vaulting off the stool and turning to face her. There was no doubt about it—under his tattoo, his skin was a mesh of scars.

"Don't." His hand gripped her wrist painfully, holding it away from his skin.

"I'm sorry," she said, pained to think that something— or somebody—had hurt him like this. She tried to back up. "I'm sorry. I didn't mean to …"

He didn't let her move, his hold on her strong. His eyes flickered green-gold, and something very feral and possessive gazed down at her from within, sending her body into heated panic. His breathing grew shallow, and desire slid through her like molten lava. Before she knew what was happening, he had yanked her to him so that she was pressed up against a hard wall of muscle, and a second later, his mouth was on hers. Her insides melted, her mind growing hazy. His kiss was hungry, needful, igniting a fire in her that threatened to consume her whole.

Strong hands grabbed her waist, lifting her onto the kitchen counter with no effort at all. He devoured her, tongue sweeping in in a possessive claim. Slowly, methodically, he trailed kisses along her jaw and down her neck, nipping the skin and sending small electric shocks through her body and down to her very centre. She gulped in air as her mind went off into a tail spin that she wasn't sure she would come back from.

"Nick," she breathed, head falling back as she gripped his shoulders.

"You have it all wrong, Helena," he growled against her skin as he nuzzled the side of her neck. "It isn't that I don't like you ..." He slid one hand down to her ass and pulled her closer, forcing her to part her legs to allow him to stand between them. "It is that I do." His erection settled intimately against her, as if to prove just how much. She gasped, digging her nails into his flesh.

"Is it wrong?" she asked, revelling in the feel of smooth, taut male skin under her hands. She could so easily drown in him.

He pressed her closer as his mouth worked on the curve between her neck and her collarbone, sending shivers along her skin and making her insides twist with delight. Heat seared her, right down to her core. "Yes," he gritted out, even as he caught her mouth in another bruising kiss.

"Why?" she rasped between short, ragged breaths.

He pulled back, breathing harsh, leaving her bereft. That beautiful green gaze bored into her. "Because you're *Human*."

He gripped the edge of the counter like he was fighting not to put his hands on her again.

Fear that he would back away any minute, she slid her legs up and locked her ankles around the back of his legs. His fingers tightened on the counter, and he closed his eyes for a long minute.

"Nick," she whispered, and he seemed to break. His hands moved to the side of her thighs, sliding up until his fingers reached the fabric of her shirt. A ragged breath left her as he slipped under the material and found the soft flesh of her backside. She shuddered, growing hotter and wetter between her legs. Hooking his fingers into the band of her panties, he started to slide them down, his gaze never wavering from hers. With a little whimper, she lifted herself up, letting him pull them down her legs so that she was left with nothing but the shirt. Her body craved him like it had never craved anyone before. She'd always been so turned off by other men. They only ever seemed to want one thing from her—the means to increase their power in one way or another. But Nick made her feel something so powerful, so strong, that it left her reeling.

His hands settled on her waist under the shirt, his thumbs circling the flesh of her abdomen and making her nipples pucker in anticipation of his touch. He growled as his eyes fell to the tight points visible under her shirt and he ground his straining erection against her core before taking her mouth in a passionate kiss that had her mind screaming from the pleasure of it.

"You're shaking," he rasped against her mouth, his hands edging up towards her swollen breasts.

"I've only ever been touched by a *Human*," she gasped mindlessly, before realising what she was saying. He tensed, lifting his head to stare down at her, jaw tight. Hurt flashed in his eyes and she regretted her words instantly. "Nick …"

"Did you fancy yourself a taste of the other side?" he bit out. "Is that what this is?"

"No …" she said quickly. "No, I—"

He pulled away from her abruptly, and she silently swore at her stupidity. How could she be such an idiot?

"I didn't mean it like that." She pulled the shirt down to cover her nakedness, feeling more than just physically exposed to him. "Please don't go."

He ran an angry hand through his hair, his beautiful face contorted into an expression of anguish. "I can't stay here. I feel like I am going mad from it all."

A cold hand of fear gripped her heart.

His hot gaze raked over her once again, and she saw the desire mixed with self-loathing. As he spun away and stalked towards the door, Helena wracked her brain for something to say. "I have to go to get some medical supplies tomorrow," she blurted out, making him halt at the door. "I was hoping you would come. I could use the help, and I have

388

no idea what threats lie in store after everything that happened at the clinic." She stared at his broad back, his shoulders stiff. "It's half a day's drive away. In Trentwich."

His head jerked to the side, his entire body freezing. "Trentwich?"

God, please say you'll come. "Yes."

He was silent for a long moment, and she wished she could see what was going on in that mind of his. "Fine," he finally grated, and left her sitting alone on the counter, her heart a million pieces around her.

Chapter Forty-Three

Stephen

Trentwich. Aiden's words echoed in Stephen's mind as he sat sullenly next to Helena in her small car—as incomprehensible to him now as they were then. The recent conundrum of Stephen's very odd and weird life. It was the riddle of riddles that, somehow; he was meant to know the answer to somewhere in the depths of his extremely overtired mind.

As he tried to stretch his long legs out in the cramped space, his knees bashed into the glove compartment, and for the hundredth time since they had set off, he wondered why he had bothered to go back for Helena's car where she had hidden it, and not just stolen a bigger, more comfortable vehicle along the way. He muttered an oath under his breath, earning himself a wary glance from Helena. The tension was thick in the air between them, and Stephen had barely exchanged two words with her the entire morning.

Keeping his eyes dead ahead, he made a great effort not to stare at her slender legs every time she changed gears, or remember what they had felt like under his hands and wrapped around his thighs. As he felt his body harden at the memory, he shifted uncomfortably in his seat and swore softly as his knees bashed into the glove compartment once again.

He focused on his destination.

So ... Trentwich was a place then. Good to know, though he still had no idea what the boy's prattling had all meant. Aiden was gone, yet he had insisted that Stephen teach him the word. How do you teach somebody who is dead—not to mention, teach things he himself did not know.

Maybe Stephen's new ability would be to see dead people, he thought wryly. It certainly wouldn't seem so strange given all the recent events in his life. Why not add another trick to the party box?

And the child's rambling about not opening a door … what the hell had that all been about? Apparently, opening doors got him killed. He should have asked which door. Maybe he should have asked for the address. That was it, wasn't it? He'd screwed up by not asking which door. Or even a date. Assuming any of this crock was true. By the time Stephen picked the right door, he would be such a mess; suffering from agoraphobia every time he needed to twist the handle. Full on panic attacks only to realise that it was the postman. Maybe Stephen would welcome death to save himself from suffering any more anxiety.

It was all so crazy.

They had left the kids and Freya with Eden. She wasn't bad for a witch, he admitted with reluctance. And for some strange reason, he trusted them to be safe with her. He hoped, at least. He sure wasn't taking them on this fucking trip to the unknown.

He and Helena drove in silence, which was mostly his fault. Whenever she asked him a question, all he offered was a grunt or a curt nod of the head. The less they said, the less her voice would stir up his *tiger* and turn him into a bloody mess.

Her hand grasped the gearstick, and his body responded as if she had just laid her hands on him. He closed his eyes briefly and gripped the edge of his seat. Damn his fucking *tiger*. Never before in his life had he wished to be separated from him.

His hands twitched, and he had to force them to stay where they were. He was pretty sure he was gouging holes into her upholstery, but better that than making her pull over so he could finish what they had started the night before. It sickened him that he still wanted her so much even though to her, he was just a lowly animal, something exciting to play out her sexual fantasies to.

"Maybe we can pick Tracey up when we're done? Take her home," Helena said after another bout of long silence. "Tell her husband what has happened."

"She lives in Fortvania." Stephen shuffled in his seat, wondering yet again why it was that women preferred to drive such tiny cars.

"Yes."

"It isn't safe to go back there." Stephen could picture walking Tracey up to her house and then getting lynched on the way in.

"I can take her." She glanced at him, and he was helpless to turn to look at her this time.

Jesus, she was so goddamn beautiful.

He swallowed hard and dragged his gaze away from her. "No." He wouldn't allow it. He knew that once Helena was seen, they'd grab her. She didn't realise it, but she was now on the Norton most wanted list, too. "We can drop her at the gate."

"Do you think Nigel and Mel and Xander will come and find us at Baxters?" she asked, trying again after more silence.

"I don't know why they would. They owe us nothing," Stephen grumbled.

She shot him a surprised look. "They believe in you. They're ready to risk their lives for you."

Exile

Stephen sighed. "This again? There is nothing to believe in."

She pursed her lips. "You don't see what everyone else sees."

Stephen focused on his reflection in the glass. Helena was wrong. They didn't see what they should see. That was the problem. "I am not what they think I am."

"Xander told us …"

"Told you what?"

"That you will be the one to make a stand against the other side … against *Humans*."

He snorted. "It is hard to stand when I am alone." He hated uttering those words, but it was true. He was one man. "There is only so much I can do."

"You don't get it. You give people courage. Didn't you feel it at the monument? You give people strength."

He barked out a laugh.

She stopped at a junction, gripped the wheel and turned to face him. "Xander hadn't walked until that moment. I thought he would give up. He stood up and walked … For you. Nigel and Mel, they came for you, too."

He scowled. "They hit me with their car."

"They saved you. They believe in you. You make everyone feel like they can do this. You make me feel like *I* can."

His gaze snapped back to hers. Did she realise she was talking about rebelling against *Humans*? Her own kind?

Her stare bored into him. "Just being near you makes me feel strong."

Her soft words hit him right in the heart. He opened his mouth to say something, but didn't have a fucking clue what it was he wanted to say. He cleared his throat and returned his gaze to the road, jaw clenching.

Realising she was getting nothing more from him, Helena pulled the car away, turning onto a longer road that looked pretty much the same as the last.

"We're here," she said after a while, nodding ahead. "Trentwich."

Stephen leaned forward as they approached. "The people of Trentwich live a fine life, I see."

The clean, high metal gates shone brightly. They would be blinding in the daylight. Even the brick was a bright red that made Stephen want to touch it to see if the paint was still wet. "This is a place for *Others*?"

"This is the main place," Helena said with an undertone of contempt in her voice. "They supply *Other* communities from here. Foods, medicinal supplies ..."

"Prison central." Stephen wondered what suffering the *Humans* had feared that made them give up a place so grand. Perhaps it was the late discovery that their luxurious homes had been built on toxic soil. If that was the case, he hoped that some of the *Humans* had perished before it was found. A few less *Humans* in the world did not do anyone any harm. With any luck, it might have even been contagious.

Stephen slumped down in his seat and pulled his hood up as Helena pulled to a stop at the gate. She rolled down her window and spoke into the small box on the side. "Doctor Helena Barnes," she said, handing over a card with her photograph on it to the hand that popped out of a small opening.

"Nice to see you again, Dr Barnes." The person in the booth stood back and then clicked a button. There was a series of noises and then the gate swung open.

Exile

How very posh, Stephen thought derisively. Fancy mechanisms and automatic. What had the *Others* in this gated community done to deserve this?

But as they rolled into the settlement, he realised that Trentwich wasn't really much of a town. Not in the same sense that Fortvania was. It was a lie—all of it. The gates, the walls, the look of pristine care. It was all shit.

Inside was a long road that led to a rather plain-looking building. On either side of the road, there were houses—lots and lots of houses. They were new, at least, but small, tiny in fact, and looked like they had been built from timber and sheets of Perspex for the windows. Maybe the brochure to this place advertised a wealthy life living beyond the gates. *Come live the life of luxury. Come beyond the gates … where we hide the shacks and the shitholes.*

As they drove up to the large building at the end of the long road, *Others* appeared from their small shacks, coming to stand at the kerb and watching like useless doormen.

Helena pulled the car into a faded parking spot and wasted no time getting out. There was no word to Stephen as she did so, not even a passing glance. He supposed that he had to follow her lead, like a good little lamb. Pulling the hood further over his head, he climbed out and walked behind her. Not that he minded the view, he thought, as his gaze fell to her sexy backside.

He had spotted his face staring out from the posters on every lamppost they had passed. What a wonderful greeting that was. It was doubtful that the *Others* here would care as much about not handing him over to the *Humans* as the ones in Fortvania had been—not that they had cared about him, but at least they hadn't turned him in.

When they entered the building, he made sure to keep his head down. A pair of old man's shoes stood before them.

There was the rest of the man, Stephen was sure, but from his position, all he could see were his scuffed shoes. Based on those alone, Stephen guessed that this man was a lot older.

"We have come to ask for aid," he heard Helena say, straight to the point. "We need some medical supplies."

"You're early, Helena." The voice belonged to a man who was well into his sixties, Stephen surmised.

"I know …" There was a moment's silence. "I'm sorry. We've had an influx of patients. The shaft at one of the mountains collapsed."

"Ah yes. I heard about that."

"I was the doctor in attendance."

"Well, you're two weeks early, sweetheart, so I don't have a lot I can give you, I'm afraid."

Trentwich was the maker of the *Humans* health care supplies, Helena had told Stephen on the drive in one of her attempts to make conversation. The people here ran the factory and produced medicines that kept the good old *Humans* alive. As payment, the residents got to keep any supplies that were not up to scratch. But they could also offer a small batch to neighbouring communities. It all worked on trade.

Stephen could sense Helena's frustration, but when she spoke, her voice was steady, determination lacing its edges. A fierce sense of proprietorship seized him. *His woman*. "We can pay."

"I don't want your money, but …"

"Come with me," the man said.

He led them to a house just a little further down from the large building. It didn't take a genius to work out that this was their version of a medical centre. Not that it was very medical—they appeared to be missing a practitioner according to the notice on the door, which stated there were no medical services until further notice, since the unfortunate passing of the good doctor.

Was there any such thing as a fortunate passing?

Maybe. If it was *Human*, Stephen decided.

The man unlocked the door and let out the bitter aroma of death. It lingered in the air, making them both catch their breath.

"Just upstairs," he said.

As they followed him, Stephen's senses stayed on high alert. They could well be walking into a trap, and though he didn't smell any *Human* scent on the air, he knew first-hand that there were *Others* that could be traitors to their own kind. Perhaps the man had realised Stephen's identity, and he wanted to cash in on the price. Or maybe it was simply that recent events were making Stephen Davies very paranoid. He hoped the latter were true.

He led them to a room at the back, almost reminiscent of a shoddy backstreet deal. Then Stephen realised that this was exactly what it was. Their trades and proposals were all backstreet deals. Behind the backs of the *Humans*. But this was more organised.

Stephen didn't expect to see a row of beds when they entered the room. He didn't expect anything, actually. The beds were empty and dirty, save for the one near the open window. The figure of a woman lay on the bed, and at first glance, she appeared dead. The stale stench emitting from the room was enough to make Stephen wish that he could never smell again. It was stale air filled with sickness and death, and he had to wait a moment before he could make himself enter.

Bloody hell.

Helena stood beside him, an expression of disgust and bewilderment on her face as she held a sleeve to her mouth and nose.

"Help her, and I will give you some supplies."

Helena furrowed her brow at his request, and Stephen wondered if the woman wasn't past the point of helping. The smell of death was thick in the air. Either way, the whole thing seemed like an awfully odd trade.

"Because you have no doctor?" Obviously, Helena thought it odd, too.

"He is dead." The words were uttered with resignation. "Do we have a deal? You take these two and I'll give you some supplies."

Two? Stephen picked up a second heartbeat … quick, frightened. His gaze swept the room and spotted the top of a small head barely visible on the other side of the woman's bed.

"We'll take it," Stephen said, cutting in before he even knew why.

Helena glanced at him in surprise then quickly turned back to the man. "Wait. Regular supplies?"

"Whatever we can spare unnoticed."

"What happened to the doctor?" Stephen asked.

The old man shrugged. "They all got sick. Bad food maybe, or water. Dr Frances died before we could do anything, and there was no one left who knew about healing."

Helena nodded her head toward the woman. "And her? She has the same?"

The old man threw a glance over his shoulder. "No, I don't think so. I'm not a doctor, but if she had the same, she would be dead. It took them in twenty-four hours." He let out a tired sigh. "She is a traveller, her and her boy. She collapsed suddenly and he won't leave her side. He …"

"I'll take a look at her for you," Helena said, cutting him off.

The man hesitated by the door, seeming to try to get a better look at Stephen.

Stephen stepped further into the room, standing in the shadows. He wasn't about to get busted by some old man who couldn't even pick out decent shoes.

Helena took cautious steps toward the woman, probably worried about contamination. "I just want to examine you … if you don't mind," she said kindly.

She pulled out a pair of gloves from her pocket, and Stephen could swear she had a massive supply of those on her person. Always the doctor, he guessed. "Can I roll you onto your back?" she asked the woman.

He went to stand at the end of the bed, hands stuffed into the front of the hoodie, his eyes going to the boy crouched in the corner—almost under his mother's bed. He was holding a comic and his head was down as he pretended to read, but Stephen would bet his life those eyes and ears were fully focused on them and what they were doing to his mother. Stephen crouched down, keeping a safe distance so as not to scare him away.

"He creates fire," said the man from the doorway. "He almost killed the kids that found his mother." He exhaled heavily. "We can't handle him. He burns everything."

"Does he have a name?" Stephen asked, his eyes never leaving the small figure in front of him.

"He said his name is Aiden …"

Chapter Forty-Four

Stephen

Stephen's heart did a somersault at the sound of Aiden's name. It was just a crazy coincidence, he told himself. Aiden was dead. Not to mention that the boy in front of him was not even the same age—probably around six or seven.

But Aiden's insistence that Stephen come to this place, and the incongruity of being led to a small child with the same name struck him as extremely odd at that moment ...

The small cry that fell from Helena's lips scrambled his thoughts and had him jumping back up.

"Oh, God—" She was shaking her head and pointing at the woman. "Sh-She looks just like me."

What was she talking about? Stephen took a closer look ... and his eyes widened.

The clothes, the flowing dress, the wavy hair ...

Fuck.

"You ..." was all he managed as he stared down at the figure of the woman who had been in his dreams.

Helena's eyes were glued to the woman, mouth open in shock. "What is going on?"

Stephen was fucked if he knew.

And as if the fates wanted to screw some more with his brain, the little boy looked up from his comic at that moment. The same orange and red, fire-filled eyes that Aiden used to have met his. There was no fear in them, but also, no recognition. He didn't know who he was. The little face—while much younger—was unequivocally Aiden's, though.

Exile

Stephen watched, dumbfounded, as the child pushed himself up and went to his mother's side, his face lighting up with a smile when he saw his mother's eyes flutter open. The innocence on his features was in stark contrast to the fear he had struck through the hearts of *Others* around him. He seemed unaware of his mother's precarious condition—but then, he was young.

"Aiden?"

It couldn't be, though … He wasn't into physics, but even he knew the laws couldn't be bent this out of shape. Dead children didn't just come alive.

His eyes began to change in colour, and Stephen tensed. He had seen Aiden do this before …

The boy's hands began to glow from the heat beneath his skin. Any moment now, flames would appear, and what he did with them was the worry. He heard the old man quickly shuffle out of the room.

Stephen guessed he had seen this before, too.

He approached Aiden slowly, slowly placing his hands over Aiden's and pressing them together. The heat was breath-taking. "No fire, Aiden. No fire."

The child raised innocent eyes to Stephen then smiled. "No fire."

"That's right. No fire." He kept hold of the boy's hands, his heart beating to the rhythm of a drum.

Helena's eyes were still on the woman, her mind lost. Yeah, welcome to my world, Stephen thought. Where nothing made one blind bit of sense.

With a simple okay, Aiden wandered back to where he was sitting before and picked up a rather battered-looking toy car, the windows of which were gone, and the paint was all but burnt off.

"Aiden …" Stephen whispered. *How was this all possible?*

"You'll take him, too?" the man asked.

"Take him?" Stephen blinked hard, trying to get a grip in this very fucked up world. "What do you mean?"

"We give you supplies, then you take them with you." He gestured to the woman and Aiden. "They can't stay here."

"Okay." It seemed like the most natural thing in the world to agree to take on Aiden's care. The child might not be his, but he was … well, *his* really... The sense of responsibility and protection he felt for him couldn't have been greater even if he had been his actual father.

There was a note of relief in the man's voice when he spoke again. "I'll get you what we can spare." With that, he closed the door behind him and left them to it.

Helena's mind was so stuck on the woman that she hadn't even seen Aiden yet. "None of this makes sense. How can she look like me?"

How indeed. That was the big thousand-pound question. And how did a dead child come back to life?

"I'm just going to talk to your mum and the doctor, okay?" For some reason, he felt like he needed to explain to Aiden … He needed to explain a lot to Aiden. If this was *the* Aiden.

It looked like Helena was going to faint or hyperventilate at any moment. Perhaps both if she didn't calm down. Stephen reached out and curled a firm hand around the back of her neck, using touch to ground her. "Just breathe. We'll figure this out." He could have laughed at his own assurances. He couldn't figure out shit right then.

"I just … I don't understand what is happening. She looks just like me …"

"I know."

The woman in the bed moved a slight bit, her eyes fluttering open and landing on Stephen. She swallowed and licked her dry lips. "Nicky," she wheezed. "You pulled me through."

Stephen shook his head. "No ..."

"Yes," she breathed. "At the school."

"It isn't possible."

"Things are only impossible to us when we do not understand how they work," she said in barely a whisper.

"You know her?" Helena frowned, stepping out of his hold.

"Yes ... No ... It's hard to explain ..." He let out a frustrated breath and turned to crouch by the woman's side. "Who are you? Tell me what's going on."

"Some things had to happen," she said slowly. "Or other things would fail." She swallowed. "I had to show you the way. I had to come to you looking like this so you would pay attention."

His brows drew together. "You don't normally look like this?"

Helena had moved in close, standing right next to him. At the woman's words, some of the tension seemed to leave her shoulders. Tentatively, she reached out and stroked gentle fingers over the woman's face. "You're a seeker?"

Stephen frowned. What the hell was a seeker?

No one had noticed that Aiden moved until he came over with a glass of water and a straw, which he held to his mother's lips. Stephen guessed that was what he had been doing all this time—tending to his sick mother. He put the glass on the side and then climbed onto the chair next to the bed and slipped his small hand into his mother's. Helena's eyes widened as she laid eyes on the small boy for the first time, but she didn't say anything about the striking similarity.

"A seeker?" Stephen asked.

Her eyes darted back to his. "You thought we'd already met. When you first saw me … that's what you'd said …" She looked as if she'd had the lightbulb moment he was missing. "You thought you knew me."

"Yeah … well, kind of," he said, bemused. "In my dreams."

"So you know this woman because you have seen her, right?"

"I thought she was you."

"Yes." Helena smiled, excited, and Stephen frowned, even more confused than he was a moment ago.

"Freya was right. So was Xander. All of them … they all knew." Helena's eyes searched his, her expression one of incredulity. "This is fate, Nick. Seekers seek."

Stephen had to bite his tongue. He was very tired of hearing people say *It was meant* and *It's fate*. Instead, he mentally counted to five. "Explain this to me."

"She's a seeker, Nick … You've never heard of them?"

"Evidently not."

"They're part of the fates. Like messengers. Everyone has a fate. You can't avoid it. Even if you change all the decisions, some things happen and we always get to the same place. If you make a wrong choice, go too far off the path, seekers come to help steer you back." The woman on the bed weakly nodded her head in agreement.

"So, if I use my free will …"

"They nudge you right back onto your path."

Stephen's frown deepened. "Explain it to me like I am thick."

Exile

"Have you heard of the book of Blight?" At his blank stare, she continued. "This guy, Blight, foresaw that one day a man would come and turn the *Human* world upside down. He would lead his people, and they would rise and form a new world—a world of *Others*."

The seeker gave a small smile, her eyes closing for a moment in contentment.

"I still don't …"

"*You*, Nick … you are that person. That's your destiny, but for some reason, you have veered off the path."

He didn't know whether to laugh at the absurdity of it all, or to worry about the fact that Helena seemed to have suddenly become just as crazy as the rest of them.

At his look of disbelief, Helena's hands went to her hips, her jaw set in a determined line. He found himself strangely aroused by her annoyed stance. "Fine. You want to explain how you have been seeing me in dreams all this time? Or why there is a look-alike of me lying on this bed? Can you explain to me every bizarre thing that has happened to you these past days?"

He scowled. The truth was he couldn't explain a damn thing. And as crazy as her explanation sounded, was it any crazier than everything that had gone on till now? "Well, maybe I don't want to do this bloody Blight thing."

"You don't get to choose. A seeker would have been sent to you because you were going the wrong way." Helena pointed to the woman. "She came to set you right. You were meant to meet me …" she paused, "for some or other reason."

The woman spoke again, a whisper. Stephen had to lean in real close to hear her. "I brought you here, Nick." Each word sounded as if it carved itself from the flesh of her throat. "We had to." She squeezed Aiden's hand. "The bus. He remembered the bus."

Frustration emanated from him once more. "I don't understand."

Helena touched his shoulder lightly. "You need to talk to her. If there is a seeker here, she can answer your questions."

Someone would finally answer his questions? he thought with derision.

She carefully pushed the pillow under the woman's head to make her more comfortable, then turned to the small boy with a kind smile, hand outstretched. "Aiden, should we go and find the man for our things?" The child hesitated for a moment, staring at her with uncertainty until his mother gave his hand another weak squeeze and told him it was okay to go with the nice lady.

From a woman who had been stunned speechless just a few short moments ago, Helena was suddenly completely unfazed by it all.

"Take my boy," the woman rasped when Helena and Aiden had left the room. "Teach him the words." She coughed, spittle running down her chin. Stephen grabbed the edge of the blanket and wiped her chin. "Teach Aiden."

"Is he—" He swallowed hard. "Is he Aiden?"

The woman gave a slow nod. "Yes."

"How? I don't understand this. And what about my … children?" It felt so strange to utter the words.

"They are yours, too." The woman's face was aging, turning itself from that of Helena's to something else. She tried to sit up and Stephen hastened to help her.

She was so small and frail as he lifted her so that she was propped up against the pillows.

"How are they my children?"

She motioned to a small bag on the floor, and Stephen grabbed it and handed it to her. She fumbled inside then pulled out a small pouch like the one Aiden had used to keep the glass balls in and handed it to Stephen. It was heavier than he had expected. "Brisingamen," she said. "Give it to Freya."

His eyes widened. "This is ..."

"Yes." She nodded. "Freya's. My boy stole it." She smiled up at Stephen weakly. "He wanted to come and save you."

"Save me?" The idea twisted like a knife in Stephen's gut.

"He loves you. He'd do anything for you. He stole Freya's necklace and used it to walk from then to now. All three of them did. They came through time for you, Stephen. But you must never let Aiden tell you what he wanted to. He came to see me, but you can't mess with the future."

"They came through time?"

The woman's head tilted forward in exhaustion. "Brisingamen is a key to other places. You need to send them back."

Aiden, Nakita and Toke had come here from the future? "Do you know how crazy this sounds?"

"As crazy as the possibility of pulling a woman from your dreams?"

He clenched his jaw. "If they came to save me, does that mean I am dead?"

The woman lifted a hand to cup Stephen's face. "Some things are set."

"They can be changed?"

"Perhaps."

"If I had ignored you in my dreams, and not met Helena, could you have made me meet her? Made me be here today?"

"We would have kept trying."

"But it isn't definite, right? I could still have made all the wrong decisions if I had wanted to?"

"It would be a new world if you did."

Another thought shot through his mind. "Who is their mother?"

The woman's hand covered Stephen's, and she smiled. "For such a bright boy, you can be dim-witted sometimes." She broke into a coughing fit suddenly, her face turning red as she struggled to breathe.

Shit.

"Helena—" Stephen called out. He tugged away the pillow from behind her to let her lie down again, but she gripped his hand.

"Take my boy with you. Like you promised him. You promised you would find him in Trentwich. He came to save you … Now you save him."

Guilt racked Stephen. Yeah, and he had fucking killed him, too. Did she know that?

"I …"

But before he could say a word, her hand tightened on his, and she drew in a deep, ragged breath.

Her hand went limp, and her eyes closed in a sleep that would now forever be peaceful.

Chapter Forty-Five

Stephen

It had grown late and dark; the day slipped by easily. Helena and Stephen drove slowly with the headlights off. It was past their curfew time and the sweepers would be out. Aiden lay curled on the back seat with a blanket draped over him, while his mother lay wrapped in another blanket in the boot of the car. Aiden had refused to go with them and leave his mother behind, so they had had no option but to take her along.

Stephen knew that if this had been his own mother, he wouldn't have wanted to leave her, either. He'd not have left her there so someone could just trash her body. The boot wasn't very civilised, of course, but they had had no other choice.

"I hold her hand when she is sleepy," Aiden had told them when they tried to explain that she wasn't there anymore. But it was a lot for him to take in—losing one's mother was a lot for anyone to take in.

Aiden's mother had prepared him, though. Stephen would guess that she had known she was going to die and that Stephen would come. He didn't really understand how it was that she was still alive after he had ... failed her. He couldn't even say it in his own head. Guilt ate at him from the inside. She had made Aiden promise that whatever happened, he was to go with Stephen and Helena.

Stephen stared out of the window with messed up thoughts. He had one hundred pieces and none of them went into the same puzzle.

The bump of the tyre on the edge of the road as Helena

pulled the car off the lane jolted him from his thoughts. She drove them into the shadows of the overgrowth at the side and cut the engine. "Is everything ...?"

She held a hand up. "Shush."

The low chug was hard to miss, although they didn't sound like sweeper vehicles—more like ... scooters.

"Kids?" Stephen murmured. Back home, scooters were teenagers' step between cycle and car.

She nodded. "I think so. Money hunters."

"Money hun—?"

Aiden woke just then, and Stephen quickly turned with a finger over his mouth to signal for him to be quiet. He pushed off his blanket and forced himself through the gap between the two front seats and onto Stephen's lap.

Helena watched him for his reaction, but Stephen found he had grown surprisingly used to children crawling into his arms and onto his lap these past few days.

"I take it the money hunters aren't driving around looking for dropped bits of change?"

Helena shook her head. "No, they're *Human* and *Others*. Groups of them. They find stray *Others* and hand them over to the sweepers for a reward. Kind of like mini bounty hunters. Or, if you fall into the hands of the wrong ones, you become their toys."

He rolled the window down slightly and listened. Aiden snuggled closer to him, and Stephen instinctively rubbed an idle hand up and down his back as he listened. The scent of the night and the darkness slipped into the car—wood and wildlife.

"Perhaps we should leave the car and walk. We can come back for it tomorrow." The idea of sitting and hiding in the car was not Stephen at all. He would either face them or avoid them.

Exile

"We can't leave the car. It is registered to me." Helena lowered her voice. "There is a body in the back, remember?"

"If we don't leave the car," he countered, "perhaps there will be another three bodies inside it soon."

He tensed and swore a soft oath.

"What is it?" Helena asked in alarm just a second before four men appeared on scooters, flanking another man who came to stand at the front of the car.

Stephen lowered Aiden to the floor of the car, slowly. *Humans* tended to be jumpy. "Whatever happens," he muttered under his breath, "do not get out of this car."

War was like anything that had a goal really. Great planning and preparation was half the battle. If that was missed, skipped or overlooked, then it was sure to be a disaster. Not that victory was always obtainable, but it was harder. Going to war, it was always better to strategically kill someone than to do it half-assed and risk becoming a statistical casualty.

Would it be stupid to get out of the car and face them? Stephen wasn't sure, but he did know them coming to the car would be a disaster. He was nothing to them. Unless they knew who he was. Perhaps the dear old man with the bad shoes had known who Stephen was and hired *Humans* out to collect money. He could purchase new shoes from his cut. It would not be too wrong to think like that. The *Humans* were damn good at turning *Others* on each other.

He eyed their weapons, having no doubt they were loaded with silver.

What a prize this was—catching a man, woman and a child. Nothing like making an example out of a child to make a point to *Others* being out late at night, and showing the world they were to be feared. The *Humans* would cheer, and *Others* would look on in trepidation, but they wouldn't stand up together and fight.

This had to stop.

Others were stronger than *Humans*—even armed *Humans*. If they stood up together, *Humans* wouldn't stand a chance.

Stephen reached for the door handle, moving slowly, but Helena grabbed his other hand. "What are you doing?" she muttered without taking her eyes off the men in front of them.

"Giving you and Aiden a chance." Stephen couldn't see the men's eyes, but he retained contact. He knew that if he looked away, even for one second, they would strike like a snake.

Helena's hand tightened around his. "Don't go."

But there wasn't a choice. Stephen knew he would never live with himself if Aiden lost his life once again.

"This is no time for heroics."

He cast her a quick glance. "Good, because I'm no hero." He gave her hand a reassuring squeeze before pulling away and opening the door. The one on foot took a step forward rather than back.

Idiot.

Standing at a distance and hiding behind their guns made things harder for *Others*. But coming up close to his kind was definitely a stupid move. The advantage was thrown back in their favour. There was no match between the two species when it came to speed and strength.

"Can I help you?" Stephen asked in his most sincere voice.

"Do not dare speak to us," the man said. "You do not have the right nor the permission for that."

He wanted to laugh. He was doing a fine job at the man act, but the problem was, Stephen could scent his fear. And it was strong. *Very* strong. If he flashed his teeth and claws, the man would probably shit his pants faster than an incontinent man on laxatives.

"I don't want to hurt you," Stephen said—which was a lie. There was nothing he'd have liked more.

The man laughed—a laugh heavy with sarcasm. The kind that Stephen would let out when the *Human* died at his hands. Right before his victory dance.

He walked toward the man, his priority right then being to get them away from Helena and Aiden. Hopefully Helena would have enough sense to get out when the coast was clear, and not look back, no matter what.

Stephen wondered what part of the fates' big plan this was. How was he to kill everyone, get the necklace back to Freya, and save the day if he was dead? He was damned if he was going to be brought back by some vampirical-style creature.

Despite the smell of his fear, the man didn't move back as Stephen advanced. He was brave, he had to give him that. But with bravery always came stupidity. He wondered whether they would follow him or go after Helena and Aiden if he were to run.

Was that a chance he was willing to take?

The man held a bat, thick and heavy and woven with threads of silver. Seems these *Humans* had Stephen's card marked already. But they were regular *Humans*, who were just out for their luck. He realised then that there must be actual stores that sold items such as these. Weaponry against the *Others*.

The balance here was really fucking screwed up.

Instead of backing away, as Stephen had hoped, the man slapped the bat against his hand and then moved closer. One beating on the menu for Stephen Davies, it would

413

appear.

But if Stephen was going down, he wasn't going down alone, and he was fucked if he would make it easy for them. The man with the bat was first on the hit list.

Stephen moved to the side, stepping once, twice. They watched his dance; predators watching prey. One of the men on a scooter moved around the back and toward Stephen, and he kept an eye on him from his peripheral vision. A pathetic attempt to sneak up. Did these *Humans* never learn? You do not sneak up on a *tiger*.

Ironically, the scent that came from him was thicker than any of the others. Musky, acrid—such a delicious aroma for Stephen. It set his *tiger* off inside, pacing, ready for its prey. But he knew, one wrong move, and the *Humans* would fucking buck like horses; Helena and Aiden were right in his reach. The *Human* wouldn't want to look soft in front of his friends. A woman and a child … easy pickings.

The man moved back until he was between Stephen and another of the men. Stephen placed his odds that this one was the planner of the group—the one that Stephen wouldn't have to lay a finger on. Just take out the bigger men and this puny thing would shit his pants and run.

"We know who you are," said the man with the bat.

"If you know who I am, then why didn't you come better prepared?"

The man sneered. "There is a big price on your head."

Stephen raised his hands, moving further to the side, trying to draw the men away from the car. "Do I look like the kind of person to just roll over and say: Yes, please, I'm sorry. I didn't mean it?"

The man's sneer turned into a grin. He was missing a tooth. Maybe when this was over, he would be missing another.

"I was hoping for a good fight," he sniggered.

The man's attention was locked onto Stephen, which was a good thing. It worked to his advantage. He moved slowly, and like sheep, the *Humans* followed. If only he could tell Helena to run, but he didn't dare glance over to her and draw these *Humans'* attention back to her and Aiden.

He stopped when he was far enough away from the car. The *Humans* moved in around him, leaving just a gap so that he could make a run for it. Stephen winked at the main man with the bat and ran.

Follow me. Follow me. Follow me. He hoped these *Humans* were greedy enough to follow the money ticket that was making an escape rather than the richer prize that was sitting in the car. What was the going rate for catching an *Other* child out after hours?

He ignored the echoes of doubt that tried to edge their darkened ways into his mind, whispering in his ears and promising Helena and Aiden's demise. His mind was fast, running through numerous scenarios for which the *Humans* would use Helena and Aiden. Leverage was probably their best chance.

However, these *Humans* didn't think like Stephen did. He was thankful for that. They were simple creatures. They took off after him, the lights of their scooters bobbing up and down in a frantic dance, illuminating the gaps between the trees. Stephen kept his pace slow, enough that they had a chance to catch him—anything to keep them coming and keep them away from the car. He gave them a visual goal; one they thought they would reach.

The *Human* on foot was the smartest of them; he kept back, eyes watching. Perhaps that was why he didn't ride. The illogical evils of riding something with two wheels rather than four. If Stephen was a betting man, he would have put money on him being the one in charge.

He could hear the river from far away, the way the water lapped against the shoreline. He could smell it, too—thick, earthy, damp soil, the lifeblood of the earth flowing freely. It wasn't too fast, but fast enough that Stephen was sure it would be substantial. A myth that tigers didn't like water. On the contrary, they loved it … weretigers, and tigers alike. Only a true moron would run through the river and then up a tree to try to escape from the waiting paws of such a magnificent cat.

Directing himself toward the river, he intended to run alongside it and then through it. It was his hope that the *Humans* wouldn't leave their scooters to follow him. He planned to run into the water and then come around to the back of them and cut them off from getting back to the car.

But the man with the bat, he was the smart-arse. As if he had read Stephen's mind, he attacked. He came at him with the bat—but Stephen was fast. He ducked and rammed into his thick body, sending the man sprawling onto the ground and the bat flying from his grip. He yelled, trying to scramble away as Stephen's fist cracked into his jaw. He caught the man in a stranglehold around the throat, squeezing so that his eyes began to bulge out of their sockets.

Too late, a flash of silver caught his eye and silver burned him as it made contact with his face and rattled his brain in the confines of his skull. It sent him reeling sideward onto the ground, pain ricocheting through him. Ears still ringing, he tried to focus on the *Human* who had come up from behind him as he crouched down and spat on the ground beside Stephen.

The bat was pushed against Stephen's jaw, forcing his

head back, the silver sapping all power from him. Perhaps these *Humans* needed Stephen alive to claim their prize. But they weren't going to take him like that, that was for sure. Stephen Davies did not get beaten by a bunch of *Humans* playing hero. No, they would be taught a lesson ... taught to respect *Others*. A lesson that would last them a lifetime.

Stephen dragged himself back, trying to sit up, but it was like his body was filled with silver, his limbs unusually heavy, even now. The man grinned and didn't try to stop him. When he backed into a large trunk, he took a moment to wipe away the blood that ran down from his nose and into his mouth before pushing himself up. The man he had been about to strangle got to his feet, wheezing, glaring at Stephen as they eyed each other.

Stephen used the tree to get himself up as another of the *Humans* carrying a bat got off his scooter behind Stephen. Maybe bats were issued as standard for arseholes coming to collect bounties against *Others*. A strike on his back had him arching and then falling forward. He turned to see the *Human's* face, imprinting it on his mind.

"They want you alive," the main man said, "but I don't think they really care if you're conscious or not."

Stephen laughed between coughing and spitting out blood. "And what about you? Do they care if you are alive?"

The man cocked his head to one side. "Oh, I will be."

Another bat smashed into his side. His side scraped the ground, and his eyes shifted, his *tiger* coming to stand at Stephen's side. He roared, his teeth elongating in his mouth. He tried to bring up the strength of his *tiger*, but it was like the *tiger* was missing ... this had to be from Lee's bite. There was no other explanation.

He couldn't shift, but he couldn't hold the *tiger* back, either. Caught somewhere between both of his kind, he was unable to avoid the bat as it came down and connected with his jaw again, snapping his head to the side. He tried to retain his vision, but the world became tinted. He blinked, clearing away the blur for a second.

Stephen's heart sank when he looked up suddenly and saw Helena and Aiden out beyond the *Humans*. They hadn't taken the chance to run. *Bloody hell*. They stood just at the edge of the water, in plain fucking sight. What was she thinking … or *not* thinking?

"Run," Stephen strangled out. "Go …"

A pair of hands grabbed the front of his shirt. "It's only you we need alive. Do you want to see what happens to children who are out after hours … or women even?" He pushed the bat under Stephen's chin, using it to cut off his airway. The silver in it burned, seeping in, rendering Stephen almost powerless. "You could watch, couldn't you? We could have some fun with her."

Stephen spluttered out an incoherent curse as he attempted to think beyond the agony of the silver on his skin. One of the men emerged just behind Aiden, and Stephen pushed against the pain. Ignoring the fire under his skin, he pushed his *tiger* back before he ripped through his flesh and ended up killing them both. The *tiger* couldn't shift, not with this much silver around. He was caged and restrained in the confines of Stephen's shaky mind.

"Pathetic," the man said, smacking his hand across his face before standing up. Like a new born animal just discovering his legs, Stephen tried to get up. But all he managed to do was roll onto his front, crawling his way to Aiden and Helena.

The *Human* came and stood by his side as he slithered toward them. "Which one?"

Stephen kept going but got a boot in his side.

418

Exile

"Which one gets to live and which one gets to come and play?"

Stephen opened his mouth to yell at them to run, but no words came out. He didn't care what the *Humans* did to him, but he was not going to let them hurt Helena or Aiden. They would have to kill him first, or him them.

He favoured the latter.

The man with the bat nodded, and one of the other men grabbed Aiden from behind, holding both of his small arms. The boy pushed against him as another man approached with a bat. He struck Aiden across the stomach, and he buckled, his childish whimper escaping his throat as he fought against the men. But they held him in place and stopped him from falling when his legs gave way. His face crumpled through his tears, but no sound came out other than strangled, winded protests. They hit him again, and this time, Aiden called out.

"I'll fucking kill you," Stephen roared, pushing himself up. Oranges and yellows danced across his vision, his head feeling like someone was crushing it from the inside. He fixed his gaze on Aiden, focusing on him and what he was fighting for. As Aiden started to cry for things he didn't understand, Stephen swore he would make each and every fucking *Human* here pay for whatever they did to Aiden or Helena. They would beg for death before he was finished with them.

Norton wanted Stephen for crimes against *Humans* and taking *Human* lives. Stephen would give that to him, then … and each of their heads.

The man grabbed Aiden by his hair and pulled his head back, smacking him across the face.

Helena fought against the man who had her, his hand over her mouth. They had pushed her down to the ground, shoving her face into the dirt. She snapped her head to the

419

side, getting rid of the hand. "He's just a child," she cried.

They made a mockery of the word humanity. Clearly, they had none. These *Humans* did nothing for their cause but further concrete Stephen's hatred for them.

Humans should be eradicated.

The *Human* backhanded her across her face. "No one asked you, bitch."

"Get the fuck away from them." Stephen pushed himself up onto shaky legs.

"Pardon me?" the *Human* beside him smirked.

Stephen's *tiger* roared, pushing the breath from him and demanding release. "They aren't anything to you. They aren't important. Let them go. Take me."

"Noooo ..." Helena was on her knees now, her captor pulling her hair back so that her back was pressed against his knee. She cried out as he thrust his hand into her top and cupped her breast. "Get the hell off me."

Stephen felt the rage spread through him like wildfire. That filthy *Human* had his hands on *his* female. His head spun in a haze of fury as he desperately tried to fight off the after effects of the silver and the beatings.

"Is this your woman?" the main man sneered. "Would be a nice prize for us."

The man who had her ripped her blouse down the front, pulling it down and exposing her breasts to them all. "Look at those," he jeered lasciviously, reaching down, but Helena caught his arm before he could touch her, sinking her teeth into his arm.

Swearing loudly, he slammed his fist into the side of her head, knocking her sideways. But she was away from him. She raced toward Aiden, pulling her clothes back together to cover herself up.

"Don't fucking touch her again," Stephen growled. All

his *tiger* saw was the woman he wanted, the woman he was claiming, being handled by another.

"We found a soft spot, did we?" Stephen visualised his claws, the sharpness of them, the darkness of them and how he would use them. Stephen pushed the thoughts though his body to his hands, feeding the images to his *tiger*. His hands started to shift, but Stephen dared not allow himself any euphoric relief that his *tiger* might well be overcoming the silver.

He swung for the *Human*, who didn't manage to move back fast enough. Stephen caught him across the chest and the man yelped in pain. He swung his bat and connected with Stephen's head. Stephen ignored the explosion of pain and agony in his skull as he lunged with both hands. There were shouts form the other men, but Stephen only had his sights on one man. He dug his claws around his ankle and yanked, and the man fell, landing on the ground with a howl and a thud.

As Stephen brought his arm back to slash at him again, somebody else's bat came down on the back of his head, knocking his momentum and scattering his thoughts. He growled, slashing air to get to him, but another strike had his vision blurring.

The next blow managed to get him flat onto the ground, and as the blows began to rain down on him, darkness speckled his vision …

The world around him went black.

Chapter Forty-Six

Stephen

The world was a faraway echo in Stephen's mind, some place that he couldn't reach nor feel. Muffled sounds and lingering traces of the acrid smell of smoke and fire assailed his senses. Prying heavily hooded eyes open to narrow slits, he was instantaneously blinded by an orange glow and heat that had him snapping them shut again.

The faint sound of a woman's voice infiltrated his consciousness. Desperation laced its edges as it called out his name. "Nick, open your eyes. Please."

His mind threatened to pull him under once again, darkness seeping into the edges.

"Answer me, God damn it, Nick."

Helena.

Stephen eyes shot open and he leapt up, fighting to get his bearings as the world reeled around him.

Shit.

Helena ... Aiden ...

He had to get to them.

He lurched forward and stumbled, falling hard on his knees.

"Nick—" Helena half-sobbed in relief as she crawled over to him.

He blinked, trying to focus. *Helena*. She was here. He grabbed her as her blurry form reached him and dragged her into a rough embrace. *She was safe*. His heart thundered in his chest as he held her tight, her face buried in his chest, the fear at seeing her abused and assaulted by that piece of shit *Human* while he could only look on helplessly making him afraid to let go. She latched onto him, her fingers digging into his back as she stifled sobs.

His gradually functioning brain in his throbbing head registered the smell of fire, and he froze, his heart plummeting. "Aiden ..."

"He's okay," Helena reassured him quickly. "He's here."

Relief flooded him as he saw the young boy kneeling a few feet away. His eyes were levelled at the ground, his little frame tense.

Stephen scanned the vicinity through still hazy eyes, trying to detect any *Humans* around. But the area seemed clear, no visible threat lurking anywhere nearby. He vaguely wondered where they had disappeared to and how long they had before they reappeared.

"Aiden, come here," he rasped, desperate to have him close and to see for himself that the child was okay. He twisted his head to the side in rejection of Stephen, refusing to look at him. Fear gripped him, a knot forming in his stomach.

With great reluctance, Stephen released Helena and crawled over to the boy, careful not to scare him away. He reached out a tentative hand, but Aiden pulled back with a jerk.

"Aiden?"

Stephen couldn't see his face, but he could see his chin quivering, knew the boy was trying not to cry.

What had they done to him?

"He thinks he did something bad," Helena said, her voice low. "The *Humans* were hitting you ... like *really* hitting you ..." A strangled sob left her. "Th-They swung bats at your arms, legs, back, face ..." She faltered. "We thought they were going to kill you."

With an inward curse, he imagined the scare the little

423

boy must have gone through. "It would take more than a bunch of *Humans* to kill me." He smiled at the boy, hiding his grimace as his painfully swollen face and pounding head rebelled at the movement.

"I tried to stop them, but they started on me and then Aiden …" She paused for a long moment. "He saved us. He saved *you*."

Stephen's vision had cleared somewhat, and he noticed that Helena's lip was swollen and that she had a cut across her face. Her clothes were torn, barely covering her breasts, and she was holding her skirt in place. His blood ran cold, and he felt red-hot fury slide through him again. Fists clenched at his sides. "Did they …."

"No." She nodded past Aiden at a bright fire burning. A bubble covered the flames, keeping them in place. As Stephen looked closer, he could make out a shape …

The remnants of a body was burning in there—a body and the last traces of a bat.

Holy shit. "He did that?"

Aiden's small sobs answered Stephen's question.

The skin of the *Human* was black, his features unrecognisable. Shit, it would have been hard now to tell if this was male or female. Skin had fallen away from the skull, leaving bits of bone exposed, and the front of the *Human's* jaw was missing, melted into a pool in the back of what remained of the throat. God, he hoped that the *Human* had felt some of this before he died. He fucking deserved it.

His eyes returned to Aiden, staying there even as Helena said, "The others ran away when it happened, but they will be back. You know they will."

Fuck. "Yes."

"We need to leave."

"How long was I out? How long have they been gone?"

424

He needed to gauge how long it had been so that he had an idea of how much time they had.

"I'm not sure. They've been gone maybe ten minutes. You've been out much longer than that. I have been trying to wake you ever since they left."

"You should have left me and run," Stephen grated. If they had just used the opportunity to escape when Stephen had led the men away from the car, Aiden would not have gone through any of this. Nor would Helena.

"Would you have left me?"

He gritted his teeth. That was beside the point. He was *Other*. He would have survived this. She was *Human*, frail. She should have run, God damn it.

He took in her tattered clothes again, and anger flared inside him, his *tiger* roaring. How dare they fucking touch her ... He balled his fists against the earth beside him—now was not the time to lose his cool. He needed to get them the hell away from here before the men came back.

"I'm sorry," he said hoarsely. Stephen didn't say sorry to anyone, ever, but he found himself saying it to Helena.

Her eyes shimmered with unshed tears. "Don't. None of this is your fault."

It was, Stephen thought. He hadn't been able to protect them.

He moved a little closer to the boy. "Aiden. It's okay."

He shook his small head, fast, the way little kids did.

"You did nothing wrong."

"I made the man get on fire," he said softly.

He reached out a cautious hand and laid it on the child's shoulder, feeling a small victory when he didn't immediately pull away. "Aiden, come here."

"No." He shrunk back.

But going with his instinct, he lifted the boy to his feet

and pulled him toward him anyway, and much to his relief, the child didn't fight him. Even on his knees, Stephen was taller than the child. "You did nothing wrong, okay? Look at me."

Aiden had his head turned to the side, and Stephen hooked a finger under his chin, making him turn to face him. His eyes glowed orange as he fixed Stephen with a stare, darker than before.

"It's bad to make people on fire."

Not if they're Human, Stephen sneered inwardly. "You are very brave," he said quietly. "You saved me. You saved Helena, too. They were very bad people. It isn't bad to help good people."

"You saved us all," Helena said softly from behind Stephen.

"It was good?" he asked in a meek voice.

Stephen tightened his hold on his arms and met his gaze head on. "It was great. I promise. You saved my life." With that, he pulled him to him into a hug, not giving a shit at that moment about how badly he hurt to hold him like this. Sudden images of how the *Humans* had hit Aiden flashed through his mind. Taking great care not to hurt him, he pushed him back so that he could inspect him. "Are you hurt?"

Aiden pulled up his trouser leg and then his sleeves and showed Stephen his scuffed knee and scraped arms. But when he lifted up his t-shirt, renewed rage rolled though Stephen. His stomach was swollen where he had been beaten, purple bruises already having formed. Those fuckers. He silently swore to himself that no one was ever going to hurt Aiden again. No one. If Stephen's fucking life depended on it.

With gentle fingers, he pulled his shirt back down

426

again. "I'm sorry they did that to you," he said solemnly, and Aiden wrapped small arms around his neck in a tight hug.

Bracing himself against the shooting pains in his body, he got to his feet with the child in his arms. From the intensity and focus of the pain, he realised he must have broken some ribs and had to have fractures in different parts of his body. He was extremely grateful for his *Other* healing abilities in that moment as he felt how much the breaks and tears had already knitted together.

Turning to Helena, he took a moment's solace in her beautiful features, then murmured, "Let's get out of here, shall we?"

Stephen was surprised to find the car exactly where they'd left it. He had expected they would have taken it or at least caused damage great enough that it would have prevented any kind of getaway. Those men must have really been scared shitless after what Aiden had done, he mused.

Stephen opened his senses to listen and scent the air for any threats. But even when he was happy there was no one around, he gently put Aiden down and kept him and Helena at a safe distance so that he could check inside the car and make sure it was safe before letting them approach.

Stephen put Aiden in the back seat of the car and strapped him in before covering his shaking frame with the blanket. He took off his now bloodied and torn hoodie, leaving himself with just his t-shirt, and waited for Helena to climb into the passenger side of the car—this time, he was driving.

Her gaze eyes fixed on the tattoo on his arm as she climbed in. He hated that tattoo, hated the way people stared at it with a question in their eyes: *Why?*

Fucking witches. That was why.

Chapter Forty-Seven

Helena

Nick had been at it for hours now. Naked from the waist upwards, the muscles of his back and arms bunched and rippled as he thwacked the money hunter's bat he had found into the trunk of a tree in front of him, again—a cycle that jolted inside Helena with each blow. He roared as he gripped the bat in his hand, the silver end searing into his skin. He counted every second he managed to hold on and then smashed it back into the tree when his body just couldn't take the pain anymore. She had lost count how many times he had hit the tree, but he had made it all the way to seventy-five at one stage. He swore, the curses becoming angrier with every blow. The tree in front of him was near dead, with a sizeable chunk now missing from the middle.

He beat the defenceless trunk until his arms were shaking, and then, with a final whack, he finally dropped to the ground, chest heaving. "Useless, fucking piece of shit," he bellowed, launching the bat into the darkness.

He sat with his head in his hands, firm back glistening in the moonlight.

Eden had gone out to him twice so far. The first time, he had told her to leave him alone. The second time, he had practically carried her back into the house, slamming the door shut with such brutality that it jammed itself into wood. He'd left them with a warning not to bother him, no matter what.

He'd been like this since coming back from hiding her car. He'd hidden it a fair trek away, Helena assumed, with the amount of time it took him to come back. He wouldn't say where it was, but he had said he would deal with Aiden's mother in the morning.

It didn't take an idiot to realise that that alone was irking him. It wasn't the most dignified way to spend the night—locked in a boot somewhere. But they couldn't afford to do anything else.

"Daddy is making himself strong," Nakita had announced as she watched him from the kitchen counter. Helena had tried to take her down, but the little girl had insisted that she watch. "This is what Daddy does. We fight what beats us until we beat it, or we are dead," she said, repeating words that she had undoubtedly memorised by heart.

But Nick was trying to beat silver. It was impossible.

They had got Aiden settled in the lounge when they had got back, where the poor thing had fallen into an exhausted sleep. Nakita and Toke hadn't blinked an eye at his sudden reappearance, their young, innocent minds never once questioning why it was that Aiden was suddenly so much younger.

Eden had eventually got Nakita away from the window and put them all to bed in the lounge. After insisting Helena go get cleaned up and helped her apply some of her special cream, she had then gone to join the others, suggesting Helena do that same.

"He's stubborn as a mule," she had told her. "He's going to sear his skin off with that thing. I'm not going to sit and watch any longer. Arrogant shifter ..."

"This is a bad idea," Helena muttered now as she filled a small bag with items. She had the cream from Eden, a bottle of water for Nick to drink, another bottle of water filled up from the well outside, and some bandages she had taken out of the bag of new supplies. Everyone else was asleep so they wouldn't witness her being handed her ass at trying to help him ... but she just couldn't go to bed and leave him out there punishing himself. Her mind wouldn't settle anyway. She kept seeing the image of the woman in the bed, her own face staring back up at her.

A seeker ...

The mere thought of it scared her. It was one thing to know about the whisperings of old tales—the prophecy of the man who would change the world as they now knew it—but it was quite another to realise that she was in some way a part of it. A seeker would not have pushed him to her if she didn't play some role. And since she was a doctor, and a war between *Others* and *Humans* was imminent, then she guessed it was quite easy to figure out what exactly her role would be. She just hoped she didn't mess anything up.

Throwing Nick one more glance, she sucked in a deep breath and prepared to go out. He was still sitting, which was a good thing. At least he hadn't gone looking for the bat just to start up his idiotic display of male stubbornness again. Maybe that was her main role—to keep his obstinate head alive.

Clutching the bag to her, she snuck out of the house through the front door and walked around to the back of the house.

"I told you to leave me alone," Nick growled without looking her way. She vaguely wondered if she would ever get used to *Others* being able to scent her and know she was there before she even arrived. "Don't any of you listen?"

She ignored his bitterness. He had a right to it. "I came to tend to your hand and to bring you some water."

"My hand doesn't need tending to."

430

Exile

His arm was covered in blood, especially the one where he had held the tip of the silvered bat in his palm. It ran in dark rivulets down his wrist, dripping onto his jeans. "I beg to differ. You look like shit."

That brought a scowl in her direction, but she refused to falter. *No, Mr Nick Mason, I'm in for this ride*, she thought sternly. And she was damn well going to take her place.

"I need to fight what beats me until …"

"You beat it or you die?" He threw her a quick look of surprise before resuming his scowling. "Yeah, Nakita imparted that little slice of wisdom to me earlier." She stared into the darkness that stretched out in front of them. "It doesn't mean you have to suffer the whole way, though, Nick" she added gently after a moment. "What are you trying to beat? Silver?"

She watched as his beautiful face grew hard, his jaw tightening in a stubborn line. "Yes." He pushed himself up, trying to hide a wince as his hand made contact with the ground. He muttered an oath and opened and closed his fist, as if feeling out the pain.

His hard chest was a mess, covered in blood and sweat and dirt. She tried not to stare at the stark beauty of his body for too long as he stood there dressed only in a pair of jeans. The fact that he was barefoot should have probably made him look less powerful, vulnerable. Yet it had the exact opposite effect. It added to that dangerous air that always surrounded him, reminding her of the very ferocious animal that lurked just under the surface.

Arousal, hot and heavy, flowed thickly through her. Nick inhaled sharply, his eyes boring into hers as he no doubt scented the air. His gaze raked over her, taking in her bare legs revealed under the oversized shirt she wore, her only shield against him.

Oh God. She swallowed hard and made a show of rummaging through her small bag. "Let me tend to your wounds. Then you can go back to beating the hell out of the tree." Her voice came out harsher than she intended, but it was herself she was angry with. Why was controlling her hormones so impossible around this man?

"I'm fine," he repeated stiffly.

Helena moved closer and grabbed his wrist before he had chance to protest and he did that thing … that look he always gave when she touched him, like shock on his face. The connection between them made Helena jump, sending an electrifying pulse through her body. This was a bad idea. A bad, bad, idea. "Jesus." Nick's hand was a mass of torn and burnt skin, the wound in the centre painfully swollen. The skin had split so many times that slivers of skin and flesh hung from the wound. Tears stung her eyes, defying the toughness she had been trying to hold onto. "Look at what you did to yourself. Why?"

He tried to pull his hand back, but she held on. "This is to beat silver?" She remotely registered that he could have easily wrenched it out of her grasp if he wanted to … but he didn't. Perspiration had flattened his hair to his head, and he had wiped blood and dirt across his face.

"Why, Nick?"

A tick worked along his jaw. "Did you see what they did to you? To Aiden?"

Yes, she had. She wouldn't ever forget it, either. The way they had assaulted both her and the little boy. But she would also never forget what they had done to Nick. The merciless beating, the cruel use of silver to control and torture him—and she could do nothing to stop them. It had taken a child to save them both … She suddenly realised that that was a huge part of his anger. Nick was used to being the

432

one doing the protecting—and he had been rendered helpless. "We're both fine."

This time he did snatch his hand back, closing his fist on it. "I didn't protect you today. I didn't protect Aiden … again …" He choked out Aiden's name. "What kind of fighter am I when I can't even protect all of you. What if *Humans* show up here? What if they come with bats laced with silver? They take me out with *Others'* fucking kryptonite, and all I do is lie down and wither." He gave an angry shake of his head. "Do you know why I am in Exile? Did Freya tell you?"

"No."

"Because I screwed up, again. That's all I ever do. My sister, right? She fell in love with my friend. They weren't meant to be because she is *tiger* and he is *wolf*, and even though the *Humans* would demand their death, they still risked everything to be together. You should see them, Helena," he said in sudden earnest. "These two, they were made to be together …"

She smiled at him, feeling a twinge of envy at two people who could experience a love so powerful they were willing to defy all odds and risk even death.

"But she got pregnant," he continued rigidly, his jaw tightening in remembered pain. "She was my sister … and I couldn't protect her, either."

The pain in his words vibrated along her skin, creating a need in her to soothe him. She desperately wanted to reach out to him, but she knew he wouldn't let her. Not like this.

"I don't protect anyone. You could have been killed, or raped. Aiden could have been killed. Again. Don't you see? I must face the silver. I must, because when these *Humans* come, and they *will* come, they will go for me first. They'll take me down and then do what they want with you all. And

I can't live with that. There is enough pain and suffering because of me."

His eyes were wild, gold shimmering in their depths. It dawned on her that that was his emotional tell. They always flickered gold when his emotions were running rampant.

Like the kiss they had shared the night before, she thought with sudden breathlessness.

"Let me help you then. Let me tend to your wounds so I can make you stronger, and you can fight." It slotted into place now. This was why the seeker needed her in his life. She grabbed the water bottle from her bag. "Give me your hand. Let me clean it." When he made no move to show her his hand again, she reached for it tentatively. "Please."

After what seemed like the longest moment, he unclenched his fist. His fingernails were caked in blood where he had dug them into his wounds. If he was *Human*, he'd have been damn lucky if he could ever use his hand again. But he was shifter, and it was already healing around the edges where the silver wasn't so deep. She uncapped the water and tipped it over his cuts, bringing a sharp hiss from him. She pulled him down with her, so that they were both kneeling on the ground. Resting her bag on the ground, she set to work with her supplies.

When the wound was clean, she pasted on Eden's cream, making the silver bubble out of his skin again, watching as it started to heal almost immediately as soon as she wiped away the offending silver. "I had a baby once," she found herself saying as she worked. "That's why I am in Exile."

Nick blinked in surprise at her revelation, an expression she couldn't quite read flashing across his features. "They exile *Humans* for illegal procreation?" he finally asked, his brow creasing.

Exile

"They do when they find out the father is *Other*." It had been so long since she had thought about that. Never did she believe she would talk about it again, and she had no idea why she was telling Nick all this now.

His gaze bored into her, and she kept her eyes on his wound, her heart thudding under his intense scrutiny. She wondered what he was thinking.

"Is the father still around?" A pause. "Did you—Do you still see him?"

She gave a short laugh. "God no. Even if he lived in Exile, I'd want nothing to do with him. "

A little of the stiffness in his shoulders seemed to disappear. "What happened to the baby?"

She hesitated. "I killed it ..." she said stiffly.

Nick said nothing, waiting for her to continue.

She could still picture the baby's face—an expressionless face, but in her mind's eye, she had been able to see the look of hurt and betrayal there. She had been its mother.

"I was six months pregnant when my mother sent me over here. Just finished medical school. I didn't even know the father was *Other*. It was stupid really. I thought he was just into reading about weird stuff. It turns out he *was* the weird stuff. A necromancer. My mother believed it was a demonic ability. Benjamin Norton told my mother that they would take me and the baby. That I could work for him, here, in Exile, and she wouldn't have to suffer the shame of what I had done."

"But?"

She pushed down the sadness that always came with remembering her mother's rejection of her. "But I made friends with one of the girls at Norton's. She told me that they were planning to take the baby from me. That they would use it for experiments." She locked eyes with Stephen. "Could you imagine what they would have done to my child? So, I went to a witch, and she gave me something to drink. The baby died."

She didn't realise she was crying until Nick raised his other hand and wiped a thumb across her damp cheek. But instead of pulling it away right after, his fingers slid to the side of her neck just under her ear, his thumb stroking her jaw. "You were brave," he said softly.

She shook her head. "I killed my own baby."

"No," he said roughly. "You saved a child from a life of torture."

Tears that she hadn't realised she had been bottling up inside ever since that fateful day started to stream down her face. It was like a dam had suddenly burst. She didn't deserve to cry. She didn't deserve to feel the loss, but it slammed into her so hard she could hardly breathe.

With a soft curse, Nick pulled her to him, big, strong arms engulfing her in a protective embrace. For a moment, she felt whole, and the incredible weight of what she'd done lifted from her in that short while.

"Sorry," she mumbled when she had cried herself out, wiping her face and trying her best to compose herself. "I've made a mess all over you." She wiped away tears from where she'd cried on his chest, running her palms over his warm, firm flesh. She had no idea when wiping her tears turned into stroking the hard expanse of his chest with her fingers, and it was only when he caught her wrists that she realised what she had been doing.

She flushed with embarrassment and tried to move back, but he tugged her back, his finger hooking under her chin to lift her face to his.

Exile

"Thank you," he said hoarsely, his eyes flickering gold. Her heart did a somersault as she watched his head descend, his mouth lowering to hers. His lips were firm and strong, brushing against hers lightly before running the tip of his tongue along the seam of her lips. She parted her lips on a breathless little gasp, and Nick took full advantage, slipping between and cutting off any protest she might have been about to make.

She moaned as he swept his tongue through her mouth, his taste rich and earthy. She wondered if he was just feeling sorry for her, but when he deepened the kiss and growled into her mouth, hauling her up against his body, any misgivings she had vanished.

She clutched at the belt on his jeans as his arms closed in around her, pressing her closer still. She revelled in the feel of hard muscle and warm male flesh, the sheer power emanating from that strong, dangerous body.

In one fluid move, he had lifted her and was lowering her back onto the cool ground, his mouth never leaving hers. When he finally tore his lips away, she was left panting, her body on fire.

He propped himself up on his hands on either side of her, and his eyes locked on hers, a bright, gold fire burning within their depths. "Tell me to stop," he said gruffly, even as he   settled between her legs and pressed his hot, hard length against her.

She gasped, her head falling back. Dimly, it crossed her mind that they were outside, but right at that moment she didn't care. "I don't want you to stop." Her long shirt had climbed up, her legs bare against his damp jeans. With trembling fingers, she reached for the top button, and Nick's eyes blazed as she watched her slowly undo each one.

She bit her lip as sharp desire lanced through her at the way he watched her, hunger in his eyes. When she had opened the buttons all the way down the shirt, she hesitated, nervous. What if he didn't like what he saw? What if he decided he didn't really want her? She stared up at him, eyes wide, breathing ragged. "Nick—" she whispered uncertainly. But his dark gaze was pinned to the line of naked flesh exposed to him where her shirt was slightly parted.

With a low rumble in his throat, he pushed the shirt open, exposing the fullness of her breasts to him. His ran his eyes slowly over her, the possessiveness in his gaze spearing desire through her, molten lava running through her veins. She shivered, the tips of her breasts tightening to hard points that had nothing to do with the cool night air, and everything to do with his hungry eyes on her. But she had little time for thought as he cupped one breast in his good hand and lowered his head, growling as his mouth latched onto a nipple, sucking it deep into his hot mouth.

"Oh, my God," she cried out, arching her back as electricity shot straight from the sensitive peaks of her breasts to her centre. Her nails dug into the firm flesh of his back, the delicious feel of his mouth on her threatening to turn her insides to jelly.

Without lifting his head, he slid both hands up along her arms, catching both her wrists in one strong grip and pinning them over her head. The dominance in the act, the feeling of being overpowered, had heat pooling at her core.

There was no going back now.

Her knees came up to squeeze his sides as he trailed his lips from one hard nub to the other, nipping and flicking the delicate flesh across both breasts. Taking one then the other deep into his mouth, he devoured her like a man who had been starving. Jolts of electricity coursed through her with each hot pull, need raging through her like wildfire. She tried to pull her hands away, desperate to touch him, but he kept her arms firmly pinned above her head. He let his other hand trail down her body, sending tiny shudders through her.

She only wore her panties under the shirt, but she was already so wet for him. She whimpered as he ran his tongue along her collarbone then nipped along her jaw to take her mouth in another searing kiss just as his hand slipped into her underwear and between her drenched silky folds. She cried out against his mouth, her hips bucking as he sunk his two fingers inside her, bringing his own pleasure-filled groan from deep in his throat.

"Fuck, you feel so good," he growled against her lips. "I want to make you come for me, Helena." He nudged her legs open wider with his strong thighs, sending her mind to crazy heights as his fingers moved in and out, drawing sharp little gasps from her.

"Nick—" she whimpered when his thumb circled the hard nub of her clitoris. She tried again to pull her hands down so that she could touch him, but his hold was vice-like, making sure she was very clear as to who it was that was in control.

Her entire body pulsed to his touch, her mind getting lost in an erotic haze as his fingers kept up their tormenting dance. As if from a distance, she heard her pleading moans, but he was relentless, pushing deeper, faster, her body bowing from the incredible pleasure of his skilled touch. Her head fell back, exposing her neck to him. He trailed scorching kisses along the silky column then nipped his way back to the rock-hard points of her luscious breasts.

He worked her body, bringing her to the brink, and when his teeth lightly bit down on one nipple as his thumb pressed down on her clitoris, she gasped, her whole body tensing as the world around her exploded.

"That's it, kitten." His satisfied growl was pure masculine gratification.

As she finally went limp beneath him, she heard Nick fumble with the buckle on his belt. When he had pulled it free, he hastily undid his jeans and pushed them down, getting rid of the only barrier keeping him from her.

The sight of his hard, perfectly muscled body had Helena's breath growing ragged once more. Her hand reached out to take his hard length in her grip, but he snatched her wrist, stopping her.

"Let me," she begged, trying to get loose, but he held her off easily.

"Later," he panted. "I need to be inside you right now." He slipped a hand under her, cupping the soft flesh of her buttocks and scooping her up in one strong, swift movement. She caught her breath at the sheer strength of him, her heart thudding in wild excitement. He leaned back, his feral gaze making her knees weak, and made her straddle his lap. His skin was hot, scorching her. Pulling her closer, he settled her so that the hot tip of his erection was pushing at her entrance.

Trembling, Helena leaned down, and nipped at Nick's bottom lip before he pressed his mouth firmly against hers and sealed the kiss. Ever-so-slowly, she lowered herself onto his full thickness, and they both moaned at the sheer pleasure of him sinking inside her. She clung to him, her head falling back on a breathless exhalation as he leaned down to suckle on her breasts once more. They moved together, his strokes matching hers as he thrust inside her, gritting his teeth as he plunged deep. His hands gripped her hips as he moved her up and down on his thick shaft, and through her own daze, she could tell he was struggling to keep the rhythm steady and not drive forcefully into her.

He was the epitome of sexy male perfection as he claimed her, his big body tense under her hands, his heated gaze possessive on her as he thrust deep. Helena's legs tightened around his hips as she felt the pressure grow once more. He picked up the pace and buried his face in her neck, biting her collarbone and sending her spiralling into yet another earth-shattering climax. As wave after wave wracked her body, Nick let out his own long, deep groan as his own orgasm spilled his hot seed inside her.

They stayed joined together for a moment, breathing hard, her legs and arms wrapped around his back, while Nick's hands gently squeezed her backside. They were both panting and damp with perspiration.

Helena pulled back slightly and smiled, brushing his damp hair back so it stood up in little black spikes. "Your eyes are so beautiful," she said, stroking a hand along the rugged stubble on his cheek. She'd wanted to say that to him for so long.

"Every part of you is beautiful," he murmured, leaning in and nipping her lip.

He moved so they were stretched out on the grass, placing her half on top of him so that she wasn't lying on the hard ground. They really needed to get back inside soon, she thought as she settled comfortably on his warm body, her head against his broad shoulder. They couldn't sleep out here.

They'd just close their eyes for a second, she promised herself as her eyelids drifted shut. As they lay together under the night sky, never had she felt safer than she did right at that moment, wrapped in his arms.

Chapter Forty-Eight

Stephen

Stephen came awake with a jolt, his head a sleep-filled, disorientated mess. It was still dark out, but it was getting close to daybreak. He sucked in a breath and listened around him. Silence.

He looked down at Helena sleeping in his arms, her lips parted slightly in relaxed sleep. He felt his heart constrict at the sight of her there, so right in his arms. Fierce possessiveness ran hot through his veins, and he held her closer, running a gentle finger down the silkiness of her cheek. His heart thumped in his chest and his body hardened in remembrance of what it had felt like to be buried deep inside her.

Swallowing hard, he carefully pulled her shirt to the side so that the creamy mounds of her perfect breasts were bared to him. He stifled a moan and gritted his teeth as he grew even harder.

Fuck. The sun would be up soon. He had to get her back inside before anyone woke. He also needed to go check on Norton, he thought grimly. It had been over a day since he had last been to the school.

Fighting not to push her back and plunge straight into her silky depths once again, and to hell with whoever saw them, he drew her shirt back into place and closed his eyes in an attempt to get his raging hard-on under control.

When he had somewhat better control of himself—though he remained rock-hard—he gently smoothed back her hair from her face. "Helena," he whispered.

She murmured lightly in her sleep and burrowed closer

Mason Sabre

to him, making his self-control slip precariously.

Unable to resist, he placed a light kiss on her lips and tried again. "Helena, wake up."

She stirred, her eyes fluttering open. He felt her tense at first, confusion flitting over her features, then immediately relax when she remembered where and whom she was with. Warm, hazel eyes climbed up to his face, a satisfied smile spreading over her features. "Hi," she murmured sleepily.

"Hey," he smiled back, kissing the tip of her nose. "We need to get up, sleepyhead."

She pulled her shirt more tightly around her and pushed herself into a sitting position. Disappointment flashed though him at the sudden loss of contact. He sat up with her, his big hand going to her back and rubbing up and down. He told himself it was to keep her warm, but the truth was he just wanted an excuse to keep touching her.

"What time is it?"

"Wee hours of the morning." Her eyes widened in surprise. "We fell asleep, but I need to go and shift." Shifting wasn't on his mind, though. Checking on Norton was suddenly weighing heavy on his mind. Stephen would bet shit that the half-breed was making himself crazy just now.

"Shift?" Helena frowned, her mind still hazy with sleep. "Oh," she said as the penny dropped. "You mean right now?"

His brow furrowed in contemplation. "It's quiet. And who knows what tomorrow is going to bring." He didn't even want to think about it. For now, it seemed that maybe fate and her bitches had taken a pause in the shit they could throw at him. It gave him time to play with his toy. In a few days, he would release him—a controlled release–with Stephen hiding behind the curtain.

Disappointment etched itself on her features. "Okay," she said softly, before reaching for his hand. He didn't pull

444

away this time, letting her turn it over and inspect his palm where the silver had bitten in. "How is your hand?"

"It's okay," he brushed off her concern. The wound was all but gone, tender-looking flesh being all that remained.

She ran her thumb over it. "I never get over how fast you all heal sometimes." Her fingers traced the raw spot then slowly glided past his wrist and up along his arm to his tattoo.

He fought his usual reaction, which was to pull away, and let her explore. His skin twitched under her touch as she stroked over his scars.

"These didn't heal?" She raised her eyes to meet his. "That is why you have the tattoo?"

"Yes," he said roughly, letting her turn his arm over so she could get a look at the other side, too. His tattoo wove around his arm like a tribal design, lacing itself around his heavy muscles and going all the way to his shoulder, then down his back and chest. The tattoo wasn't for vanity—he didn't care about the ugly scars or people being appalled by them. The tattoo was for him, and the need to not be reminded of how he had got them in the first place.

"Will you tell me about it?"

The question stabbed through him, his stomach sinking. Gemma and Cade had asked him that very same question so many times, and he had never been able to bring himself to tell them. But now, sitting here with Helena and her calming touch, for the first time, the screams in his mind didn't sound so fierce. The guttural cries didn't slam though his head like a hot poker.

"Maybe one day?" he said, not wanting to do this right now.

She smiled, the non-judgmental acceptance behind it wrapping a tight fist around his heart. Kneeling, she slid her

445

fingers up the top of his arms until they came to rest on his broad shoulders. "I will hold you to that."

She bent toward him to lay a gentle kiss on his mouth, but Stephen slid a hand around her, cupping her buttocks and drawing her against him, for a proper kiss. He loved the way her breath caught in her throat and her nervous little gasps. When he finally drew back, she was shivering, her breaths coming ragged. It took everything in his willpower not to push her back and take it further.

"I will let you go and shift," she said hoarsely, her dazed gaze glued to his lips.

The corners of his mouth lifted in a self-satisfied smile. So amazingly responsive to his touch, he thought. He planted a quick, hard kiss on her mouth. "I won't be long."

He watched as she buttoned the shirt back up and slid her panties back up her long legs. He had to clench his fist to keep from reaching out and running his hand along her soft, silky skin. She was too distracting to be near. If she didn't get in the house soon, he might be in big trouble. He forced himself to stay put, made himself watch her. His eyes raked over every luscious inch of her as she walked away from him. She stopped at the corner of the house to smile at him, and then disappeared around the side.

As soon as she was out of sight, he gathered his things back up and hastily dressed. Helena would have questioned it if he had done it while she was here. Shifters didn't need clothes to shift.

He grabbed his jeans, checking the pocket for the pouch with Brisingamen in it before pulling them back on. He hadn't returned it to Freya yet. In fact, he hadn't even seen her since getting back yesterday. He'd gone straight outside and started his fight with the silver.

The truth was, however, he didn't want to hand it over

just yet. Both Freya and the *Humans* wanted it. It was worth dying for. Perhaps it was instinct that didn't let him hand it over to her, or maybe some paranoia. He'd give it back soon ... when he could think on it first.

He'd taken a look at it on the walk back from the car to the house. It wasn't as he had expected. He thought it would have been grand, the necklace of a goddess, but it was plain, dull even. The yellow gems on it were an orange yellow, and the gold looked cheap and shiny. It was the kind of thing one would expect to find decorating a mannequin in the front of a charity shop window. Yet, as he had held it between his fingers, he had felt the power emanating from it.

Shoving it back into his pocket, he did a quick search for his shoes and shirt, finding them scattered where he had launched them at different stages of his endurance test.

He ran quickly but quietly towards the old building where he was holding his prisoner, hopping over the bits of junk he had left across the path to put off anyone coming close. Awareness prickled the hairs on the back of his neck as he drew close.

He was not alone.

As he reached the main doors, a familiar scent had him freezing. The crunch of shoes had him spinning around, bringing a gasp from Eden as she rounded the corner and almost walked into him.

"Checking on your prisoner?" she asked, head cocked to one side.

"Checking on some work, that's all." He stepped away from the door.

"I saw what you did," she said quickly. "I saw Lee."

He folded his arms over his chest, eyes narrowed in challenge.

"He didn't deserve what you did to him." She thumbed

a piece of rock that balanced precariously on the wall. Stephen prepared himself in case she decided to throw it at him or something equally idiotic.

"You don't think I should have done that?" he sneered.

Eden scoffed, rolling her eyes. "He didn't deserve to become one of us. You gave him a gift. You should have killed him."

His shoulders relaxed. "He has become the very thing he hates. What better agony for him than death?"

"But now he has power. Don't shifters have more power if they're half-breeds?" It was true, they did.

"It is not something—" A loud keening from the thick of the trees cut off his words. "Stay there," Stephen instructed, shoving Eden behind him.

The scent of copper filled the air … blood. No sooner had he scented than a hunched over figured emerged from the darkness of trees, dragging his leg. He stumbled to the ground, landing on his knees and his hands. Coughing and spitting out blood.

"Xander," Eden shrieked as he started to cough up blood. She raced past Stephen and straight for the fallen *Fae*.

Xander? *Fuck*.

Stephen raced after Eden, jumping over the rocks and the rubble as Xander tried to push himself back up to his feet. His face was unrecognisable, his leg and an arm broken for sure. Stephen reached him before Eden, catching him just before he could collapse to the ground once more.

"Don't try to move."

"Xander. Oh, God."

His breathing was raspy, short gasps riddled with pain.

"Lee," he choked out.

"Lee?" Stephen's mind worked a million miles an hour. He glared at Eden. "Did you let him out?"

448

"No," she replied vehemently.

"Open the doors?"

"Why would I?" she shouted.

He reached out and gripped the front of her shirt, desperation riding his ass all the way through the scenarios his mind was already thinking of. "What did you do?"

"Nothing," she shot. "I promise. I tossed him a squirrel and left him them."

"Fuck." Stephen thrust Xander into Eden's arms. "Stay here," he ordered her and raced back to the school. He threw open the doors, but the moment he did, he could feel the draft from further down. He could feel the difference in the place. "Shit."

He raced down the corridor, slamming into the wall in his frenzied dash to the back room. But the door was open, broken, the handle snapped from the wood. He ran down the steps, but halfway down, he glimpsed the open gate.

On the ground was a pile of bones, rat bones, where Lee had eaten his catch. But the cell was bare.

Norton was gone.

The colour drained from Stephen's face. He heard the crunch of tyres on the road, heard the screams and sounds of people …

Helena …

He ran.

Chapter Forty-Nine

Stephen

Stephen couldn't make his fucking legs run fast enough. He swore as he went, but the distance between him and the house just seemed to get greater with every damn step he took. His heart was so torn inside his chest that he was losing his mind as he ran.

Sounds of people and vehicles approaching from so many different directions flooded into Stephen's brain. Norton had brought his fucking crew already. Dread filled him as he pushed into a faster run, his mind swarming with images of Helena and the kids.

The *Humans* weren't so close yet, but from what he could estimate, it wouldn't be very long.

"Helena," he yelled as he launched himself up the steps and burst into the house, almost tripping over his own feet in his desperation to get to them.

Helena was up instantly, flying out of the lounge. Eyes watched him from within the lounge as they all jolted awake from the way he had burst in.

"What is it?" Helena stared at him with worry on her face.

He grabbed her by the arms, yanking her out. "We have to leave," he panted. "Lee Norton is on his way."

Her lips parted in shock. "What?"

He raced to the back room where Freya was just busy trying to push herself out of the chair. He jammed his hand into his pocket and pulled out the pouch.

"Brisingamen," she said, her eyes going wide as he threw it to her.

It was better that she had it than the *Humans*.

"*Humans* are coming," he said to her. "We need to leave. You need to get the kids out of here. *Now*."

Everything the *Humans* were after was here, conveniently trapped under the same roof for them—every perfect fucking ingredient to the recipe they were wanting to make. Stephen's pulse sped up, panic that they would get their hands on those who had become so important to him pumped wildly in his bloodstream.

"Daddy," Nakita yelled, racing to him.

"Can you take them? Can you take them back?" He couldn't run with them all. He couldn't save them all. He wasn't afraid of Lee nor what he could do to him. But fuck … he'd given Lee such power. He'd not be able to protect them all like this.

"I can't leave Tracey," Helena said, from the doorway. "She can't run."

"I'll carry her," Stephen barked. "Take the kids, Freya. Take them now."

He grabbed Nakita, pulling her to him. "You need to take Toke and go with Freya, okay?"

"Okay," she nodded solemnly. "Are you coming, too?"

"I can't. But I'll be there, waiting. At the other side. You need to go now, though. Okay?"

Her little face was fraught with fear, but the underlying determination filled him with such fierce pride for this little girl. *His* little girl. God, he couldn't have asked for better children. He gave her a tight hug then shoved her towards Freya. "You can take them?"

She nodded, holding her hands out for Nakita to join her. Stephen grabbed Aiden, lifting him up. "Take him, too."

Freya shook her head sadly as she pulled the necklace over her head and let it rest on her chest. "I can't. He doesn't belong."

Loud bangs and crashes from the outside had him cursing violently, and he shouted at Freya. "Run … take the kids and go."

He clutched at his temples suddenly, collapsing to his knees and dropping Aiden.

"Nick ..." Helena lunged for him, but he grabbed Aiden through the pain in his head. "You need to run Aiden," he breathed to the frightened boy. "Find Eden." He pushed him away and arched his back, roaring.

"Norton ..." he growled, voice straining as his *tiger* howled inside, pulling itself from the its confines inside. He rolled onto his front, hands on the floor, knees down. His bones moved and realigned themselves as he started to shift, his teeth elongating.

He tried to scream at them to run, to get away from him, but all he managed was a roar. His *tiger* had now fully emerged.

"Nick?" Helena asked shakily.

Stephen snarled at her, teeth bared. *Why don't you run, God damn it?*

"Nick. I don't ..."

He stalked her across the floor, making her backup, trying to force her in the same direction as Aiden.

Lee burst in, slamming the main door open, a smug grin upon his very scarred face as he spotted Stephen. But he wasn't alone. They came from all around, seeming to crawl out of every fucking piece of woodwork, surrounding him, weapons loaded with silver aimed at him.

He roared as Lee approached Helena and pushed her back into the room. His clawed hand wrapped her throat. "Would you look at this?" he said with pure glee on his face.

"Leave her the fuck out of this. She has nothing to do

with this," Stephen growled at him through their linked minds.

"She has everything to do with this," Lee grinned. "You just don't know it.

He looked at the *Human* standing behind Stephen and nodded. Helena screamed just as something was shot into the side of his neck, and the world vanished from him.

***

He awoke sometime later, lying on a mattress on the floor. It was dark— no windows and no doors. Bars surrounded him and he realised he was in a cage. Not the one at the school and not the one like his father had back at home. No, these were better. Harder.

Stephen tried to move, but his head violently refused, like he had been on some alcoholic binge for a week and had only now just woken from it. His stomach turned and threatened to spill out its contents.

A soft whimper came from next to him and a vice-like fist gripped his heart.

"Helena?" He kept his voice low, cautious not to alert anyone to his wakefulness.

But she was there. He could feel her, see her. She rolled over to face him, or at least tried to, wincing as she moved. Her face was a mass of bruises, one of her eyes almost completely closed. Rage filled him, black and murderous. She had fought them. His strong, wilful Helena.

Stephen fumbled for her hand through the bars, grabbing on tight.

"I'm sorry," he breathed, the words torn from him. "I'm so sorry."

Epilogue

Stephen

Two Years Later

The bolt on the main door slid open with a quiet clank, if there was such a thing. Stephen could pretty much guess who was coming through to his pen with how they opened that door, but the sound still caused Stephen's pulse to peak with the hope that maybe Helena was with them.

He kept himself low and still, though. He might have mentally retained every movement of those who dealt with him, but he would not fall for another of Lee's fucking tricks.

He scented the air as light footsteps clacked against the concreate floor of the dismal underground corridor, and let himself relax when he sensed the familiarity of Mel's presence. He narrowed his eyes, waiting for her to appear on the other side of the doors.

He gathered the stack of books, ready to hand them over for a trade. Who'd have thought it, Stephen Davies, reading. He rose, stretching out his aching legs and muscles—the well-behaved prisoner.

Mel smiled at him from the other side of the reinforced, sheer glass pane that separated him from the rest of the world. "Just two today," he said as he passed his books into a hatch and then pressed the button that secured his side of the panel so that Mel could open hers and take his books out.

She replaced them with another five books and a clean change of clothes for him. "Some for you too," she said, smiling slightly, angling her face so that the camera above him would not pick her up and the fact that she had spoken.

Exile

It was strict silence when dealing with Nicholas Mason. All staff knew that.

He took the books when his side opened again and nodded. She didn't nod back He waited until Mel had gone, watching her as she walked away from him, his heart thumping anxiously. It always did at an exchange. The number wasn't the number of books, no, it was the number of things exchanged between them in the stacks. The only way Stephen had found to communicate.

Lee wasn't as smart as he thought. He didn't even realise he had a traitor working for him. Stephen couldn't keep the smile off his face as he pushed the access button for the back of his pen, opening the door. It was a half-in, half-out pen, with the back of it filled with trees and plants, reminiscent of a zoo exhibition, but then that was what he was to them, wasn't it?

In the farthest corner of the pen, Stephen had made himself a personal space. He kept his books there and the small treasures of hope that Mel brought to him when she could. He hid them under the bones of the animals they released to him when his shift was needed and his *tiger* was too much, even for him. At the moment, he had an old deer roaming around his enclosure. It had taken fucking everything not to pounce and tear her to shreds, but he needed the strength from her. He had to hold out as long as possible. The *Humans* would think him on a hunger strike again.

He sat back, closing his eyes, sending up a prayer to anyone listening that Mel would get the letter out.

He could almost recite it.

Dear Xander and Eden.

This is it my friends. This is the moment. I hope you are ready. We have one shot at this and if we fuck that up, its game over. So, I need you to listen to me very carefully.

Helena is in her last six weeks, but I am not sure she will last that long. The babies are pretty big and poor Helena looks ready for them to be born, but as you know, this will be my end, and Lee will have what he wants.

On the back of this letter, you will find my plans. I have drawn you an extensive map. The parts that are shaded are areas of the facility I don't understand, but maybe Mel can help you there. I am not sure she has access to the entire building, and I cannot ask her.

I need you to follow each step as I wrote them. I need you not to question or doubt them no matter how bizarre. This will work. But above all, no matter what happens, you get Helena and the babies to safety. I can take care of myself.

We will meet as talked about in previous notes, but you know the procedure for that.

I apologise for the brief and speedy details of these plans, but time is ticking and this is our one and only chance to get the fuck out of here.

Six days.

We can do this.

Nick

Six days. Sic fucking long days. Stephen sighed. They would be free and Norton … he would die.

The End

Exile

Did you enjoy that?

Please remember to leave me a review too. Reviews are so important to us authors. Even if all you can say is, damn that book was amazing … then that is fine with me.

Thank you so much.

I love hearing from my readers and I love connecting with them.

Places to find me

Join my mailing list for news, contests and exclusive content click here.

Email me - masonsabre2@gmail.com

Find me on facebook - https://www.facebook.com/msabre3

Website – Authormasonsabre.com

My author page -

https://www.facebook.com/AuthorMasonSabre

Also by Mason Sabre

Watch Over you

The Rise of the Phoenix

Cade

Dark Veil

Hidden

Death Awakening

Broken Snow

Cuts Like an Angel

Seraph

Printed in Great Britain
by Amazon